Sold

FIONA O'BRIEN

NEW
ISLAND

SOLD
First published 2004
by New Island Books
2 Brookside
Dundrum Road
Dublin 14

www.newisland.ie

isbn 1 904301 30 4

British Library Cataloguing in Publication Data.
A CIP catalogue record for this book is available
from the British Library.

Typeset by New Island
Cover design by Glen Saville
Printed by CPD, Ebbw Vale, Wales

10 9 8 7 6 5 4 3 2 1

for Sean

PROLOGUE

March 2003

Lady Arabella Grovesbury was on the way out.

She knew it, her doctors knew it and so did the hordes of property speculators hovering like vultures to pounce on the prized carcass of her estate that would be left for them to pick over.

Lying in the vast four-poster bed of her heavily panelled bedroom, she surveyed the scenes of her long life that played out before her. The tennis parties, the balls, the marriage to her charming scoundrel of a husband Bertie and, of course, her greatest love – the horses. All gone now. Thinking of Bertie, the third Lord Grovesbury, she smiled, the most handsome, insincere and loveable of men. He had made the fatal mistake of surviving World War One when his elder brothers and friends had been slaughtered and, thereafter, had got little else right. But on a horse, he had been magnificent. His exploits on the hunting field had won her heart and exonerated him from all his many shortcomings.

Twisting feeble limbs that were growing colder by the minute, she sighed. The strangulated sound rattled through the cavernous depths of her once formidable bosom.

'Not long now,' she heard the nurse whisper to no one in particular. 'She's slipping in and out of consciousness, I'd say she won't last the hour.'

Bloody rude woman, thought Arabella, it was so symptomatic of the times. Didn't she know as a nurse that hearing was always the last sense to go? She would have retorted appropriately had she not found the effort of breathing so all consuming. Well, what about it? She was dying and the Grovesbury name would die with her. She was surprised to find that this thought did not upset her unduly. She had done her bit. The Dublin she had had known and loved had been consigned to a long and distant past and she had had the best of it. There was no place for her or her kind in the free-for-all mêlée of twenty-first century Dublin. It was time to move on.

Malcolm McBride, her solicitor, sat at the desk by the window in respectful silence, clearing his throat occasionally as he looked over the final will and testament. At her bedside, the vicar reverently recited the necessary prayers to safeguard her on her impending journey.

Lady Grovesbury wasn't listening. The ringing in her ears failed to disguise the other, far more enthralling sound that beckoned – the long, lilting call of the hunting horn. With great effort, she turned her head towards the haunting sound and saw him, her Bertie, as dashing as ever astride his fabled grey hunter Marlborough. 'Get a move on old girl!' he was saying. And beside him, straining on a leading rein, was Monty, her beloved thoroughbred, tossing his magnificent head and pawing the ground impatiently.

So this was it then, thought the last Lady Grovesbury as life at last released its tenuous hold. Pastures new were beckoning. The chase was on.

1

'Excellent!' proclaimed Chris Carroll from behind his *Irish Times*, banging the breakfast table for effect.

'What?' Alex jumped, as the rack of toast beside her hurtled to the floor.

'Grovesbury Hall's finally on the market. The old girl snuffed it – remember?'

'That's not a very nice thing to say.' Alex's big blue eyes grew wide with concern. 'Who died? Anyone we know?' Alex crawled under the table to retrieve the toast.

'Oh leave it for heaven's sake! That's what we've got a maid for.' Chris felt the familiar irritation rise. 'Lady Grovesbury, she must have been ninety-three if she was a day. She died a couple of months ago – been bedridden for the past five years,' he added dismissively.

Alex sat back down and rubbed her non-existent, four-month bump tenderly. She hated hearing of anyone dying and hoped desperately she wouldn't start to cry now she was feeling hormonal. Chris hated any kind of 'scene-making' as he called it.

Chris retreated behind his newspaper and scowled. Pregnant women were highly overrated in his opinion. Pregnant girlfriends in particular. Especially when it hadn't been part of the plan. Eighteen months ago, Alex had presented him with a daughter. He remembered her telling him, tentatively, that she was pregnant. Beseeching him with her big eyes to be as thrilled and excited as she was. Chris had listened impassively and then, without uttering a word, had got up and walked calmly from the room. He couldn't bloody believe it! He, Chris Carroll, the most eligible bachelor in Dublin, taken in by the oldest trick in the book. Sure, he had been in love with Alex, in his own way, but he had been happy with things just the way they were, and then she had to go and ruin everything. Of course he had stood by her − had done the right thing, even eventually allowing her to move into his fabulous new home in Grovesbury Road − feeling, on reflection, that it would enhance his image to play the family man. And now here she was, doing it all over again. Well it had better be a boy this time. Chris had to admit he rather fancied the thought of a son and heir. And if it wasn't, well there were plenty of other willing women about ready to provide him with one. After all, Chris consoled himself with the thought, Alex or no Alex, daughter or no daughter, he was still single − and he very much intended to stay that way for the foreseeable future.

'Will there be a lot of interest in it?' Alex asked.

Chris folded his paper purposefully and regarded her with thinly veiled irritation. 'Probably. I've been waiting for the last ten years for that piece of property to come on to the market. I don't suppose I'm alone. The sale will be a blood bath.'

'How d'you mean?' Alex was trying to sound interested although the tone Chris was using made her feel uneasy.

'Oh nothing for you to worry your pretty little head about. Anyhow, I could do with getting the bit between my teeth again. Let's just say it'll separate the men from the boys. I have to get going.' He got up from the table and made his way to the front hall, picking up his brief case and keys as Alex followed in the hope of an all too infrequent goodbye kiss.

'What time will you be back this evening?' she asked hesitantly.

'I told you.' Chris sounded bored. 'Six-thirty, we've got to be at Sheehans' for seven. Surely you haven't forgotten?'

'No, of course not,' Alex lied, panicking at the thought of the incredibly smart party that had completely slipped her mind.

'Wear your red Alaia number.' He looked her over perfunctorily, taking in the still willowy figure and the long coltish legs. 'You're hardly showing, you can still get away with it.'

'Aren't you forgetting something?' Alex inclined her head in a vain attempt to sound coquettish.

Chris turned and smiled, leaning towards her, and planted a kiss on her forehead. 'You've got jam on your mouth, sweetheart.' And with that he strolled out the door and into his new Porsche 911 Cabriolet to face the challenge of a bracing new day.

CC

Rowan Delaney savoured the stale taste of whiskey and cigarettes laying claim to his mouth and tried desperately to delay waking. Perhaps, if he stayed perfectly still, the throbbing in his temples would subside and the monstrous hangover that threatened would be avoided. The sudden ringing of the phone put paid to any further deliberations on the matter and he cursed liberally as he stumbled over an empty bottle to get to it.

'This better be good.'

'Rowan, darling, did I wake you?'

'No.'

'I left as quietly as I could, sweetie.'

Rowan grimaced as he took in the mess. Some party. The place was littered with debris.

'The thing is, I left an, er, item of underwear behind – it's probably on the sofa. Can you see it?' Marysol simpered in what she thought a suitably provocative tone.

'Yep.' Rowan regarded the lacy bra indifferently.

'Well, I'll have to come around and pick it up. Would sevenish this evening be okay?'

'Sure.' As excuses went, it was one of her better ones. Rowan did a quick calculation. He could have the place more or less cleaned up by then and, with a bit of luck, Marysol would rustle up something to eat. She was good like that. Having a Spanish mother had stood her in good stead in the kitchen – she was a fabulous cook. Generous too, Rowan admitted, reflecting on her latest gift of a cashmere jumper. Despite his dishevelled appearance, he liked having nice threads and a wealthy girlfriend or two never hurt in that department. What was that saying about being a cook in the kitchen, a maid in the living room and a whore in the bedroom? Rowan smiled. He thought it downright unfair to leave it all to one woman.

'I'll bring over something to eat.'

'Great.' The thought of food made Rowan decidedly queasy, but by this evening, he'd be glad of it.

'See you at seven then.'

'Yeah, bye.' Rowan put down the phone and stretched, half turning to check his reflection in the huge mirror. Hell, he looked rough. His dark eyes seemed even more sunken than usual and his olive skin had taken on a distinctly grey pallor. Nothing a steaming good shower wouldn't fix. Then he would clean the place up and get down to work.

An hour later, the transformation was complete. Refuse sacks were hauled outside and the cottage windows thrown open to the glorious May day. Wearing nothing but his paint-spattered jeans, Rowan stood back and surveyed his current work in progress. He decided it was shaping up nicely, though he still wasn't sure what to call it. *Communication* perhaps. Yes, that was it. An appropriate title for the piece, not to mention his obscenely wealthy telecoms neighbours who had commissioned it. Rowan enjoyed a *frisson* of perverse pleasure as he regarded the inexpertly cured (real) sheep's head surrounded by wires and hung by a telephone lead that would hang against the backdrop of the canvas. Yes, it would make a very suitable work of art for the Sykes' home on Grovesbury Road. That would teach them to commission a painting without viewing his work. Rowan's 'protest against the brutalisation of twenty-first century Ireland' was one of his current favourite themes and featured heavily in his 'art'. Dubbed the *enfant terrible* of Irish art by *The Irish Times* only last month, his misguided star was finally in the ascendant, and the commissions were beginning to roll in.

As it was such a fabulous day, he decided to work outside. The cottage was restricting enough at the best of times but, on a day like today, it would be impossible.

With his shoulder-length hair secured by a headband and a look of ferocious concentration consuming his gaunt features as he attacked the canvas, an interested passer-by was not the first woman to note that Rowan Delaney bore an uncanny resemblance to Daniel Day-Lewis in *The Last of the Mohicans*.

Niamh ní Cheavin peered out the window from behind her freshly washed lace curtains and scowled. She just knew that her ignorant neighbour and landlord Chris Carroll deliberately revved the powerful engine of his car as he was passing her little cottage purely to annoy her. It was Saturday and she had been hoping to enjoy a well-deserved lie-in. Now, to cap it all, the ferocious noise of the landscape gardeners he had employed to rearrange his vast garden yet again had started up. She thought about calling round to complain but reflected that she would only get that ninny of a girlfriend of his who would be profusely apologetic but totally ineffectual. She appeared to be as terrified of Chris as everyone else. Niamh resolved to make a formal complaint to the guards and, if that didn't work, to stoop to whatever means were necessary. Chris Carroll was nothing but a bully, and Niamh was in no way, shape or form going to let him intimidate her. Apart from being a ruthless property developer and asset stripper, he represented everything she detested in men.

Ever since she had inherited the cottage after her mother's untimely death, he had been trying to get her out of it. Well, he might have succeeded in closing down his latest acquisition in the form of a long-established, local furniture-making factory and moved production to Slovenia or somewhere else suitably cost-effective, but Niamh had no intention of being such a pushover. She hadn't worked all her life in the civil service without picking up a trick or two and constantly delighted in keeping back her rent on the basis of real and fictitious complaints to her infuriated landlord.

Pulling her sensible woollen dressing gown tightly around her, she lit the old gas stove and set about feeding her three hungry cats who were weaving around her feet and mewing plaintively. 'Now, there you go. Snowy, Queenie and, yes, Jim, I'm coming to you. Don't be greedy.'

Setting the dishes down before them, Niamh brightened, remembering today was the day gorgeous vet Steve Sorenson ran his free animal clinic from the cottage next door but one to hers, and her cats were due their booster shots. In honour of the impending visit, she ran a hot bath and added a liberal dash of her favourite English Lavender bath foam, which was kept strictly for special occasions. Slipping into the perfumed water, she regarded her bony limbs dispassionately and gave herself up to surprisingly detailed fantasies where Steve Sorenson and she were performing procedures that would have made a cat blush.

Twenty minutes later, she was ready. Dressed in her

immaculately pressed white linen trousers and a navy-and-white T-shirt, she pulled her thin hair into a tight chignon and regarded her reflection. Yes, sensible, but with a definite touch of *je ne sais quoi*.

The one and only summer Niamh had spent out of the country, in Lyons nearly thirty years previously, had been put to good use and ever since she had stubbornly endeavoured to replicate the inimitable style of the French women she had so longingly admired. A quick dab of powder and a dash of red lipstick on her non-existent lips completed the look. In a way, she thought, it was just as well she had woken early. There was a lot to do. After her visit to the vet, she would drop in on her neighbour, Nellie Murphy, who lived in cottage number four, and bring her one of the chicken casseroles she was so fond of. And, with a bit of luck, she would get her to do a reading of the tea leaves. Poor Nellie hadn't been well lately – mind you, for her ninety-two years she was remarkably sprightly. Apart from her renowned mystical talents, Nellie was also the only person left who remembered Niamh's dear, long-departed mother.

In the old days, Nellie had worked in Grovesbury Hall for the late Lady Arabella, and Niamh's mother had been the cook in the house next door, where Chris Carroll's parents had lived. The cottages in Grovesbury Gardens at the back of each respective house had been the staff quarters, and now, in turn, they had been inherited by the families left behind. Of course nowadays, the humble little cottages were prospective goldmines, nestled as they were in the heart of Dublin 4, and it wasn't only Chris Carroll who wanted to get his grasping hands on them, Niamh reflected, her mouth tightening.

Gathering her three cats into their travelling baskets, she set out into the beautiful morning sunshine with a spring in her step. She was looking forward to the afternoon ahead and wondered what the tea leaves would have in store for her. Niamh ní Cheavin may have been forty-five years of age, but she hadn't given up hope of catching a man. He would have to be an animal lover, of course, and be neat and tidy around the house, but she knew he was out there, and she congratulated herself once again that she had saved herself all these years for 'him'.

Cee

Steve Sorenson shook his head and waited for the anaesthetic to take effect on the beautiful Labrador that lay prostrate on the table before him. Another 'hit and run' on the busy Strand Road had left the dog badly injured. He had been hit in the pelvis and x-rays confirmed massive internal haemorrhaging. His owner was understandably distraught and had been sent home with the quiet but firm assurances from Lucy, the veterinary nurse, that they would call immediately there was any news.

As it was an emergency, it meant Steve had to miss his free animal clinic session in Grovesbury Gardens but thankfully, his colleague Tracey had gladly stepped in for him to take the weekly slot.

Satisfied the dog was under, Steve went to work quickly. It would be touch and go, but if he had any chance of saving him, time was of the essence. Assisted by the third, and relatively newly qualified, member of his practice, Donal Sullivan, Steve made the first and crucial incision.

'Clamp, Donal.'

'Jesus, what a mess.' Donal deftly held back the flap of skin so they could get a look at what was left of the dog's abdomen.

'Yep, it's as bad as we thought. The main area of damage seems to be the duodenum. Try and stem the blood loss, and I'll get to work on the spleen.'

An hour-and-a-half later, the operation was complete. Buddy, still under anaesthetic, was stitched up with precision and moved to the recovery room where he was hitched up to state-of-the-art drips and drains under the watchful eyes of Donal.

'That was some piece of work, Steve.' Donal shook his head

in admiration. 'Remind me to ask for you if I'm ever on the table.'

'We've done all we can,' Steve said wearily. 'It's up to Buddy now. The next twenty-four hours will be crucial. He's a strong, healthy animal, but he's taken a hell of a battering.' Steve went over to the basin to wash his hands. 'Tell Lucy I'm heading over to Grovesbury Gardens. Call me if there are any problems. Otherwise I'll check in on him at around four.'

'Sure thing. Lucy said she'd be happy to watch him.'

'Good,' Steve smiled. It was Saturday and Lucy's official afternoon off, but Steve expected all his staff to drop everything, just as he would, for a sick or wounded animal. As it was, he trusted them completely. Apart from being highly qualified, Steve made sure that anyone working with him, from his partner to the cleaning lady, shared his genuine vocation and dedication to healing the devoted companions who brought such joy to the lives of their besotted owners.

The operation had gone as well as could be expected, and if he got a move on, he could make it over to Grovesbury Gardens to catch the last hour of the free clinic he had been running there from his late father's cottage.

A lot had happened since his father's death, just over ten years ago. Steve often wished his dad could have lived to see the changes and benefited from the successful career he now enjoyed – thanks to his father's constant support and belief.

'You were born to be a vet, son,' he used to say, as a young Steve followed him on his rounds of the stables up at Grovesbury Hall, where he had worked as groomsman-cum-gardener, 'and we Sorensons were always lucky with the horses, never forget that.'

Looking back, Steve realised how much his father and mother must have scrimped and saved to educate him and help put him through college – although his dad had always put any help down to 'successful punting'. Well, he'd come a long way since those days, Steve thought, pulling his Jeep up outside cottage number three. A successful practice in Sandymount had seen to that. That, and the occasional flutter he allowed himself, ensured he had been able to buy a prime sea-front site on Strand Road and build a particularly handsome double-fronted stone house and new animal hospital beside it. When his mother died, a year after his father, Steve had inherited their little cottage in Grovesbury Gardens and had immediately set about converting it into the much-needed free animal clinic. Because Dublin 4, as Steve well knew, was as full of waifs and strays as anywhere else in the city.

'Hi Tracey, sorry I got held up.' Steve failed to notice the flutter of expectation his arrival generated among the patient queue of pet owners. 'I'll take over now and you can go home.' Steve looked over the chart of the small collie who was wagging her tail frantically.

'Nice to see you, Mrs O'Malley. Molly's due her shot, is she?' Steve injected the dog deftly in the scruff of her neck. 'There we are, good girl, all over now.'

'Oh thank you Dr Sorenson,' Mrs O'Malley beamed with gratitude. 'I don't know what we'd do without you here. You know, you're getting more like your late father every day, God rest his soul. You wouldn't remember him when he was young, of course, but he was a very handsome man! He was so helpful to all of us widows, too. Nothing was too much trouble. I can tell you he's sorely missed in the cottages.'

After seeing Mrs O'Malley and Molly out, Steve saw four more patients before finishing up for the afternoon.

As he was locking up, his attention was caught by the sight of what appeared to be a vast white tent lurching alarmingly from side to side in the garden of the Sheehans' house across the wall.

'No, no, to the right, to the right!' shrieked a high-pitched voice Steve immediately recognised as Melissa's.

Of course, Steve remembered, tonight was the Sheehans' latest shindig, some sort of belated christening for their long-awaited daughter.

Steve was fond of Pascal and Melissa. You couldn't ask for

a more reasonable landlord than Pascal, and they were decent neighbours to boot. Pascal had been particularly accommodating with the lease on Steve's cottage when he had needed planning permission to do the clinic conversion. He had all but forgotten about the party tonight, he realised. He would go back and check in on Buddy and, if everything was satisfactory, take a quick shower and head over to Sheehans'. Seeing as it was Sunday tomorrow, it would do him good to get out and have a few jars.

2

'Is this some sort of sick joke?' Rod Sykes sucked in his breath as he took in the monstrosity adorning the wall of his large, square hall.

'Well, it is *different*, I'll give you that!' Michael Moriarty tried and failed to stifle a malicious chuckle as he regarded his neighbour's work of art. 'What does Tanya think?'

'That's the problem. Clearly she doesn't – think that is.' Rod shook his head in disbelief. 'She's had to go and have a lie down apparently.'

'Can't say I blame her – it's a bit on the gruesome side, although I must say, er, very striking.'

'That fucker's taking the piss.' Rod was beginning to rant. 'Look what he's called it, *Communication*. He's got a fucking nerve!'

'Calm down, Rod, it'll probably be worth a fortune in a couple of years' time. Felicity tells me Rowan's taking the art world by storm.'

'It's *already* cost me a fortune. Funny how you've managed to avoid purchasing any of his stuff.'

'Well, he's not really our style.'

'It's going straight back. I'll teach him communication.'

'S-sweetheart?' Tanya, Rod's wife, called tentatively as she descended the stairs. 'I think I'm feeling a little better now. Do you like it? I think it might grow on us … It was just a bit of a shock, that's all.'

'Not as much of a shock as that poor sheep got judging by the look on his face,' Michael couldn't resist adding.

'Well it's meant to be arresting.' Tanya valiantly tried to defend the piece, although she still had to turn her head away and look at it through half-closed eyes.

'It's not staying there, that's for sure.' Rod was pacing the floor.

'You can't take it down.' Tanya looked petrified. 'Rowan's coming round tomorrow especially to see how it's settling in.'

Rod looked at his wife and sighed. 'Darling, he's *our* tenant, he needs to keep *us* happy. That's the way it works.'

'But he's an artist, a tormented, brilliant artist. We have to at least give it a chance, please sweetie, just for me?'

'Oh for heaven's sake, all right. Just don't blame me if Nathan starts having nightmares about it.'

'I'd better get back, we're due at Sheehans' for seven.' Michael made for the door. 'Oh, and speaking of tenants, Chris Carroll was telling me he wants a few of us to get together to discuss the cottages now that Grovesbury Hall is up for sale. Some kind of development scheme he has in mind. I'll get Pascal on board and maybe we'll get together next week?'

'Sure, I'll see you at Sheehans' later anyway.'

'Well, sport, what do you think?' Rod gathered up his six-year-old son, Nathan, and threw him up in the air to shrieks of delight.

'I think it's fucking, fucking, brilliant – that's what Rowan says! And he's going to pay me if I can collect a fucking great bucket of frog spawn for him to put in another painting!'

'Is that so?' said Rod, smiling grimly. 'Son, by the time I've finished with him, he'll be drinking it.'

Cee

Carmela Walshe put on her best loden green overcoat and checked her appearance in the hall mirror before setting off for ten o'clock mass at Donnybrook Church. On reflection, she decided, it had been a wise decision to let her immaculately coifed hair go grey naturally. Liam, her husband, didn't seem to mind and, at sixty years of age, she was happy with her regally elegant appearance. It was important to age gracefully, she felt, and not succumb to the vagaries of what was affectionately referred to these days as 'cosmetic enhancement'. Carmela shuddered at the thought. If one couldn't be comfortable in one's own skin, the outlook was, indeed, bleak. Anyway, she was sure it must be a grave sin to tamper with what the Good Lord gave you.

Checking her handbag to make sure she had her rosary beads and keys, she swept out the front door of her exquisitely elegant home on Grovesbury Road and began the short walk to the church. Although it was May, she felt there was a nip in the air and, anyway, Carmela had never adapted to this strangely damp country despite her forty years in residence. She often thought longingly of the searing hot summers of her native Madrid and reminded herself that she was due a visit home one of these days. Perhaps she could persuade Marysol to accompany her this time. Thinking of her youngest daughter, Carmela frowned. At twenty-one, Marysol was showing worrying signs of developing into just the kind of girl Carmela disapproved of most. For starters, she had far too healthy an interest in men. And her choice in clothes was becoming downright provocative to put it mildly. Thank God, she thought, for her other child, Padraig. He was balm to his mother's troubled soul. Already halfway towards completing a flawless law degree, he was seriously considering entering the priesthood. Carmela smiled. With his brains and language skills, and her contacts in the Vatican, his career would have a meteoric rise. Her relatives had always dreamed of having a cardinal in the family – but for it to be her own son! The Blessed Virgin was at least listening to her prayers in one respect.

Entering the cool interior of the church, Carmela bowed her head and walked purposefully to the front pew and genuflected gracefully before kneeling down. It was important to maintain certain standards in a community, particularly one such as Donnybrook, where the gods of materialism and worldliness were gaining such a disturbing hold. The fact that she and her husband held a good fifty-one per cent of one of the most profitable haulage companies in the country, to name but one of their many business interests, was not a consideration.

A demanding day lay ahead, with a huge charity lunch to attend among other laudable causes. But first there was mass, and after that, she would lead the weekly rosary. Then she would put the troublesome matter of her easily led daughter into the hands of her Maker.

Ce

'That, was delicious.' Rowan gobbled the last of the meatballs and spaghetti – or *albóndigas*, as Marysol insisted on calling them – down with consummate speed. 'What's for dessert?'

'I thought you'd never ask.' Marysol threw him a provocative glance as she gathered up the plates and sashayed over to the sink. 'It's such a shame you don't have a dishwasher. I don't know how you manage without one.'

Rowan was tempted to reply 'I have several' but wisely bit back the retort. He was feeling decidedly more human after satisfying at least one of his many appetites.

'You're a fabulous girl, you know that?' he ventured, his eyes roaming over Marysol's generously proportioned curves.

By some standards, he acknowledged, she would have been considered overweight. But, being an artist, Rowan prided himself on appreciating the female form in all its many shapes and sizes – and he loved all of them.

'I was just about to remind you how fabulous.' Wiping her hands on the tea towel, Marysol turned from the sink and, in one fluid movement, removed her top, revealing her quiveringly enticing 34DD assets.

Rowan sighed. In three, perhaps five years, she would have assumed matronly proportions, but for now, she was glorious.

'Go on then.'

Marysol didn't need further prompting. Quickly shedding the rest of her clothes, she positioned herself strategically on top of the old oak kitchen table, tossing her long, black hair over deliciously plump shoulders.

'Dessert,' she said meaningfully, 'is now being served.'

Cee

It was nine forty-five when Rowan woke up. 'Hell, look at the time Marysol! We've almost missed the bash at Sheehans'. C'mon, get your lovely ass in gear.'

'Hmm?' Marysol stretched sleepily. 'Who wants to go to that stupid party? It'll be full of wrinklies. My *parents* are going for heaven's sake. Besides, I can think of much better ways to spend the rest of the night.'

'No can do, sweetheart. Half of the collective bread in Dublin will be there – and, as an up and coming artist, I need to play to my public. C'mon, it'll be fun. Here, have another drink, jump in the shower and throw on your clothes – with a bit of luck things'll just be warming up. Whatever else you might say about them, Pascal and Melissa know how to throw a good party.'

As Marysol grudgingly followed instructions, Rowan busied himself with choosing an appropriate outfit for the occasion. He decided on a pair of well-worn combats and a ripped khaki linen shirt, which he wore open. Leaving his shoulder-length hair in post-coital disarray, he surveyed his reflection. It was almost perfect. Quickly slipping in to the next room, he dipped his fingers in a pot of chocolate brown paint and deftly began to contour his slightly visible six-pack. He had picked up this little tip recently from a magazine article about Madonna, where he had read that she had her make-up artist similarly enhance her abdominals prior to shooting a beach scene in her latest movie. Rowan had thought it a stroke of brilliance and had been employing the tactic ever since.

'Hey! You look gorgeous, babe!' Rowan looked Marysol over appreciatively as she wandered out to join him.

'I hope you don't mind me borrowing these, but I couldn't go in what I was wearing.'

She had struggled into a pair of Rowan's baggier jeans that, on her curvaceous form, had been instantaneously remodelled, bringing the phrase 'every stitch doing its duty' to mind. Over them, she had tied a white cotton shirt, midriff style. Her long black waves hung in tendrils still damp from the shower. The overall effect was very appealing Rowan had to admit. 'C'mon, gorgeous, let's go.'

Slipping his arm around Marysol's waist he propelled her out the door. He would hover near her attentively for the first ten minutes or so, then he would check out the talent. Even losing someone as clingy as Marysol should be relatively easy in the throng of beautiful people who were bound to be there. After all, it wasn't every day the top totty in Dublin would be paraded in front of a chap, all tantalisingly confined in the one residence for what promised to be a night full of possibilities.

*

'Melissa, what a fabulous marquee.' Tanya was awestruck as she looked around the vast tent lined with veils of floating pale-pink chiffon. At the far end, the food tables were groaning with an array of lobster, beef, elaborate platters of shellfish and mouth-watering salads. In the midst of the desserts, a huge twenty-tier cake decorated with pink iced rosebuds and studded with silver balls stood majestically.

'Thank you Tanya. Pascal and I do love to throw a party, and little Gisele's christening is a cause of great celebration for us.' Melissa smiled mistily.

'Where is the little pet?'

'Oh, Maria's feeding her, she'll be coming down later.' Maria, Pascal and Melissa's South American housekeeper, was as besotted with little Gisele as her proud parents.

'I do think it was clever of you to call her Gisele, it's such a sophisticated name.' Tanya thought Melissa to be the epitome of a glamorous Dublin 4 woman. The fact that she had named her daughter after the Brazilian supermodel *du jour* only enhanced her credibility in Tanya's impressionable eyes. At twenty-nine, Tanya was a very unsure newcomer to the hallowed halls of Grovesbury Road, and she looked up to Melissa enormously. Melissa, delighted beyond belief at having someone to impress, had taken the attractive young woman under her wing – and Tanya was proving a willing and devoted protégée.

Tanya's husband, Rod, had sold his English telecoms company just before the crash and they had immediately set about spending their multimillions, moving to Ireland and buying and renovating their dream house on Grovesbury Road.

'I don't see Rowan anywhere.' Tanya looked around anxiously.

'I did invite him, of course.' Melissa frowned. 'But you know what these artists are like, so unpredictable, I'm sure he'll show up sooner or later.'

'It's just that, well, Rod wasn't exactly, er, too keen on the piece of art he's done for us. He's quite likely to say something rude to Rowan and I'd just die.'

'Don't be ridiculous, Tanya. Everybody knows Rowan is the new Knuttel – his work is so, so visceral. Rod will come around, just leave him to me. Now, we really must circulate – oh look, there's Alex all on her own. That Chris Carroll is really so mean not to introduce her to anyone. Come on, we'll go over and say hello.

'This must be costing you a pretty penny, Pascal.' Liam Walshe's oily voice cut across the party chitchat as he joined Pascal, Chris Carroll and Michael Moriarty, who were deep in conversation.

'Ah, sure, I have to keep my girls happy.' Pascal was beaming. 'Nothing but the best for the princesses.'

'Of course, of course.' Liam was at his most effusive as he deftly claimed his fifth glass of champagne from a passing waiter. 'Carmela and I were just saying what generous hosts you and Melissa are. By the way, did you see Grovesbury Hall's up for sale?'

'Actually,' said Chris smoothly, 'we were discussing that very subject. If you're free on Wednesday evening, you might join us to hear a few proposals I have in mind.'

'Delighted to.' Liam's beady eyes lit up as he scanned the room. If the property boys were cooking up a business venture, he very much wanted to be part of it.

Marysol had lost Rowan. She wasn't quite sure when she had mislaid him, but he was definitely not at her side, as he should have been. Throwing back another quick glass of bubbly, she looked around the marquee and tried to focus on the takeover bid the mind-numbingly boring banker was regaling her with. 'You know,' he was saying, talking animatedly to her chest, 'you really should consider a career in modelling. I could introduce you to some friends of mine with very good contacts in the rag trade. There's a lot of money to be made in it these days.'

'Oh fuck off, you stupid wanker!' Marysol left him with his mouth open as she set off in search of her prey. Weaving through the throng of beautiful people, she finally caught sight of him. Surrounded by three nubile blondes, Rowan was eagerly discussing the merits of finger painting versus brush. 'It's all about texture you see. He was at his most intense. 'That's what resonates when you really *connect* with the canvas.'

'How 'bout connecting with this?' Marysol threw a drunkenly aimed punch at him and missed spectacularly, sending the nearest blonde flying backwards into a plate of oysters.

While the delighted onlookers rushed to the aid of the startled group, Rowan made his escape, sidling quickly out of harm's way.

It was then that he saw her. Alone, vulnerable and looking infinitely forlorn, she took his breath away. The clinging red dress she wore only emphasised the intense unease she was obviously feeling. He was just about to cut across the room and make his move when, to his dismay, Melissa Sheehan and Tanya Sykes appeared at her side and claimed her. But not before he had made eye contact with her, and a jolt of what felt like pure electricity shot through him.

It was after dinner, and everyone had been treated to a special late-night appearance from Gisele, the star of show, who had been proudly carried in by her doting father.

When the christening cake had been washed down with yet more champagne, Melissa rose unsteadily from her chair and called for silence. 'I just want to say that this happy occasion has been made even more joyous for us by the wonderful news that another little one is about to come into our midst.' Melissa paused for effect.

'Way to go, Pascal, ya boyo!' someone shouted to great applause.

'No, no,' Melissa trilled. 'Please listen! My husband and I ... just wanted to be the first to wish Chris Carroll and his delightful partner Alex our warmest congratulations on her pregnancy. I'm sure you'll all join me in raising your glasses to the ecstatic couple.'

There was a rumble of moving seats and confused chatter as people rose to the occasion and clinked their glasses. Rowan, lounging against the wall, did likewise. But not before he noticed the look of horrified mortification on the face of the girl in the red dress and the look of livid anger Chris shot her.

The fresh air hit Marysol full blast as she staggered out into the garden. To her right, the Romanesque columns of the swimming pool framed beguilingly still water. Still more inviting was the gently bubbling jacuzzi set into the rocks beside it.

'C'mon in, it's great!' a little voice called out.

Nathan Sykes looked on delightedly as Marysol walked unsteadily down the steps fully clothed and sank back into the frothy water, her white cotton shirt clinging magnificently to her full breasts.

'Marysol? Marysol?' A frantic voice called through the din. 'Where are you?' Carmela Walshe followed the trail of damage her wayward daughter had left in her wake after attacking Rowan's blonde audience and came upon a sight that made her stop and cross herself.

'Look,' said Nathan, holding up the Lion Bar Rowan had earlier suggested he plant in the jacuzzi. 'I've just done a great big turd, and now I'm going to eat it!'

'*Madre de Dios!*' Carmela was heard to exclaim as she was joined by her husband and Rod and Tanya Sykes who had been searching for little Nathan.

As their six-year-old son shoved the Lion Bar into his mouth and bit down hard, Rod Sykes was just in time to catch his wife as she fainted.

Cee

It was eight o'clock on Sunday morning and Nellie Murphy was already up and dressed. She found herself unwilling to break the habits of a lifetime, and being ready to face the day and whatever it might hold, bright and early, was one of them. She put in her teeth, fixed back her surprisingly plentiful grey hair and sat down in her favourite easy chair, beside the window of the little front room, to light her first cigarette of the day.

Normally she didn't see people on a Sunday, but Melissa Sheehan was one of her regular clients, and she had booked the reading weeks ago for herself and the friend she would be bringing along.

Nellie shook her head thoughtfully. Yesterday, Niamh ní Cheavin had come to see her, and the day before Marysol Walshe, and their readings had both ended with similar information. After Niamh had left, Nellie read the tea leaves for herself. It was unmistakable. *A stranger was coming into their midst. A stranger with her own troubles. A woman who would play an important part in the forthcoming upheaval about to be unleashed in their lives.* Nellie sighed. She had seen a lot of comings and goings in her time, a lot of changes, some good some not so good. But one thing she was sure of, the tea leaves never lied.

3

'Chris, good to see you,' Malcolm McBride arrived in a flurry. 'So sorry to have kept you waiting, that case at the High Court ran on longer than expected. Coffee?'

'No, thanks. Let's get down to business. What have you got for me?' Chris regarded his long-time solicitor speculatively.

'Well, I've gone over the deeds thoroughly,' Malcolm coughed nervously, 'and everything seems to be pretty much in order.'

'But?' Chris's finely attuned antennae were immediately up.

'There's a bit of a problem.'

'What kind of problem?'

'The leasehold of the final cottages.'

'What about them? They belong to the respective Grovesbury Road houses. We've bought all of them bar the final four: Rowan Delaney's, which belongs to Rod Sykes; Nellie Murphy's lease is with Liam Walshe; Steve Sorenson's is with Pascal, and I have the pleasure of that mad Niamh ní Cheavin bitch as a tenant. I'm meeting the guys on Wednesday, we'll thrash out a deal, get the tenants out – and then we're all set to move on the development.'

'I'm afraid it's not quite that simple.' Malcolm ran a fluttering hand through thinning hair. 'It's to do with Grovesbury Hall.'

'What about it?'

'Well, it would appear that the second Lord Grovesbury was quite a philanthropist for his time.'

'So?'

'As you know,' Malcolm played for time, enjoying having a rare upper hand with his client, 'I am the chief executor of Lady Grovesbury's estate. When I was going over the deeds to Grovesbury Hall, I came across a rather, er, disconcerting piece of information.'

'Let's have it.'

'You and I were under the impression that the freeholds of the cottages belonged, as you say, to the Grovesbury Road houses. In fact, as a result of the deeds being amended at a later date, in accordance with the second Lord Grovesbury's wishes, the Grovesbury Garden cottages were only *leased* to the big houses for a period of ninety-nine years. After which time, i.e., now in 2003, the leaseholds revert to the owner of Grovesbury Hall. Who was, until she died, Lady Arabella Grovesbury.

'So, we buy Grovesbury Hall – what's the big deal?'

'If you would let me finish, Chris.' Malcolm pursed his lips. 'When the freeholds of the cottages revert to the new owner of Grovesbury Hall ... he, or indeed *she*, is obliged, under the terms of the amended lease, to offer the cottages for sale to each of the current tenants for the sum of five hundred pounds.' Malcolm paused to enable Chris take in the full implications of the bombshell. 'Of course this would have been considered a *huge* sum in 1903, but today ... well, it's a mere pittance.'

'But that's utterly ridiculous! It's laughable. Those cottages are worth a fortune. Besides which, I need them to proceed with the development.'

'Precisely, but the law is the law and all that.'

'Fuck the law! Let me think about this for a minute.' Chris

got up and began to pace the room. 'Who else knows about this?'

'No one, apart from you and me.' Malcolm coughed again nervously.

'Good, then that's the way it's going to stay. Could there be any other copies of this amendment?'

'I doubt it, Lady Grovesbury kept all of her legal documents in the late Lord Grovesbury's strong room in the Hall. I'll double check but, even if we did hold another copy, it would more than likely have been destroyed in 1921 when the IRA burned down my grandfather's offices so efficiently – ascendancy grievances and all that. McBride & Whitaker have always handled the Grovesbury estate.'

'Then destroy it. As far as we're concerned, this conversation never took place. To be on the safe side, it would make sense for me to buy Grovesbury Hall. I was intending to anyway. There shouldn't be too much interest in the old place. Pascal and his cronies aren't keen on it. There'll be the usual hotels and embassies sniffing around, but nothing I shouldn't be able to see off. And, in the unlikely event of someone beating me to it, well now, they'll never know that they would also have been the proud owners of the Grovesbury Garden cottages – never mind that bunch of losers that live in them. That's all that matters to me. See that there's no other evidence, Malcolm. Naturally, I'll make it worth your while. And don't forget, there'll be some lucrative business in the development scheme for your company. Do we understand each other?'

'Absolutely.'

'Good, then I'll be on my way. Oh, by the way, the meeting's at seven on Wednesday, at my place. I'll need you to be there.'

'Of course, Chris. You can count on me.'

'I'll see myself out.'

After Chris had left, Malcolm drummed his fingers on the desk thoughtfully, gazing over at his late grandfather's portrait hanging above the mantelpiece, from where it seemed to regard him sternly. He smiled, remembering as a child the endless lectures he had had to listen to on 'moral fibre'. Then, reaching over to pick up the antique silver lighter, he walked over to the fireplace and lit the corner of the offending document, watching it burn until it fell in ashes into the grate.

'Rowan, do come in, it's so good of you to call.' Tanya Sykes ushered Rowan into the cool interior of her high-tech home.

'No problem, babe. I like to make sure my work is settling in.'

'We're so thrilled with it, aren't we, Melissa?' Tanya had invited Melissa around for moral support. Apart from being a little afraid of Rowan, if it wasn't for Melissa she wouldn't even have known their tenant was a famous artist. Melissa had encouraged Tanya to commission the work and to give Rowan a free hand, so to speak.

Of course, Tanya had made sure Rod would be at work and out of the house when Rowan called. Despite her pleas, Rod was still livid about the 'monstrosity', as he called it, and threatened daily to have it taken down.

'What does Rod think of it?'

'He thinks it's fabulous,' Melissa was quick to interject. '"Extraordinarily *visceral*" I think were the words he used. Didn't he, Tanya?'

Tanya wasn't sure what 'visceral' meant, but if Melissa said so, then that was good enough for her.

'Will you have a glass of wine, Rowan? Melissa and I were just about to have a little alfresco lunch – do join us.'

'That'd be cool, thanks. I will.'

Outside, on the multi-level deck, Rowan sat back, sipped his wine and took in the view. Between them, Tanya and Melissa sported some impressive 'plastic' but, he had to admit, they were good-looking chicks. And, apart from anything else, they must be worth millions. Tanya, he noted, bore a no-doubt carefully cultivated resemblance to Posh Spice. This, coupled with the fact that her husband had exceptionally protruding front teeth, had prompted Michael Moriarty to refer to them as 'Posh 'n' Bucks', and all of Dublin 4 now did likewise.

'You look a lot like Victoria Beckham, you know that?' Rowan commented lazily, allowing his eyes to roam over Tanya's newly acquired breasts nestling in a brief bikini top. 'You should let me paint you.'

'What a wonderful idea, Rowan,' Melissa enthused. 'Think what a fabulous present it would make for Rod! Why you were saying only yesterday, Tanya, you had no idea what to give him for his birthday. That would be such a great surprise.'

'I'm not sure.' Tanya looked apprehensive.

'Think about it and let me know.' Rowan was quick to spot an opportunity. 'I'm doing a lot more portraits right now, it'd be fun.' He made a mental note to develop an innovative portrait style immediately. With all these bored, wealthy women on his doorstep, he could clean up nicely – and get laid.

'More wine, Rowan?' Melissa waved the bottle gaily.

'Why not?'

Niamh read the letter again. There was no mistaking the official tone but, through the lines, she could sense the glee in Chris Carroll's formal notification.

> It has been brought to my attention that the lease on Number 5 Grovesbury Gardens has run its course of ninety-nine years and, therefore, expires on 15 December of this year, 2003.
>
> I am, therefore, putting you on formal notice that, as the freehold belongs to me, Chris Carroll of Number 5 Grovesbury Road, Ballsbridge, Dublin 4, I shall not be renewing this lease.
>
> I will require the cottage to be cleared and vacated one month in advance of this date.

Wishing you every success in finding alternative accommodation.
   Yours sincerely,
   Chris Carroll

Niamh sat down, her legs suddenly weak. How could she have allowed something important like this to escape her notice? More importantly, where would she go? She had lived in this little cottage all her life. And then another thought occurred to her. If her lease was up, then surely the other cottage tenants would find themselves in the same predicament? That meant Rowan Delaney, Steve Sorenson's pet clinic and poor Nellie Murphy would be facing the same situation. Reaching for her handbag, she rooted out her address book and quickly phoned her solicitor, Carol, and relayed the information.

'Leave it with me, Niamh. I'll check it out as soon as I can and get back to you.'

Half an hour later, Niamh picked up the phone and listened to the news she had hoped not to hear.

'I'm afraid he's right, Niamh. The lease is up for renewal this year – couldn't you renegotiate with him?'

'Are you kidding? That bastard's been trying to get me out of here ever since I can remember. He already owns the other thirty cottages, and there are only four left with the original family tenants. I assume they'll be in the same situation?'

'Looks like it,' Carol said. 'The lease was inclusive as far as I can make out. Unless the others can renegotiate with their landlords, I'm afraid they've run into their last year too. I *am* sorry Niamh, but you'll have no problem finding somewhere else. There's a glut in the rentals market at the moment, so you'll have plenty of choice. Let me know if I can be of any help.'

Niamh replaced the receiver weakly. So this was it. She wondered if the other tenants had any idea yet – probably not. She would organise a meeting, have them round for a drink and break the news. As a neighbour, it was the least she could do for the tightly knit little community they had become over the years.

Cee

'So you see, according to *my* solicitor at any rate, *all* our leases are up this year. The rest of you may be able to renegotiate, but Chris Carroll must have taken particular delight in letting me know in no uncertain terms that I have to be out by November.'

Steve, Rowan and Nellie sat around Niamh's kitchen table and listened to her news.

'Man, that's a bummer, Niamh.' Rowan was thoughtful as a variety of scenarios ran through his mind. On the face of it, it could prove to be a problem, but he had never planned on staying in Grovesbury Gardens forever anyway. He would just have to move a little faster on finding himself a particularly smitten, wealthy woman, or *patronne* as they were called in the old days.

'I'm surprised Pascal hasn't mentioned it to me.' Steve sipped his drink. 'I guess he's been too busy to notice.'

'Not for long, he won't be. I'm quite sure Chris will alert all the landlords to the state of affairs. He's been after these last four cottages for as long as I can remember.'

'Well, I'm fortunate in that it doesn't affect me from a residential point of view, but it would be a pity to have to close the clinic. The location here is perfect, and there's no room for expansion at my Sandymount practice.'

'It's the end of an era,' Nellie spoke softly, 'but they all have to come to an end sometime. I was born here, I've lived here all my life and I'd hoped to die here. Perhaps that's not to be.'

'Liam and Carmela Walshe would *never* put you out, Nellie. I'm quite sure of that.' Niamh was emphatic. 'Apart from anything else, that sanctimonious cow Carmela wouldn't like her "holier than thou" image to appear tarnished.'

'I wouldn't be too sure about that.' Nellie stubbed out her

cigarette. 'These people always find ways of justifying things to suit themselves, especially when there's money involved.' She looked pensive. 'The second Lord Grovesbury was a very good man, you know, far ahead of his time. I remember him coming to visit us at the cottage when I was a child. Did you know he built Grovesbury, Ailesbury and Shrewsbury roads on his estate?' Nellie chuckled. 'I suppose you'd call him a property developer these days.

'The first up-market housing estate for the new middle class, eh?' Steve quipped.

'And they haven't left yet, more's the pity,' Niamh said bitterly.

'So the cottages,' Nellie continued, '*our* cottages, were built for the staff who worked in the big houses. Of course, in those days, you needed *fleets* of staff.

They chatted for a while longer as a cool breeze blew in through the open back door. Nellie was the first to leave. 'Thank you, Niamh. It was good of you to go to such trouble.'

'No trouble. Come on, I'll see you home.'

'Sure, I'm only two doors down. Even I can make it that far.' Nellie shooed Niamh back inside. 'Look after your guests!' And, with a broad wink, she tottered off down the lane.

'More coffee anyone?' Niamh closed the door softly.

'Not for me.' Rowan stretched. 'Man that was a good bash at the Sheehans' the other night, wasn't it?'

'It sure was,' Steve agreed, with a wry grin. 'Thanks, Niamh, I'll have a top up if there's one going.' Turning back to Rowan, he added, 'I believe you've made quite an impression on Liam and Carmela's daughter, what's her name? Marysomething?'

'Marysol.' Rowan grinned. 'Yeah, she's some operator.'

'How old is she?' Niamh sounded disapproving.

'Twenty-one going on forty-five. Don't worry, Niamh, she's over the age of consent.'

'It's a matter of complete indifference to me.' Niamh pursed her lips and sneaked a longing look at Steve from under sparse eyelashes. 'Personally I find it pathetic the way grown men chase young girls. It's a sign of grave insecurity. Isn't it, Steve?'

'Gimme a break, Niamh, I'm only thirty-four!' Rowan looked peeved.

'Hmm?' Steve was lost in thought. 'What was that you were saying?'

'Niamh was lecturing on the evils of men chasing young women.' Rowan spotted his chance. 'Speaking of which, who was that stunning-looking girl in the red dress with the fat fuck?'

'Really, Rowan, your language ...' Niamh raised her eyes to heaven.

'You mean Alex? Chris Carroll's partner?' Steve looked amused.

'Is that her name?' Rowan feigned only slight interest.

'Careful, Rowan,' Steve warned. 'You don't want to mess with Chris Carroll. Leave well enough alone. Remember, so many women, so little time?' Steve got up. 'Thanks, Niamh. I'd better get going, early start and all that.'

'Oh must you?' Niamh tried not to sound deflated.

'Yeah, me too man.' Rowan got up and made for the door.

'Remember, Niamh,' Steve turned towards her, 'if there's anything I can do, you know, to help you find somewhere, or whatever, don't hesitate to call.'

'Oh, thank you Steve.' Niamh flushed with pleasure as she saw them out. 'I certainly will remember that.'

Steve and Rowan strolled along the lane until they reached Rowan's cottage. 'She's got the hots for you mate, better watch out!'

'Don't be ridiculous!' Steve laughed. 'Anyway, I'm staying well away from women for the foreseeable future.

'I think it's safe to say Niamh ní Cheavin escapes that category,' Rowan chuckled. 'See ya.'

Cee

When Steve let himself into his house ten minutes later, it was already past eleven. Wandering into the kitchen, he grabbed himself a beer and went out to the garden to sit at the old wooden table.

It was coming up to two years now since Claire had left him, and he still found coming home to an empty house strangely disconcerting. Outside, it was balmy with a bright moon – one of those nights that never quite seemed to get dark.

He finished his beer and decided to check on Buddy before turning in. The dog hadn't responded as well as Steve would have hoped and was still very weak. Looking into his kennel, he saw Buddy's condition was unchanged. The dog's breathing was weak and shallow as he slept. Steve opened the door, checked the drips he was still hooked up to and closed the door quietly. He decided, as he often did with a sick animal, to sit with him for a while, and he pulled up a chair beside the kennel, putting his feet up on the nearby table. 'Hang in there, old chap,' he murmured. 'It's what we're all doing.'

It was funny, he thought, yawning, how the very things that could attract you to a person ended up coming between you. Initially, it had been Claire's ambition and energy that had appealed to him, and in the end, it was what destroyed them. Their romance had weathered student life, exams, time spent studying abroad and apart, but not marriage. As a doctor, Claire had started out like him, an idealist, but gradually had become consumed by the endless politics and game playing that went hand in hand with the speciality she was pursuing so relentlessly. When she had been offered a place on the select training team in the famous Mayo Clinic in the US, she had begged him to come with her. He couldn't do it. For a while they had tried, but long-distance marriage wasn't what Steve had in mind. After a particularly passionate row, during which she had accused Steve of being more attached to his animals than to his marriage, they had parted acrimoniously. He often wondered if she had been right. At any rate, he had no doubt she was still cutting people up with supreme competence – just as she had him. But on nights like this, he still missed her.

Sold

He wasn't sure when he had dozed off, but it was the repetitive noise that invaded his sleep: *thump, thump, thump.*

Rubbing his eyes, Steve shook himself awake and grinned. He'd have known that sound anywhere. It was the unmistakably vigorous beat of a strong, healthy tail.

Sure enough, when he looked down, Buddy was grinning up at him, struggling to get to his feet. 'Hey, hey, take it easy, old man, glad to see you've decided to rejoin us.' Steve patted the dog warmly and gave him some fresh water.

Looking at the clock on the wall, he saw it was four-thirty in the morning and picked up the phone. It was never too early to ring a distraught owner to give them good news.

Bobbi Levinsky took a moment and looked out the window of her sixty-sixth floor corner office in the Chrysler Building for the last time. Beneath her, Manhattan spread out like a jigsaw puzzle in the early-morning haze.

Then she picked up her briefcase, turned on her heels and left, closing the door softly behind her.

At five-thirty in the morning, the lobby was empty, apart from Ed, the night porter, who jumped to his feet as Bobbi exited the elevator.

'Morning, Ms Levinsky. This is a late one, even for you.'

'Morning, Ed. I had a few loose ends to tie up. You know how it is.'

'Ms Levinsky,' Ed twisted his cap in his hands awkwardly, 'we're sure gonna miss you around here. Won't be the same without you.'

'It's time to move on, Ed.' Bobbi patted his arm affectionately. 'You take care now, I'll be seeing you.'

'I sure hope so, Ms Levinsky. I sure hope so.'

Outside, Bobbi began the brisk, seven-block walk to her Park Avenue apartment. She would finish her packing and call a few friends before the limo arrived to take her to the airport.

With everything that had happened recently, it would have been way too weird to stay around.

It was funny how she still felt like a failure, despite selling her cosmetics company to Proctor & Gamble for over a billion dollars. *The Economist* had billed it as the biggest one-off achievement for an American businesswoman ever – *Time* magazine had hailed her as 'Superbabe' with the body of a supermodel and an even sexier brain.

Whatever way you looked at it, as far as Bobbi was concerned, she had still lost out. Bobbi L cosmetics had been *her* baby, and it had been brutally wrenched away from her in a vicious, male-dominated, boardroom coup.

And Richard, well he had been *really* supportive, right up to the moment when she had found out about his fling with her personal secretary. So much for romance. Was it any wonder she felt screwed over every which way?

It was her tax lawyers who had come up with the idea of establishing residence and citizenship in Ireland. That's where the personal investment she didn't even know she had in a doggy cosmetics factory in somewhere called County Laois had come in handy.

And here she was, ten days later, all set to go.

Back in her apartment, her answering machine blinked insistently.

First Richard: 'Please, Bobbi. Can't we at least *talk* about this? You owe me that much.'

Then her best friend Susan: 'Bobbi, are you sure about this, I mean *really* sure? Ireland's so far away. I wish you'd call …'

And then, thankfully, her cell phone: 'Ms Levinsky? This is Norman downstairs. Your limo is outside ready to take you to JFK.'

'You can send for my bags now, Norman. I'll be right down.' Her voice sounded flat, she noticed. Flat and, somehow, defeated. She was surprised to find this did not bother her. She felt nothing. She was numb.

But numb was good right now. She could do numb.

4

'I'm extremely worried about your sister, Padraig.' Carmela
had had the rare pleasure of attending mass with her son who,
by chance, had a couple of free hours. Now, as they sat
companionably in the morning room enjoying a pot of fresh
coffee, Carmela felt she could broach the subject that was
weighing so heavily on her mind.

Padraig looked up from the *Irish Catholic*, concern written
all over his long, narrow face. 'Why, Mama?' he asked, reverting
to Spanish, his mother's native tongue, which he knew she
loved conversing in.

Carmela looked at him fondly. 'Of course, Padraig, you're
so *spiritually* inclined. I suppose you wouldn't even notice her
behaviour.' Carmela paused. 'I probably shouldn't burden you
with the subject, but you're so wise for your age, and I
thought, well, I thought you might be able to give me some
insight as to how I, we, your father and I, can stop this
alarming trend. You wouldn't have heard about it, of course,

but there was an appallingly embarrassing episode in the Sheehans' jacuzzi the other night.'

Padraig hid a smile. He had heard all about it in vivid detail the following day from his hairdresser-boyfriend Deke, whose sister did Melissa Sheehan's hair and who had witnessed the whole spectacle herself. And it wasn't the only interesting snippet he had heard about his sister's antics, but, for now, it would be much wiser to keep this precious knowledge to himself.

'Perhaps she's having problems at work? Public relations is such an obsessive business, Mama, only concerned with image and so forth, that people can lose sight of the really important things in life … I could talk to her if you like?' Padraig's two-pronged reply was brilliant on both counts. Firstly, he knew his mother couldn't bear to entertain the thought that Marysol's behaviour might have anything to do with her upbringing, and secondly, he knew Carmela was slightly afraid of Marysol, not to mention finding discussing immoral behaviour of any kind utterly abhorrent.

'Oh would you?' Carmela was overwhelmed with relief. 'It would mean so much to your father and I. She'll listen to you, Padraig.'

Padraig wasn't so sure, but it was only fair to tip her off. Marysol was getting way too uppity since she had landed that tasty job in the flash PR company and had already twice refused to get him backstage passes to meet his favourite boy band. It was high time she got a wake-up call.

'Leave it with me, Mama. I shall choose my moment.'

Ce

'Everyone okay for a drink?' Chris sat back in the old leather chair in his study and puffed slowly on his cigar. 'We're just waiting for Liam, he's been held up but should be along any minute.'

'His daughter, what's her name?' Michael Moriarty asked.

'Marysol?'

'Yeah, that's the one. She put on a good show the other night, eh, Pascal?'

'Now, now, don't be bitchy Michael,' Pascal grinned broadly, 'it doesn't suit you. Sure she's just a little high-spirited, that's all.

'She didn't get that from her mother.'

'Shush, here's Liam now, I think.'

'Hello, hello, hope I didn't keep you waiting?' Liam glided towards the drinks cabinet.

'Help yourself, Liam.'

'Thanks, I'll have a Jameson.'

'So, what's all this about the cottages, Chris?' Rod Sykes asked expectantly.

'As you all know, Grovesbury Hall is finally up for sale – an interesting piece of property I'm sure you'll agree. While I was looking over the legal documents with my solicitor, Malcolm, he brought to my attention the fact that the leases on the remaining four cottages in Grovesbury Gardens are up at the end of this year, which you may, or may not, be aware of.

'Weren't those cottages originally part of the Grovesbury estate?' Michael asked.

'They were, Michael. They were built by the second Lord Grovesbury to house the staff who worked in the Hall and the very houses we now live in.' Chris cleared his throat. 'My late parents, I'm fortunate to say, had the foresight to begin buying them up one buy one. I, of course, have continued the process, with the result that, bar the final four remaining cottages belonging to you guys, Grovesbury Gardens is now part of my property portfolio.

'Michael and I are interested in developing the site, which lends itself perfectly to an exclusive apartment complex – which is where the rest of you come in. Obviously, we need the last four cottages to go ahead with the development. Any of you who are interested are welcome to come in on the deal with us. All I'm asking, is that you get your tenants out as soon as possible, and we can move straightaway. Malcolm will take us through the details in a moment. What do you say?'

'I'm not sure I like the idea of putting someone out of their home.' Rod looked doubtful.

'Oh come, there's a glut in the rentals market right now. No one is going to have any problem finding alternative accommodation,' Chris said briskly.

'Nellie Murphy's in her nineties. She's lived in Grovesbury Gardens all her life.' Liam sounded nervous.

'All the more reason for her to go into a good residential home – there are some very good ones in the area. It would be worth your while to organise it, Liam.'

'I, er, I'm not sure, Chris. I'll have to consult with Carmela. I'll approach Nellie, of course, but if she's not keen I'd feel obliged to let her end her days in the cottage. Do unto others and all that.'

People began to shift uneasily in their chairs. Chris glowered at Liam. This was exactly the kind of mealy-mouthed talk he had hoped to avoid.

'I didn't realise the lease was up so soon.' Pascal looked concerned. 'It would be a pity to have to move Steve Sorenson's animal clinic. Melissa likes having a vet on hand for Dolce and Gabbana. I was going to renew the lease anyway, he's a great tenant.'

Chris was livid but he moved on smoothly. 'That leaves Rowan Delaney. What about it Rod?'

'To be honest, I wouldn't be sorry to get shot of him. He's having a very bad influence on my boy, Nathan.' Rod looked uncomfortable. 'But he is a struggling artist and all that. Can you imagine the publicity?'

'What about Grovesbury Hall? Where does that fit into the picture?' Liam asked.

'Good question.'

'Actually, Michael and I are proposing to bid for that. A few pals of mine in the UK are keen to form a consortium. It's a unique property, fantastic development potential, the location's ideal. Any of you who are keen, of course, can come on board with that too. But, regardless, it suits us to move on both developments as soon as possible. Overheads and all that. So what do you say? Any of you keen to join us?' Chris looked around the room expectantly. 'Pascal?'

'Sorry, Chris, count me out. I've got my hands full with my own developments, and I'm really not sure about moving Steve's animal clinic. I think I'll renew his lease. What would all the old biddies and their pets do without him?'

'I see.' Chris smiled thinly. 'What about you, Rod? Now's your chance to play with the big boys. You won't get a chance like this again to break into the property game in Dublin.'

'Thanks, Chris, but no thanks.' Rod might have only hit thirty, but he was still sensitive to the tabloid-press experiences he had gone through when he made his multimillions in England. He had an aversion to any kind of negative publicity.

'That leaves you, Liam?'

'Well, as I said, I'll have to talk to Carmela. I appreciate the offer, Chris, but unless Nellie Murphy is happy to go into a home, well, I'd feel obliged to let her stay on. It's the least we can do really ...'

Malcolm MacBride tapped the pile of papers on the table in front of him after the others had left, 'Looks like you've got a problem.'

'Correction, *we've* got a problem.' Chris took a swig from his glass. 'Find me a way to get those tenants out, Malcolm. There must be some legal stunt you can pull. Failing that, when I buy Grovesbury Hall, I'll just have to inform the chaps that the cottages have reverted to me – there's no need to mention the business of selling them on to the tenants for a pittance. So, either way, I'd say it's a win–win situation.'

'Ms R Levinsky': the sign held up by the portly little man waiting in Arrivals was clear.

Bobbi made her way out through the gates, pushing her trolley in front of her. 'Hi, I'm Bobbi,' she held out her hand to the man, who was immersed in the racing pages of a newspaper. He looked up, quickly put away the paper and shook her hand vigorously. 'Welcome to Dublin, Ms Levinsky, I'm Jack. Follow me, your car is outside.'

As the long black Mercedes cruised along, Bobbi revised her opinion that all airport routes were basically the same soulless drive. The watery sunlight hinted at the promise of a warm, balmy day ahead, and even the little motorway leading into the city seemed fresh and uncluttered. As Jack chatted companionably, Bobbi searched in vain for the relentless traffic he reliably informed her would be descending upon them at any given moment. At six forty-five in the morning the road was clear, even when they came upon the curious low-rise clusters of redbrick houses interspersed with funny little shops. She had expected something along the lines of London, except smaller, and found the hotchpotch arrangement of buildings vaguely intriguing. Soon, they were crossing the river and heading for the suburbs and, after that, somewhere called Ballsbridge, eventually pulling up outside the Four Seasons Hotel.

A uniformed young man opened the car door for her and, as she got out, she was greeted by the hotel manager, who warmly welcomed her. 'Welcome to the Four Seasons, Ms Levinsky. Your suite is waiting for you and may I say what a pleasure it is for us to have you here. Michael will show you up. If there's anything we can do to make your stay more comfortable, please don't hesitate to let us know.'

'Thank you, I will.' Bobbi followed Michael into the lift and was brought up to the Premier Suite. It was a suite, just like all the others she had stayed in over the years – beautiful, sumptuously luxurious and blissfully anonymous.

'Will you be needing anything, Ms Levinsky?'

'No thanks, Michael. This looks great.'

When she was alone, she stripped off, headed straight for the shower and washed off yet another wearisome journey. Then, wrapped in a fluffy bathrobe, she drew the blinds, flung herself on the vast bed and wondered for about thirty seconds what the hell she was doing before falling soundly asleep.

Marysol was in the kitchen when Padraig finally got a chance to talk to her alone.

'Mmm, that smells good. What is it?'

'Nothing for you to get excited about. I'm taking it round to a friend of mine for a late supper.'

'Ah, that would be your painter friend, would it not?'

'Rowan's an artist, not a painter.'

'And clearly not a starving one, judging by the way you've been looking after his appetite.'

Marysol shot him a look. 'Why the sudden interest in my social life, Padraig?'

'Oh, I always have my big sister's interests at heart, you know that. Actually, I feel it only fair to point out that you're treading rather a fine line at the moment.'

'If you're referring to the Sheehans' party, I was a bit squiffy and responding to the plaintive cries of a small child who had fallen into the jacuzzi. Actually, if it wasn't for me he might have drowned. Rod and Tanya Sykes should be down on their knees thanking me.'

'Mama is very worried about you, to say the least. She feels your behaviour, not to mention your dress sense, is becoming increasingly inappropriate, quite apart from the company you appear to be keeping. I said I'd have a word with you.'

'Well you've had your word, now piss off. I have to get this sauce just right and you're distracting me. What are you going to tell her?'

'That you've seen the error of your ways and are willing to

apologise for letting the family down and are determined to lead a henceforth unblemished existence.'

Marysol snorted. 'That's rich coming from you.'

'Alternatively, of course, I could inform Mama that dinner is not the only thing you've been supplying that painter chappie with.'

'What are you talking about?'

'Oh, come now, Marysol. How long did you think your sordid little secret would be safe for? Do you really think you can get away with pilfering from the family home? A particularly nasty pastime, if I may say so. Even for you.

'I have no idea what you're talking about.'

'Oh, I think you do. And while I'm on the subject, you should tell Rowan to be careful where he wears that cashmere jumper you nicked. It was Father's particular favourite. He's been looking everywhere for it. And, as we speak, Mama is blaming the builders for the disappearance of her smaller solitaire, the three-carat one I believe. You must have quite a lot of dosh if you've offloaded that. I'm sure they'd love to know their beloved daughter is stealing from them.'

'And I'm equally sure they'd love to learn their beloved only son is as gay as Christmas.'

'They'd never believe you, not in a million years. It would only confirm their opinion of how depraved you've become.'

Marysol sighed, 'What do you want?'

'Backstage passes to Westlife's concert in the RDS and an invite to the party in Renards afterwards. Oh, and I'll have a helping of that pasta, now that you mention it.'

Ce

Bobbi awoke with a start and, for a moment, had absolutely no idea where she was. The electric alarm clock beside the bed was beeping insistently and registered four p. m. Gradually, her eyes grew accustomed to the dim light and she got up to draw back the blinds, blinking at the strong shaft of sunlight that lit up the room. Going to bed had probably not been a good idea, given the tyrannical demands of jetlag, but the events of the last few weeks had totally exhausted her, emotionally and physically, and she felt better for her few hours' sleep.

As it was such a beautiful afternoon, she decided to go out and get her bearings. A gentle run was just what she needed to shake off the grogginess of transatlantic travel, and she could take in the neighbourhood at the same time. She pulled on a pair of sweatpants and a cropped sports top, fixed her shoulder length hair up in a ponytail and headed downstairs.

Outside, Bobbi followed the directions the concierge had given her and headed left out of the hotel and across the main road in the direction of Sandymount Strand. The late afternoon sun was still strong and she was glad of the baseball cap she had pulled on to keep the glare from her eyes. At a quarter-to-five, the traffic was already building, and she was struck by the number of convertible cars she saw, their drivers lounging nonchalantly in the static progress, sneaking surreptitious looks from behind designer shades to make sure they were being noticed.

Gradually, she picked up her pace and, before long, found herself at the seafront, just as she had been told. The tide was out and, as mothers sunbathed, a few intrepid children paddled at the shoreline, while a steady flow of dogs and their owners meandered lazily along in the heat. Feeling more invigorated with every stride, Bobbi followed the shoreline for a while, and then made a right turn, coming back to the main road again and crossing over to Ailesbury Road. Here the houses took on grander proportions, and she realised she was entering the exclusive embassy belt she had read about. Stately Victorian mansions reposed regally in the shade of elegant chestnut and beech trees, and an air of quiet reserve prevailed. Judging from the amount of luxury cars parked in respective driveways, affluence sat easily with the inhabitants of this neighbourhood.

She was beginning to tire and slow her pace to a gentle jog

when a large sign caught her attention in the distance. Drawing closer, she continued down Grovesbury Road, where the impressive houses took on more of a high Victorian Tudor style. More than one of them seemed to be in a state of refurbishment. Approaching the sign, she slowed to a walk, pausing to take in the magnificent, decaying old mansion. You couldn't miss the For Sale sign, yet despite its imperious proportions, there was something terribly forlorn about the old place, like something out of a romantic novel from a bygone age. 'Grovesbury Hall', the sign read. 'A unique property comprising ten thousand square feet on grounds of ten acres. For Auction 4th June. Joint Agents Mitford & Cantrell, UK.'

In the evening sun, the honeyed stone of the house glowed softly, and a magnificent portico flanked with columns framed the impressive doorway, where peeling strips of paint unfurled a lonely path. Beautifully proportioned windows, behind which heavy drapes were drawn, hinted at an interior rife with history and intrigue. Bobbi had travelled extensively in Europe, and its other-worldy architecture had always held a fascination for her, particularly in contrast to the instantly manufactured 'old homes' of America. This, she thought, was the kind of house that people wrote about. A romantic house. And she'd bet her bottom dollar it had a story or two to tell. Lost in thought, she was backing across the road to get a better look at the house when a screech of brakes brought her to a startled halt.

'You ought to look where you're going, babe,' the driver of the silver convertible Porsche admonished, giving her an appreciative once over. 'Shame to put a dint in that fabulous bodywork.' And, before she could think of a suitably curt reply, he was gone, roaring off down the road before turning in to one of the gateways further down.

'Asshole,' Bobbi muttered under her breath, looking after him. All the same, she had got a fright. She was still jetlagged, and the close shave left her jangled. Although the driver's last-minute swerve and screech of breaks seemed excessive – after all, he had the whole road to get around her – she still hadn't been paying proper attention. Breaking into a gentle jog back to her hotel, she shook her head and grinned. At least the natives appeared to be friendly.

5

Phillip O'Sullivan fidgeted with the lapel of his new Louis Copeland suit and went over for the hundredth time what his boss, Tom Knight, had told him.

'This is the big one, Phil. The sale we've been waiting for. You won't see another property like Grovesbury Hall coming onto the market. Now, I've told you the drill. The call from New York will come through to my mobile at a quarter-past two. You'll speak to a Mr O'Hara of Finnegan O'Hara and keep him abreast of the bidding. Sit at the front of the room where I can see you. When he puts in a bid, give me the nod – got it?'

'Yes, Mr Knight.'

'And make sure Susan has set out enough chairs in our upstairs room. Thirty should be more than enough – I don't anticipate there'll be that many people throwing forty million euro about.

Chris Carroll pulled up outside the Shelbourne Hotel and handed the keys of his Porsche to Jimmy, the porter.

'Mr Moriarty's gone in ahead of you, Mr Carroll. Not five minutes ago.'

'Thanks, Jimmy. Look after the car will you? We'll be a couple of hours.'

Chris strolled through the lobby to the side bar where he had arranged to meet Michael for a quick lunch before the auction, which was being held a couple of doors away. At one thirty, the bar was still busy, but Chris saw that Michael had managed to get a window table and had already ordered.

'Hi, Chris, I took the liberty of ordering two smoked salmon platters. Okay for you?'

'Fine.' Chris helped himself to a glass of sparkling water. 'I told Malcolm we'd see him there.'

'I spoke to Tom Knight earlier. Apparently there's a fair bit of interest.'

'Well he would say that, wouldn't he? But nothing we shouldn't be able to see off, eh? The usual suspects I suppose?'

'Yeah, I figure the main competition will be Mitchell's gang of medics. They've been hot to trot for months to find a site for their new private clinic.' Michael referred to the well-known plastic surgeon who was behind many of the new private hospitals springing up around the city.

'Shouldn't be a problem. He should stick to what he knows best – he's not in our league when it comes to carving people up.'

Michael chuckled. 'There are two embassies at least and some interest from another UK consortium. That's about it as far as I can make out.'

'Well, they're wasting their time.' Chris raised his glass. 'Here's to you and me becoming the new owners of Grovesbury Hall.'

'I'll drink to that!'

Niamh sat in her little office in the land registry department and leafed idly through the *Irish Times* property section as she sipped her mid-morning cup of tea. She had taken to checking the apartments-for-let column but, as yet, she could only be half-hearted about it. Somehow she could never see herself living anywhere but in her dear little cottage. The thought of a bleak, modern apartment block left her absolutely cold. And the only cottages for rent seemed to be miles out of town, which would mean serious commuting expenses. If only she could think of a way to stop Chris Carroll putting her out but, as the lease was up, there was absolutely nothing she could do. She had already gone over the situation with her solicitor several times and researched the matter thoroughly herself, all to no avail. Come November, she would say goodbye to the little cottage once and for all.

She was just about to turn the page when the notice caught her eye. Of course, Grovesbury Hall was up for auction today; she had almost forgotten. If she could swap her early lunch hour for a later one, she could slip into the auction in time for the bidding. At least it might take her mind off things, and as Chris Carroll was bound to be there, she could have the pleasure of pushing the price up a couple of notches for him. No one would suspect that she wasn't a legitimate bidder, except Chris, of course. Anyway, he and his cronies could well afford it – but even the super-rich resented having to pay a penny more than they had to for anything. That's how they stayed rich, she supposed.

Feeling decidedly better about things, Niamh folded away the paper and settled back to the pile of work in front of her. There was nothing like a little retail therapy to look forward to in a lunch hour, particularly when it was somebody else's money you were spending.

Cee

At two o'clock, people were beginning to drift in to the estate agent's and upstairs to the private room where the auction would be held. Philip O'Sullivan and Susan, Tom Knights' PA, had set the room out meticulously. At the front of the room was a long table from behind which Tom would conduct the auction. In front of this were rows of chairs where the interested parties and their legal teams would take their places and, of course, the inevitable reporters anxious to grab the scoop on the biggest private property sale to hit Dublin in decades.

By the time Niamh had slipped quietly in to take her place, there was only standing room and the excitement was palpable. Looking around the room, she soon spotted Chris Carroll, sitting with Michael Moriarty on the right-hand side, deep in conversation.

At two fifteen on the dot, the mobile in Philip O'Sullivan's hand began to ring. He answered it promptly and confirmed to the brisk American voice on the other end, that the auction was starting imminently and he, Philip, would be liasing with him on behalf of Mr Tom Knight.

Right on cue, the ceremony commenced. Tom Knight, along with his colleagues and the solicitors of the late vendor, strolled in from the side door and took their places behind the desk.

In his brisk, charismatic fashion, Tom began the sale. 'Can I have twenty million. Twenty million to start for this unique property?'

Silence.

'Come now, we all know what this property is worth. Twenty million anyone?'

Still silence.

It was customary to make the auctioneer pitch a little lower even though everyone in the room knew the stakes would soon soar. Tom was just about to drop to eighteen million when he got a firm nod from Phillip, sitting eagerly in the front row.

Delighted, Tom threw himself into what would be the most talked about auction ever held in the country, despite the ludicrous price of property in Dublin 4 – at present anything from three to five million per acre. 'Thank you, sir!' he smiled confidently. 'I have an opening bid of twenty million euro for this amazing property. Twenty million ...'

'Who the hell is that little twit on the phone?' Chris muttered to Michael.

'No idea. Guess he's one of Tom's boys, could be anyone he's bidding for.'

'Twenty-one million, thank you on my right ...' Fred Mitchell, the plastic surgeon, studied his notes as his solicitor put in the bid on behalf of the private hospital group.

'Twenty-two million. Do I have twenty-three million anywhere? Thank you, at the back of room. To you, sir. Twenty-five million, anyone?' Another nod from Phillip, a wide smile from Tom Knight who paused and, having conferred with the legal team to confirm that they had reached the agreed reserve price, announced formally, 'Ladies and gentlemen, I can now confirm that Grovesbury Hall is officially on the market.'

This was the moment of truth, when the really heavy hitters would come in. 'Twenty-five million. I have twenty-five million. We're only getting started ladies and gentlemen! Any increase? Yes! Twenty-six, on my right. Against you, sir, at the back. Twenty-seven, thank you, sir. Do I have thirty? Let's get down to business. Is there thirty million in the room?'

'Let's get in there,' whispered Michael to Chris, who gave the nod to Malcolm McBride across the room.

'Thirty million. Thank you, sir. This is more like it for this unique property, Thirty million. Let's not be coy here, gentlemen. What's that? Thirty-five? Well done, sir! Thirty-five million I'm bid.'

'Thirty-six! Thank you, sir. Thirty-six million against you, sir.' Tom indicated to Chris that the counterbid was against him.

'This is ridiculous, forty's our max. Who the fuck's pushing the price up – it's not worth nearly this much.'

A tense silence settled on the room as the last of the

competitors dropped out leaving Chris and Michael and whoever was bidding by phone.

'Thirty-six million, gentlemen. It's against you,' Tom said with a gleam in his eye.

'Let's up it – wrap it up for God's sake and scare them off,' Michael urged as Chris nodded grimly.

'Forty million, thank you indeed, sir. This is more like it! Forty million I'm bid for Grovesbury Hall, I'm going to sell ...'

Niamh, standing squashed up against the wall at the back of the room could hardly believe her ears. Such huge sums of money were being bandied about so nonchalantly – and there had hardly been breathing space to throw an extra bid in, fictitious or otherwise.

'Forty-two! Thank you, sir.' Tom grinned at Phillip who had indicated the bid and looked as if he was about to faint at the amount of money he was spending vicariously.

'Go for it,' urged Michael. And Chris nodded again.

'Forty-three. Thank you, sir. Forty-three million euro I'm bid for Grovesbury Hall. I'm selling. Are there any other bids?' Tom looked theatrically round the room full of disbelieving faces at the unheard of price for a house in the heart of Dublin 4.

Phillip held the phone tensely, listening acutely as there was a brief, 'Hold the line a minute there, Philip.'

'I'm selling at forty-three million ...' Tom continued.

In the front row, Phillip held up his hand, indicating to Tom to pause for a second, which seemed to fill eternity. The voice on the end of the phone came back decisively. 'Phillip? You still with us?'

'Yes, sir?'

'Let's wrap this up,' the American voice said briskly. 'Fifty million, and we'll keep going if we have to ...'

Phillip got up unsteadily and went up to the table where he whispered in Tom's ear.

'Fifty million!' beamed Tom. 'Fifty million, I'm offered for

Grovesbury Hall. For the last time, any advance on fifty million?

'Let it go.' Chris sat looking grim faced as Michael shook his head.

'The property is sold! Fifty million euro. Congratulations, sir!'

In the furore that ensued, nobody noticed the tall, beautiful, elegantly dressed brunette slip quietly from the room. Outside, she answered the insistent ring of her mobile phone.

'Ms Levinsky? Following your instructions, we are happy to inform you that you are now the new owner of Grovesbury Hall. On behalf of Finnegan O'Hara, I'd like to offer you our heartiest congratulations. That must be one hell of a house you've got yourself!'

'It sure is,' said Bobbi happily, reflecting that she hadn't even been inside the front door.

6

Alex couldn't figure out where she was going wrong.

In the beginning, when she had been a beautiful young model, Chris had been besotted with her. He had first seen her at a charity fashion show at the Point Theatre, which he had been attending with his then girlfriend, and from the moment he had set eyes on her, he had wanted her. At first, she had resisted his persistent phone calls and invitations. Chris was ten years her senior and, apart from coming from a rich and successful family, had acquired quite a reputation as being a veritable whizzkid in his own right, not to mention enjoying superlative success as a ladies' man.

To be truthful, she had been rather frightened of him, but Chris Carroll wasn't used to taking no for an answer. Her repeated refusals only made him even more determined. Eventually, his tenacity paid off, and she had agreed to have dinner with him. He had arrived at her family home in Templeogue in his chauffeur-driven Bentley coupé and whisked her to dinner in Paris, courtesy of the private jet he had chartered for the night. It was heady stuff for a young girl, and she had never looked back. When Chris set his mind on something, he was totally concentrated, and he had set about wooing her with the unwavering determination that generations of Carrolls had employed to get whatever, and whomever, they wanted.

After three months, she was giddily in love with him, and the feeling appeared to be mutual. Despite her parents' concerns – 'he's too old for you', 'he's not one of us', 'he'll never marry you' (this last one from her mother) – she was won over. She truly thought her prince charming had arrived, just like Richard Gere in *Pretty Woman*.

That the marriage proposal hadn't been forthcoming did not initially concern her. They were in love. That was all that had mattered. Chris couldn't get enough of her and regularly told her so. When she found she was accidentally pregnant after just six months, she was thrilled, if nervous, and couldn't wait to tell him the wonderful news. Of course, it would be a shock, she knew, but it was 'meant to be'. Wasn't that why these things happened?

Chris hadn't taken the news well initially. He was in the middle of a big property deal and was stressed and under pressure, but she knew he'd come around and see it for the wonderful surprise it was. And, sure enough, he had asked her to move into the fabulous home he had bought and renovated where his late parents had lived before him. Six months later, Cindy had been born, and Alex thought she would die with happiness. What did it matter that they weren't married? They didn't need a piece of paper or a church service to proclaim their love to the world.

Her parents were not happy about the situation, but fell in love with their first granddaughter the moment they saw her, and wisely said nothing about how they felt.

That had been two-and-a-half years ago. And, if she was truthful, Alex admitted to herself that things had never been quite the same between them. She had kept herself in good shape, regaining her willowy figure a ridiculously short time after Cindy's birth, but while the physical side of their relationship was still regular, she could feel Chris slipping away from her, losing interest steadily day by day. The thought of losing him was constantly on her mind and made her blood run cold with fear.

They'd been together for almost three years now and, lately, it seemed he couldn't stand to be around her. No matter what she did, she irritated him. Getting pregnant this time had been deliberate. She just *knew* Chris would love to have a son, no matter what he said about not wanting any more children, and it would be lovely for Cindy to have a sibling close in age to her. Apart from anything else, Alex was desperate. Giving Chris a son and heir seemed like the only flicker of light at the end of the awfully cold and lonely tunnel she had somehow found herself in.

Cee

'Good to meet you, Ms Levinsky.' The good-looking architect shook Bobbi's hand heartily. 'This is quite a project you've taken on here.'

'That's why I've employed you.' Bobbi smiled as she took in the six-foot four physique and immensely attractive face that had earned Sean O'Rourke the nickname of 'The Body'. 'You and your firm come highly recommended, Mr O'Rourke, and, please, call me Bobbi. I look forward to working with you.'

'Let's take the tour, shall we? We'll start at the top and work downwards.'

'Ready when you are.' Bobbi followed Sean up the magnificent staircase that began in the middle of the vast hallway and divided into two parts as it ascended on to the return, where an extraordinary multicoloured stained-glass window filtered the outside sunlight into the dim interior. They continued to climb the flights leading up through four majestic floors until they finally reached the top of the house and a small door, leading to what Sean informed her would have been the servants' quarters.

'Oh!' cried Bobbi. 'What a darling little room.' Before her was a small room, full of nooks and crannies and helter-skelter proportions, topped by a steeply sloping ceiling. Following the inter-connecting door through to the next room, another door appeared, which, when opened, led onto a hidden flight of stairs.

'The turret room,' said Sean, smiling at his client's obvious delight. 'These were a common feature of houses built at this time.' As he talked into his Dictaphone, giving the proportions and measurements as he went along, Bobbi followed like an excited child. The turret room was on the east side of the house and looked out onto both the front and back of the extensive grounds, from where the old stables were just visible.

As they worked their way down the house, exploring room after room and admiring the fabulous proportions and period features, Sean chatted about some of his ideas and the immense possibilities involved in totally renovating the place, without of course losing any of its unique charm.

'It'll be a long haul, Bobbi. You do realise that, don't you?' Sean asked, as they arrived back down in the hall. 'I don't know how soon you'd hoped to move in, but we're talking at least nine months here, maybe a year.'

'That's okay, I'd kind of figured we'd be talking that amount of time. For now I'm quite happy in the Four Seasons. It's comfortable and the staff are friendly, and it's good not to feel I'm on my own all the time, if I feel like company,' Bobbi smiled.

'Well, as long as you're sure. We could find you somewhere to rent if you'd prefer?' Sean said, thinking he'd bet his bottom dollar this was one woman who would not be short of company – if she wanted it, that is.

'Nope I'm fine, I'll stay put. Anyway, it's nice to be near enough to my new home to keep an eye on things.'

'What about the contents?' Sean asked.

'There are a few nice pieces I've noticed, but most of it's not exactly to my taste, shall we say. This portrait is fabulous, though,' Bobbi said, walking closer to examine the huge painting that hung over the central fireplace of a beautiful young woman sitting side-saddle in full hunting regalia on a magnificent horse. 'Who is it of do you suppose?'

'Looks like it's a young Lady Grovesbury,' said Sean, rubbing gently at the faded signature of the artist. 'Yep, here we are, "*Lady Arabella Grovesbury and Monty, 1919*".'

'Wow, she was some beauty, huh?'

'She certainly was,' agreed Sean. 'Let's head outside. I'm keen to see the old stables in particular – I have a couple of interesting ideas for them.'

Outside, their feet crunched on the gravel as they followed the rundown path framed by beech trees and came to the stables, which had certainly seen better days. There were about forty in all, built around a courtyard, all beautifully pro-portioned and spacious despite their woebegone appearance.

'They don't make 'em like this anymore,' Bobbi said admiringly, stroking a marble manger. 'Oh look,' she cried, brushing aside some stray brambles to reveal a coat of arms and a plaque, 'they have the name of the horse engraved, how lovely.'

'Like you said, they don't make them like this anymore,' Sean replied, looking at Bobbi who had become silently absorbed in thoughtful admiration. 'Did you ever keep horses?'

'I used to ride quite a bit as a kid. You know, the usual stuff, pony camp I think you call it here.'

'Right.' They continued to walk around the courtyard, finding all the loose boxes in much the same state of disrepair, coming finally to a corner one, which was bigger than the rest. Suddenly, a low-pitched growl emanated from the back of the box.

'What was that?' Bobbi jumped. As Sean turned round to follow the sound, there was a rustle from the far corner. From behind a bale of straw, a long white nose poked around, followed by a pair of sturdy forelegs, and a pair of small eyes regarded them beadily. As Bobbi watched, the butchest dog she had ever set eyes on appeared before her. It was all she could do not to laugh as Sean approached and the dog growled even more menacingly.

'Er, I think we should probably leave now,' said Sean backing off uncertainly, as the dog crouched tense and ready to spring.

'Hey, boy, it's okay. C'mon, here fella, come here.' Bobbi sat down on her hunkers and held out her hand. 'C'mon, come and say hello.'

As Sean watched apprehensively, the dog's ears twitched, and he looked towards Bobbi uncertainly. Then, never taking his eyes off Sean, the dog came towards her, slowly approaching the hand she held out.

'Careful, Bobbi,' warned Sean.

'C'mon baby, it's okay,' Bobbi cajoled, as the dog sniffed warily at her hand. Then, allowing her to stroke him, he suddenly rolled over on his back and began to lick her hand effusively. 'There you go, big guy. Who's a good boy, huh?'

'That', said Sean, 'is the ugliest dog I've ever seen. It looks like a pig!'

'Shame on you, Sean! He's an English Bull Terrier, aren't you, baby?' The dog was now frantically wagging his tail and covering Bobbi with licks. 'You're a beauty. Yes you are.'

'Well, I guess it's true what they say – it must be in the eye of the beholder.'

'He's awfully thin though, and I bet you're thirsty, baby. C'mon, let's go find you some water.' Outside in the courtyard, Bobbi found a tap and turned it on. The dog lapped hungrily from it.

'Looks like you've found a friend,' said Sean, looking amused as the dog followed Bobbi like a shadow.

'Well, I sure could do with one. This one looks like he could do with a good feed.'

There was only one more box to check out, which turned

out to have been the old tack room. Pushing through the worn half-door, they were greeted with a musty smell and an array of bits, saddles and bridles all hanging from stands on the wall. Over each, again, hung a plaque engraved with a horse's name. As Sean wandered around taking measurements, Bobbi suddenly whistled. 'Hey look at this,' she said, fingering a beautiful leather bridle.

'What?'

'Somebody's been taking real good care of this.'

'What do you mean?'

'Well, see for yourself, it's sparkling clean. Look at all the others, all covered in dust and mildew. This bridle has been polished very thoroughly by somebody. Look, it's pristine, I can smell the fresh wax. There's a name on it.' Bobbi held the old bridle to the light, where a small brass plaque revealed the name Montyson. 'How strange, that's the same name that was on the stable we found this little guy in,' she said looking down at the dog, who sat at her feet looking up enquiringly.

'Not strange at all,' said Sean wryly. 'He was in the best stable. Dogs know how to look after themselves.'

Bobbi replaced the bridle on its hook thoughtfully. 'Maybe, but I think it's strange.'

'Okay, I've got all I need here. Shall we go back to the house?' Sean started to gather up his tapes. As they made to leave the stables, the dog started to whine, hovering agitatedly outside the stable where he had, presumably, been living.

'C'mon, fella, it's okay,' Bobbi called to him. The dog still waited, whining even louder.

'I told you, he knows when he's on to a good thing. Looks like he doesn't want to leave.'

'I don't think that's it.' Bobbi looked concerned. 'C'mon, you can come with me now, it's okay.' The dog waited for a moment and looked inside the stable as if to check on it before deciding to follow his new friend, trotting at her heels.

'Not that it's any concern of mine, Bobbi, but what are you going to do with him?'

'Take him back to the hotel with me of course.'

'Do they, er, have a policy on keeping pets?'

'If necessary, I'll pay for an additional room, but I hold the Premier Suite indefinitely, so I'm sure we can come to some arrangement.'

They reached the house and made their way back to the front hall, the dog following Bobbi adoringly.

'Let's meet next week, shall we? I'll give you a call when I've put some ideas and initial plans together and we'll talk?'

'Sure thing, Sean.' Bobbi shook the proffered hand heartily.

'And good luck with your new friend.'

Bobbi was just about to reply when a voice called out. 'Sean! I thought I recognised the car. I hope you don't mind me stopping by, but I've always been fascinated by the old place. Oh,' the stranger said with feigned surprise, 'I'm so sorry. Do forgive my intruding. I'm Chris Carroll. Sean, won't you introduce me to this delightful creature?'

Bobbi turned in the direction of the confident voice to see the man who had almost run her down with the silver Porsche stride over to her and hold out his hand.

'Bobbi, this is Chris Carroll. Chris, Bobbi Levinsky.'

'Congratulations, Ms Levinsky. It's a pleasure to meet you finally, I've heard so much about you.' Chris looked directly into Bobbi's eyes. 'Grovesbury Hall will make an impressive home, although I would have thought it rather a large one for a single woman.' Chris allowed the comment to hang in the air. 'Anyhow, welcome to Grovesbury Road. You must come for dinner some evening and meet a few of your neighbours – they're all certainly dying to meet you.' Chris was at his most charming.

'Thank you, that's very kind. I'm sure I'd enjoy that, er, Chris.'

'Good, that's settled then. Sean, give me a call later on this afternoon, will you? I have a couple of things I'd like to talk to you about.'

'Sure, Chris. I'll be in touch.'

'Well, I'll be off. Sorry for dropping in unannounced as they say, and may I wish you every happiness in your new home, Bobbi. Bye, for now.'

'Who is that guy?' Bobbi asked, when Chris had left.

'One of our biggest property developers. I think he was the under-bidder from what I'm told. He was planning on turning the Hall into a luxury hotel. He's usually got a few projects on the go at any given time. Looks like you pipped him to the post on this one. I wouldn't say Chris is used to being upstaged. Personally, I'm delighted the old place is going to become the home it was always meant to be.'

'Me too,' said Bobbi. 'The minute I saw I it, I knew I had to have it.'

'Well, I'd better be off. I'll be in touch next week, okay?'

'Sure, I'll look forward to it.'

After Sean left, Bobbi wandered over to the old portrait of Lady Grovesbury and Monty and looked at it for a long while. Then, with her new four-legged friend close at her heels, she locked up and headed out into the bright summer's day. 'Looks like it's just you and me, pal. Don't know about you, but I could murder a burger. Let's see what the Four Seasons can rustle up for us, huh?'

They were half-way down Grovesbury Road when the dog picked up his pace and trotted down a little lane to the left. Curious, Bobbi followed him. She turned left again at the end of the lane and came upon a row of the cutest little cottages she had ever seen. 'GROVESBURY GARDENS' read the well-worn sign overhung by ivy on the old brick wall. The dog paused for her to catch up with him before trotting off again, stopping to sniff happily at various gates and lampposts.

Suddenly, what sounded like crashing metal and a volley of curses intruded on the up-till-then peaceful picture. Drawing closer to the sound, Bobbi stopped in her tracks as she watched someone dragging what appeared to be the top half of an old and rusted car through the gateway to one of the cottages. The dog sat down and watched too, wagging his tail back and forth, eventually letting out an excited bark. At this, the cursing stopped and, from behind the rusted metal, one of the sexiest men Bobbi had ever set eyes on appeared.

'Bruiser!' he said delightedly as the dog rushed up to him. 'Well what do you know? Where the hell have you been, you mutt! Nellie's been frantic with worry about you!'

'Bruiser?' said Bobbi, totally confused.

'That's his name, Bruiser.' A pair of deeply set brown eyes regarded her speculatively. 'Speaking of names, what's yours?'

'Bobbi.'

'Hi Bobbi, I'm Rowan. I don't know where you found this guy, but I know at least one person who'll be very happy you did,' he said, patting the dog casually, although Bobbi had the distinct feeling he was undressing her with his eyes. 'Why don't you come in for a drink and I'll find Nellie to tell her the good news?'

'Who's Nellie?' asked Bobbi, following him inside the cottage.

'You're about to find out,' said Rowan as he picked up the phone.

Minutes later, a surprisingly pretty old lady appeared at the door. 'Rowan, I can't believe it, where is he, the rogue?' And then seeing Bobbi sitting at the table, 'Oh, I'm sorry. I didn't realise you had company.'

'Come on in, Nellie, and sit down. The prodigal son has returned as you can see.' Bruiser had the grace to look sheepish as he trotted over to Nellie who patted him warmly. 'Where on earth have you been, you scoundrel? I was worried sick about you.'

'He turned up with Bobbi here,' said Rowan. 'Bobbi, this is Nellie, a neighbour of mine. Nellie, this is Bobbi. You're an American, aren't you?'

'Is it that obvious?'

'Well it's obvious you're not from around these parts, and the accent is a bit of a give away all right.' Rowan smiled handing her the glass of water she had asked for.

'I'm a New Yorker, but my parents were Polish.'

'Ah, said Nellie, regarding Bobbi thoughtfully. 'So you're the stranger. I was wondering when you'd turn up.'

Bobbi sipped her water uncertainly. Whatever about being regarded as a stranger by this funny, fey old woman, the way Rowan Delaney was looking at her was making her feel very peculiar indeed.

7

Melissa and Tanya were lunching in One Pico after a particularly prolific morning of shopping. For once, the topic of conversation was far more riveting than their usual debate over which was the least calorific option on the menu.

'Can you believe it?' Melissa sipped her champagne gleefully. 'Bobbi Levinsky actually *bought* Grovesbury Hall. We're going to have an international celebrity living on our road! She paid fifty million for it and beat off Chris Carroll and his UK consortium. Pascal told me Chris is absolutely *livid*!'

'I heard it went for fifty-five. Who is she anyway? And how come she has that kind of money? Was she married to someone famous?' Tanya wasn't as up to date on the international celebrity circuit as Melissa.

'No, no, no,' Melissa sighed. 'She started Bobbi L cosmetics, you know, and sold out to Proctor & Gamble or someone for absolute squillions. It was all over the papers a few months ago, even Pascal has heard of her.'

'Why on earth is she coming to live in Dublin?'

'Probably tax reasons,' Melissa said knowingly. 'Anyway, who cares? She'll add such style to the road. She keeps a very low profile of course, as I do, but even so, she's always mentioned on the best-dressed lists. I've ordered the complete range of her cosmetics from Harvey Nicks, and there's an incredible waiting list.'

'But you always use MAC, Melissa.'

'That's not the point, Tanya,' Melissa explained patiently. 'I want her to feel right at home when I give my first dinner party for her, and a sensitive hostess always caters to her guests preferences.'

'Of course, how clever of you Melissa. I'll have to order a set too. Can you do it online do you think?'

'I have no idea.' Melissa sniffed, not yet being able to regard imitation as the sincerest form of flattery. 'Anyhow, she's hired Sean O'Rourke to do the whole place up, so it'll be absolutely fabulous.'

'Where's she going to live in the meantime?'

'Well, it's supposed to be confidential,' Melissa lowered her voice and looked covertly around the restaurant, 'you know, because of security and all that, but apparently she's taken the Premier Suite in the Four Seasons indefinitely.'

'Wow. The whole top floor?'

'Exactly.'

'Have you seen her yet?'

'Er no, not yet, but I intend to leave my card at the Four Seasons for her. Of course, I'll give a party to introduce her to a few select neighbours. It's really the least one can do.'

'What if she doesn't come?'

'Don't be silly, Tanya. Of course she'll come. You know how Americans attach such importance to hospitality. Anyway, how else is she going to discover who's who in Dublin? A woman like Bobbi Levinsky will understand the importance of making the right connections as soon as possible,' Melissa said with more confidence than she felt.

'Oh, you will invite Rod and me. Won't you, Melissa. Please?' Tanya begged.

Melissa smiled indulgently. 'Of course I will, Tanya. But you must make sure Rod doesn't bore her with his techno-talk all evening. And you should do a bit of research yourself, you know, just so you can appear *au fait* with her situation.'

'What does *au fait* mean?' Tanya was bewildered.

'Never mind, Tanya, just go online and look up the Bobbi L web site. You'll find everything you need to know there.'

'I'll do it the minute I get home.'

'Good girl, now let's hurry, and we'll stop off at Havana on the way home. Nicky told me the new collections are in today, and there's a Maria Grachvogal outfit I just *have* to have.'

*

'So you see,' said Nellie, 'I promised Lady Grovesbury that I'd look after Bruiser when she, well … after she'd gone. It was the least I could do, she had always been so good to me.'

'You were good to her, Nellie. Sure what would she have done without you?' Rowan interjected.

'Ah, well, we went back a long way. I'd worked for her ever since I was a young girl. She was a real character – I miss her a lot. When Bruiser disappeared, I thought he'd gone for good too. He was pining you see, and there's not a lot you can do for that. Where was it you said you found him?'

'In one of the stables,' said Bobbi. 'He gave us quite a start.'

'Ah,' said Nellie, 'that makes sense, pet. You were looking for your old friend, weren't you?'

Rowan looked at Bobbi and raised his eyes to heaven, tapping his head with his finger. 'He's back now, Nellie, that's the main thing.'

'Well, I'll take him home with me now,' said Nellie. 'C'mon, Bruiser. Your basket awaits you.' Nellie got up and made for the door. But Bruiser remained lying at Bobbi's feet. 'Come on, Bruiser, time to go home,' Nellie said from the door. Bruiser didn't budge. He looked at Nellie and then up at Bobbi and whined.

'Looks like you've found a friend,' said Rowan chuckling.

'You're the second person who's said that to me today,' said Bobbi. 'Look, I know this might sound weird to you guys, but I've really taken a shine to the little guy. If it's not being too presumptuous, I'd like to take care of him for a while. If it's all right with you, of course,' she said, looking uncertainly at Nellie. 'If he settles in with me, he can come back and live in his old home in Grovesbury Hall when I move in. In the meantime, I'm sure the hotel will work something out for us.'

'Well, if you're sure.' Nellie looked bemused. 'He doesn't seem to want to leave you, and to be honest, he was a bit of a handful for me to deal with, even though my neighbour, Niamh ní Cheavin, was kind enough to walk him every day. If he's any trouble, just let me know and I'll take him back.'

'It's a deal,' said Bobbi, smiling.

After Nellie had left, Rowan invited Bobbi to stay for lunch. 'Nothing fancy, just some cheese and fresh baguette, and I'm pretty sure I can rustle up a glass of wine if you fancy it?'

'Thanks, that'd be cool.'

'And I can even offer Bruiser here some left over lamb casserole.' Rowan put a dish down in front of the dog, thinking that Marysol would be delighted if she knew how much her cuisine was about to be appreciated.

'What's with the, er, piece of metal you were dragging in through the gate earlier?' asked Bobbi, as she helped herself to a generous piece of baguette and cut a slice of delicious-looking Brie.

'It's going to be a pivotal part of my next piece of work,' said Rowan, biting hungrily into a large chunk of bread, washed down rapidly by a slug of chilled Pouilly Fuissé, also courtesy of Marysol.

'You're an artist?'

'Yup, you could say that.'

'There's some really interesting stuff here,' said Bobbi, looking around the room. 'You're obviously very talented.'

'Not as talented as the artist who dreamt you up.'

'Puh*leese*!' Bobbi laughed out loud, although she was mortified to find herself blushing under the intensity of Rowan's admiring gaze.

'I mean it. You should let me paint you. I'm working on a new portrait style, and I could do with some serious inspiration.'

'Thanks, but no thanks.' Bobbi looked away feeling vaguely embarrassed. 'But I'd be really interested to look at your stuff. I've just bought Grovesbury Hall, and I'm renovating the place completely. It's going to need some serious art.'

'Well, as we say around these parts, "I'm yer man".' Rowan's dark eyes were laughing. 'But I really would like to paint you. I concentrate on the "inner woman", and I've a feeling yours has a lot to say for herself.'

'I've never had a problem with making my views clear, if that's what you're wondering.'

'Ah, but it's what we *don't* say that is always so much more interesting, don't you think?'

'Maybe,' said Bobbi, feeling pleasantly light-headed. She didn't usually drink in the middle of the day and found she was unwinding for the first time in months.

'Why here? Why Dublin?'

'It's a long story.'

'I'm not in any rush, are you?'

'Well, no but …'

'So tell me.'

'Let's just say I got screwed over in spectacular fashion.'

'A man?'

'Several actually.' Bobbi sipped her wine.

'Go on, it sounds riveting.'

And for the first time since the takeover coup, Bobbi found herself telling the whole story – to this man with the strangely compelling eyes, whom she had just met.

'Forgive me for stating the obvious,' said Rowan, 'but selling your company for billions doesn't exactly sound like a disaster to me. In fact I'd call that a kind of luxury problem.'

'But that's not the point. I didn't want to sell, I didn't need to and I certainly shouldn't have been forced to. But that's business for ya. When the big boys gang up against you, there's still not an awful lot one lone voice can shout about.'

'Why Ireland? Do you have roots here?'

'Not a one. But I'm eligible for beneficial tax breaks because part of the Bobbi L cosmetics portfolio was a doggie cosmetics company in County Laois, which I was totally unaware of. My lawyers sorted the deal for me. Actually, I must get around to visiting it one of these days.'

'So Bruiser here really has landed impressively on his four little paws!'

'I've always been an animal lover. Though really my thing was horses.'

'Do you keep any?'

'Not anymore.' Bobbi looked away. 'So, are you going to do me a deal on one of your paintings, or what?'

'That was a deft change of subject.' Rowan looked amused. 'But we starving artists are always open to offers.'

'Why don't you take me though some of your stuff?'

'Sure, follow me,' said Rowan, giving Bobbi the once over.

Steve sat in his tiny office taking advantage of a welcome lull in proceedings to listen to the three-thirty from Cheltenham. He had a lot riding on it, but word on the horse was good. His trainer was having a successful run, and a particularly talented young jockey was in the saddle. Listening to the tense commentary, it was going to be a closely run race, but Harlem's Honey was well placed and holding his ground nicely with just a furlong to go.

'Sorry to barge in, Steve, but there's an urgent call from the

Four Seasons. They want a vet up there as soon as possible, like *now*.' Lucy looked flustered as she stuck her head around the door.

'The hotel?'

'Yep, something about a dog.'

'Can't they bring it down?'

'I already asked but apparently not. They didn't go into detail, but it sounds bad.'

'Tell them I'm on my way. Probably the poor mutt has been run over by some ponce in a Porsche.' Steve turned off the radio and reached for his emergency kit, the Cheltenham three-thirty forgotten.

Arriving at the hotel, there was no sign of carnage. Steve pulled up outside the main entrance, handed his keys over to the uniformed valet and headed inside to enquire at reception.

'I'm Steve Sorenson, the vet. There was an emergency call about a dog?'

'Ah, yes, doctor.' The concierge looked relieved. 'Thank you for responding so promptly. Sheila will show you up to the Premier Suite directly.'

'Please, follow me, doctor.' The pretty receptionist swept ahead of him, but not before Steve noticed the look of amusement she exchanged with the concierge.

'Could you tell me what the problem is?' Steve asked her in the private lift leading to the suite, thinking that it looked suspiciously as if some neurotic tourist and their pampered pet were probably overreacting dramatically. 'Is the dog badly hurt or disturbed? I hope this is a genuine emergency, I really don't have time to –'

'Oh it's an emergency all right,' confirmed Sheila hurriedly. As they exited the lift, she knocked firmly on the door of the suite, which was opened directly.

For a moment, all Steve could take in was pandemonium. But that was before the smell hit him. Fleets of maids scurried around ferrying buckets of bleach and scrubbing frantically at what was the most spectacular case of doggie gastroenteritis he had ever seen. As soon as one pool of vomit or diarrhoea had been dealt with, it was replaced instantaneously with another spurt. No corner of the room, it would appear, had remained unscathed.

'For heaven's sake, don't just stand there! Do something!' yelled a panicked American voice. 'He's been like this for the last hour, he'll die for sure. You have to help him!' cried the most beautiful woman Steve had ever set eyes on. As the culprit escaped the woman's clutches and darted out of the bathroom, he threw himself at Steve's feet panting furiously, before spewing impressively over Steves brand-new suede boots.

'Bruiser!' said Steve disbelievingly, before dropping to his knees to attend to the dog. 'What the hell are you doing here?'

'You know him too?' the woman sounded incredulous.

'I should know him,' Steve replied curtly, checking the dogs vital signs before deftly injecting him in the scruff of his neck. 'I'm his vet. More to the point,' Steve looked up at her accusingly, 'what, may I ask, are *you* doing with him? And what, in God's name, have you been feeding him?'

'He was given to me, not that it's any of your business,' she retorted hotly. 'And I haven't fed him anything. The last time he ate was around lunch-time, at a friend's house. I think he said it was, er, lamb stew.'

'More like chilli stew, judging from the evidence,' said Steve, finding it hard to breathe with the impressive stench assailing his nostrils. 'Don't they teach you the difference between animals and humans in America? There's a reason we have dog food manufactured, and it's a good one.' The exasperation in Steve's voice was evident.

Bobbi quelled the tart response that threatened to escape, knowing from previous experience there was no point in aggravating people more than necessary. In truth, she felt shamefully responsible for poor Bruiser's troubles. If she hadn't been so distracted by Rowan and his patter, she would have paid more attention to what he was feeding Bruiser. 'Will he be okay?' she ventured.

'He'll live. I'll take him back with me to the surgery. He's going to be seriously dehydrated. It's best if we hook him up to a drip as soon as possible.'

'I'll come with him.'

'No need,' Steve said firmly. 'Call me in the morning, and I'll let you know how he's doing. If everything's okay, you can collect him in a day or two.' A pair of piercing blue eyes looked directly into hers. 'I'll need proof of ownership before I can release him to you.'

'Now just a minute, mister, what do you think I am? This was an accident. Bruiser will have the best care with me any dog could have.'

'That remains to be seen,' said Steve. 'But your track record so far isn't looking good. Bruiser's a particularly fine specimen of his breed, not to mention an old friend. It's only right that I ensure he's going to a good home – and a five-star suite offers no guarantees whatsoever. Call the surgery in the morning and we'll discuss the matter further.' Steve handed her his card. And without so much as asking her name, he took Bruiser in his arms and strode out the door.

In the surgery, Bruiser was immediately given a thorough check and put on a drip. 'Can you believe it? Feeding a dog bloody chillies! The stupid cow could have killed him,' Steve said to Lucy, who had listened to him recount everything that happened at the hotel.

'It'd take more than that to knock old Bruiser out. Anyway, it's nice to see him again, even if he is recuperating.' Just then the phone rang and Lucy answered it. 'It's for you Steve.'

'Hello.'

'Steve, Paddy Byrne here, bad luck mate,' the voice of his bookie came down the line.

'What?' Steve was confused.

'Didn't you watch the three-thirty?'

'I was out on a call, why?'

'Harlem's Honey was pipped at the post. Unbelievable finish, beaten by a nose. Look, I know your account is pretty up to date and everything, but, well, I'd appreciate if you'd settle up a.s.a.p. If that's all right?'

'Of course, Paddy. I'll call in to you first thing tomorrow.'

'Great, see ya then.'

What had started as an irritating afternoon for Steve had just deteriorated dramatically. He was now fifteen thousand euro poorer.

℃

'So,' drawled a familiar voice, 'I see you and the American billionairess have been getting cosy.'

Rowan had just returned from a quick pint in Kiely's to find Marysol lounging on his comfortable, if decrepit, sofa. Judging from appearances, she'd been drinking and, if he was reading the signs accurately, was spoiling for a fight, for which he was definitely not in the mood.

'Since when has who I have in my house been any business of yours?' The irritation Rowan increasingly felt in Marysol's presence was finding an opportune outlet.

'"House" is a bit of an overstatement, don't you think?' Marysol smirked.

Rowan ignored the barb. 'Who've you been talking to this time, or were you just peering through the windows perhaps?'

'I was in with Nellie for a tea-leaf reading, if you must know,' Marysol slurred. 'She wouldn't shut up about the stupid bitch. Seeing as I was in the vicinity, I thought I'd drop in and say hello, and it doesn't take a detective to work out what two empty wine glasses suggest. And, I notice, you had the nerve to feed her that lamb casserole I cooked for you the other night.' Marysol's anger was rising.

Rowan was tempted to tell her that it was Bruiser who had enjoyed her cooking but wisely stopped himself. 'You're pissed, Marysol, and I'm busy. I have work to do. Why don't you push off and annoy someone else?'

'How dare you! I am *not* drunk! I just helped myself to the bottle of Premier Cru Chablis that *I* gave *you* if you remember. Before you decided to share it with one of your tarts.'

The irritation Rowan felt was now building to something more dangerous. 'I'm a free agent, Marysol. I've always made that clear.' Rowan's eyes narrowed. 'But actually, I'm glad you've brought the subject up. I've been meaning to talk to you about it.'

'What subject?' Marysol was becoming confused.

'Women.' Rowan strolled over to the window and looked out, before turning back to face her. 'I don't like clingy women, Marysol, I never have, and you've become a veritable limpet. I think it's better if we don't see each other any more. It's been fun, but it's not for me.'

'Wh—what?' Marysol was almost shocked into sobriety.

'You heard me. It's over. Not that anything ever really began.'

'You can't, you couldn't mean that!'

'Oh but I do, emphatically.' Rowan looked bored. 'You've finished your wine, now I think you should leave.' Secretly, he was pleased that the opportunity to dump Marysol had arisen so opportunely. Normally, he found it hard to end an affair, particularly if the girl in question was upset, but Marysol had been bugging him lately, and now, with this gorgeous, not to mention obscenely wealthy, American woman on his doorstep, his prospects, romantic *and* otherwise, had suddenly brightened considerably.

'B—but, you can't. After everything I've done for you.'

'I have always been appreciative of your, er, generosity, Marysol. But it was *you* who insisted on it, not me.'

'You bastard! If you think you can dump me just 'cos that American bitch has batted her eyes at you, you're very much mistaken.' She was ranting now. 'You'll regret this Rowan Delaney, I'm warning you. Nobody dumps me, least of all a jumped-up gurrier who calls himself an artist. You're a piss artist maybe, but that's about it. Your work's a bloody joke! Even Rod and Tanya can't abide that piece of piss you did for their hall. Rod calls it "the monstrosity"!'

Rowan's face was white with anger. 'Is that a fact? Well, I wouldn't expect you, or them for that matter, to understand the nature of my work. You're nothing but a spoilt, ignorant, Dublin 4 bimbo, and a boring one at that.'

Marysol was momentarily struck dumb. When she did regain the power of speech, the words she spat out were laced with venom. 'Maybe you've forgotten that I am a *superb* cook and a dedicated career woman. But you'll remember this conversation, Rowan Delaney, before I've finished with you. Oh, I almost forgot, you wouldn't understand what public relations is about, would you? Well, you're about to find out.' The little cottage shook as Marysol slammed the door behind her.

As Rowan dialled directory enquiries for the telephone number of the Four Seasons, he wondered idly if someone as beautiful and rich as Bobbi Levinsky could possibly count cooking amongst her very obvious attributes.

8

Alex was extremely nervous. *It's only a dinner party*, she kept telling herself, *nothing to get worked up about*. Only a dinner party to introduce one of the most famous and successful women in the world to her excitable and extremely curious neighbours.

'Organise it,' Chris had told her. Just a small dinner party, twenty-eight of his carefully chosen business associates, neighbours and a few colourful characters to add a bit of local interest.

The formal dining room had been set out immaculately. The vast George III mahogany table was surrounded by a full set of Heppelwhite chairs, and looked resplendent laid out with the Sèvres dinner service, Waterford crystal and Irish-silver candelabra.

The caterers were busy in the kitchen, and all that remained was for Alex to go upstairs and get ready for the night ahead. It was just six o'clock, and guests were expected for pre-dinner drinks at eight. Alex went over everything just one more time:

it was vital that tonight was a success. Chris was a perfectionist and expected everything to be flawlessly organised. Everything was just as it should be. And then she remembered, just in time, *the wine*. Chris had warned her to take the Bordeaux up from the cellar that morning. She had shown Fred, their houseman, the cases to be brought up, and the wine had been sitting in the kitchen since. She would remind the caterers to let it breathe and decant it – then that was it, there was nothing more to do. She would only be in the way of the staff, who were well used to the drill, and truth be told, they terrified her. She wasn't very good at giving instructions at the best of times. Satisfied that everything was under control, she went upstairs to the nursery to spend some time with Cindy before beginning her transformation.

When Cindy had drifted off to a contented sleep, Alex went up to her bedroom to select an appropriate outfit. Looking half-heartedly through the racks of designer labels, she found herself becoming more and more confused. What on earth do you wear when you're six months pregnant and one of the best-dressed women in the world is coming for dinner? Panicking, she went through one outfit after another, but none of them seemed to fit the bill. In the end, exhausted and deflated, she settled on the red Alaia dress Chris liked so much. After all, he had told her to wear it to the Sheehans' party only six weeks ago, so at least she could be sure of a favourable reaction – and any sort of positive reaction from Chris was top of her list of priorities at the moment. Satisfied she had made the right choice, she laid the dress out and went to take a long, relaxing bath and wash her hair. She had meant to make an appointment for a blow dry earlier but hadn't got around to it, and anyway, she preferred to do her hair herself. It was, she reflected mournfully, one of the few things left she felt she could manage with any degree of confidence.

Forty-five minutes later, she was ready. Checking her appearance in the full-length mirror, she felt slightly more self-assured. She had done the best she could under the circumstances and had to admit the overall effect was pretty good. The red dress was figure hugging, and although it accentuated her bump, she looked good in it. The strappy high-heeled Jimmy Choo's she wore matched the dress perfectly, and elongated her already endless legs. It was time to go downstairs.

Alex wandered down to the sumptuously luxurious drawing room and gratefully accepted a glass of champagne offered to her by one of the catering waiters and sank back into a sofa. Sipping her drink, she found, after all, that she was quite excited at the thought of the evening ahead. A dinner party was just what she and Chris needed – perhaps it would help relieve some of the stress he seemed to be under lately and help lift his spirits. Hearing his key in the door at just half-past seven, she called to him as he passed through the hall. 'Hi, sweetheart, how was your day?'

'Bloody endless, I only just got away in time.' Chris didn't even put his head around the door. 'I hope everything's under control. Hell, I've barely got time for a shower.' She heard him racing upstairs.

Alex got up and went into the dining room to have a last-minute look. It was magnificent, not even Chris would be able to find fault with anything. She was still there, ten minutes later, admiring the beautiful setting, when Chris came into the room, his navy silk Hong Kong tailored suit fitting him a little more snugly of late. Alex neglected to point out he had put on a considerable amount of weight in the last few months, although she worried about it given the extraordinarily demanding life he led. She resolved to have a word with him about it soon, when he was in a more approachable mood.

'Well, what do you think?' Alex hoped Chris would be pleased.

'I think you should change *now*.' Chris's tone took Alex totally by surprise.

'What? Why? I … I thought you liked this dress,' Alex stammered.

'*Not* when you're obviously pregnant.' Chris looked her up

and down disparagingly. 'Bloody hell, Alex, I've bought you a whole roomful of designer clothes – surely you can find something more appropriate? Doesn't the word "elegance" mean anything to you?'

Cut to the quick, Alex felt tears sting her eyes. 'B-but it's, I thought –' Then the doorbell rang. Checking his watch, Chris muttered something under his breath, 'Well, it's too late now. Forget it, we have guests to greet.'

From the hall, Alex heard Liam and Carmela Walshe's gushing tones as they arrived as punctually as ever. 'Chris, good to see you.' Liam's nasally voice drifted into the sitting room. 'We're looking forward to a great evening, good of you to include us.'

Alex threw back her remaining half-glass of champagne miserably. As far as she was concerned, it was already a fiasco.

Soon, the room began to fill as various couples arrived. All the women were decked out in seriously glamorous numbers and weighed down with a staggering amount of jewels.

'Wow,' muttered Michael Moriarty to Chris. 'There's enough ice flashing here to put Torville and Dean to shame. I hope for their husbands' sake it isn't real.'

'Fat chance,' chuckled Chris. 'Restraint isn't a word that has found its way into these girls' vocabulary. Felicity looks as ravishing as always though. I must say, you did well there, Michael.' Chris had always admired Michael's wife, who was notorious for her good taste and sense of style. Tonight she looked svelte and elegant in a backless, violet Valentino dress that set off her dark-red hair beautifully.

Even Rowan Delaney had made a special effort and looked extremely handsome, if dishevelled, in a black Armani linen suit he had purchased specially for the occasion. It had cost him an arm and a leg, but he felt it was a worthwhile investment in his future. The invitation to the select gathering had come as a very welcome and unexpected surprise and, he guessed correctly, had more to do with livening up what could have been a rather stuffy evening, than neighbourly inclination on Chris Carroll's part. Whatever the reason, Rowan didn't care. He was determined to make the most of it, and judging by the champagne-charged atmosphere, it had the promise of shaping up to be quite a night.

He looked around for Alex, whom he had seen briefly across the room looking utterly ravishing in the red dress she had worn to the Sheehans' bash, but now she was nowhere to be found. Wandering out into the hall, he followed the trail of one of the caterers and found himself in the most opulent dining room he had ever seen. Immediately, his attention was caught by the place names set out before each person's setting. Judging correctly that Chris would be at the head of the table, he worked out that Alex, presumably, would be at the other end. He was right. Liam Walshe had been seated on her left and Michael Moriarty on her right. Rowan deftly found his own place setting and immediately swapped it with Michael's, then, feeling considerably better about the evening's prospects, returned to the sitting room and went over to chat to Tanya and Melissa, who were positively gibbering with excitement.

At exactly half-past eight, Fred, Chris's houseman, came in and discreetly murmured something to Chris, who immediately made his excuses to Pascal and Michael and slipped from the room.

He returned, moments later, with what Michael Moriarty would refer to later as the apparition. A hush descended on the entire room as Chris proudly introduced the guest of honour. 'Everybody, I'd like you to meet the new and, if I may say so, very beautiful *chatelaine* of Grovesbury Hall. May I introduce Ms Bobbi Levinsky. Welcome to Dublin 4, Bobbi.'

'Thank you, Chris,' Bobbi smiled. 'It's very kind of you to invite me to your home and make me feel so welcome.'

As all eyes in the room took in the staggeringly beautiful brunette, every man in the room felt weak, and every woman immediately felt over dressed. Bereft of jewels and wearing a deceptively simple white halter-neck silk shift dress, which skimmed, but failed to disguise, the gracefully toned figure and accentuated the glowing olive skin, Bobbi Levinsky was a picture of exquisite understatement.

One by one, Chris made the personal introductions, moving swiftly through the room. And people began to relax as Bobbi chatted easily and amiably to them all. He had just about completed the introductions, when he noticed that Alex, smiling nervously, had just come into the room and was walking towards them. 'Ah, there you are,' Chris said smoothly. 'Bobbi, this is Alex, my, er, partner. Alex, our new neighbour, Bobbi Levinsky.'

For an awful moment, Alex felt her mouth opening and closing as her carefully rehearsed words of welcome deserted her then, mercifully, she was rescued.

'Alex, it's a real pleasure to meet you,' Bobbi said warmly, immediately sensing the other woman's insecurity. 'What a terrific dress! And I see congratulations are in order. If junior takes after his or her mom in the gene-pool stakes, you'll have a real looker on your hands, guys!' Chris smiled thinly, and Alex beamed, visibly relaxing.

'We're so happy you were able to join us tonight, Bobbi. Have you met everybody?' Alex suddenly felt as if she had known this woman for years and immediately forgot she was an international celebrity and enormously wealthy businesswoman.

It was exactly the impression Bobbi wanted to create, and years of socialising in the most hallowed halls of fame and otherwise had taught her how to put people at ease. To those who knew her well, it was one of her many, and very endearing, charms.

'Bobbi,' Chris snapped his fingers at a passing waiter, 'what would you like to drink? A glass of Cristal?'

'Thank you, Chris.' Bobbi accepted the glass of champagne graciously. Turning back to Alex, she said, 'So Alex, when is your due date? I guess it must be months away, you're hardly showing.'

'Actually, I've only got a few months to go.' Alex was

thrilled to be able to discuss her pregnancy with someone who seemed so genuinely interested and allowed the waiter to refill her glass of champagne.

Chris was beginning to feel excluded and spotted his chance to intervene. 'Alex, you shouldn't be drinking. It's extremely unhealthy for the baby.'

The intended remark stung, and Alex immediately felt her composure desert her. 'My doctor said a glass or two occasionally won't do any harm. This is only my second. But you're right, I'll drink water now,' she said, exchanging her champagne for a glass of sparkling water.

Just then, one of the caterers came in to announce that dinner was served if people would like to make their way in to the dining room.

Chris put an arm around his guest of honour and gently propelled her away from Alex. 'Let's go and eat, shall we, Bobbi?'

The first course passed without incident, and fuelled by a seemingly unceasing flow of champagne, the lively group was gearing up for a seriously good night.

Chris, at the head of the long table, had Bobbi seated on his right and was regaling her with an intimate account of his latest property development scheme in London. Beside Bobbi, was Michael Moriarty who, unable to get much of a look in with Bobbi, was chatting to the well-endowed blonde actress on his right.

At the other end of the table, Rowan Delaney was like a dog with two mickies. Having switched seats with Michael to sit next to Alex, whom he had very definitely got the hots for, he realised with a pang he had relinquished his chance to sit beside Bobbi all evening. Alex, although she looked absolutely ravishing and was doing her best to chat and look interested, seemed nervous and on edge. No wonder, he thought to himself, living with that smug bastard would take a toll on anyone's nerves. He followed Alex's gaze and noticed her unease as she watched Chris flirt outrageously with Bobbi.

Immediately, Rowan resolved to move in for the kill. He

realised he would have to move carefully. Alex was like a timid colt and would most certainly bolt if he came on too strongly. But she was also vulnerable and, Rowan guessed, extremely lonely. In fact, perfectly ripe for an affair with a man who could understand her and make her feel loved. The fact that she was pregnant with another man's child did not deter him in the slightest. The fact that the other man was Chris Carroll only added to the attraction as far as he was concerned. And Rowan, like most men, loved a challenge. It was a pity she was drinking water all evening, but it was nothing he couldn't work round.

'Pregnancy obviously agrees with you, Alex. You're looking particularly beautiful tonight. Chris is a very lucky man.' Rowan sat back in his chair and smiled at her, gazing intensely into her eyes.

'Oh, er, thank you, Rowan.'

'I always think pregnancy must be a very sensual experience for a woman.'

'Sensual?' Alex looked flustered. 'Well, I don't know about that.'

'Think about it,' Rowan leaned closer. 'It's the ultimate act of creativity. You're contributing to something utterly unique.'

'Do you have any children?'

'No, not yet, but I'd love to – with the right woman of course. I adore kids.'

'I'm sure they love you too.' Alex smiled at him.

'You should let me paint you, you know.'

'Oh, I don't think so.'

'No, really, now, while you have that inner radiance. It won't be the same after the baby's born. This is the time when there's a secret bond between the mother and child, I can see it in your eyes. It would be a wonderful present for Chris. Think about it anyway, we can discuss it another time.'

Michael Moriarty took advantage of the blonde actress's visit to the bathroom to lean over to Pascal. 'Isn't she incredible?' he said looking towards Bobbi. 'I've never seen anything like her.'

'Sure she's like a lovely, glossy racehorse.' Pascal was enjoying himself thoroughly.

'One I'd very much like a chance to ride,' Michael couldn't resist adding.

'You're incorrigible, Michael,' Pascal chuckled.

'I can't make up my mind whether she's more like Cindy Crawford or a young Ali McGraw,' mused Melissa.

'Who's Ali McGraw?' asked Tanya, looking blank.

'Oh never mind.' Melissa immediately regretted dating herself so obviously.

The second course was now being served: rack of lamb and summer vegetables, accompanied by a particularly fine Bordeaux. Michael, being one of the first to sample the red wine, was impressed. 'Hey, Pascal, try some of this red – you won't get a chance to glug this back very often.' He poured a generous glass for Pascal. 'I realise we have a distinguished guest in our midst, Chris,' Michael raised his glass to Chris, 'but you're seriously pushing the boat out tonight. If I'm not mistaken, this is a Lafite '82, eh?' Michael prided himself on being a wine buff.

'What's that, Michael?' Chris had only been half-listening.

'The red. Just saying this is quite a celebration.'

Chris smiled thinly, raised his glass to his nose and breathed the bouquet before tasting it. 'Alex,' he muttered to her as she passed him on her way back to the table, 'the red wine I asked you to select this morning?'

'I know, it's going down well, isn't it? I've just told the caterers to open another dozen bottles.' Alex was pleased she had anticipated the demand.

Seeing as he was surrounded by guests, not to mention having Bobbi Levinsky beside him, Chris smiled graciously and tried very hard not to choke. Instead, he raised his glass to Bobbi, reiterated his welcome to her and sat back to watch the last cases of the most coveted red from his cellar being demolished.

After dinner, the party returned to the sitting room, where

coffee was served along with yet more champagne. Melissa and Tanya claimed Bobbi, anxious for a girly chat and, with a bit of luck, a few tips on make-up. 'After all,' as Melissa pointed out to Tanya, 'she started out as a make-up artist, you know, before she created her own range of cosmetics.'

'However,' commented Rowan, under his breath to Michael, 'unlike the majority of women who use cosmetics, Bobbi certainly needs no enhancement.'

'Liam,' Pascal sat down beside him and Carmela, 'any decision yet on the new car? You mentioned last week you were thinking of changing.'

'Actually, Pascal, yes.' Liam was delighted to broach the subject, particularly in the midst of such a select gathering, 'I've decided to get an Aston Martin, it's on order as we speak. I should be taking delivery next month.'

'Ah, grand motor, grand motor. You and Prince Charles, eh?' Pascal chuckled.

Felicity smiled benignly as she whispered to her husband, 'Bloody copycat. *We're* the only people on the road with an Aston, you've *always* driven one. That smarmy git wouldn't have known what an Aston was till he saw yours.' Felicity didn't take kindly to competition.

'Don't worry, darling,' Michael said snidely. 'Since they've been taken over by Ford, the new ones have lost their cachet. At least ours is the genuine article.'

'Quite,' agreed Felicity, her composure regained. 'I suppose imitation *is* the sincerest form of flattery.'

Across the room, Chris was refilling his glass and feeling increasingly belligerent. He spotted Liam and Carmela and decided to go over and join them. If Liam wouldn't listen to what he had to say about the cottages, maybe his sanctimonious wife would see the sense in it. Seeing as they were drinking him out of house and home, it was the least they could bloody do.

'Chris,' Carmela gushed, 'we were just saying what a delightful evening this is turning out to be.'

'Yes, yes,' agreed Liam. 'You're doing us proud.'

'Have you had a chance to discuss the little matter of Nellie Murphy's cottage and my proposal with your wife, Liam?' Chris was pleased to see Carmela's gaze sharpen.

'What about the cottage, Liam? You haven't mentioned anything about it to me.'

'Er, as a matter of fact, dear, I was going to. We've just been so busy lately, it must have slipped my mind.' Liam coughed nervously.

'I was just saying to Liam,' Chris continued, 'that you and he hold the freehold on one of the last four cottages in Grovesbury Gardens, which I'm interested in buying to proceed with a very lucrative development I'm planning. I was suggesting to Liam that he find Nellie, er, alternative accommodation and come on board with the deal. After all, Carmela, Nellie's getting on now, isn't she? I mean surely she won't be able to manage for much longer on her own.'

'No, you're quite right, Chris.' Carmela could sniff an advantageous opportunity a mile off. 'She certainly won't be able to manage on her own. In fact, I don't know how she does as it is. Of course, I keep a close eye on her and drop in regularly, but she's becoming increasingly frail.' Carmela looked concerned as she turned to Liam. 'Why, wasn't I only saying to you the other day, dear, how worried I was about her?'

'Yes, yes, dear. Indeed you were.' Liam readily agreed with his wife although he had no recollection of such a comment.

'Tell me more about this proposed development, Chris. What would our involvement entail?' Carmela was already visualising the new wing she had been thinking of adding to her home.

'Well, that's up to you and Liam, really, but here's what Michael and I are proposing.' As Chris related his plans to Carmela, she listened carefully, occasionally patting her hair. 'I think that sounds extremely interesting, Chris. I can't think why you didn't mention this to me, Liam. Leave it with me, Chris, I'll have a word with Nellie as soon as I can. In fact, I'll probably call in to her after ten o'clock mass during the week.

There are some excellent homes for the elderly in the vicinity, and, of course, Liam and I would see that she's well looked after.'

'Good, let me know how you get on.' Chris was satisfied that at least one member of the community was seeing sense.

It was coming up to one o'clock in the morning and the party showed no signs of breaking up. But Bobbi had a way to go before she adapted to the Dublin 4 levels of stamina. She stood up, thanked Chris and Alex for a great evening, and said it was time she went home.

'Oh, must you?' Alex sounded disappointed.

'Yes, Bobbi. What's the rush?' Chris walked somewhat unsteadily over to her. 'Things are just getting going. Anyway, you've only got a lonely hotel suite waiting for you.' The insinuation wasn't lost on Bobbi. 'It'll still be there in a few hours.'

Bobbi smiled, but there was coldness in her eyes as she faced him. 'Thank you again, Chris. It's been a wonderful evening, but I really must go,' she said firmly. 'Alex, let's get together soon. Maybe we can do lunch some time?'

'I'd love to, Bobbi, take care. Can we order you a taxi or do you have a driver?'

'I just have to call the hotel.'

'No need.' Rowan spotted his moment. 'I'm just about to leave myself – I'd be happy to see you back, if you fancy a walk. It's only down the road.'

'Great, I could do with some fresh air, and it's a beautiful night.'

'Well, that's settled then, let's get your coat and we'll go. Chris, Alex, it's been great, talk to you soon. Oh, Alex, think about what I was saying earlier won't you?'

'Yes, I will, Rowan. Goodnight guys, safe home.'

After the guest of honour had departed, people began to say their goodbyes and make for home. Alex was relieved it hadn't turned into an all-nighter as it so easily could have. She was exhausted and couldn't wait to get to bed. Chris seemed agitated even though the evening had been a resounding success, and everybody had thought Bobbi charming.

'So unaffected,' trilled Melissa. 'Why it's hard to believe she's so rich.'

'Is she really that rich, though?' Tanya wasn't convinced.

'You'd better believe it,' Chris said. 'She's worth more than the rest of us put together, and then some.'

When everyone had left and the caterers were busy clearing up, Alex went up to check on Cindy, who was fast asleep, before wearily climbing the next flight of stairs to the bedroom suite. Chris was there ahead of her, standing gazing out the window, his jacket thrown on the bed and a glass of whiskey in his hand.

'Well, that was a great night, wasn't it?' Alex said as she went to draw the curtains.

Chris turned to her, breathing whiskey fumes in her face, making her feel immediately nauseous. 'You're some stupid bitch, you know that?'

'What?' Alex backed away in shock. He had never, ever spoken to her like that, and for a moment, she felt herself reeling.

'Well that was a great night, wasn't it?' Chris mimicked her cruelly, a sneer curling his mouth. 'It certainly was a great night, Alex, you really pulled it off this time.' Chris took a swig of his drink. 'Not only did you embarrass me by looking like a Braeburn apple in that ridiculously inappropriate dress, but then, your *pièce de résistance*! You serve the Château Lafite '82 for dinner.'

'But, that's the one you told me to have brought up,' Alex cried, the look on Chris's face chilling her to the bone.

'I told you to have the Lafite '85 decanted, if you'd bothered to listen,' he ranted. 'Not only is the '82 fourteen thousand euro a case, it's bloody unobtainable now. So you, you stupid cow, have wasted my entire stock of the most prized wine in the country!'

'Chris, I'm sorry, it looked … I thought … The cases must

have been side by side in the cellar ...' Alex trailed off, feeling utterly defeated. She sank down on the bed.

'Sorry isn't good enough, not this time Alex.' Chris looked down at her disdainfully. 'I wouldn't mind if that crowd had even vaguely appreciated what they were drinking, but apart from Michael Moriarty and Bobbi – now there's a woman who knows her stuff – it was a case of pearls before fucking swine.'

Alex began to cry. 'I'm so sorry, Chris, it was a mistake. A stupid, stupid mistake,' she sobbed.

Chris made for the door before flinging his parting shot. 'Save the apologies, I should have known. I guess the only label you ever saw on a bottle before you met me was Blue Nun. If I were you, I'd try to make friends with Bobbi Levinsky. She seems to have taken to you for some reason. You never know, some of her polish might rub off on you.' And with that, he slammed the bedroom door behind him.

Ce

A bright moon shone down as Bobbi and Rowan walked amiably along Grovesbury Road. Ahead of them was the turn to Grovesbury Gardens and the cottages. 'Hey, why don't you come in for a quick nightcap?' Rowan suggested to Bobbi. 'It's early by our standards, and tomorrow's Sunday, so you can't possibly decline.'

Bobbi laughed at Rowan's obvious enthusiasm; it was hard to be immune to his charm when he decided to turn it on. 'Well, okay, just a quick one.'

'Then I'll call you a taxi and pack you off home. Or "back to your lonely hotel suite" as Chris would say.' Rowan grinned. 'Judging from appearances, I'd say he'd be more than happy to keep you company any time.'

'Don't be ridiculous!' Bobbi retorted. 'He's got Alex, hasn't he? He was just a bit under the weather towards the end of the evening, I guess.'

'Uh-uh.' Rowan shook his head. 'He's definitely got the hots for you, Bobbi. I can tell.'

'Well, even if he did, he's very definitely not my type. Besides which, I'm off men at the moment.'

'What *is* your type?' Rowan was curious.

'You're asking *me*? Heck, if I knew, I'd have had my personal life sussed long ago.'

'Well, here we are.' Rowan put his key in the door and turned the lock. 'As you know, it may not be a mansion, but it's home.'

Inside, Bobbi wandered around looking at the various paintings and works in progress while Rowan went to the kitchen to open a bottle of wine. When he returned to the small sitting room with two glasses, she was sitting cross-legged on the sofa. 'I don't see any evidence of the portraits you were talking about,' Bobbi said curiously.

'Ah, I never leave my portraits out on display.' Rowan poured two generous glasses of wine. 'There's an intimate quality about an unfinished portrait that I always think you risk losing if you show it before it's fully finished. Not even the sitter gets to see it until it's absolutely ready.'

'What if they don't like the finished work?'

Rowan shrugged. 'That hasn't happened yet, but if it does, I'll deal with it.' *It hasn't happened*, he thought, *because I haven't done any portraits yet*. Though how the idea had escaped him for so long was a mystery. 'Speaking of sitters, who's looking after Bruiser tonight?'

Bobbi shifted her position ever so slightly. 'He's, um, in residence at the Strand Animal Hospital tonight. They're keeping him in for a couple of days' observation. I forgot to mention it, but that stew you fed him, it was a little heavy on the chillies.'

'Crikey, poor ol' Bruiser. Did it affect him badly?'

'You could put it like that,' Bobbi grinned. 'Let's just say he made a pretty decent stab at redecorating my entire suite. The vet was not at all impressed when he arrived to treat him. I guess he thinks I'm some kind of deviant animal abuser.' Bobbi took a swig of her wine. 'He pretty much accused me of as much on the spot.'

'Not Steve Sorenson?' Rowan enquired.

'Yeah, I think that's what his card said. I don't know what kind of a vet he is, but he could sure use some improvement on his people skills. You know him?'

'Everyone around here knows Steve. He runs the free animal clinic here from the cottages, just two doors down from me. I've known Steve since we were nippers.'

'What is it with this place, everyone seems to know everyone else – and their business.'

'Welcome to Dublin, Bobbi,' said Rowan as he got up to return the bottle to the fridge. 'It's a small, small town.' Just then there was a knock on the door. 'Get that would you, Bobbi?' Rowan called from the kitchen.

'Sure.' Bobbi jumped up from the sofa and reached the door just as there was another loud knock. She opened it to find not one, but four gardaí lined up, the first of which said brusquely, 'Does Rowan Delaney reside here?'

'Well, yes, but I'll just have to see if he's available.' Bobbi was taken aback.

'No need, Miss, we'll see for ourselves. We have a warrant to search the premises. If you'd just step aside, please.'

'Who is it?' Rowan appeared from the kitchen just as the four guards, complete with sniffer dog, pushed their way inside. 'What the hell is going on?'

'Rowan Delaney?' the first guard asked unceremoniously.

'Yes, that's me. What the hell is this about?'

'We have reason to believe you are in possession of Class A illegal substances. We intend to search the premises.'

'Now just a minute, there's got to be some mistake.'

'No mistake, and you might as well co-operate: we have a warrant to search the place. Go ahead, lads.'

'I don't believe this.' Rowan ran a hand through his hair. 'Well be my guests, you won't find anything. Watch my fucking paintings – if you damage anything you can fucking well pay for it!'

'Jaysus, Bobbi, I'm sorry about this. But I honestly have no idea what brought this on.'

'Do you do drugs?' Bobbi whispered, as the lads went to work.

'No. Alcohol's my drug. Do you?'

'Not really, some grass maybe, now and then, that's about it. They look like they mean business,' she added, standing beside Rowan as the guards went through everything with a fine-tooth comb, following the trail of the German Shepherd who was sniffing eagerly all around him.

Moving upstairs, they continued their search. Bobbi and Rowan listened as they lifted, shifted and rummaged around, watched by the fourth guard who had remained downstairs. Suddenly there was a shout from upstairs, 'Hey, Sarge, you better take a look at this.' As the three men trundled downstairs with the German Shepherd, one of them held out a bulky package to the sergeant. 'Found it in the bathroom cabinet.'

'Let's have a look.' The package was passed over. 'Well, Mr Delaney, thinking of having a party were you? I think you'd better come down to the station with us. You both have quite a bit of explaining to do.'

'Look, leave her out of this,' Rowan said angrily. 'She's just a friend. Whatever is going on, it's got nothing to do with her.'

'That may be, Mr Delaney, but we'll let the lads at the station work that one out. Now, if you'd like to follow me, the cars are waiting outside.'

As Rowan and Bobbi were ushered into separate police cars, more than one lace curtain in Grovesbury Gardens twitched.

At Donnybrook police station, the cars pulled up and Bobbi and Rowan were escorted into the bleak-looking building and shown to separate rooms for questioning.

This is turning out to be some evening, thought Bobbi to

herself, as a burly inspector and a policewoman made their way into the small room.

'Name, please.'

'Bobbi Levinsky.'

'Address.'

'The Four Seasons Hotel.'

'You're a tourist?'

'No. I'm a resident. I'm staying at the Four Seasons while my house is being renovated.'

'Previous address?'

'Park Avenue, New York.'

'Ah, you'd be an American then.' The first flicker of interest showed on the until-then impassive faces. 'How do you know Rowan Delaney? And for how long have you known him?'

As Bobbi answered the interminable questions as clearly and concisely as she could, she couldn't help feeling a bizarre sense of unreality about the whole thing.

'Look, do I need to get a lawyer?'

'No, this is all entirely routine, Ms Levinsky. You'll make things much easier for everybody concerned if you just co-operate with our line of enquiry.'

'Of course. Anything I can do to help.' Bobbi didn't need the impending headlines she could imagine covering the national and international press.

'Well, I think that's it for the moment. I'm afraid we'll have to do a full body search, Ms Levinsky. If that proves negative, you're free to go.' The inspector nodded at the policewoman. 'Helen? Take Ms Levinsky through to the search room, would you?'

'Yes, sir. Come with me, please, Ms Levinsky.'

Bobbi wasn't expecting this, nor was she used to taking orders, but in this instance, she reconciled herself to taking the line of least resistance. Disappearing through the glass double doors and into another small room, she wondered, not for the first time, if coming to Ireland had been such a smart idea after all.

9

In the dream, it was always the same.

She was galloping along the beach astride Moonflower, faster and faster. The sharp taste of salt in the air, the wind whipping her hair from her face, and Danny behind her on Sundown, almost, but never quite, catching her. Then she would wake, her face wet with tears.

For a moment, Bobbi had absolutely no idea where she was. Then, shielding her eyes from the shaft of sunlight that was assaulting her, she pulled a pillow over her face and groaned. Never, ever, in all her life had she had a hangover like this. Her head felt as if it belonged in a freak show. Her eyes didn't fit their sockets and seemed to have spent the night in a sandstorm, and as for her mouth, well, the less said the better. What was it with these Irish people and alcohol? And how on earth could she have managed to drink so much?

She had been all right at the party, and then – and then she remembered. Rowan. The cops. The police station. And then afterwards, when they had been let go, they had gone back to Bobbi's suite and got well and truly smashed. Bobbi got out of bed gingerly, testing the floor with her foot to see if it hurt. Then she tottered bravely to the enormous living room, where the remnants of the mini-bar were displayed in glorious abandon. Cringing, Bobbi remembered Rowan's insistence that they drink it dry, and they had, every last drop. At the time, it had seemed amusing. Thinking of Rowan, Bobbi hurtled back to the present. Where was he? She had vague memories of things becoming amorous. After that, it was a bit of a blur.

Well at least she had woken up in her own bed, alone, which was a reassuring start to the day. Apart from the master bedroom, there were at least three other bedrooms in the vast suite. Padding down the long corridor, Bobbi looked cautiously around the first two doors, before finally finding Rowan in the last bedroom. Looking at him fast asleep and sprawled across the bed, Bobbi smiled. A white linen sheet was draped across his torso, and his long dark hair trailed along the pillow and onto his outstretched arms. Bobbi thought he resembled a particularly beautiful Renaissance painting.

Closing the door softly, she made her way back to her bedroom and headed for the shower. She couldn't face breakfast, and a steaming hot shower was the only possible thing that might make her feel just the slightest bit more human. Luckily, she had nothing more to do today than make a few transatlantic calls, one of which involved her lawyers and catching up on her doggie cosmetics factory. Which reminded her, suddenly, of the conspicuous absence she had felt in the suite. Bruiser! He was still at Strand Animal Hospital. She would have to go down and claim him at lunch time. That's if that arrogant vet would release him to her. Bobbi scowled. What did he want? References? Well she could produce harder evidence than that. All the same, she found, for some inexplicable reason, the thought of facing Steve Sorenson intimidating. Perhaps she would ask Rowan to go with her when he woke up. Yes, that's what she would do. Apart from anything else, he could confirm that Nellie *had* given Bruiser to her and that it was *his* fault, not hers, that Bruiser had had his unfortunate run-in with the chillies.

After a particularly brutal shower, Bobbi emerged feeling marginally more human to find Rowan, wearing only the black linen pants of his now rather rumpled Armani suit, making coffee in the kitchen.

'Hi gorgeous,' he drawled sleepily, as he wandered over to the many kitchen cupboards. 'How's the head?'

'Not sure,' Bobbi smiled ruefully. 'The one I seem to be wearing couldn't possibly belong to me. How about you?'

'Ah, I'll live, I suppose. All the same it was fun, wasn't it?' Rowan grinned.

'I guess, although I'm not sure I could handle that level of "fun" on a regular basis.'

'Course you will. It's only a matter of building up your stamina.'

'Rowan,' Bobbi said, 'I need to ask you something.'

'Sure, shoot.'

'I have to go down to collect Bruiser from the vet today, and, well, I was wondering if you'd come with me, as a sort of character reference y'know. It's just that I feel uncomfortable about the whole chilli incident.'

'No can do, kiddo.' Rowan shook his head. 'I would if I could, Bobbi, but I've got a reporter from *The Guardian* coming to interview me, and I need to be back like *now*.' Rowan glanced at his watch. 'Good job I didn't oversleep anymore than I already have.'

'Oh,' was all Bobbi could think of to say.

'It'll be cool, Bobbi. I don't know what you're worried about. Steve's a pussycat, really! If it makes you feel better, I'll ring him myself and confirm that you *are* Bruiser's legitimate new owner and that the chilli stew was entirely my fault.'

'Would you?' Bobbi brightened.

'Sure, now I really have to run. Call me later and let me know how it goes. See ya.'

Sold

After Rowan had left, Bobbi got dressed and set off on the short walk down Sandymount Avenue that led to the Strand Animal Hospital. She carried with her a very smart new collar and lead with a shiny silver doggie tag with her mobile number on it. Reaching the door of the practice, she rang the bell and checked her watch. It was just coming up to twelve o'clock. The buzzer sounded and the door clicked open. There were just two other people sitting in the small waiting area, one with a cat basket and the other with a pair of Golden Retriever puppies. Bobbi gave her name to the girl behind the desk and sat down to wait. Twenty minutes later, the veterinary nurse popped her head around one of the doors and called Bobbi's name. As Bobbi went in to the little room, she was greeted effusively by Bruiser, who looked as large as life and, despite his ordeal, was gratifyingly pleased to see her. Bobbi immediately felt relieved: if the nurse was dealing with her then she might escape another lecture from 'animal champion' Steve Sorenson.

'Thanks, Lucy.' Bobbi's hopes were dashed as Steve appeared around the door. 'I'll deal with this. Donal needs you in the surgery.'

As Lucy left the room, Bobbi was about to explain about the chillies when she was cut short.

'It's all right, Ms Levinsky. Rowan Delaney has filled me in on the situation. I'm sorry if I was, er, somewhat abrupt with you the other day, but one never knows with these things. I always feel it's better to be safe than sorry, don't you?' A pair of disturbingly blue eyes questioned her.

'Yes, of course. Please, call me Bobbi.'

Steve held out a hand and smiled. 'Let's start again then, Bobbi, shall we? I hear you've bought Grovesbury Hall, fine old place. It'll be nice for Bruiser to have his old stomping ground back.'

'Do you know it well?'

'Not the interior. But I know the grounds like the back of my hand. My father used to be head groomsman for the

Grovesburys. I spent many a happy hour hanging out in the stables.'

'Oh,' said Bobbi, not quite knowing what to make of this piece of information.

'Now, Bruiser here is a fine example of his pedigree. I'll just run through the basics with you and give you one of these leaflets and that's it, really.'

'It's quite all right, Dr Sorenson. I've kept dogs all my life. Despite the earlier culinary lapse, I really am quite capable of looking after Bruiser. In fact, an aunt of mine in Connecticut used to breed English Bull Terriers. With respect, I probably know more about them than you do.' Bobbi smiled as she patted Bruiser. 'You can rest assured he'll be in good hands.'

'Well, fine,' said Steve. 'Any problems, you know where we are. Lucy will make sure you're on our register.'

'Thank you,' said Bobbi, putting Bruiser's new collar and lead on. 'And I – *we* appreciate your concern, don't we Bruiser?'

'Not at all,' said Steve, feeling strangely deflated as he watched Bobbi exit the room with Bruiser looking adoringly up at her as he trotted happily out into the sunlight.

Rowan had just seen off the surprisingly attractive female journalist who had come to interview him for *The Guardian* and was about to sit down and have a reviving beer when there was a knock at the door.

'Rowan!' Niamh ní Cheavin stood on his doorstep. 'I hope you don't mind me dropping by. It's just, the other night, the cops and everything. Well, Nellie was worried about you and I said I'd call around to make sure things were okay?'

'C'mon in, Niamh,' Rowan said with more enthusiasm than he felt. 'You might as well get the original version. Fancy a beer?'

'Well, eh, yes. Why not? Thanks, Rowan.' Niamh sat down

primly on the old sofa as Rowan went to fetch her a beer. 'What were the police doing calling to your place?'

'You might well ask.' Rowan took a swig from his bottle of Bud. 'They were looking for drugs.'

'Drugs?' Niamh looked horrified.

'Yep, they claimed they had a tip-off and barged in with a search warrant and an attitude. The fact that I was entertaining a guest at the time didn't deter them in the least.'

'Who?' asked Niamh, mesmerised by the turn events had taken.

'Bobbi Levinsky.'

'I don't believe it! What did the poor girl do?'

'There wasn't a lot she could do. She was very cool about it, considering she had every right to throw a hissy fit at being bundled off to Donnybrook station and subjected to a full body search.'

'Jesus, Mary and Joseph!'

'Oh, I almost left out the best bit. They found a good party pack of cocaine upstairs in the bathroom cabinet of all places. That's when we were taken to the station for questioning.'

'Oh, Rowan. I didn't think you did drugs.' Niamh looked crestfallen.

'I don't – that's just it – no one was more surprised than me. But try telling that to those guys when they get their blood up.'

'What's going to happen now?'

'We've been let off until the impending charge and court case, which they'll let us know about in due course.'

'I can't believe it, really I can't.' Niamh looked baffled.

'I wouldn't either, only I was there.' Rowan looked grim. 'Believe me, Niamh, those drugs were *not* mine. Somebody planted them there. God knows who, or indeed why, but this was definitely a setup.'

'I don't like the sound of this, Rowan. I don't like the sound of it one little bit. If you ask me, this has all the hallmarks of a Chris Carroll stunt.'

'Chris Carroll? Why would he pull something like that?'
Rowan was gobsmacked.

'Think about it,' said Niamh. 'There are only four cottages
left that he doesn't own, and he wants to develop the site. He's
already terminated my lease, and he won't be reticent about
putting the pressure on you, Nellie or Steve for that matter. If
your landlords won't get you out, he will, by fair means or
foul. Knowing the way he operates, my money's on the latter.
Mark my words,' Niamh drew a long breath, 'you need to get
yourself a lawyer, Rowan, and a sharp one at that.'

Leaving Rowan to ponder her theory, Niamh went home
and let herself in to her own little cottage. The cats came to
greet her, weaving around her feet plaintively. She fed them,
opened the kitchen door to let some air in and made herself
a cup of tea. Wandering back into the front room, she turned
on the television and sat down in her favourite chair to watch
the six o'clock news. She would ring Nellie later and bring
her up to date on the situation. When the news ended, she
flicked off the remote control and watched the screen fade to
dark. For some reason, she felt unreasonably low today. She
looked around the room, noting each nook and cranny as she
had a million times since she had got her eviction notice. She
still couldn't imagine for the life of her leaving her home. It
would be like leaving her life behind her. Mentally, she
reprimanded herself. It's only bricks and mortar. There's
always somewhere else, she said to herself sternly. But where?
And when? And how could she possibly be happy anywhere
else, away from the little community that was the only family
she had?

It was then that she noticed the leaflet lying on the floor
beneath the letterbox. Picking it up, she turned it over and saw
that it was from An Post. 'We tried and were unable to deliver
a package to you today,' it read. Niamh noted that she was
requested to pick up the package at the sorting office in
Ballsbridge. She couldn't think who would be sending her a
parcel. It wasn't her birthday, and as far as she could remember,

she hadn't sent away for any books or any of the *Reader's Digest* offers she was so meticulous about. She put the notice on her tiny hall table to remind her to collect the parcel in the morning on her way to work and, yawning, went to run herself a long, hot bath.

Padraig was in the den watching television when Marysol came home after a work function she had been attending on behalf of a design company that was a prestigious client of the firm she worked for. She came into the room, threw her handbag on a chair and flopped down into a sofa, putting her feet up on the antique footrest. 'I am totally, totally exhausted,' she proclaimed. 'I must have been working late every night this week.'

'I must say, Marysol, you look remarkably well for someone who's just been very unceremoniously dumped,' Padraig remarked.

'I was not dumped, you little prick. Rowan was beginning to bore me. It was a bit like watching paint dry after the initial excitement wore off. Artists are *so* self-obsessed.'

'That's not the version I heard. Word on the street is you were blown out – in favour of our American billionairess. I must admit, I almost felt sorry for you. She's pretty much beyond competing with, isn't she?'

'Just goes to show you're way out of the loop, Padraig, as usual. You really shouldn't rely on your little gay friends for gossip. They clearly make a habit of getting it arseways, if you'll forgive the analogy.'

'*Very* witty, Marysol, one of your better attempts, I'll grant you.' Padraig allowed himself a smile. 'Regardless of the circumstances, I'm sure mother and father will be delighted at the outcome. As you know, they were very worried about you.'

'Well now you can all breathe easily again, Padraig, and shut up, would you? I really am exhausted.'

'With pleasure. Oh, just one more thing while we're on the subject. I heard Rowan got busted the other night for possession and possibly dealing. Apparently a sizeable stash of cocaine was found on his premises.'

'Doesn't surprise me in the slightest.' Marysol put her hand to her mouth as she yawned leisurely. 'That man is positively depraved.'

'It was a tip-off.'

'So?'

'I was wondering why you'd off-loaded mother's solitaire. Now it's all making perfect sense.'

'I don't know what you're talking about.'

'But I know your dealer, Marysol, and he's been talking about nothing else. If I say so myself, sister dear, I think you acted with not only alacrity, but inspiration. Rowan was getting ideas way beyond his station. I shall look forward greatly to the court case.'

'Not as much as I will.'

'I'm so glad to see you haven't lost your touch, Marysol. I was almost beginning to believe that chap had you for a fool. Bravo, sister, now we'll say no more about it.'

10

'Alex?'

'Yes, this is Alex speaking.' The clear voice on the other end of the line took Alex by surprise.

'Hi, Alex, it's Bobbi Levinsky. How've you been keeping?'

'Oh, Bobbi, hi. Well I've been fine, thanks,' Alex lied. 'How are you?'

'Great. Listen, if you're free, I was hoping you'd have lunch with me today.'

'Well, I'm not sure.' Alex looked at her reflection in the mirror and winced. Her face was pale and wan, her hair was limp and in need of a wash and the comfortable sweat pants she had despondently pulled on earlier did nothing to enhance the overall image.

'Oh, come, on, Alex. I don't know about you, but I sure could do with some female company. Meet me here in the dining room at the Four Seasons at one o'clock, okay?'

'Okay, Bobbi, that would be lovely. I'll see you there.' Alex replaced the receiver hurriedly. If she got a move on and washed her hair she could just about make it. Bobbi was right, it would do her good to get out.

Since the night of the dinner party and the awful scene with Chris that followed, Alex had been wandering around in a daze. Chris had been leaving the house early and coming home late, sometimes very late. He barely exchanged a word with her if he could avoid it. There was no point trying to reason with him, or talk to him. He made it abundantly clear that her very presence in the house was a source of immense irritation. If she hadn't been pregnant, she would have moved out and taken Cindy with her. *Who are you kidding?* her inner voice demanded scornfully. *You wouldn't have the guts. You never have. And anyway, where would you go? Back to your parents? That would thrill them. At least your mother would be able to say 'I told you so.'* To say Alex was miserable was the understatement of the century.

At one o'clock, Bobbi was seated at a window table for two in the main dining room of the Four Seasons. She had thought about having lunch served in her private dining room, but dismissed this idea in favour of the restaurant. She had been couped up in the suite all morning, and indeed for the most of the last three days, on conference calls to her lawyers and, as a result, had a massive dose of cabin fever. Just watching the various business people and lunching ladies wandering into the room and being shown to their tables was making her feel more human.

Bobbi told the hovering waiter she would wait for her friend to join her before ordering and took a sip of her mineral water. At exactly five-past one, Alex appeared through the doors looking flustered. Bobbi had to stop herself from doing a double take. It was only two weeks since she had seen Alex, but she would hardly have recognised her. The girl had become a shadow of the bloomingly lovely creature Chris had introduced her to at the party. Apart from her bump, she looked downright gaunt. Her face was drawn, and there were dark circles under her eyes that no amount of carefully applied concealer could hide.

'Hi, Alex. It's good to see you.' Bobbi stood up to greet her enthusiastically.

'Hi, Bobbi. I hope I haven't kept you waiting.' Alex was breathless. 'I've been a bit disorganised lately, and Cindy's getting clingy now every time I try to leave the house. I think she senses things are going to change when the new baby arrives.' Alex was trying to sound light-hearted, but Bobbi immediately picked up the forced brightness in her voice.

'You're perfectly on time, Alex. Now let's order. I don't know about you, but I'm ravenous.' Bobbi signalled for the waiter, thinking she had never seen anyone look as if they needed a good feed as much as this frail girl sitting beside her.

Over starters of Caesar salad, the two women chatted amiably, unaware of the curious glances thrown regularly in their direction as people began to recognise Bobbi and whisper to each other about Dublin's most glamorous new resident.

By the time their main course was being served, Alex was looking less harassed and starting to relax.

'Will you have a glass of wine, Alex, with your pasta? I think I will – this is the first time in days I've had a chance to chill,' Bobbi asked, glancing at the wine list.

'Oh I don't think I will.' Alex sounded hesitant. 'Chris doesn't like me drinking when I'm pregnant.'

Bobbi laughed. 'C'mon, just the one glass, Alex. Chris will never know. After all, your doctor said a glass or two was okay. And you are doing all the hard work at the moment.'

'Well, okay then. Actually I'd love one.'

'Good, that settles it. We'll have two glasses of Pinot Grigio.'

'How are you finding Dublin, Bobbi? It must be a real culture shock for you.'

'Well, it's different, that's for sure, but I'm becoming acclimatised. People have been very friendly. I won't really feel at home until I can move into Grovesbury Hall, I guess, and that won't be as soon as I'd hoped.'

'How's the work going?'

'Slowly, but it's going to be great.' Bobbi's face lit up. 'Sean O'Rourke has some fantastic ideas. Actually, if you're not rushing, why don't you come around with me after lunch and take a look at it? I need to drop in myself.'

'I'd love to.' Alex was thrilled to think she'd get to see inside the house that was the talk of the neighbourhood. More importantly, it would be something interesting to tell Chris about later when he got home – if he got home.

'Alex,' Bobbi looked concerned, 'I don't know you hardly at all, and I certainly don't want to pry, but is everything okay with you? It's just, well, you're looking tired, and you seem a little preoccupied.'

For a moment Alex looked intensely uncomfortable, making Bobbi immediately wish she'd kept her mouth shut. Her direct manner seemed to take people by surprise here, and she had to remind herself constantly that this small little place was not New York. Then, to Bobbi's horror, two big tears began to roll down Alex's face, which she hurriedly tried to brush away with her napkin.

'Oh, God, Alex, I'm so sorry. I didn't mean to upset you, really. Just forget I said anything.'

'No, no.' Alex tried to compose herself. 'It's okay, really, it … it's not your fault. I'm just … well, I'm going through a tough time at the moment, and …' Two more big tears followed, and Bobbi leaned forward anxiously.

'Look, Alex, why don't we take coffee upstairs in my suite? We can have some privacy there, and if you want to talk you can talk, and if you want to tell me to mind my own business, well you can do that too,' Bobbi smiled as Alex brightened and sniffed.

'I'd like that Bobbi. In a way, it would be a relief to talk to someone.'

'Then let's go,' Bobbi said.

Once inside her suite, Bobbi instructed Alex to make herself comfortable on the huge velvet-covered sofa while she went to get them each a large glass of water. A discreet knock on the door announced the arrival of the coffee, served with the accompaniment of delicate *petits fours*. When the table had been laid and the coffee poured, Bobbi sat down beside Alex. 'Like I said, Alex, you don't have to say a thing. For heaven's sake you're practically about to have a baby! I guess that would have most of us feeling a little over-wrought.'

'No,' said Alex in a small voice, 'it's not about the baby, well, not directly. It's about me and Chris.'

'Ah, I see.' Bobbi had expected as much.

Alex began, tentatively at first, to tell Bobbi everything from the beginning. How she and Chris had met. How he had pursued her relentlessly and swept her off her feet. How she had fallen in love with him and so, she believed, had he with her. As Bobbi listened, saying nothing, just nodding occasionally, Alex found the floodgates opening. She began to cry again, telling how Chris had walked out of the room when she had told him she was pregnant with Cindy. How he had gradually come around and asked her to move in with him, then became increasingly distant after Cindy's birth. And finally her latest and, if she was honest, desperate attempt to keep him with this second pregnancy. It made a sorry tale to listen to, and Bobbi's heart went out to Alex, clearly so upset and undone by her current situation.

'So you see, Bobbi, I really don't know what to do. Whatever I do seems to be wrong, and he makes it so obvious that I'm irritating him, it's awful. I'm just trying to stay out of his way. But that makes me feel even worse. I'm at my wits' end.' Alex looked worn out. 'I just hope beyond hope that I have a boy. I just *know* Chris would love a son, and then maybe things would get better,' she trailed off.

Having listened to the story, Bobbi very much doubted it. Things certainly wouldn't improve if Alex continued to behave like a doormat. Bobbi had come across plenty of men in her time just like Chris Carroll, and she knew exactly how to treat them. If she was honest, she was shocked at Alex's obvious naïvety, but, she reminded herself, the girl was young and obviously overawed by her bully of a partner.

'Oh, honey.' Bobbi patted her hand affectionately. 'I'm no one to lecture on personal relationships, believe me, but you've got to understand one thing here.'

'What's that?' Alex sniffed.

'You can't let him treat you like this. You can't let anyone – man or woman – treat you like this. I don't care how much you love him, honey, you're gonna have to make him "step up to bat", as we say in the States.'

'But how? Chris holds all the cards. He knows how much I love him, how much I need him.'

Bobbi sighed. 'That's not true, Alex. You don't need him. You sure as heck don't need him if he's treating you like you say. And let's remember something here, you happen to be the mother of his children – like that doesn't count for anything in this country?'

'It's just, well, I'm terrified of losing him.' Alex looked stricken. 'You probably wouldn't understand, Bobbi, I mean, you're so gorgeous and clever –' and loaded she almost added '– you can probably get anyone you want. But Chris has always been the only one I've ever wanted.'

'You're wrong, Alex. I may look like I've got it all going for me, but believe me, I know what it's like to lose someone you love.'

'I can't imagine you losing anyone. He must have been off his trolley,' Alex said.

'Being a big-noise success can attract men initially, mostly out of curiosity,' Bobbi smiled wryly, 'but most of them can't stay the pace for long. They either feel intimidated or resentful, and neither one works for me.' Bobbi paused. 'The thing about men is, well, they'll always come and go. But where there's life, there's hope. The person I'd give everything in the world to get back is gone forever.'

'Who was that?'

'My little brother Danny. He was killed when he was just eight years old.'

'Oh, Bobbi, how awful. What happened?'

'We were both horse crazy. I had been picked for the junior American show-jumping team. He was a natural too. We were far from rich, but we had an aunt in North Carolina who kept horses, and every year we'd go to her for most of the summer with our mother. We lived for that holiday. All year we'd be counting the days. Every day, Danny and I, we'd take our horses and ride down to this beautiful stretch of beach and race each other along the water's edge. It was just magic.' Bobbi paused.

'Go on.'

'One day, we went down, just as usual. Me on Moonflower and Danny on Sundown, and we set off, galloping along the beach. We were going pretty hard, but no faster than usual. I was in front and Danny was trying to catch me. I never saw it happen till it was too late.' Bobbi's voice began to tremble. 'Something spooked his horse I guess. Anyway, he came off, hit his head on a rock in the sand and by the time I got him back he was dead. He died in my arms.'

'Oh, Bobbi.' Alex was lost for words.

'I carried him over my saddle. I knew his horse would follow mine. Remember – this was way before cell phones. They rushed him to the hospital, but we knew it was too late. He was already gone.'

'Oh, Bobbi. I'm so sorry. I can't imagine what I'd do if anything happened to Cindy, or, or –'

'Exactly. I guess what I'm trying to say, Alex, is that you need to concentrate on the important stuff right now. I know it must be difficult when things are tough between you and Chris, but you've got Cindy and another little one on the way. You really need to take care of *you*. Stop worrying about Chris, for heaven's sake! Let him worry and wonder about you for a change.'

'You're right, I know you are. It's just, well, it's not easy for me. How did you manage, Bobbi? I mean after … the accident?'

'Badly, I guess. I was twelve years old, I blamed myself for it – still do, truth be told. Not a day goes by that I don't miss him. My father and mother never forgave me or got over losing Danny. Dad bailed out shortly after, and mom became a serial man hunter. She left soon after, and I stayed with my aunt in North Carolina. Mom remarried a couple of times but never kept in touch. As soon as I was old enough, I went back to New York and got work as an apprentice make-up artist, and the rest, as they say, is history.'

'And the show jumping?'

Bobbi gave a wintry smile. 'I've never gotten on a horse since, and I doubt I ever will.' Bobbi looked Alex directly in the eye. 'All I'm saying, I guess, is that there are more important things to worry about than some pig-headed man. I ought to know, I've had dealings with most of them. You've got Chris, right now – whether you want to keep him or not remains to be seen. But he's here, and you've got a chance to take control of your relationship, Alex. Before it's too late.'

'Do you really think that's possible?'

'I *know* it's possible. Stick with me kiddo, I'm going to teach you a thing or two about the male of the species.' Bobbi was pleased to see Alex give a little smile. 'Now come on, you've got your car, right?' Alex nodded. 'Good, then you can drive us to Grovesbury Hall, and I'll walk back afterwards.'

Downstairs, Alex went out ahead to get the car from the valet while Bobbi stopped to have a quick word with the concierge. She was just about to leave when she heard her name being called. She turned to see Chris striding across the lobby towards her. 'What a pleasant surprise to bump into you like this. I'm just finishing a business meeting, come and join me for a drink.' He looked her up and down appreciatively. 'I must say you're looking as gorgeous as ever. Dublin must be agreeing with you.' As Chris leaned in to plant an unwelcome kiss on her cheek, Bobbi became aware of a blonde looking none too pleased to see Chris greet Bobbi so enthusiastically.

'Well, Chris,' said the blonde smiling icily. 'Aren't you going to introduce me?'

'What? Oh, yes, of course. Bobbi, this is Meredith Lacey, a colleague of mine. Meredith, our new neighbour, Bobbi Levinsky.' Bobbi shook hands politely with the girl, who, she decided, definitely didn't improve on closer inspection. 'Meredith and I were just finishing up, weren't we?' Chris said meaningfully to the blonde, whose expression became even colder if possible. 'Give me a call on Tuesday, there's a good girl, and we'll chat some more about your, er, ideas.' As the girl turned on her stiletto heels and left none too happily, Chris turned his full attention back to Bobbi. 'Now, about that drink. I won't take no for an answer.'

'I'm afraid you'll have to, Chris,' Bobbi said coolly. 'Alex is waiting for me outside, you must have just missed each other.'

'Alex?' Chris looked startled. 'What's she doing here?'

'We've just had lunch, and now we're going back to Grovesbury Hall. I want to show her how the work is coming on so, if you'll excuse me, I really must rush.'

'Of course, another time then,' said Chris, failing to hide his obvious irritation.

Outside, Bobbi quickly hopped into Alex's car. 'I just bumped into Chris, you must have just missed him.' Bobbi could feel Alex tense up at this news. 'He was just finishing a business meeting or something,' she added. 'We didn't have time to chat.' Bobbi neglected to mention that she'd bet her bottom dollar that business was the last thing on the agenda for that particular meeting.

'Chris is always having some kind of meeting or another. I just wish he'd pencil me in for one.'

'Now, now,' admonished Bobbi. 'Remember what we agreed? That, my dear girl, is all about to change.'

Pulling up outside Grovesbury Hall, any unease Alex was feeling suddenly evaporated as she was confronted by more activity than she had ever thought possible on one site. Living on Grovesbury Road for the past two years, she had become accustomed to fairly constant bouts of refurbishment, both in Chris's house and the others on the road where, at any given moment, complete wings of houses were demolished and replaced or added to. But nothing prepared her for the fleets of builders and landscapers working inside and outside the Hall. Watching her astonishment as they got out of the car and went up the steps to the house, Bobbi smiled. 'That's one of the advantages of having obscene amounts of money, I guess,' she said, pushing open the imposing hall door leading into the vast square outer hall. 'When Sean O'Rourke informed me we were looking at nine months to a year for the renovation work, I just told him to hire three times as many builders or however many it would take to get the job done quickly. I'm happy to say, things seem to progressing right on time.'

'Oh, Bobbi. It's amazing, it's just amazing.' Alex had never seen anything like it.

'Come on, I'll give you the guided tour.'

Alex followed, exclaiming time and time again at the magnificent, yet understated, air of elegance Bobbi had achieved in the renovation. A group of Italian plasterers had been flown in especially to restore the delicately hewn ceilings, which, in themselves, were works of art. An interior design firm from Paris had provided the sumptuously elegant fabrics and soft furnishings that blended so beautifully with the overall look.

Just as she had sworn she had never seen anything as beautiful as one bedroom, the next one took her breath away. All, of course, with incredible *en suite* bathrooms.

Downstairs, they descended three steps into a state-of-the-art kitchen that was the size of an aircraft hangar but still managed to look inviting. 'The kitchen's the giveaway,' Bobbi grinned. 'Europe's good for the other stuff, but nobody does kitchens like Americans.'

'I can see what you mean.' Alex looked around in wonder at every gadget known to man, and a good few others besides, all beautifully and seamlessly fitted into the gleaming white and stainless-steel space.

'Anyhow, I like to cook, when I can, so I guess I'll be spending quite a bit of time in here. Now that the bedrooms and kitchen are almost finished, I should be able to move in at the end of the month,' Bobbi said, checking one of the power switches for electricity, which immediately blinked on. 'The rest of the work can go on pretty much around me. Of course, outside will take longer, but that's not so much of an inconvenience.'

'It's the most incredible house I've ever seen,' Alex said as they walked back into the hall. 'I really do hope you'll be happy here.'

'I know I will. And it'll be good to have you down the road.'

'I'd better get back.' Alex looked at her watch. 'Cindy will think I've abandoned her for good! Thanks for lunch and, well, for listening. It means a lot.'

'You take care now, and remember what I said. And Alex?' Bobbi hesitated.

'Yes?'

'Always remember I have plenty of space here, you know, if things get rough for you.'

'Thanks, Bobbi. I will.' Alex felt her eyes welling up again. 'But let's hope it doesn't come to that.'

'I'm sure it won't. But it never hurts to have a bolthole.'

Bobbi waved as Alex got into her car and drove away. Closing the front door behind her, Bobbi started to walk back to the Four Seasons, where she would collect Bruiser and take him for his evening walk on Sandymount Strand. Just thinking about Chris Carroll made her blood boil. He represented everything she found detestable in a man, and the fact that he was picking on someone as vulnerable and clearly unable to fight back as Alex made him all the worse in her opinion. What Alex needed, Bobbi thought to herself as she strolled along, was a serious distraction. And she knew just the man to provide it.

11

Niamh was on her way back from work after a particularly arduous day made all the more wearisome by the suffocating heatwave that had descended upon Dublin. Even with all four windows wound down on her little Nissan Micra, she still could hardly feel a breath of air. As it was Wednesday, she would need to stop at the Merrion Centre to do her weekly shop, although the mere thought of it made her feel weak. She could have put it off, but, being a rigorous creature of habit, Niamh took a peculiar comfort in the certainty of her various repetitive duties, however tiresome. Pulling in to the shopping centre and descending to the underground car park, she was pleased to find it unusually empty and parked easily.

Upstairs, she popped her coin in the slot and pulled a trolley from the line. Setting off around the aisles, she completed her shop in record time, thanks, she presumed, to the fact that half of Dublin was sitting outside having a well-earned drink after work. Having stocked up on necessities, she headed over to the off-licence to check what was on special offer. She was rewarded with finding a rather interesting-looking French white on offer at half price and decided to treat herself to two bottles. In weather like this, it was always nice to have something crisp and refreshing to drink in the fridge, and she might invite Rowan and Nellie in for a bite to eat over the weekend. The queue at the checkout was mercifully brief, and soon Niamh was heading down to her car.

Ten minutes later she was home. She opened the front door of the cottage and went back to unload the bags when she suddenly remembered the parcel she had collected from the post office on her way to work that morning. It sat now on the front seat of her car, a rather long, oblong, package, wrapped in uninspiring, run-of-the-mill brown paper. Once she had brought in the shopping, she picked up the parcel and set it down on the small hall table while she went to unpack the groceries. When everything had been put away, and the cats fed, she made herself a cup of tea and went to open the mysterious package. Turning it over in her hands as she sat down, the only distinguishing aspect of its appearance was the English postmark, which did nothing to enlighten her. She tore off the paper, opened the corrugated cardboard flap and then the lid of the white plastic box underneath.

For a moment she was genuinely puzzled as she looked at the strangely shaped object she held up to examine, and then she let it fall to the ground with a resounding thud, from where she viewed it with unspeakable horror. Niamh ní Cheavin had just had her first encounter with a huge, black, extraordinarily lifelike dildo.

Chris was deep in thought as he sat in traffic on lower Baggot Street on his way into Fitzwilliam Square. Running into Bobbi in the Four Seasons the other week had not exactly come as a surprise. He had been frequenting the hotel in the hope of just such a chance encounter. That she had been lunching with Alex presented rather more of a problem. The pair, it would seem, had struck up quite a friendship, and although Chris had affected the introduction, not to mention encouraged Alex to be friendly to Bobbi, he had not anticipated that the two would get along as well as they did. It could spoil everything.

Initially, he had been livid at being pipped to the post on Grovesbury Hall, particularly by some jumped-up American chick, but that was before he had met Bobbi. Like most men, he had fallen instantly in lust with her, and her astonishing wealth was only an added attraction. Intimidation was not a term Chris was familiar with, and he could hardly believe his luck when he learned that, at thirty-four years of age, she was still, unbelievably, single. After that, the way forward was blindingly clear. What a team they would make! Her, the self-made billionairess with supermodel looks, and he, Chris Carroll, property developer and business brain *sans pareil*. Why, with Bobbi's class and money behind him, there would be no heights he couldn't scale. He'd be richer than any of them! *And* have a babe on his arm to boot. Chris got a hard-on just thinking about it.

The only fly in the ointment was Alex. She was one problem he could do without right now. He had been growing steadily tired of her: she was no challenge for him anymore and was always mooning over Cindy instead of devoting her attentions to him. What Chris needed, he thought, was some serious stimulation, someone to get his pulse racing again, and Bobbi Levinsky was just that person. Thank God he hadn't married Alex. He had known he never would. Whatever the circumstances, it would have been far too time consuming. This way it was easy. She had no rights whatsoever to his fortune or businesses. Of course, he would see she was well looked after, and Cindy too, but she would be dispatched nonetheless. And then a thought occurred to him:

this baby, suppose it was a boy? Chris contemplated the possibility. He certainly wouldn't have any son of his living with Alex. If Chris had a son, *he* would be bringing him up, not the string of unsuitable men that his mother would undoubtedly hook up with.

Pulling up outside his solicitor's office in Fitzwilliam Square, Chris made a mental note to accompany Alex when she next went for a scan. Regardless of what she said, he had every intention of finding out the sex of his unborn child.

'Chris, good to see you.' Malcolm stood up to greet his most important client as Chris was shown in to his office. 'Coffee?'

'Yes, I will actually. I've been on the go all morning,'

'Margaret,' Malcolm nodded at his secretary, 'make that two, will you?'

'I have a couple of things I want to discuss with you.'

'I gathered as much from our telephone conversation yesterday.' Malcolm pursed his mouth and inclined his head at what he thought was a suitably intent listening angle.

'Time's running out, Malcolm. I need you to find a legal way to get those tenants out. Or I'll have to take things into my own hands.'

'Now, now, Chris. Let's not be hasty here.' Malcolm risked giving his client a sternly disapproving look. 'These things have to be done by the book. I'm looking in to the matter rigorously. But I'm afraid legally, unless you can persuade the landlords not to renew the leases, those tenants have every right to stay just where they are.'

'There must be some sort of stunt you can pull.'

'I am not in the game of pulling stunts, as you so quaintly put it. These matters have to be handled with kid gloves. Anyhow, we've already served Niamh ní Cheavin her notice. She'll be out by November.'

'That's only one of them. I need the other three out as well. And, anyway, it's not soon enough. I'm not having those weedy bastards holding up my development scheme. It's utterly ridiculous to think they can hold me to ransom like this.'

'As I've said, Chris, unless you can persuade the current landlords *not* to renew the leases, you don't have a leg to stand on. Failing that, you, er, could always come clean and let the new owner of Grovesbury Hall know she is now in possession of the freehold on the cottages. Perhaps she would be more, er, open to a little gentle encouragement. I hear she's quite a beauty.' Malcolm let the words hang in the air.

'Bobbi Levinsky? She's a looker all right. And no, it's out of the question. We can't possibly let her in on the lease situation. She's American for God's sake. There's no knowing what she'd do.'

'She's also a phenomenally successful businesswoman,' Malcolm said knowledgeably. 'How do you know she wouldn't be interested in coming on board with the whole thing?'

'No, it's too risky. If she refused we'd be ruined.' Chris finished his coffee. 'Like I said, Malcolm, find some way of getting them out – or I will. I'll see myself out.'

As Chris got back into his car and revved up the powerful engine, he couldn't resist grinning to himself. By now that dried up old bitch Niamh ní Cheavin should have received his little 'gift' in the post. And that was only for starters. By the time he had finished with her, it would be *way* before November that she'd get the message to fuck off out of his property. And the rest of them wouldn't be long after her.

Cee

'Mareeeya!'

'Yes, Mrs Sheehan?'

'Are you sure, *absolutely* sure, that the Bobbi L cosmetics have been arranged on display as I instructed in the bathrooms?'

'Sí, Mrs Sheehan. Everything is perfect. Just like you told

me,' Maria, Melissa's South American housekeeper, assured her for the umpteenth time.

'And Jesus' (Melissa pronounced it correctly as 'Haysoos') 'will be ready with the silver tray of champagne cocktails as people arrive? I want everyone to be handed a drink the minute they cross the threshold.'

'Sí, Mrs Sheehan. Jesus is in position at this very moment. I mysel' have checked.'

'Hmm.' Melissa teetered out to the front hall on her six-inch Manolo's to see for herself. She didn't trust Jesus as far as she'd throw him. His fondness for drink had landed her and Pascal in hot water on more than one occasion. But, to give Maria her due, her husband stood imperiously, and indeed soberly, in the front hall, looking every inch the immaculately tailored butler. As far as appearances went, he measured up, for now.

It was ten to one, and the girls would be arriving any minute. Melissa shivered with anticipation. Imagine, Bobbi Levinsky, a fully blown *international celebrity*, was coming to her house for lunch. Melissa took a few deep breaths. It wasn't that she was nervous. She hadn't met Bobbi since that night in Chris Carroll's house, which was weeks ago, and it was important that the lunch should be a huge success. Melissa had been practising drawing out her vowels in that attractive mid-Atlantic fashion that Catherine Zeta-Jones had espoused, and her elocution coach was pleased with her progress. She had all but eradicated any evidence of her earlier, less fortunate inner-city background, but all the same, despite her bravado, the thought of having Bobbi in her home gave Melissa veritable palpitations. *Get a grip*, she chided herself. *Bobbi's a self-made woman, just as you are. She won't have been any stranger to hardship. And besides, she's American. If anything goes wrong, she'll just think it's a quaint little Irish custom.* Reassured by this staunch self-affirmation, Melissa took a last look in the hall mirror, reapplied a quick touch of Bobbi L's Frantic Fuchsia to her expensively plumped-up lips and awaited the arrival of her guests.

'Darling!' Angela Lemass, Melissa's next-door neighbour, swept into the hall in her relentlessly elegant fashion, looking every inch the glamorous, if ageing, Hollywood star she was. '*So* sweet of you to include me, Melissa.' Angela looked theatrically around her as she exhaled a cloud of smoke. 'Oh, Lord, don't tell me I'm the first to arrive!' Angela had been torn between making a late, grand entrance or missing the arrival of Bobbi, and had decided to forgo the entrance. After many years spent in Hollywood, she knew, more than most, how relentlessly punctual Americans were.

'Angela. Delighted, you could join us,' Melissa air-kissed her assiduously on both cheeks. 'Do make sure you have a champagne cocktail. They're the house speciality!'

No sooner was Angela in the door than Tanya Sykes arrived breathlessly on her heels. 'Melissa, I'm so sorry I'm late, but Nathan got his head stuck in the railings. We had to call the fire brigade to get him out.'

'Never mind,' Melissa said lightly, 'you're here now.' Although privately she was annoyed with Tanya, who had promised to be there early for moral support.

'Let's move outside, shall we? It's such lovely weather I thought we'd have an alfresco lunch.' The girls followed Melissa through the French doors and out into the sunshine. Outside, steps led from a large balustraded patio down to the swimming pool. Beside the pool, a table for six beautifully laid out with crisp linen, sparkling crystal and gleaming silver was waiting.

Seconds later, Jesus appeared with the champagne. He was closely followed by Carmela Walshe, her hair freshly coifed into her favoured upswept do.

'Someone should really tell her the bicycle pump is *not* the appropriate instrument to add lift to one's hairstyle,' murmured Angela to Tanya Sykes, who immediately started to titter. Angela couldn't stand Carmela, whom she thought of as a hypocritical, holier than thou gossipmonger. The feeling was mutual, and Carmela regularly referred in private to Angela as 'that frightful lush of a woman who was nothing more than a third-rate B-movie star'. Occasions such as this, however, demanded appropriate Grovesbury Road neighbourly behaviour, and the two women greeted each other warmly.

'Carmela, how lovely to see you again, and looking as elegant as ever.'

'Angela, how *are* you? It's been simply ages since Liam and I have seen you. You must come to dinner soon.'

Just then, Bobbi and Alex arrived together and were shown down to the pool by Jesus, closely followed by Maria, who couldn't wait to see their famous guest.

Melissa rushed to greet them and made the necessary introductions.

Initially, Melissa hadn't been sure about inviting the two older women to join them. But Angela was her next-door neighbour and terrific fun and would be bound to have a lot to talk to Bobbi about, as she had spent much of her earlier life in Hollywood, before coming back to Ireland to marry. As long as she didn't go over the top with the champagne, she was fabulous company.

Carmela was a different kettle of fish, but Liam and Pascal did a lot of business together and Melissa couldn't afford to offend her. Although she was well aware that, behind her back, Carmela looked down her supercilious Spanish nose at her and only barely tolerated Melissa and Pascal because of their immense, if recently acquired, wealth.

As the girls settled down to a delicious lunch of lobster, Melissa found herself beginning to relax. The sun was shining, and the champagne was having the desired effect. Everyone seemed to be enjoying themselves thoroughly. Bobbi was deep in conversation with Angela, who had just discovered that her son-in-law, Sean O'Rourke, was Bobbi's architect on Grovesbury Hall.

'It's almost finished now. He's done a fabulous job,' Bobbi was saying. 'I couldn't have believed some of the changes he suggested could have enhanced the house without taking away from its character. I should be able to move in at the end of the month.'

'You should see it,' agreed Alex. 'It's out of this world. I've never seen anything like it.'

'What are you going to do with the stables? They'd make a wonderful mews development,' Carmela commented.

'I haven't really decided yet.' Bobbi paused. 'They certainly would lend themselves to a mews development or workshops perhaps, but they're so beautiful it seems a shame not to restore them to their former glory.'

'But why on earth would you do that unless you're going to keep horses?' Tanya asked.

'I know. It's silly really.' Bobbi shrugged.

'She was insane about her horses,' Angela mused aloud, shaking her head.

'Who?' Tanya looked confused.

'Lady Grovesbury. I only met her once or twice, in the sixties, with my late-husband,' Angela continued. 'She threw a seriously good party – apparently she was quite a goer in her day. But her horses were her life. She bred some of the best show jumpers in the country. What was her famous one?' Angela paused, 'Montysomething or other, I think.'

'That's it! There's a magnificent portrait of her on a horse that I intend to keep. It's titled *Lady Arabella Grovesbury and Monty*, dated sometime in the twenties,' said Bobbi, looking interested.

'But how could anyone possibly keep horses on Grovesbury Road?' Tanya asked.

'Don't forget Grovesbury Hall backs onto the RDS. It was a perfect location, really,' said Angela. 'Which reminds me, the Horse Show will be coming up in August. You must make sure to go Bobbi, especially on the Friday for the Aga Khan trophy, the Nations Cup competition. It's such a lovely afternoon out. Of course, not nearly so elegant as it used to be in the old days, but nonetheless, worth attending.'

'Liam and I will be giving our annual Horse Show lunch

on the Friday.' Carmela inclined her head. 'Of course you must join us, Bobbi.'

'Oh, er, thank you Carmela, that's very kind of you. If I'm in the country I'll certainly take you up on that.'

Carmela smiled. She had deliberately not extended the invitation to any of the others around the table. She was meticulous about bestowing her favours and determined to keep her guest list as exclusive as possible, preferring to restrict it to the *old* Dublin families she could identify with. Unfortunately, this was becoming increasingly difficult, particularly as Liam's business contacts had to be included, which meant Pascal and Melissa. This invasion of new money, and the *excesses* that accompanied it, was, in Carmela's opinion, a very unwelcome addition to Dublin 4. However, Bobbi was such a celebrity, she felt she could make an exception.

'Melissa, lunch was really lovely.' Carmela stood up regretfully as coffee was being served. 'But I'm afraid I must be on my way. I have appointments to investigate one or two retirement homes in the area, and I mustn't be late. However much I'd love to stay and chat.'

'How very wise of you, Carmela,' Angela said mischievously. 'One can't put one's name down soon enough these days. The waiting lists are endless, I believe.'

Carmela shot her a withering glance. 'It's on behalf of a very dear friend of ours, actually. Liam and I feel it's our duty to look out for the elderly.'

'What a pity you have to rush,' said Melissa, giddy with relief that she was going. 'I'll show you out, Carmela.'

'Goodbye ladies. So nice to see you again, Bobbi.'

As Carmela left, a collective sigh was breathed around the table. 'Thank God she's gone,' said Angela. 'I have no idea why Melissa invited her. She's about as much fun as a wet weekend.'

'I'm terrified of her,' Tanya took a gulp of her champagne. 'She's always so polite but somehow disapproving.'

Melissa arrived back at the table with Dolce and Gabbana trotting behind her. 'More coffee on its way, girls,' she said gaily as she rejoined them. 'Are you all right, Alex? You're looking a little pale.'

'I'm fine, thanks. It's just this heat.' Alex took a sip of water.

'Would you prefer to move inside?' Melissa was concerned. 'How remiss of me. You must find this weather so oppressive in your condition.'

'No, I'm fine, really. I just think I'll run in to the bathroom.' Alex got up.

'Bobbi, why don't you go with her?' Melissa had spotted her chance to show off the carefully arranged rows of Bobbi L cosmetics that had pride of place in all her bathrooms.

'Sure, c'mon, Alex. You know the way, right?'

As Bobbi and Alex disappeared inside, Angela inhaled deeply on her slender cigarette holder. 'That girl doesn't look well. I've never seen anyone look so frail.'

'She *is* well on the way to having a baby, Angela,' Melissa said reprovingly.

'Mark my words,' Angela pronounced, 'that has nothing whatsoever to do with pregnancy, and everything to do with that smug man she's living with, very unwisely in my opinion. He'll never marry her.'

'Angela, how can you of all people be so conservative?' Melissa was shocked. 'What does it matter whether or not they're married?'

'Not a jot, Melissa, to you or me. But I'll wager you it matters rather a lot to Alex. Not that I'd wish that overbearing creep on anyone. But she *is* the mother of his children, and old fashioned or not, I bet if he proposed Alex would accept.'

'Too bleeding right,' agreed Tanya, who was becoming more boisterous with every glass of champagne. 'The minute I told Rod I was pregnant with our Nathan, he had me up the aisle in three months flat.' There was an embarrassed silence for a moment as this piece of news was digested.

'Of course, we were engaged anyway,' Tanya added quickly, realising her gaffe at relinquishing the information. 'We just moved the wedding forward a bit.'

'How sweet,' said Melissa, relieved to see Bobbi and Alex reappearing through the doors of the conservatory. 'Did you, er, find everything you needed girls?'

'Sure. Great place you have here, Melissa. Love the pool, do you swim every day?'

'Er, not *every* day, no. But as often as I can,' said Melissa thinking it was really time she took a dip sometime this year. 'We were just saying how well you look, Alex dear. Pregnancy obviously agrees with you.'

'I'm not so sure about that, but thank you anyway, Melissa. I'll be glad when the baby's born though. I'm finding it more tiring this time round for some reason.'

'Any idea whether it's a boy or a girl?' asked Tanya.

'Not a clue,' smiled Alex, 'and I have no desire to know. As long as he or she is healthy, that's all I care about. Although,' she paused, biting her lip, 'I'm pretty sure Chris would prefer a boy.'

'Not necessarily,' Tanya interjected. 'Rod would love a little girl. He's always trying to get me to go again. But I'm only just getting used to having my figure back. Speaking of boys, I was talking to Rowan Delaney the other day. You know, the artist? He said he was really keen to do more portraits. You should have a family one done of you, Chris and the children when the baby's born, Alex.'

'Why wait till then?' Bobbi was quick to interject. 'Rowan is absolutely *dying* to paint you right now, Alex. He told me so himself. In fact he never quits talking about it.'

'What a wonderful idea,' enthused Angela. 'My late husband insisted I was painted several times – he adored them all. It would be a wonderful surprise for your, er, partner, Alex. Nothing like looking at you through another man's eyes you know.' Angela let the thought hang in the air.

'I don't know,' said Alex hesitantly. 'I'd feel so self-conscious.'

'Don't be silly. For heaven's sake, all you have to do is *sit* there for a few sessions. The worst part about it is the boredom – depending, of course, on the artist,' Angela added wickedly.

'I think it's a great idea, Alex. I'm going to tell Rowan to call you and set up an appointment,' Bobbi said firmly.

'Well, maybe, but –'

'No buts, that's settled then.' Melissa raised her glass and giggled. 'Let's drink to painted ladies!'

It was coming up to five o'clock, and the girls were still sitting around the table outside when Melissa heard Pascal's voice and looked up to see him appearing through the doors. She waved up at him to come and join them. 'Pascal's not usually home this early. Maybe he's come home to have a swim before going out this evening.'

'He's not alone, Melissa,' Angela noted, looking over the top of her sunglasses. 'Who is that *devastatingly* attractive man with him?'

Before Melissa had a chance to answer, Pascal arrived at the table looking harassed. 'Sorry to barge in on your lunch girls, but I invited Steve in for a drink. We've had some rather unpleasant news, to put it mildly.'

'Of course, sweetheart.' Melissa immediately moved aside as Pascal pulled up two more chairs. 'Steve, let me introduce you to our new neighbour, Bobbi Levinsky. Steve,' she said to the girls, 'is our local and much depended on vet.'

'Hi, Bobbi.' Steve nodded across the table at her.

'You two know each other?' Melissa seemed surprised. This girl was getting around.

'We were introduced by a mutual friend.' Steve smiled, although he seemed distracted. 'How is Bruiser these days?'

'He's great. The hotel staff are his willing slaves. I don't know what they're going to do when he leaves.'

'Leaves?' Steve sounded perplexed.

'We're moving in to Grovesbury Hall at the end of this month, sooner than expected I'm happy to say.'

'Oh, good for you. It'll be nice for Bruiser to be back home.'

'Pascal, what's this bad news you were talking about?' Melissa enquired, as Jesus, refilled everyone's glasses and poured two fresh ones for Steve and Pascal.

Displeasure crossed Pascal's normally cheerful face, 'Steve rang me with it this morning. The cottage in Grovesbury Gardens that Steve leases from me to run the free animal clinic –' there was a pause '– it was vandalised last night.'

'What?' There was a collective gasp from the girls. 'Who on earth would do a thing like that?' Bobbi was incredulous.

'Who knows? Thugs, vandals, druggies?' Pascal shook his head.

'How bad is it?' asked Melissa, gathering Dolce up on to her lap.

'Very bad. The place has been completely wrecked – not to mention my equipment. All I'm grateful for is that there were no animals there at the time.' Steve looked angry.

'It'll take a lot of fixing, that's for sure,' Pascal said grimly. 'Whoever did this knew what they were about. That's what's so odd about it all.'

'How d'you mean?'

'Well, it hasn't just been roughed up. This wasn't a few thugs out of their heads on whack or something – whoever did this was thorough. When I say the place has been wrecked, it's all but destroyed really, inside at any rate.'

'What about the free animal clinic, Steve?'

'I'm afraid that's the end of it – for now at any rate. I couldn't possibly risk an animal being hurt. There's no more space at my Strand practice and I'd never be able to find anywhere else to set up – even temporarily. It's a bloody shame though.'

'Not necessarily.' Bobbi heard herself piping up.

'What?'

'I can think of somewhere you could run it from, and it would be just as convenient a location for people.'

'Where?'

'The stables. At Grovesbury Hall. They'd be perfect. All it would mean is fixing up one or two of them and some sort of waiting area for people. The builders are at work there anyway. I'm sure they can set something up temporarily, until your cottage is fixed.' Bobbi looked expectantly at Steve.

'Well, I, er, don't know, it's very generous of you but –'

'But what?' cried Melissa. 'It's a fabulous idea, why we were all just talking about the stables earlier. They'd make a perfect temporary animal clinic.'

'Sounds good to me.' Pascal grinned. 'You'll get new equipment easily enough, the insurance will take care of that. So, while I get to work on the cottage, you set up in the stables. What could be better? The locals can't afford to do without the service, Steve.'

'Well, if you're sure it wouldn't be too much of an intrusion.' Steve looked over at Bobbi.

'No intrusion at all, Steve. I'd be delighted.'

Wouldn't we all, thought Angela to herself, smiling. An intrusion by Steve Sorenson would be a very welcome one on any girl's part. She inhaled deeply on her cigarette as she scrutinised Steve from behind her sunglasses. Such a pity she was twice his age, because that was one man she would very definitely *not* have let slip through her fingers.

12

'Tanya, he's going and that's that,' Rod Sykes said firmly, as he finished up his morning workout in their state-of-the-art gym.

'But we can't, Rod. It'll be awful. Where'll he go? And he's just arranged for Alex to start sitting for him next week. We can't put him out.'

'Watch me.' Rod was uncharacteristically deaf to his wife's pleas. 'Look, he's a bad enough influence on Nathan as it is – all those weird things lying round the place he uses for his "art" – but I'm not having anyone involved with drugs in any property of mine, let alone near my son. You of all people should see how inappropriate it would be. Rowan's a nice enough guy – but he's got to go.'

'But he said the drugs weren't his, it was a set-up. They haven't proved anything yet,' Tanya pleaded.

'Well he would say that, wouldn't he? He's hardly going to say, "Whoops, it's a fair cop gov, you've caught me out", to four policemen in front of Bobbi Levinsky now is he? I bet she wasn't pleased. Think of the trouble he could have got her into.'

'Bobbi says she believes him. She thinks he was set up too.'

'Oh, for heaven's sake. Who cares? Either way, I am *not* having him in my property, and Nathan is *not* to spend a minute more in his company. I'll expect you to see to that, Tanya. I'll get my solicitor to serve him a month's notice.'

From his favourite vantage point, monitoring the in-house surveillance system in Rod's office, six-year-old Nathan considered his parents' conversation. Something as important as this required action.

Cee

Bobbi was in her office checking her e-mails. It was just seven-thirty, and already she had been for her morning run and showered. She sat now in the turret room, with a pot of fresh coffee beside her and Bruiser lying contentedly at her feet. Looking out over the grounds, which were finally beginning to take shape, she could see the beginnings of what would become meticulously manicured gardens and, beyond that, the stables, whose cobblestones glowed in the early-morning sun.

The builders had set up two prefabs, one of which served as their on-site office and the other as a waiting area for Steve's clients, who were more than happy to make the transition from Grovesbury Gardens to get a glimpse of the grandest house in Dublin.

It was hard to believe she had been in the house for just over a month. Already she felt completely at home and thought of her previous fast-track lifestyle in New York with vague amusement. She had been back there only last week. Although she loved the buzz of the city, and it had been great to catch up with her friends, she had been relieved to board her Aer Lingus flight and surprisingly happy to catch a glimpse of the greeny-grey coastline that emerged when they finally broke through the cloud over Dublin.

There was no doubt whatsoever in her mind that she had done the right thing in moving to Ireland. Sure, it had been a culture shock, and initially she had found people friendly but in their own way, suspicious – not that she could blame them. Anyhow, over the years, Bobbi had become used to being an object of curiosity.

Then one day, she couldn't quite say for sure when exactly, she felt that she had finally become accepted. It wasn't just the numerous invitations she received from her neighbours – it was more subtle than that. It might have been the day the postman had called a cheery 'Howya, Bobbi', as she set off on her morning run with Bruiser at her heels. Or maybe the day the taxi driver had confided to her that 'Everyone thought yis'd be a right royal-pain-in-the-arse movie-star type but sure yis are a bit of craic, wha?' Or maybe it had been the day that she had been leaving for New York and Steve had casually mentioned that she must come around to his place for a bite to eat when she got home. That had been over a week ago, and she hadn't seen him since. But he would be here on Saturday for his free animal clinic come hell or high water.

Stretching back in her chair, Bobbi thought about the day ahead. She had a meeting with Sean O'Rourke at ten o'clock, and then she was due to meet Alex for lunch in town. Alex was becoming increasingly nervous about the 'first sitting' for her portrait with Rowan, which she had agreed to and now very much wished she could renege on. Bobbi was meeting her in Patrick Guilbaud's in the Merrion Hotel at one o'clock, and then afterwards Alex said she 'had something fun planned'. What exactly, Bobbi had absolutely no idea.

She finished up her e-mails and headed back downstairs to the kitchen, pausing to admire the latest acquisition in her art collection. It was a beautiful painting of a young girl by Orpen, and Bobbi had fallen in love with it when she had seen it at Sotheby's Irish art auction in London the month before.

Studying the picture, she realised it was slightly askew on the wall, as if someone had brushed by it. As Bobbi straightened it, a puzzled expression passed over her face. That was the second time in as many days the picture had moved, and it had been hung perfectly and with immense care by the man sent from the gallery. As Bobbi continued down to the kitchen, she remembered other little things she had noticed since she had moved into the Hall. Nothing major but, considering the matter now, there had definitely been a succession of things being mislaid, or turning up in unusual places. She had checked with Polly, her housekeeper, but she was meticulous about not touching or moving anything without checking with Bobbi first. Keys seemed to be a particular favourite and, more than once, Bobbi's handbag, and now, this new painting. Polly had even become quite alarmed by it, and although she didn't come right out and say it, Bobbi knew what she was thinking. Bobbi smiled. She didn't believe in ghosts, and anyway, if the late Lady Grovesbury wanted to check out her old home every now and then, it was okay by her. There was nothing but a good, warm, happy feeling about this house, and that was what mattered as far as Bobbi was concerned.

*

'Niamh, any luck with that file I asked you for?'

Niamh jumped as her boss's voice interrupted her thoughts. She had totally forgotten to request the wretched file from the land registry. 'It's on its way, Conor. I'll chase them up, you know what they're like,' she lied.

As soon as he had disappeared within the safe confines of his office, Niamh hastily rang through and requested the file. She made a mental note to shake herself out of the morbid frame of mind that had taken over since the phone calls began. It was ridiculous to let this kind of thing get to her, but no matter what she did the calls kept coming, and whatever sort of a pervert was behind them, he was having the desired effect.

Niamh hadn't told a soul about them. The calls were of such a sordid and overtly sexual nature that she couldn't possibly discuss them with anyone. The very thought brought a hot flush to her cheeks. She had tried everything – hanging up, taking the phone off the hook, telling the caller just what a sad, perverted, sick bastard he was and even blowing a tin whistle loudly into the receiver – all to no avail. Sooner rather than later, the phone would ring again and it would be him. She knew she should go to the guards, but the thought of them sniggering at her, a spinster living alone, was even worse than the calls themselves.

Lately, though, there was another, far more sinister undertone to them that was really beginning to disturb her. Not only were there the usual sexual implications and insults, but now her cats had been included in the veiled threats. Niamh's blood ran cold even thinking about it. Whoever was making the calls knew where she lived and had obviously been watching her. It was all very well people saying that these sort of sick people got off on simply upsetting the victim and rarely carried out their threats. But then Steve Sorenson's cottage had been ransacked – maybe there was some weird sicko with animal rights issues out there, just waiting to strike again.

Niamh knew she should do something – but what? She hated drawing any sort of attention to herself, and this would be the worst kind possible. She couldn't bear people pitying her and tut-tutting about her poor, sad, lonely life. No, she would wait a little bit longer and give things a chance to work themselves out. As if to confirm the validity of her decision, the file from the land registry landed at that very moment on her desk.

C

'A tea-leaf reading? Are you crazy?' Bobbi was incredulous in the face of Alex's enthusiasm.

'But she's brilliant, Bobbi, really uncanny. She reads hands too, if you prefer,' Alex added. 'Honestly, she's been so accurate with everyone I know, and I haven't been to her for *ages*. I've made the appointment for three-thirty, so if we get a move on we'll be in perfect time.'

'I can't believe you go in for that stuff. It's pure charlatanism. All they do is ask a few leading questions, watch your reactions and bingo, they're off!'

'Not Nellie. I promise you, Bobbi, she really has the gift. Look all I'm asking is that you give it a go. What have you got to lose?'

'Don't get me wrong, I like Nellie. I think she's a sweet old dear, but all this "you'll meet a tall, dark, handsome stranger" stuff leaves me cold. But hey, if that's what you want, I'll go along – but only to prove you wrong. And let's not forget, she knows me pretty well by now. It wouldn't be difficult for her to spin out a plausible yarn.'

Twenty minutes later, they pulled up outside Nellie's cottage. They rang the bell, and the door was opened promptly by Nellie, looking fresh and sprightly in a cool cotton blouse and rather fifties-looking dirndl skirt. She ushered the girls in and offered them tea or coffee. Bobbi hadn't been in Nellie's cottage before and was struck by its quaint, old-world charm. The walls were a pristine white, and the pretty, if faded, materials and soft furnishings lent a cosy feel to the little place.

'Now, who's first?' Nellie got straight down to business.

Alex looked at Bobbi who shook her head meaningfully. 'You go ahead, Alex. I'll enjoy my cup of coffee out here.'

While Alex disappeared into the little room off the sitting room with Nellie, Bobbi picked up one of the many magazines provided and glanced through it. A few doors down, she could hear crashing and banging and presumed Rowan was at work on one of his 'masterpieces'. A radio burbled from a little table across the room and on the far wall an old clock tick-tocked soothingly. She was almost about to nod off in the comfortable little chair when the door opened and Alex appeared. Looking at the clock, Bobbi was surprised to notice half an hour had passed, although it had felt more like ten minutes.

'Go on in,' said Alex. 'She's waiting for you.'

Bobbi shook her head as she pulled herself up from the chair. 'Only because I think it would be rude not to,' she said under her breath.

'Hurry, go on. I'll wait for you here.'

Reluctantly, Bobbi went into the tiny room, where Nellie sat behind a small table. In front of the table was another chair. 'Sit down, Bobbi and give me your hands. Palms up, please.'

Silently, Bobbi did as she was told, feeling faintly ridiculous as Nellie took both of her hands in hers and studied them intently. Suddenly, a warm, tingling sensation was running through Bobbi's fingers, into her hands and up her arms. She stiffened in surprise, and Nellie looked up at her and smiled, 'Don't worry about that, it's only the energy field. It doesn't happen with everyone, but the connection's quite strong with you. It'll settle down in a moment.'

'You've had great success in your life,' Nellie began, 'but it has been built on tragedy.' She paused and looked up at Bobbi. 'I'm not interested in asking questions – I just tell what I see and what the spirits tell me. If you want to stop me at any stage and ask me something, feel free.' Bobbi nodded.

'There's been a loss here, a great sense of loss, and help-lessness – I feel a great sense of helplessness.' She paused as Bobbi's face went pale. 'There's a little boy here. He passed over quite some time ago. Do you know who he is?'

Bobbi tried to speak but didn't trust her voice. When she eventually found it, she faltered, 'It … it's my little brother. He died when he was eight years old.'

Nellie shook her head and paused again as if to listen to someone. 'No, no it's not him. This little boy is much younger, *much* younger he's telling me. Though he's with the older boy. Did you have any other younger brothers?'

'No, and I'm pretty sure I'd know about it if I had.'

'Well he's telling me he was separated from you very early on, and he's sorry about that. But he's watching over you from the other side.'

'The other boy you mentioned?' Bobbi urged.

'He's telling me it wasn't your fault, what happened,' Nellie said gently. 'And you mustn't go on blaming yourself. He's very happy you know, in the spirit world. He wants you to move on.' Nellie looked up as tears began to stream down Bobbi's face.

'There, there, love, it's all right. I'll stop for a little while if you like. I know it can be upsetting sometimes.'

'No, no,' Bobbi gulped, 'go on. I'm sorry, it's just such a shock. I forgot how much I miss him.'

'This new house of yours.'

'Grovesbury Hall?'

'You know it found *you* – you didn't find it.' Nellie looked up and smiled. 'This house, there's very strong parallels I'm getting here. It's seen tragedy, but it's a happy house. It'll be a homecoming for you in more ways than one.'

'What's the connection with horses?' Nellie smiled. 'The boys are telling me about horses?'

'Oh, I guess horses played a big part in our lives when we were young. I used to ride a lot but I gave it up,' Bobbi paused, 'after … the accident.'

'Well they're about to come back in to your life,' Nellie said firmly.

'Oh, I don't think so.' Bobbi shook her head.

'Mark my words,' Nellie said firmly, 'horses are going to play a big part in your life again – and not in the too-distant future either. Now I'll have to stop there, Bobbi,' she said. 'Let me know if you ever find out about the other little boy. He was quite insistent you know!'

'Er, sure, I will, Nellie.' Bobbi looked directly at her. 'And thanks. I, well, I was a bit sceptical you know. Guess it's the New Yorker in me.'

'You take care of yourself now, and come and see me again

sometime.' Nellie waved the girls off as they got into Alex's car and went back inside. She sighed. She was definitely getting too old for this. There was a time when she could have seen ten, even fifteen people a day, but now even a short session wore her out.

She made a cup of tea, sat down at her little kitchen table and lit a cigarette, inhaling thoughtfully. That last sitting with the American girl had left her feeling drained all right. It had been a long time since the spirits had come through so forcefully, although often with the young it happened that way – they were as impatient to communicate on the other side, just as they would have been on this one. But that girl had been through a lot, no doubt about it. Nellie hadn't delved too deeply into the tragedy or accident, but she knew it had affected Bobbi deeply, and she no doubt bore the scars on the inside.

Putting out her cigarette carefully, she drained the remains of her cup of tea. Just for curiosity, she peered into the cup to examine the tea leaves. It was just as she had expected. There was more upheaval to come, and there were the parallels again, staring her right in the face. She wondered should she have told Bobbi about Lord and Lady Grovesbury's only son and heir who had died so tragically – and at such a heart-breakingly young age. She had sensed his presence strongly at the sitting but had deliberately tuned him out. He was restless, that was for sure, the poor little chap. Only ten years old he was when he'd been thrown from his horse in a horrible hunting accident. His little neck had snapped like a chicken bone before he died in his father's arms.

They had never gotten over it. And that had been the end of the horses. Lord Grovesbury himself had shot the horse; deranged with grief he was. He would have shot all the others in the stables too, when he got back to the Hall, only he had been restrained until old Dr Johnson had been called to sedate him. After that, horses had been well and truly banned from Grovesbury Hall. Every last one of them, even Lady

Grovesbury's beloved Monty, had to go. Some of the finest bloodstock in the country had been bred by her ladyship at the Hall. Between them, the National Stud and the Aga Khan had bought them up. And, if losing her only son had broken her heart, Nellie knew that letting Monty go had finished Lady Arabella off completely. Horses had been in her blood. She had a way with them no one else even came close to. Nellie knew Lady Arabella used to sneak away to visit Monty in the Aga Khan's stud farm as often as she could and had personally seen to it that he was guaranteed a safe and peaceful retirement and, when the time came, a painless and merciful death.

But all that had been so long ago, Nellie sighed. Thinking about the past made her tired and seemed these days to take up more and more of her present. What was done was done, and what did any of it matter now when everyone was dead and gone anyway, and she wouldn't be long joining them herself.

A cool breeze blew in through the open kitchen window, stirring the white muslin curtain softly. It was only six o'clock but, Nellie thought, she would go and have a little nap. She was all done in. Niamh had said she might drop by later, and she would hear the bell if she rang. Nellie emptied her ashtray, rinsed her cup and saucer out at the sink and walked slowly to her bedroom. She lay down on the bed and drifted off to a deep and peaceful sleep.

Not surprisingly, she never heard a sound when, half an hour later, a figure slipped in through the kitchen window. It moved quickly and stealthily to the kitchen table, where Nellie's cigarettes and lighter sat. The figure lit a cigarette, inhaled for a few moments and dropped the half-smoked remains into a waste-paper basket, which had been stuffed with firelighters and several sheets of torn newspaper. As the flames obligingly leapt to life, the figure walked calmly to the front door and left, closing it softly behind him.

13

'What on earth am I going to wear?' Alex moaned to Bobbi over the phone.

'Didn't you discuss that with Rowan when you spoke to him?'

'He said it would make no difference whatsoever.'

'Oh,' said Bobbi. 'I would have thought he'd be quite particular about what you wore.'

'So did I, now I haven't a clue.' Alex paused and took a breath. 'Bobbi, you don't think, well, you don't think he'd, well, that he'd –'

'What?'

'Well, that he'd expect me to undress or anything?'

'Don't be ridiculous!' Bobbi laughed at Alex's vivid imagination. 'Of course he wouldn't. It's a portrait for Chris, isn't it? He's hardly going to expect you to strip off – unless you want to of course,' she couldn't resist adding mischievously.

'As if!'

'Well, Rowan's an extremely attractive man, Alex. You never know.'

'What I know is that I'm eight months pregnant and feel like a beached whale. It'll be bad enough sitting in front of him, never mind getting up to anything else.'

'Well, whatever you wear, you'll look fabulous.'

'You wouldn't come with me Bobbi? Just for the first sitting, please?'

'Are you crazy? Even if Rowan allowed it, which I'm sure he wouldn't, there's no way I'd go with you to hold your hand. You're having your portrait painted – not having the baby! Ring me the minute you get back, though. I want to hear every last detail.'

When Alex put down the phone, she went back to her wardrobe and looked helplessly at the collection of designer labels hanging neatly on the rails – none of which fitted her in her present condition. Eventually, she settled on a stretchy navy and white striped cotton lycra dress with a deep V-neck and threw a navy cashmere sweater around her shoulders in case it got chilly. Her hair had been freshly washed, and her make-up was minimal. She had a good colour thanks to the fabulous weather they had been having, and checking in the mirror for one last time before she left, a healthy, glowing reflection looked back at her. She had taken Bobbi's advice regarding the situation with Chris and was concentrating on the forthcoming birth and had been eating healthily and taking regular long walks. The benefits, both outside and inside, of getting out of the house were paying off. She was looking like her old self again and feeling a million times better.

As it was such a nice day, she decided to walk the short distance around to Rowan's cottage. And, on the off-chance that Chris would pop home and find her out, she had told Theresa, their Filipino housekeeper, to say she had gone to meet Bobbi.

Five minutes later, she was outside the cottage door, having edged her way precariously through various pieces of scrap metal that littered the tiny front garden. She was just about to press the doorbell when the door opened, and Rowan stood before her, a wide grin creasing his very tanned face.

'Good, you're punctual. I like that in a woman. Come on in.'

'Er, thank you.' Alex couldn't help her eyes flickering over the tanned torso and long tanned legs that emerged from the well-worn pair of cut-off jeans that appeared to be all that Rowan was wearing.

'Now, sit yourself down over there.' Rowan indicated an ancient chaise longue in front of the window, which he had draped in yards of scarlet silk taffeta that fell in folds to the ground. 'I want to make sure the light is just right.'

Alex did as she was told as Rowan walked over to the easel that held the huge canvas that dominated the centre of the room. 'Perfect,' he proclaimed. 'It won't last long. It's important we get to work quickly.'

'I, er, wasn't sure what to wear,' Alex said tentatively. 'Is this all right?'

'Hmm?' Rowan sounded distracted as he adjusted the easel and moved the high stool he would be sitting on to the left. 'Oh, it doesn't matter at all at this stage – I just need to get the lines right. We can work the clothes in later. At a more finished stage.'

'Oh,' said Alex sounding relieved.

'Here,' he said, filling two glasses with a generous helping of Moët & Chandon. 'Have a little sip of that. It's part of the ritual and it'll help you relax.' Again there was the wide grin.

'Oh, no thanks, I don't drink. That is, it's not a good idea when you're pregnant.'

'I heard you say at your dinner party that your doctor told you a glass now and again wouldn't hurt.' Rowan raised a questioning eyebrow. 'I'll get you a glass of sparkling water gladly,' he smiled, 'but please, just one glass? For good luck? It's a ritual, strictly water after this, I promise.'

Alex couldn't help laughing at him. 'Oh all right, but just the one.' While Rowan went to fetch the water, Alex took a sip of her champagne and tried to relax. Really, she was becoming ridiculously uptight these days. After all, it wasn't every day you had your portrait painted by an up-and-coming artist. She might as well enjoy the experience.

When Rowan returned, he placed the water on a small table beside her and took a few steps back. 'We need to work out how this is going to look,' he said, squinting. 'Why don't you try lying down? There, put your feet up, that's it.' Rowan regarded Alex as she manoeuvred her legs onto the chaise longue rather awkwardly. 'Now, lie on your side, facing me, that's it, and bend your arm back behind your head, see, like this.' Rowan moved Alex's arm into position. 'That's it, now lie back and rest your head on your hand so that the crook of your elbow is facing towards me. That's it. Perfect. Absolutely fabulous.' Alex lay reclining on the chaise, feeling suddenly rather soporific, thanks to the champagne. 'Okay, now you can go and change in there.' Rowan indicated the door leading to his bedroom.

'Sorry?' Alex sat bolt upright. 'B–but I thought you said it didn't matter what I was wearing,' she found herself gibbering.

'It doesn't. But I have to get the lines of your body right. Go into my bedroom. There's a sheet of muslin I've left on the bed. Get undressed and wrap the sheet around you, under your arms.' Seeing Alex's horrified expression, Rowan tried to sound reassuring. 'Relax Alex, you'll be totally covered, and even if you weren't, I wouldn't be seeing anything I hadn't seen before.'

'I … I can't,' Alex bleated. 'Chris would kill me if he even thought –'

'But he won't, will he? And let's leave Chris out of this, shall we?' Rowan's voice took on a serious tone. 'Look, Alex, either we do this properly or we don't do it at all. I need to see the lines of your body until I get the basic shape right. It'll only take one, at the most two sittings. After that you can dress up as Little Bo Beep for all I care. The muslin will cover your, er, modesty, so to speak, but it's fluid enough not to interfere with the lines of your body. Now let's get on with it and go and get changed.'

Something in Rowan's voice, or maybe his expression, propelled Alex into action. He was right. She was being childish and, as usual, feeling both guilty and intimidated by Chris. She got up and went into the room and quickly undressed, then wrapped the length of white muslin around her, tying it under her arms, sarong style. When she came back into the front room and reassumed her position, Rowan appeared to be concentrating ferociously on mixing oils.

When he finally looked up, his breath caught. Reclining back on the chaise longue, her arm draped casually behind her head and the thin muslin only accentuating the magnificent lines of her voluptuously full body, Alex looked like a goddess of fertility. Her skin glowed golden in the late-afternoon light, her lips (fresh from nervous biting) were slightly parted and cherry red, and her dark blonde hair fell in a sheath around her shoulders.

'Great. Yeah, great,' said Rowan, brush in hand, retreating behind the virgin canvas. This was going to be sensational. He began to paint furiously, smiling to himself as he was hidden from view.

Alex was apprehensive enough as it was – but if she had been able to see the very obvious evidence of his erection, she would have bolted for sure.

Cee

'This settles it, Liam,' Carmela said, shaking her head reprovingly at her husband. 'She'll have to go into a home immediately. Why, she could have burnt in her bed! I dread to think what would have happened if that Niamh woman hadn't called on her when she did.'

'I suppose you're right, dear.' Liam looked up from behind his newspaper and nodded.

'Of course I'm right. We're only lucky the cottage wasn't burnt down in the process. I knew those cigarettes would be the death of her sooner or later. She must have left one burning and nodded off.'

'Maybe you could look in on her in hospital in a day or two when she's feeling better and broach the subject?'

'That's exactly what I'll do. She's in St Vincent's. I'll make enquires and drop in on her in the morning, if she's up to it. In the meanwhile, why don't you get in touch with Chris Carroll and tell him the cottage is now vacant and we're ready to talk business?'

'Whatever you think, Carmela.'

*

'I don't believe it!' Niamh sat down, feeling suddenly weak at what the young guard was implying. 'Who on earth would do a thing like that?'

'That's exactly what we'd like to know,' he said grimly. 'It's very lucky you turned up when you did, otherwise things could have ended very differently. Do you know of anyone who'd want to harm her?'

'What?' Niamh's head was reeling. 'No, no, of course not. Who would want to harm an old woman? Why Nellie's never hurt anyone in her life.'

'Well whoever got in through that window came prepared. Fire lighters and newspapers don't end up in a wastepaper basket accidentally, only to be lit by a burning cigarette. Whoever did this wanted to set the place on fire and the old woman with it.'

Niamh was lost for words and just sat shaking her head.

'Well Miss ní Cheavin, if anything strikes you or comes to mind that might throw any light on the incident, call us at Donnybrook station.'

'Of course I will, Guard.'

'And, well, you might want to be careful yourself. I don't

want to alarm you or anything but, well, there's been funny goings on in the area recently. A woman living on her own can be vulnerable. Just make sure to lock up securely and take the usual precautions.'

'I will,' said Niamh weakly, thinking of the nuisance calls she had been getting. She was very nearly going to tell him about them, but then bit her tongue. What were a few nuisance calls from some pervert compared to a poor defenceless woman being almost burned alive in her bed?

Ce

It was four o'clock the following day when the youth swaggered nonchalantly down through Grovesbury Gardens. He was no more than fourteen or fifteen years old, and his tough, aggressive gait was not tempered by the cheerful tune he whistled. Slowing down as he drew close to Niamh's cottage, he looked round surreptitiously to check if the coast was clear. He rubbed a grubby hand over his closely shaved head, lit a cigarette and paused to consider his options. Looking up instinctively at the first sign of movement in the area, a grin creased his face as a large marmalade cat strolled around the corner and sat down on the steps in front of the brightly painted front door. Perfectly located to bask in the late-afternoon sun, Jimmy, Niamh's oldest cat, settled down to wash himself assiduously. The youth took a last drag of his cigarette and threw it to the ground where he trod on it. Then, from inside his jacket he produced a pair of battered leather gloves, which he quickly put on. In one swift move, he picked up the surprised cat, held him firmly in his arms and walked around to the back of the house. Holding Jimmy with one gloved hand round his neck as the cat struggled, he dragged a couple of pills from another pocket and shoved them roughly down Jimmy's throat.

It wasn't out of kindness he decided to sedate the animal. Mikey had been one of those kids who had never lost the thrill of pulling the legs off live insects. The request from a mate who knew someone who wanted to use a cat to make a point and needed the procedure carried out effectively for a generous amount of cash had come as manna from heaven to him. The only reason he was sedating the animal was to keep him quiet, at least initially, so he would have a chance to make a clean getaway. After that, it could yell as much as it wanted.

He waited a few moments until the pills took effect (he had known they would come in handy the night they had ransacked that vet's place) and the cat became drowsy. Mikey went to work quickly, dragging a hammer from his jacket and the nails from another pocket. The cat tried to struggle, but it was no use. Four thuds was all it took, and then Mikey got the hell out of there.

He definitely didn't want to be around when some old biddy came home to find her cat nailed by its four legs to her front door. As he legged it towards the main road, Jimmy's plaintive yowls were just beginning.

14

Chris sat at his corner table in the old bar of the Four Seasons puffing on a particularly good cigar and sipping a glass of his favourite Château Lafite. He had just left Meredith Lacey after an eventful two hours spent in her conveniently located Ballsbridge apartment and was availing himself of the opportunity to gather his thoughts and congratulate himself on the supremely successful turn of events that had transpired.

He sat back in his chair and sighed. Meredith hadn't half put him through his paces. He would have to lose some of this weight that had crept on over the last year or so, or risk croaking it in most unsavoury circumstances. He chuckled quietly. Meredith was quite a girl – hard as nails and a great ride. Not into all this emotional stuff either, thank goodness. And the fact that she was located a mere ten minutes from his home, his office and his favourite watering hole was an obvious bonus he had shrewdly factored into the attractively packaged equation. She was clever too. Chris had had his fill of the pretty airheads who abounded in D4, two a penny, constantly on the prowl, gold diggers every one of them. Anyway, they were too easy. They were all very well for a quick fuck, but then the silly little tarts expected you to talk to them! Some of them even hinted heavily that they were available for a trip away to an exotic and romantic (read expensive) location. At least Meredith had her head screwed on. She didn't bug him and knew when to keep her mouth shut and – more importantly – when not to. In fact, she was the perfect interlude to amuse him until he could get around to the real quarry he had set his sights on in the extremely pleasing shape of Bobbi Levinsky. And Meredith, being a smart girl, wouldn't make a fuss when it was time for him to end their little arrangement.

So much for his personal life. Business-wise, things were progressing even more advantageously. At least three of the four cottages had been vacated. The vet had been easily disposed of once his precious clinic had been ransacked, and that weird old woman who told fortunes had practically gone up in smoke – high time she went into a home anyway. And Niamh, that dried up old spinster who had caused him so much grief, wouldn't be in her cottage long either. The best of all though, thought Chris with a malicious smile, was that piss-artist painter Rowan Delaney. He hadn't had to lift a finger to get him out of the place – he had managed it all on his own. Drugs no less. His timing couldn't have been more opportune. Chris had been worried about him, particularly since his landlord, Rod Sykes, was such a wimp about any adverse publicity that getting his tenant out might have involved. Yes, everything was coming along very nicely indeed. It was amazing how easily people crumpled when a little bit of pressure was applied. Still, as the old saying went, if you can't stand the heat, stay out of the kitchen.

The only thing left on his current agenda was to accompany Alex to her scan in the morning. She had been pathetically grateful when he had suggested the idea. Of late, Chris had been a little perplexed regarding Alex. She had been very unlike herself – happy, cheerful and out from under his feet for a change. He almost wondered momentarily if she was seeing someone else. She had become quite mysterious, evasive even, when he asked where she had been – and she wasn't showing her usual avid interest in him. Probably she was becoming obsessive about the new baby. Well, tomorrow he would have the information he needed and he could think about what to do next.

Cee

'Oh, Bobbi, I think it's working.' Alex's excitement was tangible as she confided her latest news over coffee in Bobbi's kitchen.

'What is, hon?'

'Your advice, you know, about Chris.'

'Really? In what way?' Bobbi kept her voice deliberately neutral.

'Well, he's been much more interested in what I'm doing lately. And yesterday he said he wanted to come with me to see the scan. He's *never* shown any interest in babies before – not even when I was pregnant with Cindy.' Alex's eyes were shining.

'Really?'

'Well that proves he must still care about me, doesn't it? And it means he's excited about the baby too.'

Not by a long shot, Bobbi sorely wanted to say but couldn't. Instead she smiled at Alex's beaming face and reiterated her earlier advice. 'One step at a time, honey. I'm glad things are going well between you two but just remember you have to keep taking care of *you* – no slipping up, right?'

'Of course not.' Alex looked indignant. 'Why would I when your strategy is obviously working so well?'

'Speaking of strategies, how's the portrait coming along?'

'I never thought I'd say it, Bobbi, but I'm really enjoying it. Rowan's such a laugh, he really makes it fun.'

'I thought he might,' Bobbi grinned. 'By the way, I told him to drop in today to have a look at some artwork I need to have framed,' she added casually. 'How many more sittings have you got?'

'I don't know, he's very evasive. Every time I ask him, he says you can't always judge these things, that a portrait will let you know when it's completed.' Alex giggled.

'Of course.' Bobbi made a face. 'Silly me.'

Just then the doorbell sounded and Polly, the housekeeper, went to answer the intercom. 'Rowan Delaney is here to see you, Bobbi?' she called down the kitchen.

'That's okay, Polly, I'm expecting him. You can show him down here.'

A moment later Rowan appeared, looking even more dishevelled than usual. 'Hey guys, howya?'

'Good, thanks, sit down.' Bobbi smiled as he kissed them both. 'Will you have some coffee?'

'Yeah, man, great. Actually if it wasn't so obscenely early I'd ask for something stronger.'

Bobbi and Alex looked intrigued. Rowan seemed unusually stressed, and normally he was so laid back he was horizontal.

'It's almost twelve o'clock, Rowan,' Bobbi said, looking at the kitchen clock. 'You're welcome to a drink if you want one. What's up?'

'No, you're grand. Coffee'll be fine.' He pushed his hair back over his shoulders as Bobbi put a mug in front of him and Alex poured the coffee.

'What's going on?' Alex asked.

'I have to get out of the cottage. I got a letter today from Rod Sykes' solicitor giving me a month's notice.'

'What? Why?'

'That's exactly what I asked when I rang him. Rod gave it to me straight. He said he didn't want anyone dealing in drugs

in his property and that I was to stay away from Nathan.'
Rowan looked downcast.

'Who's Nathan?' Bobbi was confused.

'Rod and Tanya's son,' Alex explained. 'Oh, Rowan, that's awful, I'm so sorry. Where will you go?'

'Hold on a minute,' interjected Bobbi. 'They can't prove those drugs were yours. They haven't even had the court case yet.'

'They were found on my, or rather Rod's, premises. That's enough apparently,' Rowan said wearily. 'I could fight it, but what's the point? He's rotten with money – he'd make mince meat of me. And, frankly, I don't need the publicity.'

'But all your paintings – what will you do with them?' Bobbi asked.

'Put them into storage, I suppose. What else can I do?'

'It's so weird, first Steve's place, then poor Nellie nearly going up in flames and now you having to move out. What is it with Grovesbury Gardens?' Bobbi shook her head.

'Well, I wasn't planning on staying there forever but, for the moment, it was home. I'll just have to find somewhere else – and sharpish.'

'And Alex's portrait? What about that?'

'Well, we might be able to get it finished, but there's going to be awful upheaval going on.'

'Wait a minute, I have an idea.' Bobbi held up her hand. 'Why don't you move in here for a while? Lord knows I have tons of space, and to be honest, I'd enjoy the company. In fact, I know just the place you could use for your studio. The light would be perfect. What do you say?'

Rowan looked surprised. 'Jeez, Bobbi, that's really good of you man, but I couldn't really –'

'Why ever not? I have tons of spare bedrooms here. You'd have absolute privacy, and you could paint all day every day. I don't see the problem?'

'Neither do I,' Alex added. 'It's an extremely generous offer, Bobbi. You'd be crazy not to take it, Rowan.'

'Well, I dunno. It seems a bit, well, like taking advantage –'

'Nonsense. Do I look like a woman you could take advantage of? Just say yes, Rowan, and we'll get started on moving you in right away. Besides,' she added slyly, 'I have an awful lot of free wall space that needs covering. This way you can really get a feel for the house and the kind of art it needs. C'mon, don't be a moron, it makes sense – you know it does.'

'Well, if you're really sure.'

'Sure, I'm sure.' Bobbi held out her hand. 'Deal?'

'Deal,' said Rowan, shaking it heartily in his own. 'I really appreciate this, Bobbi.'

'No problem. Like I said, I'll be glad of the company. Now let's have that drink shall we?'

Cee

They made a strange pair: the dark-haired, dark-skinned little girl, dressed in a long, ill-fitting skirt, a brightly coloured scarf tied about her head and worn, brown leather sandals on her feet leading the woebegone-looking animal behind her on a long trailing rope. The unlikely travelling companions proceeded slowly along the Merrion Road, before turning into Grovesbury Road, the uneven clip, clop of the lame horse's hooves clattering incongruously along the quiet, tree-lined pavements.

Reaching Grovesbury Hall, the girl paused to read the name on the large brass plate on the gate before continuing up the driveway. The horse followed, his hooves leaving a trail of indents in the perfectly arranged gravel. The little girl then threw the rope around one of the pillars at the bottom of the steps leading to the front door. There, the horse remained tethered, his left foreleg slightly bent and lifted and his head drooping listlessly as his companion marched up the front steps and boldly pressed the door bell.

'Yes?' said Polly as she opened the door and looked out. Seeing the young Romanian gypsy girl she added, 'I'm sorry, there's no one at home now. You'll have to come back another time.'

'Wait,' the little girl said in lilting English pointing to the horse. 'People told me there is vet here? No? He is sick horse, he need help.'

'What on earth?' Polly looked aghast as she noticed the animal for the first time. 'Look, you'll have to take him away immediately. You can't leave him here, this is a private residence. Off you go now, and take your friend with you. Go on now, honestly!'

The girl shrugged her shoulders helplessly and turned to go down the steps when Bobbi appeared at the door. 'What is it, Polly. Who's there?'

'Beautiful lady,' the girl addressed Bobbi with a well-practised smile. 'I bring sick horse. I find him on the beach. Bad boys have hurt him. I bring him here, for vet. Yes? Please, I am hungry, you give me money?' she added hopefully.

'What? Oh hang on a sec.' Bobbi retrieved her handbag and got some cash out to give to the little girl, who couldn't have been more than seven or eight years old. 'Here, honey, go get yourself an ice-cream or something. But you can't leave your horse here.'

'You look after him, beautiful lady.' The girl shot her a wide grin, and before Bobbi could say another word, she ran down the steps and out on to road, pocketing the notes in one of the many folds in her long skirt.

'Well I never!' said Polly, her mouth open and hands on her hips. 'The cheek of it. What does she think you're going to do with a horse? We'll have to call the guards to take it away.'

'No, Polly, it's okay, I'd better take a look at him. He's in pretty bad shape.' Bobbi walked down the steps and approached the horse slowly, trying to ignore the churning that was beginning in her stomach. 'Hey, there boy, it's okay. I won't hurt you.' The animal flinched as Bobbi tentatively ran a practised hand over his back, noticing the open wounds and sores, continuing down his flank and feeling her way gently down the injured foreleg. 'Looks like this leg is badly infected to me. Poor guy, you must be in a lot of pain.' She rubbed the horse's nose gently as he blew into her other hand.

'What are you going to do with him?' Polly stood a safe distance back on the steps.

'He's in no state to be moved anywhere,' Bobbi said, taking a deep breath. 'He's painfully thin and, from the feel of this coat, he's running a fever. I'll take him around to the stables and have one of the stalls cleared out for him. Call Steve to come see him as soon as possible.'

'C'mon old boy. Let's get you some food and water and see if we can't fix you up some.' Bobbi took the rope from the pillar and led the old horse slowly around the back of the house and down the path towards the stables. He followed her obediently, head down, going short on his lame foreleg. When she reached the temporary prefabs that had been set up, she called to the foreman to ask two of the builders to clean out the largest stall thoroughly. She would take care of the rest of it herself. 'Look, I know this isn't in the usual line of work for you guys, but it won't take long. It *is* in a good cause – we've got a very sick horse here.'

'Right away, Bobbi,' said the foreman, ever conscious of the triple-time pay he and his men were on. 'Not a bother. We'll have the place cleaned out in a jiffy.'

'Good, I appreciate it, guys. Now I need to send out for some fresh straw, some hay and horse nuts and oats. Any idea where I can get my hands on that kinda stuff?'

'With the Horse Show approaching, I'd say you'd get it in the RDS. I'll send one of the men down now to find out.'

'Great, I'll just get a bucket of fresh water and go see if Polly's arranged for the vet to call.' Bobbi tied the old Chestnut up to the stable door and went back inside.

As it turned out, Steve was out on an urgent call, so Polly had left a message for him to ring Bobbi at the house as soon as he could.

An hour later, Old Chestnut, as Bobbi had called him, was

ensconced in the newly cleaned out stall. Fresh straw lay on the floor and freshly warmed oats filled the manger. The horse had sniffed the food half-heartedly and left it untouched. He stood still, with his head hanging, only responding to Bobbi's caresses with a slight movement of his ears and a soft muzzle thrust into her hand. Bruiser watched the scene intently, never once bothering the horse. Although Bobbi was reluctant to leave him, she had to go back to the house to finish up some business letters. For once, Bruiser didn't follow her. He stayed in the stall with Old Chestnut and lay down quietly beside him, head resting on his paws, looking for all the world like a long-lost friend. The horse seemed to take comfort in his presence, and Bobbi decided to leave him there.

It was only on her way back up to the house that she remembered that that was exactly where she had found Bruiser the day she and Sean O'Rourke had been going over the stables. It was that very stall Bruiser had been hiding in and had seemed so reluctant to leave. Strange, she mused, the attachments animals had to places. Anyway, she reasoned, the company would do the old horse good. She only hoped Steve would get here sooner rather than later. She didn't like the look of that infected leg at all.

Rowan, Steve and Niamh sat in Rowan's front room. Rowan was filling the glasses he had set out beside them with wine. Niamh's hand shook very slightly as she took her first sip. Overnight, it seemed, she had aged at least ten years. 'I still can't believe it,' she said tremulously. 'I can't believe *any human being* would do something like that to a poor innocent, harmless animal.'

'I'd like to say it never happens, Niamh.' Steve sounded weary. 'But, unfortunately, there are still too many people out there who get some kind of kick from inflicting pain and suffering on defenceless animals. Why only last week –'

'Stop!' Niamh covered her ears. 'I don't want to hear it, I couldn't bear it.'

'Sorry.'

'I don't like to even *think* what would have happened if you hadn't come along when you did Rowan. Poor little Jimmy.' She shook her head and took another gulp of wine.

Rowan was about to say he couldn't believe that half the neighbourhood hadn't turned up, the screams from the cat had been so loud, but thoughtfully refrained. He had had to return to his cottage as he'd forgotten his wallet, which was when he had heard the eerie yowls and found poor Jimmy. Wisely, Rowan hadn't touched the cat but had called Steve, who came out straightaway, with his partner Tracey, to rescue the unfortunate animal. Luckily, not a lot of harm had been done, and apart from the wounds to his paws which had been cleaned and dressed, Jimmy was going to be fine. He was recovering in suitably sedated bliss in Steve's surgery.

Niamh, however, was not faring so well. The incident had shocked her greatly, and both Rowan and Steve were worried about her.

'I should have known,' she said to nobody in particular. 'I should have known something like this would happen. How could I have been so irresponsible?'

'What? Don't be mad, Niamh. How could you possibly have known anything like this would happen? I've heard about survivor guilt, but this is ridiculous!' Rowan protested.

'I'm not mad,' Niamh continued in a small voice. 'I could have prevented this. I could have saved poor Jimmy from that bastard.'

Rowan and Steve exchanged a concerned look. 'Niamh, listen to me. Jimmy's going to be absolutely fine, it hasn't taken a feather out of him. He'll be as right as rain in a couple of days.'

'You don't understand.' Niamh looked directly at them. 'I was warned.'

'What?'

Slowly, Niamh launched into the story of the phone calls, the threats and even the obscene gifts she had been sent.

Rowan and Steve listened in horrified silence.

'You silly bitch!' Rowan went over and put an arm around her. 'Why on earth didn't you say something?'

'I don't know, really. I suppose I thought the guards would laugh at me, and I didn't want everyone feeling sorry for me – pitying me living on my own with my cats. It was pride, nothing more than stupid, stupid pride, and poor little Jimmy was punished for it.' Niamh began to sob quietly.

'For heaven's sake!' Steve shook his head in disbelief. 'But we're your friends, Niamh. I can't believe you wouldn't have come to us if you had a problem – *any* problem.'

'I suppose I've got used to coping on my own over the years. This seemed like just another hurdle to get over. Since Chris Carroll has given me notice to leave the cottage, nothing else has seemed to matter very much really. Now even my last few months here have been ruined.'

'D'you think he could be behind this?' Rowan ventured.

Niamh sniffed. 'I wouldn't put anything past him. But not even Chris would be sick enough to nail an innocent cat to a door. Besides, he knows he's got me moving out in November.'

'Maybe, but he could easily find someone else to do his dirty work for him. And maybe November isn't soon enough for him to get his hands on your cottage.'

'You don't really think ...' Steve looked appalled.

'Think about it. Three months ago, we were all getting along just fine in Grovesbury Gardens. Now Niamh's been cruelly harassed, you've been ransacked and Nellie's place was set on fire. Even I've been set up with drugs. It's got to be more than a coincidence.'

'But why?'

'Who knows? But clearly somebody wants us out of the cottages,' Rowan said grimly.

'And the only person who could benefit from that is Chris

Carroll, or someone connected to him, for sure.' Niamh nodded in agreement.

'It does seem a bit extreme. Although, I grant you there have been weird things happening.' Steve looked doubtful. 'I mean, even if it were a possibility that he's behind this in some way, how could we possibly prove anything?'

Rowan looked thoughtful. 'I don't know, but I know a girl who does.'

'Who?' asked Niamh and Steve.

'Alex. I'm painting her at the moment, and something she mentioned the other day has just come to mind.'

'What can she possibly know?' Niamh sounded scornful. 'She's terrified of Chris herself, and anyway, she's not going to be disloyal to him and tell *you* anything that might compromise him.'

'That remains to be seen,' Rowan said mysteriously. 'In the meantime, you're not staying on your own, Niamh. You must come and stay with me.'

'I couldn't possibly, Rowan. Although it's very kind of you to offer. I'll tell the guards, I promise, but I'm more comfortable in my own place. God knows, I won't have it for much longer.'

'Well, in that case, I'll kip down on your sofa at night. I'm only two doors down anyway. I'll be up and out in the morning before you even know I've been there.'

'There's no need, really, Rowan.'

'No, I insist.'

'Rowan's right, Niamh,' Steve agreed. 'You shouldn't be on your own. Not after what's happened.'

'Well maybe just for tonight then. Thank you, Rowan. It's not that I'm ungrateful, I'm just used to my own space and routine you know.'

'Like I said, you won't even know I'm there.'

15

'Well, what do you think?' Bobbi stood back as Steve examined the horse thoroughly.

'It's infected all right, and that's not the only problem,' Steve said, running his hand along the horse's foreleg. 'He's been badly hurt, not to mention neglected. Hard to say for how long. He's not in good shape, Bobbi.'

'What are you saying?'

'Nothing – yet. But you've got a very sick horse on your hands. It may be too late for him to respond to treatment. I'll lance the leg, of course, and antibiotics should take care of any remaining infection, but whether he can make a full recovery or not depends on what strength he has left to fight back. Is he eating?'

'No, hasn't touched a thing.'

'I'll do the leg this afternoon, under local anaesthetic. Hopefully, if we can get the fever down, he'll start to eat, but if he doesn't, well, I think it would be kinder to put him out of his suffering.'

'I don't want him to suffer any more than you do, but at least let's give him a fighting chance.' Bobbi stroked the old horse's neck. 'He deserves that much. Don't you, old man?'

'That's another thing,' Steve commented, 'he's not that old either. I'd put him at about fifteen. He just looks a lot older. He has a beautiful head, though. I'd say he was quite a looker in his day.'

'I really appreciate you doing this, Steve.'

'No problem, I mostly get to deal with small animals in my practice, but I think I can remember enough from my training to handle this.' Steve looked amused as he watched the concern on Bobbi's face. 'Don't worry, Bobbi, I have my full equine licence. It'll be a pleasure to work on this guy. Like I said, I'll be back this afternoon with Donal. We'll take care of it then. It's good of you to take him,' Steve commented. 'Stables or no stables. A lot of people would have just called the ISPCA.'

'Oh, I don't have anything against horses.' Bobbi's expression became guarded. 'I just don't like being around them.'

'I see. By the way, sorry I couldn't get down earlier, but when you called I was out rescuing a cat from a particularly gruesome predicament. Luckily Rowan Delaney arrived just in time, otherwise it would have been a very upsetting sight for his neighbour to come home to.' Bobbi listened to Steve's account of the unfortunate cat incident in growing disbelief. She had already heard about Nellie's accident from Polly who had been only too keen to share the local gossip. Now, hearing about this latest distressing incident, Bobbi's razor-sharp instincts were instantly on the alert. 'Steve, surely you all can't possibly think these incidents are unrelated?'

'I don't like to jump to conclusions.' Steve paused, thinking of what Niamh had said about Chris Carroll. 'But you could say there's a growing train of thought that someone, or some people, are behind this, yes. I just find it hard to believe that anyone could be so callous as to target people in their own homes – and why?'

'Well,' Bobbi said thoughtfully, 'that depends. It's amazing what people will do when there's money involved. Call me a hard-nosed New Yorker, but I smell a helluva rat here.'

'At least Niamh ní Cheavin has promised to go to the guards about it. I think we'll all feel better about things when the law is involved.' Steve looked serious. 'Anyway, I'd better get moving. I'll see you later on. I should be back at about three-thirty to lance this leg.' Steve patted the horse as he was leaving. 'Poor old chap, at least it'll relieve the pain at any rate.'

'See you later then.' Bobbi waved him off and began the walk back up to the house. Something sinister was going on for sure, but just what could Grovesbury Gardens cottages have to do with anything?

Cee

'Well, Malcolm.' Chris sat back in the leather chair in his solicitor's office and grinned broadly. 'It seems things have progressed rather more quickly than we anticipated. Fortuitous, don't you think?' Chris regarded the little bird-like man that sat across the desk from him, who seemed, if possible, even more agitated than usual.

'Let's not be hasty, Chris.' Malcolm pursed his lips and drew in a measured breath. 'I agree it would seem that things appear to be moving in our favour. But many's the slip twixt cup and lip, and all that.' Malcolm took care to deliver an admonishing look to his client.

'On the contrary, Malcolm, I think it's imperative we move with the utmost speed.' Chris smiled thinly. He was in no mood for mealy-mouthed warnings. 'I want you to apply for planning permission immediately. Two of the cottages have already been vacated, and I have it on good authority the remaining two should be clear in the next week or two. While you're at it, draw up the necessary legal papers. I'll deal with the landlords. When the development goes ahead, I'm sure they'll be more than happy to exchange their cottages for an apartment each in the complex. It's a more than generous offer on my part.' *Too bloody generous by half,* thought Chris to himself, but he couldn't afford to cut off his nose to spite his face. This way, none of the relevant Grovesbury Road residents would object to planning, and it would only cost him four apartments out of a luxury complex of at least fifty. Peanuts, really, in the scheme of things.

'As I understand it, Chris, the situation is still, how shall I put it, delicate. Not to mention unstable. I would advise we proceed with caution.'

'Just get on with it man, for heaven's sake. I don't have time to waste. Apply for planning and draw up the legal papers. I've got a very lucrative development to get underway. One, I might remind you, that your firm is going to benefit from.'

'Er, yes, quite Chris. but I must reiterate –'

'Save it, Malcolm. Just do the job I pay you handsomely to do, will you? I'll expect to hear from you in a day or two.' Chris got up to leave. 'Call me when things are moving.'

Malcolm sighed. There was no use arguing with Chris Carroll when he got the bit between his teeth. But really – legally – it was a most unsatisfactory state of affairs, *most* unsatisfactory.

As his bolshie client left the office, Malcolm got up from his desk and went over to his grandfather's Victorian drinks cabinet, where he kept a variety of spirits for strictly celebratory use with his most esteemed clients. He poured himself a large whiskey and reassured himself that, whatever the outcome of this outlandish scheme, McBride & Whitaker, the revered firm of solicitors set up by his late great-grandfather, would emerge unscathed.

Cee

Rowan Delaney was, for once, lost in thought. The portrait, if it could be reduced to such a confining term, was simply magnificent. He had excelled himself far beyond his wildest dreams. Alex had proven a more than inspiring subject. She sat now, brushing her hair, as he put the final touches to what would be their last sitting in his cottage. He was due to move in to Grovesbury Hall over the next day or two, and the sittings would continue from the makeshift studio that Bobbi had arranged for him in the small room adjoining the stables. The builders had put in a long glass window running the full length of the wall and the light, as a result, was excellent.

Alex, in many ways, had been a revelation to Rowan. He had never lost the wild physical attraction he had felt for her from the first moment he had set eyes on her. But, as the sittings progressed and Alex began to relax more and more in his company, she blossomed visibly in a way he could never have predicted. She had an extraordinarily sensual quality about her, enhanced, in many ways, by her very genuine innocence. And it was this almost ephemeral quality that Rowan was endeavouring to capture on canvas. Rowan wasn't stupid. He was aware full well what a shit Chris Carroll was and, from his discreet conversations with Bobbi, gathered in no uncertain terms that she was of the same opinion. The thought of Alex wasting her loveliness on that boor of a man, who had done his utmost to eradicate any sense of self-esteem she might have had, enraged him beyond belief.

The trouble was – after all his careful plotting and planning – now that he had Alex in the same room on a twice-weekly basis, he had absolutely no idea how to move things on. It wasn't so much the fact that she was going to give birth any minute that made him hesitate – more a deeply buried sense of chivalry that seemed to be manifesting itself whenever he was in her presence. He felt extraordinarily protective of Alex. So much so that he was prepared, for the first time in his life, to rein in his own, extremely demanding, urges. But now time was running out, and besides, there were other important avenues he wanted to explore. 'Why do you stay with him, Alex?' The question was out before it had barely formed itself in his head.

'What?' The brush in Alex's hand paused in mid-air.

'You heard me. Why do you stay with the shit?'

'You … you shouldn't speak about Chris like that!' She sounded horrified.

'Why not? Everyone else does. And you still haven't answered my question.'

'Because I love him.'

'No you don't, you may be in awe of him. But you sure as hell aren't in love with him.'

'Oh really.' Alex adopted an outraged tone. 'And I suppose you'd know all about that, wouldn't you? Not that it's any of your business.'

'I do know you couldn't possibly love someone who treats you so badly. It may be a personality defect, but it's not love.'

'How dare you suggest I have a personality defect. Just who the hell do you think you are?'

'I could never suggest there would be anything even remotely defective about you. I merely think you are in denial about your real feelings towards Chris. Probably because, like most people, you're afraid of him. But he's nothing more than a bully Alex – a very rich bully I grant you, but a bully nonetheless.'

There was a pause, and then Alex said in a small voice, 'He's the father of my children.'

'That's not a good enough reason, Alex. Is it the money?'

'You bastard!' Something in Alex finally snapped. 'What the hell do you know about anything? Of course it's not the money – I'd love Chris if he was penniless. If, if –'

'If what?' asked Rowan gently.

'If … oh, Rowan.' Alex looked at him helplessly as two big tears began to roll down her cheeks. 'If he only loved me, just a little bit even, in return.'

'Darling.' Rowan went over and put his arms around her, rocking her gently as she began to sob. 'Shh, don't try to be brave, sweetheart. You've been having a rotten time. Any one can see that.'

'Oh, Rowan. What am I going to do?'

'Nothing – for now. You're very vulnerable Alex. You're about to have a baby and, oh God, you're *so* beautiful. So very, very beautiful.' Rowan looked into the big, blue eyes brimming with tears and traced the trembling lips with his finger and then his lips were on hers. There was a moment's startled hesitation – and then Alex was kissing him willingly, openly returning his passion with an intensity she hadn't known she was capable of.

It was Alex who pulled away. 'Oh God, Rowan. Stop! What are we doing? What am I even thinking of?'

'We weren't thinking Alex. That's just it, you can't deny something like this. It's too strong to rationalise. I've wanted you since the moment I set eyes on you,' Rowan said.

'You're crazy, I'm about to have another man's baby for heaven's sake. A man I love and I'm –'

'You don't love him, Alex,' Rowan whispered as he nuzzled her throat gently. 'You know you don't.'

'Oh God, I don't know what to think, I *can't* think,' Alex wailed.

'Of course you can't, and you shouldn't try. Look, I'm going to make you a cup of tea, and you're going to dry your eyes and drink it. Alex, the last thing in the world I want is to upset you, but I can't hide the way I feel about you anymore. I don't care if you're having twenty babies, I'm crazy about you, and I have been since the first time I saw you in that red dress.'

'But –'

'No buts. I expect absolutely nothing from you. I just want you to go home and, whenever you're feeling lonely or threatened, remember that someone close by is very much in love with you.'

'Oh, Rowan.'

'Now stop looking so miserable. Anyone would think you'd just had bad news, and I happen to think someone loving you is extremely good news.'

'It's him. He's definitely behind it.' Rowan looked grim as he sat with Bobbi in the kitchen late that night.

'Are you sure?' Bobbi asked thoughtfully.

'As much as anyone can be. Alex mentioned he was caught up in some big development scheme due to start on Grovesbury Road. When he went with her to see the scan of the baby, apparently he couldn't get away quickly enough. Dashed off to some bloody meeting about a Dublin 4 development and put Alex in a taxi – charming sort, our Chris.'

'That's not exactly concrete proof, Rowan.'

'No, but it's a start. I bet, if we do a little research, we'll come up trumps. Niamh ní Cheavin is on the case as we speak.'

'How so?'

'She works in the land registry. It'll be a doddle for her to check out the latest planning applications. If it's true, and he *is* going to develop the cottages, that's where we'll find our proof.'

'Proof that he intends to develop the site, sure, but no proof that he's behind all the harassment of the tenants. And let's face it, if no one objects and the landlords, for whatever reasons, have terminated their leases and ousted their tenants, well, there's nothing stopping him going ahead with the development.' Bobbi looked meaningfully at him.

'You could object.'

'What good would that do? I'm hardly a stalwart pillar of the community.'

'You live in the biggest house on the road. And you're an international celebrity, Bobbi, people would listen to you.'

'I don't think it's a good idea for me to start throwing my weight around, certainly not without proof that Chris Carroll is, as you say, behind this. Besides, I came to Ireland to avoid that sort of notoriety.'

'We can't let him get away with this, Bobbi. He's a bully, an influential bully. You're the only person who could take him on,' Rowan added slyly.

'I think we should wait until we know for sure, Rowan. Anyway, it's late and I'm off to bed.'

'Crikey, that reminds me, I'd better get over to Niamh's, she shouldn't be alone in that cottage after what happened.'

'You mean the cat incident? Steve told me about that.' Bobbi shook her head. 'How is she taking it?'

'That's the least of it, Bobbi,' said Rowan, going on to tell about the series of threats and unwelcome attention Niamh had been subjected to over the past weeks.

'I can't believe it!' Bobbi was appalled as she listened. 'Why on earth didn't you say so – Steve never told me things had gotten so out of hand. The poor woman, of course she can't stay on her own. You're to go down there right now and bring her back here. Tell her I won't take no for an answer, and if she doesn't come back with you, I'll go and fetch her myself. This puts a completely different perspective on things.'

Rowan grinned. 'It'll be my pleasure.'

Cee

'Have you lost what few marbles you have left?' Niamh couldn't believe what she was hearing. 'Why, in the name of God, would I up sticks and go and move in to Grovesbury Hall, of all places, with a woman that I barely know to say hello to? I've never heard of anything so ridiculous!'

'You do know her, Niamh, come on, she's lovely.'

'I know she's a multimillionairess, and she's pally with that Alex girl who happens to be Chris Carroll's consort,' snorted Niamh. 'That's a good enough reason for me.'

'Alex is a sweetheart, and Bobbi is under no illusions regarding Chris Carroll. In fact, she's our only chance to take the bastard on.'

'What gives you that impression?' Niamh was suspicious.

'Trust me. Anyway, I'm going to be living there. Steve's running his animal clinic from the stables. She's got tons of space, the house is like a feckin' hotel for heaven sake! And I happen to think she's lonely,' Rowan added slyly.

'Humph! How could a woman like that be lonely? Sure she's stunning looking and loaded to boot!'

'That doesn't guarantee friends at all – quite the opposite, Niamh, as you well know.'

'I'm not going to be a charity case.'

'You can pay her rent for pity's sake – and think about it, it'll give us a chance to put our collective heads together and figure out what Chris Carroll really has up his sleeve.'

'What about Nellie? She's due out of hospital any day now. I couldn't leave her.' Niamh looked triumphant.

'I was just coming to that, if you'd get off your high bloody horse and give me a chance to explain,' Rowan sighed. 'Bobbi's been in to see Nellie in hospital. She's invited her to stay and recuperate at the Hall until she's feeling stronger. Nellie, unlike you, had the good sense to take her up on her offer without a moment's hesitation.'

Niamh's mouth fell open. 'I don't believe it!'

'It's true, Nellie's moving in tomorrow. I'm going to collect her from hospital, and Bobbi's already hired a full-time private nurse to look after her.'

'She's a regular Lady Bountiful, isn't she, this Bobbi Levinsky?' Niamh couldn't help the snide remark escaping. She had always prided herself on looking out for Nellie, her late mother's oldest friend, and now she had been outdone by this American Florence Nightingale.

'I know you don't mean that, Niamh,' Rowan said with a reproving look. 'You know the offer makes sense, and like I said, I think Bobbi could do with the company. Anyway, it'll only be for a while, just until things get sorted out.' Rowan could see Niamh was weakening. 'And think of it – if Chris Carroll *is* behind the goings on lately, it won't half put the wind up him if he thinks we've got Bobbi Levinsky's ear to bend.'

Niamh considered this legitimate point of view. 'Well, I'll

think about it, but only because I don't want Nellie to feel uncomfortable in a strange house, among strangers, mind.'

'That's very noble of you, Niamh.'

'Don't get smart with me, Rowan Delaney.' The beginnings of a smile tugged at Niamh's firmly set mouth.

'I wouldn't dream of it.'

'I suppose if you have a house as big as that one, you might as well have a few bodies rattling around it,' Niamh conceded.

'My sentiments exactly.'

16

'What is it?' Bobbi asked Alex, who had just come from a sitting for her portrait, while the pair were having a welcome cool drink.

'What's what?' Alex looked flustered.

'There's something you're not telling me.' There was an interested gleam in Bobbi's eye.

'I don't know what you mean.' Alex immediately looked guilty.

'Alex, I wasn't a cosmetics queen for nothing – this is *me* you're talking to. I realise you're in the final stages of pregnancy, honey, but that very definite bloom you've been sporting recently has very little to do with an impending birth – I'd bet my last dollar on it. Come to think of it, our artist friend has had a very pronounced spring in his step these days too, if I'm not mistaken.' Bobbi's astute observations were rewarded by a deep flush suffusing Alex's cheeks.

'Oh, Bobbi, I don't know what's got into me, really I don't,' Alex said helplessly.

'Go on, tell Auntie Roberta.'

'I think I'm going crazy. Maybe it's my hormones or something.'

'I like the sound of this already.'

'You mustn't tell a soul.' Alex chewed her lip.

'Who am I going to tell? The international press?'

As Alex launched into her account of what had happened between her and Rowan during the sitting, Bobbi listened avidly.

'But I think that's *great* honey, just great. You and Rowan would make a *wild* couple.'

'Are you crazy?' Alex looked alarmed at the thought. 'Anyway, it was only a kiss. That's all, nothing else has happened, *nothing*, I swear.'

'You don't have to defend yourself to me, Alex. I happen to think this is exactly what the doctor ordered.'

'No it's not!' Alex protested. 'It's disastrous.'

'Give me one good reason why.'

'Well I'm about to have a baby, for one thing.'

'Doesn't seem to bother Rowan.'

'Oh be serious, Bobbi. I don't know whether I'm coming or going. And he's so – so, well, so kind, and considerate and gentle with me.'

'Men usually are when they're in love.'

'I just, well, he's just been such a revelation. I thought he was a complete wild child y'know.' Alex smiled. 'And I know it's totally mad, but I think I'm beginning to feel the same way about him. But that's impossible, because I love Chris. Oh, Bobbi, I'm such a mess, I feel as if I'm going out of my mind.'

'Of course you're not, don't be ridiculous. You're just a beautiful young woman who's responding perfectly naturally to the attentions of a very attractive man who's clearly head over heels about her. Though I could have told you that ages ago. Rowan has been mooning around you for months. You've just been too caught up with that selfish man you insist on living with to notice. There, I've said it.' Bobbi paused to draw breath and watch Alex's reaction to her rather unintended burst of opinion.

'You think so, too?'

'Me and the rest of the world.'

'But I love Chris, and he's the father of my children and –'

'And he doesn't make you happy.'

'But he did, in the beginning.'

'How long ago was that, honey?'

'But –'

'Alex, Chris has been making you thoroughly miserable ever since the night I first met you at that dinner party. You may have loved him once, sure, but you certainly can't go on loving someone who treats you so badly. If you do – you're doing yourself and your children a great disservice.'

'But what am I going to do?'

'Take it one step at a time. You have to come to terms with this yourself, Alex. Maybe Chris will change, as you seem to keep hoping. Only you can decide how long you're going to wait for that to happen. But, in the meantime, he's not doing you any good. And you're wasting valuable time neglecting the possibility of a fabulous relationship with a man who truly does love you.'

'Do you really think Rowan loves me? You don't think it's just some mad artist's whim or something?'

'Honey, I know so. He's been boring me rigid telling me exactly that for the last six weeks at least.'

'And what did you say?'

'I told him to shut up telling me and to tell you. And from the look on your face, I'm pleased to see he's taken my advice. Right?'

'Well, he did, um, mention it once or twice.'

'Then for heaven's sake stop looking so worried and go and enjoy yourself. You have a new baby on the way and at least one man who's crazy about you. There are a lot of women in the world who'd happily trade places with you.'

'Oh, Bobbi.' Alex looked worried.

'No more "Oh, Bobbis", I don't want to hear another word about it.'

'I don't mean that. I think the baby's coming!'

Cee

Chris was enjoying a reviving drink at Meredith's place when he switched his phone back on and got the message. He listened to Bobbi Levinsky's voice telling him that Alex had gone into labour and had been rushed to Mount Carmel Hospital half an hour earlier.

'What is it, darling?' drawled Meredith, slipping her excessively toned arms into a silk robe. 'You don't have to rush off do you?'

'No, no. Nothing important,' smiled Chris, watching her admire her reflection in the full-length mirror. 'Nothing that can't wait till later at any rate.'

'Good,' said Meredith, turning back to him, 'because there's a very pressing matter I need you to attend to when you've finished that drink.'

Chris checked his watch. There was no need to rush. Since he had found out (unbeknown to Alex) from the ultrasound technician that the baby was another girl, he was damned if he was going to waste precious time mooning round a labour ward. These things took forever, anyway, and he had much more enticing matters to attend to.

It was good news though, that Alex had finally gone in to have the baby. She'd be in hospital for the best part of a week, which would give him ample time to conjure up a reason to have a meeting with Bobbi Levinsky, and there would be no chance of Alex appearing at an inopportune moment to spoil things.

Cee

'Where the hell is he?'

'Who knows?' Bobbi shrugged. 'I've left three more messages on his phone. It's obviously switched off.'

'He should be here,' Rowan hissed. 'The nurse said Alex keeps asking for him.'

'There's nothing more we can do, Rowan. The text message was definitely delivered, so he must know she's gone into labour.'

'Poor Alex.' Rowan was pacing the floor as he muttered. 'I wish I could get my hands on that smug, selfish bastard.'

'Shh. He's probably on his way as we speak.' Bobbi's nerves were beginning to fray and Rowan's demented pacing was making her even more jumpy.

'How long has it been?'

'About an hour and a half, I guess. Look, why don't you go home, Rowan? I'll stay for a while – this could take hours.'

'No way, I'm not leaving her here on her own. I'll kill that bastard if he ever shows up.'

'That's another good reason for you to go home, hon. Whatever about me – I can't see Chris Carroll being thrilled to see *you* sitting outside his partner's room while she's bringing his child into the world.' Bobbi smiled wryly. 'And I'm sure the hospital staff have enough to contend with without you throwing a hissy fit.'

'Mr Carroll?' The nurse's crisp voice startled them.

'Er, no,' said Bobbi. 'We're friends of Alex. We came in with her.'

'She's ready to see you now.' The nurse beamed. 'You can follow me.'

'Already?' Bobbi looked surprised.

'It was a very quick and easy delivery. It happens that way sometimes with a second baby.'

'Oh, I almost forgot – the baby?'

'Mother and baby are doing just fine.' The nurse smiled at the anxious faces as she pointed to Alex's private room. 'Not long now, mind, she's very tired, but she's just dying to show off her new son to the world.'

Ce

'It's a boy!' said Bobbi triumphantly, as she arrived back at the Hall, worn out by the unexpected excitement.

'Did everything go all right?' Niamh was concerned. Since she had moved into the Hall, she had got to know Alex better and had to admit she was a genuinely nice girl – albeit one with desperate taste in men, as she had pointed out to Rowan with relish.

'Yes, mother and baby are positively blooming. Alex is just thrilled skinny, and the baby is the cutest little thing I've ever seen.'

'Can't take after his father then,' Niamh couldn't resist adding. 'God, Chris will really be insufferable now. I don't envy that child having a father like him. I suppose he was all puffed up like a peacock?'

There was a pause. 'Actually, I couldn't say. He hadn't shown up by the time I left.'

'What?'

'I left several messages on his phone and called his office number – but he still hadn't arrived at the hospital. No word either.'

'Oh he'll show up all right,' Niamh raised her eyes to heaven, 'if only to take all the credit. What about Rowan?'

Bobbi grinned. 'Anyone would think he was the proud father! It was all I could do to prise the baby away from him.'

'I was sure it was going to be a girl. I don't know why, I just was,' Niamh mused.

'I told her it would be a boy,' Nellie said, sitting at the kitchen table finishing the remains of the delicious chicken casserole Niamh had cooked for everyone. 'I told her that the last time she came to see me, with you, Bobbi. And I never say unless I'm absolutely sure.'

'Well, looks like you hit the nail on the head again, Nellie. Anyway guys, I'm going upstairs to shower and change, and then I'll be going back to the hospital. There are a couple of things Alex wanted me to pick up for her. What with Master Carroll's sudden insistence to make his presence felt, it was all we could do to get Alex to the hospital, never mind her suitcase.'

Cee

It was ten o'clock when Chris strolled into the hospital and announced his arrival at the nurses' station and asked to be directed to Alex's room. He had thought about picking up a bottle of champagne and some flowers but reckoned there was time enough for all that sort of thing tomorrow, when he could get his secretary on the case. Anyway, he'd had quite enough to drink with Meredith as it was. With a bit of luck, the whole thing would be over soon. When Cindy was being born, Alex had been in labour for twelve hours. A pretty young nurse approached him as he rounded the corner.

'I'm looking for Alex O'Gallagher's room?'

'That's it, just on the right there.' The nurse smiled broadly. 'They're such a lovely couple and delirious about their little boy.'

'What did you say?' Chris wheeled around.

'It is Alex O'Gallagher you're looking for?' The nurse sounded perplexed.

'Yes, Alex O'Gallagher,' Chris repeated slowly.

'Well, like I said, she and her little boy are in that room there.'

Chris opened the door soundlessly and took in the scene that wouldn't have looked out of place on the front cover of *Hello!* magazine. Alex, looking utterly radiant, was beaming up at Rowan, who was walking around the small room rocking the baby in his arms. Neither one heard Chris come in until the nurse, who had become concerned, popped her head around the door. 'Everything all right?' she asked.

'Everything will be perfectly all right,' said Chris thinly, 'if somebody would kindly take the trouble to introduce me to my son!' Chris glared at Rowan who looked up in surprise. 'And just what the hell do *you* think you're doing here?'

Cee

'Well,' said Niamh to Nellie as they sat in the kitchen chatting, 'it's all go at the moment, that's for sure.'

'It is that,' agreed Nellie, who was rapidly regaining her strength and enjoying every minute of her new luxurious surroundings. 'I'd like to be able to say things will settle down, but I'm afraid this is only the beginning, Niamh.'

The telephone ringing interrupted any further prompting from Niamh, and she went to answer it. 'Hold on, one minute please, I'll get her for you now,' she said, then pushing the appropriate button to transfer the call to Bobbi's room, she hung up.

'Hey, Masie,' Bobbi picked up the call. 'How the heck are you?' Bobbi was delighted to hear from her aunt in North Carolina who was the only relative she kept in touch with. Her father had died some years previously, and her mother, who was probably on her fifth marriage by now, was only ever interested in her if she needed a quick cash injection. Since the death of her younger brother, neither parent had bothered to maintain any sort of relationship with Bobbi. Her aunt, however, had stepped into their absentee roles and loved Bobbi as if she was her own child. Bobbi chatted to her for a few minutes and, yawning, told her how she had nearly got to deliver her first baby. Telling her aunt about the baby boy suddenly jogged something in Bobbi's mind. 'Masie?'

'Uh, huh?'

'This might sound like a weird question, but humour me, okay?'

'Sure, honey. Shoot!'

'Did I ever have any other brother or cousin or something,

besides Danny? You know, was there a younger boy in the family? It's just something this psychic woman said to me a few weeks ago, and it's been bothering me.'

There was a pause on the other end of the phone.

'Masie?'

'I'm here,' she hesitated. 'I told them they should have told you. But it's all so long ago and, in those days, well, no one thought that kind of stuff was important.'

'Go on, what stuff?

'You had a twin brother, Bobbi. He only survived a few days, honey. You were always the stronger one.'

Bobbi felt the breath sucked out of her. She struggled to find her voice. 'Wh–what was his name?' She couldn't quite take this in.

'They called him Danny.'

'Oh, God,' Bobbi gasped. 'So they lost two sons, both times because of me.'

'Bobbi, don't be ridiculous, honey. The first Danny was never going to survive. He was a weak baby, and they didn't have the technology back then. They … they named the second boy after him, and then when the tragedy happened, well, your father never really got over it. He took to the bottle and it was downhill from there, I guess. Bobbi, I really wish I wasn't talking about this on the phone to you. It's upsetting and I understand how you must be feeling, but –'

'He blamed me, Masie. They both blamed me.' Bobbi sounded pathetically vulnerable to her aunt across the miles.

'It was a tragedy, Bobbi, but it was nobody's fault. You can't go on blaming yourself for that accident on the beach. There was nothing you or anyone could have done. The tragedy is what it did to *you*, honey, after he –'

'Don't, I can't think about that.'

'What it must have done to you, watching him shoot that horse and then your own beautiful Moonflower. I never saw a better partnership between horse and rider. You would have won everything, everything.'

'Don't Masie, please.' Bobbi's voice caught as the horrific memories came crowding back.

'I'm only saying it, honey, because you have a gift with horses. You know it, and so does anyone who knows the slightest thing about the animals. It's an even bigger tragedy if you let what happened get in the way of that.' Masie paused. 'Come over soon, Bobbi, and we'll talk about this some more. I'm sorry if I've upset you, but you really need to deal with this. You can't go on burying yourself in work anymore. You're in the country of great bloodstock now. You should think about that – maybe it's happened for a reason.'

'I have to go now, Masie.'

'I love you, honey. Come see me soon.'

'I will, and I love you too.' Bobbi put the phone down with a trembling hand. She wouldn't think about it now, she couldn't think about it now. It was way too weird and way too painful.

She remembered she had promised to pick up Alex's suitcase and bring it with her when she returned to the hospital. But now the thought of going back to see the new baby boy suddenly proved too much to handle. She would phone a cab instead and have them deliver it and check to make sure that Rowan was still there. Tonight, Bobbi needed to spend some time alone.

After sending Alex's things to the hospital, she pulled on her oldest sweatpants and shirt, went downstairs, avoiding the kitchen where Nellie and Niamh were still chatting, and slipped outside.

The balmy air enveloped her the minute she stepped out of the conservatory doors. The sky was clear and a million stars twinkled from its inky velvet. Slowly Bobbi walked the grounds, veering first towards the right, where the intricately landscaped gardens were beginning to take shape, hugging her arms around her, although the night was warm. She had felt chilled ever since the phone call. It was just too spooky. She couldn't take it in. And yet, somewhere in the depths of her, she felt she had known it all along. Known she had never been complete, that something, a part of her, had always been missing. Something – no matter how hard she tried – she could never make up for. She continued walking, stalked by the comforting shadows of immense trees that had, in their time, seen it all before.

Snatches of long-past conversations and exchanged knowing looks between relatives all suddenly made sense. The need to belong she had craved but never felt and, finally, the unrelenting, awful loneliness.

She had tried *so* hard, so very, very hard. And in a way her work, her business and her ultimate phenomenal success had filled the void – but never for long. Sooner or later, she would be on the run again, striving, always striving for something that remained just beyond her reach. Lost in thought, she kept walking until she found herself on the old path lined with beech trees leading to the stables. Stepping onto the old, cobbled stones that surrounded the stalls, she felt, if possible, that the night appeared to have taken on an even more profound stillness. Nothing stirred, even the leaves on the trees seemed immovably etched against the sky, and her footsteps sounded in eerily enhanced echoes beneath her. Suddenly there was a movement, and Bobbi tensed instinctively. Then, over the open half-door of the corner stall, a head appeared, and Old Chestnut looked out, thrusting his nose into the night. For a long moment, Bobbi and he looked at each other and neither moved. Old Chestnut's ears twitched enquiringly, and then he gave a low whinny in her direction. Despite herself, Bobbi headed for his stall and held out a trembling hand. The horse pushed his nose into the proffered hand and blew gently. Slowly, Bobbi drew back the bolt on the stable door and moved inside, flicking on the light on the wall as she did. The horse moved back slowly and then stood still, regarding her from ineffably beautiful, trusting brown eyes. Steve had operated on him the previous day, and his infected leg had been lanced and dressed. Slowly, Bobbi ran her hand along the leg and noted that the swelling had all but disappeared. His coat, too, seemed smoother to the touch, and his eyes were definitely brighter.

They stood there in the stall for what seemed like a long time, neither one moving. Both wounded, wary and broken in different ways, regarding each other in the still of the night. Old Chestnut made the first move. Taking a tentative step forward on his bad leg, he moved towards Bobbi and blew gently into her shoulder, his ears moving enquiringly, and dipped his head into the crook of her arm. Just like her beloved Moonflower had done a thousand times before, in that other, long ago, forgotten lifetime. It was that simple, unconditional gesture that unlocked the floodgates. They came then, the memories, unrelenting, uncompromising, like the rerun of a bad movie. The smell of the salt spray, as she and Danny galloped along the water's edge. The panic and then horror as she realised Danny had lain unmoving on the sand. The frantic, pounding gallop that still sounded in her head as she had desperately urged Moonflower faster and faster to get them both back to home and help. And then, finally, the unspeakable, horrifying reality that it was all too late – that Danny was gone, forever.

But the nightmare had only just begun. She heard her father's roars of grief and rage tear through the night. Cowering in Moonflower's stable, Bobbi had tried to shut it out, to cover her ears, but it was no good. Clinging to her horse, she had buried her face in Moonflower's neck and desperately tried to block out the raucous sound of the gunshot that ripped through the early evening air as her father shot Danny's horse. She had stayed there, stock still, praying to a God she only vaguely knew to stop this – to somehow stay the horrifying events unfolding before her eyes. She had known then, even as she had prayed, that it was useless. She had heard the drunken, swaggering footsteps, the roaring and swearing and the plaintive, impotent cries of her mother and Aunt Masie – and then he had found them. The horse had sensed the danger, her nostrils flaring as she stiffened while Bobbi's arms clung to her neck. 'Get away from that friggin' creature,' he had roared, 'or so help me, I'll shoot you too.' In the years to follow, Bobbi often wished he had. He had wrenched her away from Moonflower, flung her against the wall and, swaying drunkenly, had aimed the pistol at the wild-eyed mare. The shot rang out into the night. The ghastly sound of the magnificent animal collapsing to her knees and falling to the ground where she groaned quietly had become the living nightmare that Bobbi had consciously shut out in a supreme effort to survive.

Now, twenty-two years later, the savage scene unfolded before her again. Bobbi sobbed and sobbed until her tears soaked Old Chestnut's mane and the strength drained from her body. Racked with inconsolable grief, she sank to her knees and lay curled against the stable wall, moaning softly as she relived the pain again and again. All the while, Old Chestnut stood over her, blowing warm air onto her tear-stained face, and nuzzled gently into her hair.

She wasn't sure how long she had lain there – it could have been minutes, hours, days – when the half-door opened and the Old Chestnut lifted his head.

'What the –' Steve could barely make out the figure curled against the wall. 'Jesus, Bobbi! What's happened? Are you all right?'

Bobbi nodded mutely, afraid to trust herself to speak, and got slowly to her feet.

'What the heck happened?' Steve was beside her in a flash. 'Was it the horse? Have you been kicked? Are you sick? Here, let me help you.'

'I'm fine, really.' She rubbed her face.

'You don't look fine to me,' Steve said gently, relieved that at least she didn't appear to have been hurt.

'I'm okay, really.' Bobbi tried to sound casual although she realised she must look like a total wreck. 'Or I will be. I'm, uh, sorry you had to find me like this.'

'I was coming by to check on Chestnut here and saw the light on in the stable. Look, are you going to tell me what all this is about?' He lifted her chin gently with his hand and took in the tear-stained face and red-rimmed eyes that began to brim again, letting two big tears roll down her cheeks.

'Hey.' Steve's arms went around her. 'It's okay, Bobbi. Whatever it is, it's okay.' He rocked her gently, murmuring to her and stroking her face as if he were soothing a frightened animal. Gradually, the tears stopped and were replaced by the occasional sniff.

'Here,' said Steve, pulling away to retrieve a handkerchief from his pocket. 'I knew it would come in useful one day.'

'Thanks.' Bobbi managed a tremulous smile.

'You look like you could do with a stiff drink, purely for medicinal purposes, of course.' Steve was relieved to see the smile. 'I wouldn't mind one myself, come to think of it. You gave me quite a fright.'

'I could use a drink,' Bobbi agreed. 'But I don't want to go up to the house – the others might be up and I don't particularly want anyone else to see me in this state.'

'Come back with me to my place, I'm only around the corner. I'll fix you a stiff drink of your choice, and you can talk or just get plastered. I'll have you back before midnight.'

'God.' Bobbi blew her nose again. 'What time is it?'

'A quarter-past ten. Let me just have a look at Old Chestnut's leg here and we'll be off.'

'It's healing beautifully. I had a look earlier.'

'I thought you didn't like horses.'

'I never said that. I said I didn't like being *around* horses.'

'Same thing, isn't it?'

'Not exactly.'

'Are you afraid of them?

'No,' Bobbi sighed. 'It's a long story. I'll try to explain, but first I need that drink.'

After Bobbi and Steve had left, Old Chestnut stood quietly in his stall, swishing his tail occasionally, unperturbed by the ghostly figure that hovered by the wall, and remained with him through the night as he drifted into a contented sleep.

17

'What's your poison?'

'Bourbon, if you've got it.' Bobbi sat at the table and watched Steve as he moved about the rustic-styled wood and stone kitchen.

'As it so happens, I have. Courtesy of my ex-wife. C'mon, let's sit outside. It's not often we get such a good summer.'

'You were married?' Bobbi was curious to find out more as she joined him outside at the old wooden table. Steve didn't usually give much away, particularly about his personal life, but Bobbi sensed there was a story there.

'For five years. It didn't work out. She's a surgeon, she lives in Connecticut these days.'

'Any kids?'

'Nope, just as well really.'

'I'm sorry.'

'Don't be, I'm not. At least, not now. It took a while, but I realise at this stage that we would never have made it.' Steve frowned. 'We were too much alike in many ways. Anyway, this isn't about me. What's going on with you? If I'm prying just tell me to mind my own business.' Steve's turquoise-blue eyes regarded her seriously. 'But you don't seem like the kind of woman who gets upset easily. Something must have really got to you.'

Slowly, as the bourbon burned a comforting trail down her throat, Bobbi told her story. Haltingly at first, and then more freely, as Steve listened intently, saying nothing, just nodding and prompting her from time to time when she paused. She told him of her love of horses. Her future as a member of the American Olympic show-jumping team. Her beloved Moonflower. The accident and the horrible, haunting after-math.

Steve shook his head in disbelief when she got to the part about her father shooting the horses. 'Jesus, Bobbi, I can't even imagine. That must have been so tough on you.'

'So you see,' Bobbi said as he topped up their drinks, 'it wasn't that I was afraid of horses. I just couldn't bear to be anywhere near one. It was too painful. It brought back memories I couldn't deal with.'

'And now?'

'I don't know.' Bobbi was pensive. 'Something happened tonight, something that I guess went some way to explaining my father's reaction.' She went on to tell him of the conversation with her aunt on the phone and the revelation that she had had a twin brother who had died in infancy. 'I just wanted to get out of the house, to walk, and I found myself down at the stables, and then, well, I don't know. Old Chestnut looked about as lonely as I felt.' Bobbi smiled. 'I went in to check on him, and then, well it all kind of came out, the floodgates opened I guess. It was kinda weird.' She looked sheepish.

'Not weird at all.' Steve sounded concerned. 'That's a hell of a lot to deal with.'

'Then you arrived.'

'Do you think you might be able to come to terms with horses again? I mean, it's such a waste, particularly if you have a talent with them.'

'I don't know. I'll never compete again, if that's what you mean. But maybe, if I take things slowly. Who knows?'

'Would you ever think of breeding?'

'What? Here?'

'The Grovesburys bred some of the finest horses in the country. Lady Arabella played a big part in promoting the combination of the famous Irish draught horse with thoroughbreds. We call it the sport horse. Most of today's show jumpers are that particular breed. You've got the stables and the grounds. It's a tough but lucrative business if you know what you're about.'

'And I don't.'

'Bet it wouldn't take you long.' Steve grinned. 'It would be a change from cosmetics, I grant you, but tremendously rewarding. I could put you in touch with the right people.'

'I don't know. It's not something I ever even thought about, never mind seriously considered.'

'It's just a suggestion. Think about it.'

'Oh, I almost forgot,' Bobbi changed the subject quickly. 'Alex had a baby boy this evening. Rowan and I just got her to the hospital in the nick of time.'

'Rowan's playing with fire there.'

'But he really loves her, and I think the feeling's mutual.'

'Chris Carroll isn't the sort of person you want to mess with. That goes for both Rowan and Alex.'

'He's a bully, that's all. I've come across plenty of them in my time.'

'Well, if it's the real thing, Alex should leave him.'

'I think she will, given time. She just needs to believe in herself a bit more. Rowan's good for her in that respect.'

'He certainly seems smitten, I'll give you that much.'

'That was said with a certain amount of cynicism.'

'I'm not cynical, just wary – once bitten and all that.'

'That makes two of us.' Bobbi yawned widely. 'Sorry, it's been a helluva day.'

'Look, I can leave you back now, but why don't you stay here tonight? I've plenty of space and you look completely exhausted – beautiful – but exhausted.'

Bobbi blushed, taken aback by the unexpected compliment. 'I, well, thanks, Steve. I guess I'll take you up on that offer. If you're sure it's no trouble.'

'No trouble at all. You'll have your own room, and if you need anything, you can yell. I'll be just down the corridor.'

Steve got up to go inside and, before she could stop herself, Bobbi put a tentative hand on his arm. 'I'd much rather you weren't.'

Steve turned and faced her, looking searchingly into her eyes. Suddenly Bobbi found his nearness overwhelming. She took in the tall, lean body, the dark-blond hair and chiselled features and reached up to touch his face.

'Are you propositioning me, Bobbi Levinsky?' he murmured as a quizzical eyebrow was raised above his startlingly blue eyes.

'I guess it looks that way, doesn't it?'

'This wasn't what I had in mind, you know.'

'Me neither, but I'm willing to take a risk if you are.'

Maybe it was because she had been celibate for months, or maybe it was because her emotions were all over the place, or maybe it was just good, old-fashioned chemistry, but suddenly they were devouring each other as if their lives depended on it. Steve spoke first. 'Would you rather continue this conversation inside?'

'Fresh air's good for me,' Bobbi managed to gasp.

'I won't argue with that.'

And then his lips were on hers again, crushing them deliciously, his tongue insistently searching her eagerly responsive mouth, until they sank onto the sun-warmed ground where, shedding their inhibitions faster than their clothes, they raised the temperature of the already balmy night.

$\mathcal{C}_{\ell\ell}$

Bobbi wasn't the only one who had had a sleepless night. Back at the Hall, Nellie had slept fitfully for an hour or two before finally switching on the bedside lamp and getting up to make herself a cup of tea in the new-fangled tea maker Niamh had bought for her. She would have loved to have a cigarette with it, but didn't dare light one since the awful fire. Even though she knew the fire had been started deliberately, it had given her a bad fright, and she didn't want to risk setting the Hall on fire on top of everything else that was going on. She settled the cup of tea on the bedside table and climbed back into bed. Suddenly, the bedside light flickered, dimmed and went out, only to light up again instantly.

'I know you're there,' she said, shaking her head as she took a sip of the warming tea, propped up against four large pillows. 'There's no need to go moving things around and making a song and dance about it. You young people are always so impatient,' she sighed. She had sensed him, of course, the minute she had come into the Hall. His presence had been quite insistent. Polly had hinted at strange goings on and cautioned against the risks involved in renovating an old, historic house and 'disturbing' things.

Of course, they all assumed it was Lady Arabella. Nellie chuckled to herself at the thought. No, if it had been Lady Arabella, they'd have all known about it in no uncertain terms. There was one woman who had never believed in the softly, softly approach. No, it was her late son, so tragically killed on the hunting field at the age of ten, who had returned to his old family home. If Nellie concentrated very hard, she could just about make out his aura, standing over by the window. She frowned. It took so much energy now and she was so much weaker. She knew he was trying to tell her something, but she was tired and her senses weren't what they used to be. 'I know you're restless, pet, but I'm not much help to you now,' she murmured. 'I'm old, sonny, and I need to go back to sleep. Maybe I'll be of more use to you in the morning.'

Nellie drained her cup of tea and settled herself back on

her pillows. She wondered if she should tell Bobbi about him and decided against it. Leave well enough alone for the moment. She would ponder the matter tomorrow; now she needed to get some sleep. As if in obedient response, the bedside lamp obligingly switched itself off.

At six-thirty the following morning Bobbi tiptoed into the Hall and ran quickly upstairs to her suite of rooms. Flinging off her sweatpants and shirt, she headed into her walk-in wet room and turned the shower on full blast. The powerful sprays pummelled her weary body and blasted her still tingling skin. She had thought about going back to bed to catch a few hours sleep, but even though she was exhausted, she felt completely wide awake. She smiled broadly as she wrapped herself in a towel and began to dry herself vigorously, reliving the electric feeling of Steve's touch that still burned on her skin. Boy but that guy knew what to do with his hands.

They had eventually retired to Steve's bedroom and continued making love for the remainder of the night, until finally they had fallen asleep in an untidy tangle of limbs. Bobbi had woken at five-thirty and tried, unsuccessfully, to slip out of bed, only to be dragged back by Steve, who had no intention of letting her get away so easily.

She dressed quickly, pulling on a pair of jeans and a fresh shirt, and went quietly downstairs. Bruiser, who was sulking at having been abandoned for the night, followed closely as she went through the kitchen and on down to the stables.

Old Chestnut heard her approaching, and his head appeared over the door as he whinnied in greeting. Bobbi opened the door, and the horse moved back and nudged her shoulder. 'Hey, fella, how're you doin'?' Bobbi ran a hand down his leg and was pleased to see that there was no sign of swelling. His coat was looking better too, and though the cuts and welts would take time to heal, the fever appeared to have gone down. He was still painfully thin but nibbled eagerly on the carrot she had brought him. With the right nutrition and a lot of loving care, she felt sure he would improve. Steve had told her if the swelling had gone down it was important he got to walk on the leg as soon as possible.

Leaving the stall, Bobbi walked across to the old tack room, where the door gave after a good push, and she entered the dim, dusty interior, which, despite years of neglect, still smelled of wax, leather and horses. She rummaged around and found what she was looking for – a long disused lunging lead, which she shook free of cobwebs. She was about to pick up one of the many bridles hanging nearby on their various hooks, when the one over to the far right of the room caught her eye. Walking towards it, Bobbi remembered noticing it the first time she had been down here with Sean O'Rourke.

The bridle had caught her attention then – as it did now – because of its gleaming condition. Reaching up to take it from its place, she read again the brass identification plaque above it – 'Montyson'. Bobbi fingered it curiously. The leather was well worn but meticulously cared for and had been thoroughly polished, very recently. Inset to the foreband was a smaller brass plate, which also bore the name Montyson. Bobbi was perplexed. Obviously someone cared a great deal about this bridle, but as far as she knew, no one bar herself and the builders were ever around the stables. It was a puzzle for sure.

She shrugged, took the bridle and lunging lead and returned to Old Chestnut, who stood patiently while she fixed the bridle in place and attached the lunging lead. Then, coaxing him to follow her, she led him out into the early morning sunlight. Outside the stable, he paused for a moment, lifted his head and blew a bit and then slowly at first, and then with mounting confidence, he followed Bobbi as she led him to what used to have been an old paddock. There, she moved away, still holding the lead, while he stood at the edge.

When she had established the correct distance between them, she urged him to walk on. Immediately, his ears pricked up and he set off as he should, in a wide circle, going slightly short on his bad leg but gaining confidence all the time. Bobbi watched him carefully as he walked, never letting him break into a trot and noticed the leg and the stiffness loosening up with each stride. 'You've done this before, Old Chestnut,' she said to him as they worked together slowly and deliberately. Old Chestnut just swished his tail in response.

Chris sat in his study and pondered the situation. The development scheme was poised to begin any day now, once they got the planning through – and that was a done deal as far as he was concerned. The tenants were all out, and after that, it had been easy to persuade the landlords to exchange their cottages for apartments in what would be the exclusive new development. Of course, he had thrown in a generous cash incentive as well, just to be sure. Cheap at the price, he reminded himself. He needed this scheme to go ahead and go ahead fast. Property had stabilised in the last year or so, and the wildly climbing prices of property were a thing of the past, even in Dublin 4. He was mortgaged up to the hilt as it was, and this apartment scheme would get him nicely back on track, but he needed it to happen immediately.

Chris looked up irritably as there was a knock on the door. 'Yes,' he barked.

Maya, their Filipino nanny, tentatively popped her head around the door. 'Mr Carroll, Cindy has been put to bed. She would like for you to go up and say goodnight before she goes to sleep. She is missing her mummy.'

'Please don't disturb me unless it's absolutely urgent, Maya.' Chris glowered at the girl. 'Tell her to go asleep and I'll look in on her later.'

'Yes, Mr Carroll,' Maya said meekly, closing the door behind her quietly. As she went upstairs she could already hear Cindy crying. She felt sorry for the little girl who was too young to understand where her mummy was and that she would be coming back very soon. Maya sighed. There was so much luxury in this house but little or no love. She thought of her own three children back home with their grandparents. Every month Maya sent money back home religiously. They had so little compared to the children here – but at least they knew they were loved.

Chris flicked through Alex's address book and found the number for Grovesbury Hall. He would have rung the mobile number but wisely decided that would have appeared a bit presumptuous. He checked his watch and dialled the number – it was seven-thirty. With a bit of luck, Bobbi would be in and he'd take it from there.

'Grovesbury Hall.' Chris paused for a split second as he listened to the voice on the other end of the line. If he hadn't known better, he could have sworn it was that bitch Niamh ní Cheavin. Well, he had sent her well and truly scuttling back under whatever stone she had crawled out from.

'May I speak to Ms Levinsky?'

'One moment.' Niamh recoiled in mock horror as she recognised Chris's pompous voice immediately. 'Who shall I say is calling?'

'Chris Carroll.'

A moment later Bobbi picked up the line. 'Chris,' she said briskly. 'What can I do for you?'

'Bobbi, I'm glad I caught you,' Chris began. 'It's Alex, I … I well, I'm worried about her, Bobbi. She hasn't been herself lately. I know she's been spending a lot of time with you and I thought, well, I thought maybe you might be able to give me some insights.' Chris took a breath, 'I'm *very* worried, Bobbi. I wouldn't be calling you otherwise. I'd really appreciate it if you could meet with me and we could discuss this properly.'

There was a pause as Bobbi weighed up the situation. Chris did sound genuinely concerned; maybe he was finally waking up to the fact that he had something very much worth holding on to in Alex. 'I could meet you this evening, Chris. How about in half an hour?'

'I appreciate this, Bobbi, really I do. The Four Seasons? In the Old Bar?'

'I'll be there.'

Bobbi put the phone down thoughtfully. She didn't like the man, but Alex clearly still had feelings for him, no matter how misplaced Bobbi felt they were. She sighed. She had been supposed to meet Steve that night, but she would put him off until later. Whatever Chris had to say couldn't possibly take long.

When Bobbi arrived at the Four Seasons she made her way straight to the Old Bar, which was unusually empty, presumably because of the still fabulous weather Dublin was enjoying. Chris was there ahead of her, already seated at a table for two by the panelled wall. He stood up to greet her as she approached. 'Bobbi, thank you so much for coming down at such short notice. Will you join me in a glass of champagne?'

Bobbi was just about to decline when he added quickly, 'It's not every day a man gets to celebrate the arrival of his first son!'

'Well, yes, of course, Chris. Congratulations!' Bobbi sat down, took a sip of her drink and got straight to the point. 'You said you were worried about Alex?'

Chris took a deep breath, 'Yes, very worried frankly, Bobbi. I realise the past few months haven't been easy for her, with the baby on the way and everything, and I've been under phenomenal pressure with work, but she's become very withdrawn. Her behaviour has become well, underhand I suppose would be the best way to describe it. She goes out all the time, mostly on her own, and then, to cap it all, when I go into the hospital to meet my new son – that painter chappie's in the room. Holding the baby, if you don't mind!' Chris waited for that little snippet of information to sink in.

So that was what this was all about, thought Bobbi. You're not in the slightest bit worried about Alex, you're just trying to pump me for information.

'Actually, Chris, Alex was with me when she went into labour. I'm sure she's already told you the story. Rowan and I got her to the hospital just in time. I understand you were somewhat detained?'

'Yes, I was unavoidably held up at a meeting. That's why my phone was switched off. Of course, I got to the hospital the moment I could.'

Liar, thought Bobbi, although she smiled serenely. She wasn't going to give this fucker an ounce of information unless it was something that made him sit up and think for a moment. Clearly he'd been drinking, his face was flushed and he was beginning to have to articulate very carefully. Suddenly, he leaned in towards her and put his hand on hers.

'How about we continue this conversation over dinner, Bobbi? I haven't eaten. I'm sure you haven't either. I've reserved my usual table in the dining room. What do you say?' Chris's eyes glittered hopefully.

Bobbi withdrew her hand abruptly. 'Sorry, Chris, I have a date.'

'So cancel it. We should get to know each other, Bobbi,' he leered. 'We'd make a great team. You know it as well as I do. It must get lonely in that big house all on your own.'

'Let's get this straight, Chris. Firstly, I'm frankly horrified that you would drag me down here under false pretences. Clearly, you're not remotely concerned about Alex, and if you're trying to pry, you'll get no information from me. As far as I'm concerned, she's way too good for you. Secondly, I'm not on my own in the Hall. I happen to have the company of several extremely entertaining house guests. You might know of them? Nellie Murphy, Rowan Delaney and Niamh ní Cheavin. They seem to have run into some sort of trouble with the leases on the cottages. And, thirdly, if you were the last man on earth, I wouldn't have dinner with you. Do I make myself clear? And now I really must leave. I'm late already.' Bobbi got up from her chair.

Chris leaned back watching her through narrowed eyes.

'Don't let me detain you,' he drawled. 'I hear lesbians can get very irate when they're kept waiting.'

Bobbi looked down at him scornfully, 'That's exactly the kind of cheap, boorish, unimaginative remark I'd expect from someone like you, Chris. But I'm afraid your tactics don't work with me. I've dealt with men like you all my life, and I've come out on top every time.' Then still smiling, she lowered her tone threateningly, 'Don't mess with me, Chris, you're way out of your league.' With that, she turned on her heel and left him sitting there, seething with anger.

18

'It's preposterous, that's what it is.' Carmela's nostrils flared with indignation.

'What is, Mama?' Padraig looked up from the dinner table, mildly surprised at his mother's unusually vehement tone. Marysol was out at one of her many functions, so it was just himself and his parents dining together.

His father sighed, bracing himself for another diatribe.

'She's taken them all in – *all* of them!'

'Of whom are you speaking, Mama?' Padraig repeated.

'That American woman.' Carmela could hardly contain herself. 'She's taken all of the tenants in to live with her.'

'Now, dear, we can't be sure of that.' Liam was already feeling uneasy.

'Of course we can be sure,' Carmela almost spat. 'I heard it myself when I rang to enquire about Nellie Murphy. Chris Carroll himself confirmed it to me when I rang to speak to him.'

'I'm sure it's only a temporary situation, dear. There's no need for you to upset yourself.' Liam hastily poured himself another glass of wine.

'How could I not be upset? How do you think this looks, Liam? It makes it look as if we put that old woman out on the street! She's an … an ungrateful old trout!'

'Really, dear, there's no need –'

'I fully understand how you must be feeling, Mama,' Padraig interjected smoothly. 'You have been so good to Nellie over the years, and all the trouble you were going to, to find her a comfortable retirement home.'

'Exactly.' Carmela was momentarily mollified. 'Thank you, Padraig. It's reassuring to see that at least *someone* in this family has a little sensitivity.'

'You mentioned *all* of them, Mama? There are others?'

Carmela snorted. 'I don't know what she thinks she's doing. She's got Nellie, that Niamh ní Cheavin woman and that awful artist fellow, what's his name?'

'Rowan Delaney?' Padraig prompted.

'That's the one. It won't go down well on the road. It certainly will not.'

'I really can't think why you're letting it upset you so much, dear. At least the cottages are vacant now – and Chris can proceed with the development. That's in all our interests.'

'I don't like it, Liam. It's just not proper. She has no right. Why she might as well be running a charitable institution.'

'I agree, Mama, it will lower the tone of the road considerably. Who knows who, or what, she'll take in next.' Padraig was intrigued at this latest information. Just wait till he told Marysol! That would give her something to think about. Rowan Delaney, up living with the billionairess!

Privately, Padraig was impressed with the American woman's lateral thinking. Whatever they might say about her, she certainly seemed to have a flair for public relations.

Ce

'It's true!' Tanya Sykes told a nonplussed Rod. 'I met Rowan in Donnybrook today and asked him how he was getting on with somewhere to live, and he told me. He, Niamh and Nellie are all staying with Bobbi.'

'I couldn't give a fig where he was living as long as it's not in my cottage,' Rod said. 'Anyway, it's all for the best seeing as how Chris Carroll has offered us one of the apartments in the new development in exchange for it. It'll be much more valuable in the long term and a good investment for our Nathan.'

'I was mortified,' Tanya continued. 'I thought Rowan was getting a dig at us, you know. But he was really friendly. Said everything was working out great.'

'Well, it's no wonder. They're probably having rave ups every night – drink, drugs and Ouija boards, I don't doubt. I must say, though, I'm surprised at Bobbi, I thought she had more class about her. Still, whatever turns you on and all that. We're well rid of him.'

Ce

'I don't believe it!' Melissa gawped at Pascal.

'It's true apparently,' Pascal chuckled. 'I met Steve Sorenson today in Sandymount, and he said he had just been about to ring me to let me know he wouldn't be renewing the lease on the cottage after all. Bobbi's quite happy for him to continue his Saturday clinic from the stables.'

'Are you sure you didn't pick it up wrong, Pascal?' Melissa wasn't convinced.

'Quite sure, pet. He was laughing about it himself. Rowan, Nellie and Niamh have *all* moved into the Hall. Of course it's only a temporary thing, but I must say I think it's admirable of Bobbi. Who'd have thought it? She's really become one of us now.'

'Well, it's easy for her, isn't it?' Melissa was put out. 'I mean she has all those empty rooms. She can afford as many staff as she wants. She won't even know they're there.'

'Ah now, pet, it's big of her all the same. You have to admit.'

'Humph! She fancies Rowan Delaney that's what it is. What better way to snare a man than to lure him under your own roof?'

'I don't think Rowan ever needed that much luring when it came to attractive women, pet.' Pascal looked at her fondly. 'Sure wasn't he always saying he wanted to do *your* portrait?'

Melissa smiled, momentarily appeased, 'That reminds me, I must ring Alex immediately to find out about that portrait Rowan was doing of her. Now that she's back home, it must be nearly finished. I didn't get a chance to talk to her about it when I visited her in hospital.'

Chris was beginning to feel the strain. He had been careful of late to be at his most attentive and charming around Alex now that she was home with little Christopher, and he was finding it a chore. Particularly when all he wanted to do was find out what the fuck was going on and what exactly Bobbi Levinsky thought she was playing at. Since that night a couple of weeks ago in the Four Seasons, he had to admit he was feeling rattled – and he didn't like it. Still, at least all was quiet on the home front. Alex was besotted with their new son, and he had to admit he was a terrific little fellow. As he sat in the television room, idly watching the nine o'clock news, Chris felt distinctly uneasy. He didn't like being threatened by anyone – never mind a bloody woman – but Bobbi Levinsky certainly wasn't just anybody. She had very definitely been warning him off. And taking that bloody bunch of losers into the Hall! What was that about? Chris didn't like it. He didn't like it at all. She had even made some snide remark about them having 'run into trouble with their leases'. For a moment Chris wondered could she possibly suspect anything, but then he dismissed the thought as ridiculous. What could she possibly know? Anyway, there was absolutely nothing any of them could do to stop him now. The planning permission had come through, and he wasn't going to waste a moment. The bulldozers were already lined up to start clearing out the site. After that, well, it would be full steam ahead.

He was just about to light a cigar when the baby monitor that linked the room to the nursery made an unusual noise. For a moment, he couldn't make it out and then recognised the tone – it was Alex's mobile phone. Immediately, Chris turned down the sound on the television and listened carefully as he heard Alex's voice answering.

Initially, he figured it was one of her girlfriends on the end of the line. Alex was talking animatedly about Christopher and how Cindy was thrilled with her new brother and seemed to be adjusting well. Then her voice lowered and became more hesitant.

'I … I don't think I can do this for much longer, Rowan, really I don't. I know I said I'd see it through and I will. I just need some time … I will finish it, I promise. You'll just have to be patient for a little while … Please?'

Chris sat still and alert as the conversation continued, anger beginning to burn inside him.

'Well, maybe I could do tomorrow … Yes I know how much it means to you … I want it as well. You know I wouldn't let you down.' Another pause. 'It means a lot to me too … All right, tomorrow then, tomorrow afternoon … I'll see you at the usual time … Okay, bye, me too.' And then there was silence.

Chris lit his cigar and sat back thoughtfully. So it was true. Alex did have something going on with that Rowan Delaney character. And, by all accounts, it had been going on while she had been carrying *his* son. The bloody little whore! And to think he had been feeling sorry for her – feeling guilty that he had maybe, just maybe, been a little hard on her of late. This put a wholly different perspective on the situation. Chris's face was grim. And that American bitch had known all along. No wonder she had sneered at him at their last meeting.

Chris felt his blood beginning to boil. And as for Alex, well, he would deal with her later. Right now, there was something more important to get to the bottom of. He checked his watch – nine-thirty and just beginning to get dark. He tried to remember what Carmela Walshe had told him on the phone – as far as he could recall she had said that Rowan Delaney was working out of the stables in Grovesbury Hall. Well, he would find out soon enough. There shouldn't be anyone about at this time of night, though, in the mood he was in, he didn't care if there was. He was going to find out exactly what that little fucker Rowan Delaney was up to. And when he did, he would make very sure that he'd regret the day he was bloody born. No one messed with Chris Carroll. No one. He stubbed his cigar out forcefully and strode out of the house, slamming the door behind him.

In less than five minutes, he arrived at the Hall. The gates were open, and from inside the house, light filtered out from behind the drawn blinds and curtains of several upstairs windows. Outside stood Bobbi's Range Rover along with a few other nondescript cars he presumed belonged to staff, or one or two of her house guests. Chris trod quietly on the gravel – he knew the layout of the property well, having gone over it several times prior to the sale – and, keeping close to the wall, made his way around the side of the house until he found the path that led to the stables. He moved stealthily watched only by the enormous chestnut trees in whose shadows he was concealed. Reaching the cobbled courtyard that was dimly lit, he paused to get his bearings. Just as he had thought, the place appeared to be deserted. Slowly, he made his way around the stables, checking each one to no avail. Suddenly, he heard a movement and stiffened as he leaned back against the wall. It came from the next stall, he was sure of it. He sucked in his breath sharply as something emerged over the half-door and then almost laughed in relief as he realised it was a horse. He continued on, passing the old tack room, and still finding nothing was about to give up when he came upon what he was looking for. Just beyond the stables, around the back of the courtyard was what looked like a deserted studio.

The little one-roomed building was built of brick, with the entire front section of the roof in glass. Swiftly, Chris made his way to the door and found it unlocked. He quickly found the light switch and, knowing he was well hidden from the main house, switched it on. As his eyes became accustomed to the light, he looked around the small room. Stacks of canvases rested untidily against one wall, and against the other a chaise longue draped in scarlet silk taffeta provided a splash of unexpected colour. In the centre of the room stood a large easel supporting a huge ten by twelve foot canvas, covered by a swathe of oil-streaked rags. Glancing over to a row of shelves, several empty bottles of Moët & Chandon and two glass flutes caught his eye. Clearly this was where Delaney practised his so-called art.

Chris rummaged through a few of the canvases leaning against the wall but found nothing of interest. They appeared to be either background scenes or something entirely beyond his visual comprehension. He was about to leave when something drew him towards the covered canvas on the easel. Out of curiosity, he pulled off the layers of material and then, confounded, stepped back unsteadily, trying to take in the sight swimming before his eyes.

It was Alex all right, there could be no doubting it. But an Alex he could never have imagined in his wildest dreams. The images that stared back at him were so staggeringly erotic they defied belief or description. In the main portion of the canvas, Alex reclined completely nude on the chaise longue, the scarlet material lending a superb vividness to her creamy pallor. One hand was thrown behind her head, her lips were parted and her dark golden hair cascaded around her beautifully sculpted shoulders and voluptuously swollen breasts. Her other hand rested on her heavily pregnant stomach, beyond which her long, slender legs stretched lazily. Surrounding this main image, were a series of facial studies of other Alexs: her head thrown back laughing; another looking ineffably sad; another looking wanton and another pensive, and so on. All blending one into the other and yet unutterably individual. It was as if one were looking at a kaleidoscope of the most extraordinarily beautiful woman, portrayed in a myriad of inescapably intimate images.

For a moment, Chris was too stunned to take it in. He shook his head in disbelief. So this was how Alex, *his* partner, the mother of *his* children, was spending her time. Cavorting shamelessly with that debauched, junkie of a piss artist. *This* was how she repaid him! He, who had stood by her when she had deliberately got herself pregnant, who had allowed her move into *his* home and assume the role of *his* partner. No wonder that bitch Bobbi had been laughing at him. It had been taking place under her very own roof! Chris seethed with rage. All that simpering, innocent façade Alex had tricked him with, and behind it she was nothing but a cheap little whore! And he had fallen for it. Chris brushed a damp piece of hair back off his head. Well, he would deal with the pair of them later. Right now, he was going to make sure that piece of pornographic filth never, *ever* saw the light of day. He looked round wildly for something to destroy it with and saw, in the corner of the room, some pots of whitewash and a bottle of white spirit. He ripped the lid off the pot and was poised to hurl it over the offensive piece of art when an icy voice stopped him in his tracks.

'Just what the hell do you think you're doing?'

Chris wheeled round to see Rowan Delaney standing in the doorway, his face white with anger.

'What am *I* doing? That's rich, you little fuck! What may I ask do you think *you're* doing painting this, this filth of my, my —'

'Your what, Chris?' Rowan's eyes glittered. 'Alex doesn't belong to you, she's not even your wife, and you certainly haven't made her feel wanted. It's a bit late to be playing the role of the possessive lover. If you must know, Alex was having her portrait painted to give to you as a gift, which is at this moment up in the main house. This', Rowan indicated the exotic painting, 'is totally my own doing. Alex knows nothing about it. It's *my* vision of her. The real Alex. The real, live, flesh and blood woman that you've all but managed to destroy.'

Chris snorted. 'Do you really expect me to believe that, you miserable piece of piss? You must be even more out of your head than I thought! I'll remind you that Alex is the mother of *my* children –'

'Yes, just as you're the father of *hers* – and a particularly inadequate one as far as I can see. One that couldn't even be bothered to turn up at the birth of his own child.'

'You –' Chris threw the pot of paint aside, splattering its contents onto the floor and walls and lunged at Rowan, catching him squarely on the chin. Rowan staggered backwards and then hurled himself at Chris, head-butting him straight in the mouth, where, despite the excruciating pain he inflicted on himself, he heard the satisfying crunch of several teeth, which Chris spat out as he fell against the wall.

Livid with rage, Chris hauled himself up, quickly grabbing one of the empty champagne bottles and breaking it forcefully against the windowsill. Dizzy from the head-butt, Rowan frantically tried to gather his wits, as the two circled each other warily. Chris was heavy-set and, although not as quick on his feet as he used to be, was nonetheless a menacing opponent, and Rowan was feeling disoriented. Chris was closing in on him, brandishing the bottle menacingly, when he slipped on the freshly thrown paint. As he fell heavily against the wall, the bottle flew out of his hand and smashed through the window, shattering splinters of glass into the night.

Chris, muttering obscenities, was in the process of dragging himself up and about to lunge for Rowan again when they heard the sound of running feet.

'What the hell's going on here?' Bobbi stood incredulously as she took in the scene.

'Stay out of this you Yankee bitch. I'm going to kill him with my bare hands,' Chris yelled.

'That's enough, Chris!' Steve was behind him in an instant, pinning his arms back. 'I don't know what the hell's going on – but one more word to Bobbi and I'll finish you off myself.'

'Rowan?' Bobbi ignored Chris. 'I think somebody here owes me an explanation?'

'I found him down here snooping around.' Rowan looked at Chris with revulsion as he touched the beginnings of a spectacular black eye. 'Things got out of hand.'

'So I see,' said Bobbi, turning to fix Chris with an icy look. 'And you, Chris, are guilty of trespassing on private property. I suggest you leave before I call the guards.'

Chris shook himself as Steve released him and made unsteadily for the door. He turned and spat at Rowan, 'You haven't heard the last of this. I'll see to it that you're run out of town before I'm finished.'

'Are you okay, mate?' Steve shook his head as he looked around at the mess.

'I'll live.'

'What the heck happened?'

'I guess it might have something to do with this.' Bobbi had caught sight of the painting of Alex. 'Oh, my God, Rowan. It's … it's unbelievable. It's incredible. Get over here Steve and take a look.'

'Not surprisingly, Chris doesn't share your opinion,' commented Rowan. 'He wasn't meant to see it, obviously. I was doing it for Alex, she doesn't know anything about it.'

'Well she won't be long finding out,' said Steve wryly.

'Oh God, Alex,' Rowan muttered. 'I'll have to go to her. He's on the rampage, he'll bloody kill her.' He made for the door as Bobbi put a restraining hand on his arm.

'Wait, Rowan, I really think you should leave it. Alex is going to have to fight this one on her own. Chris would never hurt her, I'm pretty sure about that, and they're going to have to resolve things one way or the other. If you show up, it'll only make things worse for her.'

'Bobbi's right, Rowan. C'mon inside, let's have a drink and think this through.'

'If he lays a hand on her, I'll kill him!'

'I'll call her in a while to make sure she's okay,' said Bobbi. 'But you really have to leave them to work this out themselves. Alex needs to stand up to him, and this looks like it might be make or break time.'

Luckily for Chris, he made the five-minute journey back to his house without running into anybody. When he got to his front door, he fumbled for his keys, only to discover they must have dropped out of his pocket during the fight. Cursing, he rang the front doorbell insistently. When Maya opened the door, her hand flew to her mouth to stifle a scream. With his clothes liberally splattered in white paint, a cut and swollen mouth, Maya thought she was about to be accosted by an aggressive intruder. 'Mr Carroll!' she gasped. 'What has happened to you?'

Chris ignored the question and pushed past her into the hall, 'Where's Alex?' he barked.

'She is taking a bath, Mr Carroll.'

'Tell her I want to see her in my study in exactly twenty minutes, Maya. Do you understand?'

'Yes, Mr Carroll.' Maya looked worried as she scurried upstairs.

In his study, Chris strode over to the drinks cabinet and poured himself a large whiskey, then sitting down behind his desk, he took a gulp and touched his mouth tentatively as the liquid stung his lips before burning its welcome trail of warmth.

Fifteen minutes later, Alex knocked on the door as she always did before entering Chris's study.

'Come in, Alex,' Chris said, keeping his voice deliberately neutral.

'Oh my God!' Alex gasped at his appearance. 'Chris, what happened? Were you mugged?'

'Sit down.' Chris nodded towards the chair across from him.

'But, Chris,' she cried, 'we need to get the doctor. You've been hurt –'

'Shut up and listen.' Chris silenced her with a look as she sank into the chair. He rubbed his jaw which was beginning to turn an interesting shade of purple, while his eyes bored into her. 'How long have we been together now, Alex?'

'Chris, please –'

'Answer me!'

'N-nearly three years, Chris. Why? What's –'

'Ah yes, nearly three years. Three years since I invited you into my home. Three years during which I have given you unlimited access to what many would agree are the considerably finer things in life. I have always been generous to you – have I not?'

'Yes, of course, Chris.'

'You have a room full of designer clothes, several holidays a year, a more than generous bank account which I top up regularly – not to mention two children which, I might point out, I was not consulted about.' The cruel comment hung in the air.

'Chris, I've never been ungrateful –'

'And now, three years later, as you so accurately remind me, I find out just how you repay my generosity.'

'I don't understand.'

'You repay me by conducting an underhand, sordid little affair with a junkie piss artist. Captured most appositely by him on canvas in all its glorious Technicolor.'

'Chris, I don't know what you're talking about, really.'

'I haven't finished!' Chris leaned forward. 'That piece of filth you and he choose to call a portrait has finally been your undoing. And if you think for one second that I am going to sit back and be made a laughing stock of by you and your new American lesbian friend, your stupidity has reached giddier heights than even I would have thought possible.'

Alex was finding it hard to breathe. Clutching the arms of the chair, her knuckles were white and her whole body seemed to clench in horror.

'Chris, for God's sake, the portrait is beautiful. It … it was a present for you, a surprise. I can't understand why you're so angry about it.'

'Pornography was never my strong point, Alex. Possibly where you come from it's held in higher esteem.' Chris got up and began to stroll thoughtfully around the room. 'I want you to listen carefully to what I'm going to say, Alex, because I won't be repeating myself. Do you understand?'

'Chris, please!'

'There was a very good reason that I didn't want to rush into having children with you, Alex. I have long held the opinion that you would not be a good mother, and this latest example of your flagrantly out-of-control behaviour has proved the point without a doubt. That portrait as you call it, will provide ample proof to any court that you are an unfit mother. And I will not have my children suffering such a debilitating handicap.'

Alex gasped, the very breath sucked straight out of her body.

'I overheard your conversation with Rowan Delaney earlier this evening in the nursery and I went around to Grovesbury Hall to find out for myself just what was going on.'

'Chris, you've got it all wrong, I swear. If you'd just listen to me I can explain –'

'That was when I came across the painting, and Rowan came across me. The irony that I received these injuries attempting to defend your non-existent honour is not lost on me, I can assure you.'

If possible, Alex went even whiter. The mention of Rowan's name and the realisation that he and Chris had clearly been fighting was dawning on her through the mist of mis-understanding that held her prisoner. But what could Rowan have said? What had he implied? Alex's head began to spin with horror.

'Chris, I swear, there's never been anyone but you.'

Chris continued to pace the floor, thoroughly enjoying the effect he was having, 'Clearly, we shall have to come to some arrangement. I think it's best if you find yourself an apartment, which I will naturally pay for – initially. The children, of course, will stay here with me. I'm going out now, frankly I can't bear to look at you after this incident. I'll be speaking to my solicitor in the morning. I believe these things can be drawn up reasonably quickly these days. In the meantime, I suggest you find yourself alternative accommodation – and a solicitor.' Grabbing his jacket, Chris walked out the door and out of the house, while Alex sat numbly, listening to the roar of the Porsche's engine and spraying gravel as Chris tore off down the road.

She wasn't sure for how long she sat there, trying to take it all in. Despite the hot bath she had taken, she felt chilled to the bone and began to shiver uncontrollably. After Chris's departure, the house was strangely still, and the silence screamed at her. Pulling her bath robe around her tightly, she got up and, as she had seen Chris do on many an occasion, poured herself a large gin, adding a splash of flat tonic from a previously opened bottle. Grasping the glass with both hands, she brought it trembling to her mouth. The very action of taking a drink seemed to buy her a moment of normality which she clutched at. Sitting back down in the chair, she forced herself to go over the extraordinary scene that had just unfolded and, piece by piece, decipher what had apparently transpired.

That Chris had overheard her talking to Rowan on the phone was evident. That he had then gone up to the Hall and somehow confronted him was also understandable. But what Alex for the life of her failed to understand was why Chris had been so livid about the painting. Alex had asked Rowan to keep it in the Hall until she was ready to give it to Chris, and the portrait had been exquisite. She couldn't understand his reaction – and to call it pornographic? He must have lost his reason. The portrait had been luminously beautiful, sensitive and, above all, demure. Alex just couldn't comprehend it. *But never mind all that,* a little voice reminded her. *What are you going to do now? You've been given your marching orders in no uncertain manner, the party's over, Alex.* She finished her drink and got up slowly, mustering what little sanity she felt she had left, to pack. She didn't need much, it was the children's stuff that would take up the most space. Alex thought carefully as she methodically put one item of clothing into the case after another, then Cindy's favourite teddy bear, little Christopher's babygros and, finally, she made up the carrycot.

'Where are we going, Mummy?' Cindy was delighted at being woken up and dressed quickly.

'Just out for a little while, darling. Shush, now be quiet.'

'Can we leave the baby behind, Mummy?'

Alex smiled, despite herself. 'Now that wouldn't be very kind of us, would it? What if he woke up and got frightened in the night?'

'Silly baby! Not brave like me, Mummy.'

'Well he's only little, darling, he'll get better. Now be a good girl and carry teddy for mummy.'

As Cindy clambered down the stairs clutching her teddy, Alex carried Christopher and, once downstairs, placed him in the carrycot where he began to cry.

'Miss Alex?' Maya appeared from the kitchen. 'It is late. What is happening? Where are you going?' she asked, concern written all over her anxious face.

Alex sighed, there was nothing for it but to be straight. 'I'm leaving, Maya, and I'm taking the children with me.'

'But Mr Chris … He will. What will I say?'

'Tell Mr Chris that I will speak to him when I have thought things through.' Alex took a deep breath. 'Maya, thank you for all your help these last few months.' Alex patted her arm.

Maya looked if she were about to burst into tears. 'You take care of yourself, Miss Alex.'

With Maya's help, Alex loaded up her Mercedes Jeep, and then after hugging the Filipino woman warmly, she got into the car and started the engine with a trembling hand.

The drive to Grovesbury Hall, Alex reflected ironically, would take all of about three minutes, but it was the first leg of a very long overdue journey.

19

The planning permission was through. The notice had been so artfully hidden in the fronds of ivy hanging over the walls of Grovesbury Gardens that few had noticed it. And to those who did, it was of little or no interest. The main troublemakers who might have objected, being the Grovesbury Road houses, had all been taken care of and were happy for the development to go ahead – although they dreaded the noise and upheaval that it would undoubtedly entail. Bulldozers were moving into position on the proposed site, and work was beginning to clear away the little paths and well-worn footways before actually knocking down the cottages.

With all that had been going on in his personal life, it was a welcome breakthrough for Chris, and he needed a little distraction. Since Alex had moved out two days ago, he hadn't heard from her. He was livid that she had taken the children with her and guessed she had probably run back to her parents' house. Anyway, he didn't care where she was as long as he gained custody of the children, and his solicitor was on the case. She wouldn't have a well-toned leg to stand on by the time he'd finished with her.

Today though, he was celebrating his development finally getting the go-ahead by sharing a very liquid lunch hour or two with a journalist pal from a well-known Sunday broadsheet.

Chris liked staying in touch with the word on the street: it meant he kept his finger on the pulse and knew what was going on. Always important from a business point of view. He, on the other hand, served as a useful mole who leaked, when necessary, the savoury or unsavoury details of the Grovesbury Road set to the press.

He sat now with his companion, over a table in the dining room of the Four Seasons, enjoying a vintage port and a cigar.

'Your famous neighbour, the Levinsky woman.' The journalist looked enquiringly at Chris. 'There's been some interesting talk about her lately.'

'Really? Like what, Gerry?'

'Apparently she's seeing some vet. The name Steve Sorenson mean anything to you?'

Chris forced himself to smile although his jaw clenched, this was news to him, 'Yes, as a matter of fact I do know him. He runs a practice in Sandymount, I believe. Charming fellow. They're an item you say?'

'From what I can gather. She sounds like quite a character. I'm interested in doing a double page spread on her next Sunday. She refuses to talk to the press though. I thought you might be able to, er, shed a little light on the subject.'

'I'd be happy to Gerry. Ask away.' Chris puffed thoughtfully on his cigar.

'There are rumours that she's taking in waifs and strays at Grovesbury Hall. Is it true?'

Chris snorted. 'The woman's as mad as a brush! Very odd altogether. I have no idea why someone as balanced as Steve Sorenson would want to get involved with her.'

'How so?'

'Well, between you and me,' Chris lowered his voice, 'I'd say she's a dyke.'

'Get away! What a waste! She's incredible looking.'

'I know, it's a shame. Although maybe she swings both ways. What with that crowd she's let in to the Hall, you wouldn't know what was going on.'

'What are you getting at? Who's in there?'

'Very unsavoury types altogether.' Chris warmed to his theme. 'That artist fellow, Rowan Delaney, some old spiritualist woman and a spinster who used to be a tenant of mine. The artist is behind it, of course.'

'Delaney? How do you mean?'

'Well the rest of them are mates of his. They're all from Grovesbury Gardens, and now that their leases have been terminated, they can't be bothered to find alternative accommodation – much easier to move in with a screwed up little rich girl who has to buy herself company. Delaney was caught with drugs on the premises, you know,' Chris added for extra mileage.

'Are you serious?'

'Absolutely. The guards were called and everything. Of course, you can't use that as the court case is still pending, but you get the drift?'

'I'm beginning to.'

'Think about it. Bobbi's money, Rowan's contacts and an oul' wan who calls herself a psychic. Well the mind boggles as to what's going on in that place. I'd say poor old Steve is just a convenient smoke screen.'

The journalist's eyes widened ever so slightly. 'You've got a point there. Crikey, I wish I lived on The Road. From what I hear, there's more women going through those houses than traffic at Dublin Airport!'

Chris smiled knowingly. 'Don't believe everything you hear, Gerry.'

'How well do you know her?'

'Oh, not that well. I've had her in the house a couple of times, you know, for the odd dinner party. But, well, really, her behaviour was so outrageous we had to stop including her.'

'What did she do?'

'Well, let's just say it wasn't safe to leave your belongings lying around.'

'I don't believe it! She's a klepto! Brilliant!'

'Of course, you can't mention that, it's such a sensitive issue. But women hold on to their handbags a lot more tightly when she's around.'

'And all that money she has.'

'It's not uncommon for rich women to steal – enough of them shoplift. It gives them a rush, apparently.'

'She sounds like quite a girl this Bobbi.'

'That's one way of putting it.' Chris smiled thinly. 'Of course, you'll have to be careful writing about her. She has enough money to drag you and your paper through every court in the country.'

'True, but she's so scrupulous about protecting her privacy that I doubt she'd retaliate. It would only draw more attention to her. She's noted the world over for avoiding any sort of press.'

'You have a point there,' said Chris. 'All the same, generalise it. I don't want any fingers pointing in my direction.'

'Have they ever yet?' Gerry smiled.

'No, not yet.'

'Exactly. Lunch was as entertaining as ever, Chris. I'll be in touch. My shout next time.'

꒰ꛃ꒱

The arrival of Alex and her children at the Hall had created quite a stir to say the least. Fortunately, Bobbi, Steve and Rowan had still been up, even though it was nearly midnight. They were going over the details of the fight with Chris, which Rowan was gleefully exaggerating in his favour with every drink.

When they heard the urgent ringing at the front door they all jumped. Bobbi immediately went to answer it. 'Alex! Are you okay, honey?' Bobbi was relieved, although not surprised, to see her. 'Come on in and let's get these little guys settled down and then you can tell me all about it.'

'I'm sorry to descend on you like this, Bobbi. But I really couldn't take any more. And the thought of having to listen to my parents telling me "we told you so" was just unbearable. Is it okay if we stay for a few days? Just till I get my head together.'

'I'm annoyed you'd even question that, Alex. You know there's always been a bed for you here. You can stay as long as you like.'

'Oh, Bobbi, it was awful,' Alex began to sob quietly once they were upstairs.

'I thought it might be.' Bobbi hugged her.

'I don't even know what happened. Chris was ranting on about how the painting was pornographic filth and that it would prove beyond a shadow of a doubt that I was an unfit mother. He said he was going to make sure he took Cindy and Christopher away from me.' Alex's face was stricken.

'Now you listen to me. Chris Carroll is nothing but a bully. There is nothing he can do to you unless you allow it. You and the children will be safe here. You've been through a lot, Alex, and you need some time to just let all this sink in and decide how you're going to deal with it. In the meantime, there's someone downstairs who has quite a bit of explaining to do to you.'

'Rowan?' Alex sniffed.

'Yes, Rowan. Let's just say your obvious charms inspired him more than any of us realised.'

'What do you mean?'

'Come on downstairs when you're ready. We'll be in the kitchen.'

Twenty minutes later, having put Cindy and Christopher down for the night, Alex made her way to the kitchen where

Rowan immediately got up. Without saying a word, he went over and put his arms around her.

'I think it's best if we leave you two alone to talk this over,' said Bobbi, as she and Steve left the room, closing the door softly behind them.

'Was it bad?' Rowan stroked her face. 'Are you okay?'

'I don't know.' Alex sat down and put her head in her hands. 'What on earth happened? I don't understand. Chris overheard me talking to you on the phone and came down here to confront you, I suppose. But, after that, I didn't have a clue what he was talking about.'

'It was supposed to be a surprise for you.'

'What was?'

'The painting.'

'What are you talking about? I've seen the painting – it's beautiful.'

'Not that one, there's another one I've been working on. I was going to give it to you when the time was right, but things have got a bit ahead of themselves.'

Alex looked even more bewildered. 'I still don't understand.'

'Come on.' Rowan took her by the hand. 'There's something I need to show you.'

He led Alex outside, and they walked slowly towards the stables and around to Rowan's makeshift studio. The light was still on, and the obvious disarray in the small room bore testimony to recent events. 'I was coming down to do some work when I heard a noise and realised someone was in the studio. It was Chris, having a good old rummage around. It was only a matter of time before he came across this.' Rowan indicated the large canvas that had been covered up again.

'What is it?'

'It's you,' Rowan said with a smile. 'Well, the you *I* see at any rate.' He pulled off the paint-spattered covers and stood back to watch Alex's reaction.

For a moment she was utterly speechless as the full force of the portrait hit her and she gasped as her hands flew to her mouth. Then she began to cry.

'Hey, hey, come here.' Rowan held her and stroked her hair tenderly. 'It wasn't meant to make you sad, baby.'

'Oh, Rowan,' Alex raised her eyes to his face, 'it's amazing.'

'You're amazing.' Rowan kissed her forehead, her eyes and then her nose. 'Chris, however, didn't share your opinion and, well, things sort of deteriorated from there.'

Alex smiled through her tears. 'No, I don't suppose he would. At least now I know why he was ranting and raving about it. Oh, but, Rowan, he said he's going to take the children from me and that this portrait will prove I'm an unfit mother.'

'Alex, look at me.' Rowan lifted her chin. 'Firstly, neither Chris nor anyone else has a right to access this painting. Secondly, if I thought it would bring you *anything* other than happiness I'd destroy it with my own hands. Even if I do happen to think it's my finest piece of art to date.'

'Do you mean that?'

'Absolutely. You can hack it to bits yourself right now if you want to.'

'No, I don't want to do that.'

'What would you like to do, right now?'

'I … I don't know.'

'Yes you do.' His hand travelled down to the small of her back as he pulled her close to him. 'And I certainly know what I want to do.'

'What's that?' Alex asked breathlessly, feeling him hard against her.

'Get to know you better. Every gorgeous little bit of you in fact.' Rowan nudged her gently back towards the chaise longue that was still draped in folds of scarlet silk taffeta. Pushing her shirt gently off her shoulder he began to nuzzle and bite her neck insistently, until she was moaning with pleasure. 'To quote one of my favourite chat up lines,' Rowan muttered, '"Lie down, I think I love you."' Pushing her down onto the chaise and kissing her hungrily, he was pleased to discover the only protest he met with was the enthusiastic creaking of long disused springs.

Cee

Although it was late, and he had an early start, Steve was unable to sleep. He tossed and turned, even tried reading for a bit. Dragging himself out of bed and down to the kitchen, he sat down to drink a cup of tea at the table. Rubbing bleary eyes, he looked at the clock and shook his head wearily when he saw it was already three-thirty in the morning.

After Alex had turned up at the Hall, he and Bobbi had come back to his place for a nightcap. He had wanted her to stay the night, as she usually did, but understandably, with all the goings on and the latest new arrivals at the Hall, she thought it best to go home. Thinking about her now, he frowned. Bobbi was one unique woman, and there was no doubt they got along famously, in every respect. She was undeniably strong. And yet, in many respects, surprisingly vulnerable. It was a very unusual and beguiling combination. Steve found himself becoming more and more captivated with her. *Oh get real,* his inner voice mocked, *you're in love with the girl. You have been since the first day you set eyes on her.* Steve smiled at the memory, but the truth was, it scared him to death. Bobbi was as close as he had ever come to meeting his ideal woman. Since they had been seeing each other over the past few weeks, he had never once thought of Claire.

Bobbi was everything he had ever hoped for in a woman and more. She was intelligent, funny, endearing, compassionate, challenging, vulnerable and unbelievably sexy. As good as it gets. There was just one huge and, as far as he was concerned, insurmountable problem. The money. They had never actually talked about it, but Steve knew and felt the subject was hanging heavily between them. He also knew it shouldn't matter to him, but it did. Bobbi Levinsky had the annual income of a small, independent state. While he, well, sure he was doing well, but you couldn't compete with that sort of wealth. He knew he shouldn't feel as if he had to, but something deep inside of him just couldn't reconcile the situation. He frowned, leafing idly through the pages of the latest edition of *The Turf*. Once had been enough. He had gone through all that crap with Claire. She had come from a very wealthy family by Irish standards, and he had never been allowed to forget it. That, quite apart from anything else, had thrown up problems enough. But no one was in Bobbi's league. Why the hell was he ending up falling for another wealthy woman? It was ridiculous. No good could possibly come from it. Experience had taught him that much, if nothing else.

Talk about a bloody conundrum. The powers that be were obviously having a huge celestial laugh at his expense. That he, Steve Sorenson, vet and professional gambler, should meet and fall in love with one of the richest women in the world was indeed a joke.

Grovesbury Hall basked in the late-afternoon sunshine of a glorious September, enlivened by the long-forgotten sound of children's laughter. Sitting outside on the patio, Nellie closed her eyes and breathed in the lingering scent of the Indian summer that, despite its heat, was drawing to an inevitable close.

From the stables, high-pitched shrieks of fun could be heard as little Cindy tried in vain to run away from Nathan Sykes who was chasing her, and anyone else he could find, with a garden hose. It hadn't taken Nathan long to work out where his hero Rowan had disappeared to. Artfully listening in to his parent's conversations, and the odd phone call or two, he had realised that Rowan was only down the road. After that, it had been easy. His new nanny was an extremely pretty and bored Spanish girl, and once they were out on their daily afternoon walk around the neighbourhood, Nathan had little trouble persuading her that he was allowed to come and play in Grovesbury Hall where his new friend Cindy was living. Since there were a horse, a dog, endless beautiful gardens and, in the shape of Rowan, a smoulderingly sexy artist to gaze at, his nanny didn't need much encouragement.

Alex, too, was delighted for Cindy to have a playmate, which allowed her more time to spend with little Christopher, and the stables provided an idyllic distraction for the children.

'Hey, hey, that's enough!' Alex cried, shielding herself from attack. 'Calm down you guys!'

'Looks like this is where the action is!' The clip clop of hooves announced Bobbi's arrival as she led Old Chestnut on a leading rein back to the stables after their work out. In the last couple of weeks, the horse had changed beyond all recognition. The welts and wounds on his flanks had healed beautifully and his strength and muscle tone were recovering daily thanks to Bobbi's dedicated workouts with him. Constant grooming and nourishment gave his coat a healthy sheen, and his eyes were bright and lively. He was certainly a very different animal from the woebegone creature who had turned up on Bobbi's doorstep.

'He's looking really good, Bobbi. You've worked wonders with him,' said Alex admiringly as Cindy and Nathan rushed over to beg for a ride.

'Only a little one, guys. Here, I'll give you a leg up Nathan, and Cindy can sit behind you and hold on,' said Bobbi. As she led the children around the courtyard for a short walk on Old Chestnut, Alex, watching from her seat under the shady tree, saw Rowan looking out from his studio waving at them and, to the right, Niamh coming down from the house with a tray of more drinks.

Smiling as she lazily brushed a stray hair off her face, she couldn't help thinking that staying at the Hall was really a lot like living in a particularly luxurious commune.

A week had gone by and Chris had heard nothing from Alex. Initially, it hadn't bothered him, in a way it had even been a relief. Now he was becoming irritated. He had expected histrionics, weeping, begging – but not this. He checked his watch. It was eleven o'clock, and he had a few minutes between meetings. He lifted the phone on his desk and instructed his secretary to call Alex's parents' home. It was exasperating, but it had to be done.

'Mrs O'Gallagher?' Chris had never gotten around to calling Alex's mother by her first name. 'It's Chris.' He paused, waiting for a suitably apprehensive reply.

'Chris?' Alex's mother sounded concerned. 'Is everything all right? Why are you calling?'

'I would have thought that was obvious.' Chris wasn't going to waste time with niceties. 'Put me on to Alex, please. I need to discuss a few things with her.'

There was a pause. 'I'm afraid I don't understand, Chris. Alex isn't here. We haven't seen her since she called to visit us last Sunday with the children.'

'I see.' Chris's mind worked quickly, but there was no backtracking now.

'Chris, you're worrying me. What's happened? Are Alex and the children all right? Nothing's happened has it?' Panic was beginning to rise in Mrs O'Gallagher's voice.

'No, no, everyone's fine,' Chris said briskly. 'Alex and I are having a few problems, that's all. She left the house a week ago – I presumed she was with you.'

'So you don't know where she or the children are?' Mrs O'Gallagher said with a coldness that astounded him. 'I wouldn't say things are all right at all, Chris. You must have upset Alex a great deal for her to leave with the children.'

'Now just a minute Mrs –'

'No, just you listen to me for a minute young man. If anything has happened to my daughter or my grandchildren I will hold you fully responsible. Do you understand me? Now I want you to find Alex and tell her to contact me the minute you hear from her. Otherwise I'll be on to the police.' And the phone went dead.

Chris couldn't believe his ears. How dare she? The silly ignorant old bat! How dare she have the gall to suggest that *he* might be responsible for this! Livid with fury he dialled his home number, which was picked up after three rings by a subdued Maya.

'The Carroll residence?'

'Maya, it's me,' Chris barked into the phone. 'If Alex calls to the house or phones you, I want you to let me know immediately. Do you understand? Immediately.'

'But Mr Chris —'

'No buts, Maya. She's bound to need to collect more things for herself and the children, and when she does —'

Maya interjected quickly, 'But, Mr Chris. Miss Alex is staying at Grovesbury Hall with the children. I thought you knew.'

Chris clenched the phone more tightly. 'What did you say?'

'Miss Alex and the children are at Grovesbury Hall.'

'How do you know? Are you sure?'

'Of course, Mr Chris. I was speaking to Polly, Miss Levinsky's housekeeper, just the other day. She was saying how nice it was to have children around the place and —'

Chris cut her off brusquely. 'Thank you, Maya, that's all I need to know.'

Maya put the phone down weakly. She hoped against hope she hadn't made more trouble for Miss Alex. The house was so quiet without her and the children, and she missed them dreadfully. She shook her head sadly and went back to her housework.

In his office, Chris sat seething. So she had run to Grovesbury Hall to make a laughing stock of him with her lover and that American bitch. Well, that wasn't very smart of her — not very smart at all. But what else would he expect from Alex? Intellect had never been her strong point. She didn't know it, but she was playing straight into his hands. Once that piece the journalist was doing on Bobbi and that bunch of weirdos living in the Hall was published on Sunday for the whole of the country to read and ponder on, Alex would be bleating a very different tune.

Cee

It was Niamh who spotted it first. She had gone to half-past ten mass in Donnybrook Church as she did every Sunday and then had driven up to Donnybrook Fair to pick up the papers and a jar of horseradish sauce to accompany the roast beef she was cooking for Sunday lunch. When she got back to Grovesbury Hall, she made a cup of tea and settled herself down on the sofa in the kitchen to have a good read of the papers while all was quiet. You couldn't miss the double-page spread dominated by a huge shot of Grovesbury Hall with an only slightly smaller one of Bobbi, taken at the height of her fame when she had just sold her cosmetics company. The headline read: 'BOBBI LEVINSKY: WORTH MILLIONS – BUT MONEY CAN'T BUY HER LOVE'. And then, along the side of page, was a smaller shot of Rowan looking respectively mad, bad and extremely sexy.

Niamh gasped in astonishment. She began to read avidly, disbelief written all over her face as she scanned the article, which left little to the imagination. Basically, Bobbi was portrayed as a poor little rich girl whose millions could not buy her the love that, apparently, she craved desperately. Instead, the article implied, she had to pay people to live with her. Niamh's mouth fell open as she read about herself, 'middle-aged civil servant and cat lover', and Nellie, who was described as an elderly 'spiritualist', and, of course, Rowan, who needed no introduction as an extremely 'unorthodox' artist and wild child. The words 'drugs' and 'orgies' were not exactly mentioned but heavily hinted at. Alex's name, mercifully, had somehow escaped. Obviously the paper had gone to press before that snippet of information could have been included, and Niamh was relieved for her. Although if

Chris knew she was here, once he got his hands on that article there was going to be trouble.

'Hey. Any coffee going?' Rowan wandered into the kitchen looking dishevelled.

'You'll need more than coffee when you've had a read of this!' Niamh handed him the article.

Rowan sank down beside her on the sofa and began to read. 'Jaysus! How could anyone dredge up such codswallop?' Rowan jabbed a finger at an offending paragraph. 'Look, it says here –'

'I know, I've read it all.' Niamh shook her head. 'It's unbelievable!'

'Bobbi's gonna go ape when she sees it!'

'Sees what, exactly?'

Niamh and Rowan looked up from the paper like a pair of guilty children as Bobbi came into the kitchen.

'This,' said Niamh weakly, handing her the paper.

Bobbi set it down on the counter top and began to read. When she had finished, she looked up grimly. 'Normally, I don't let this kind of shit get to me,' she said, flinging the paper aside, 'but this smacks of Chris Carroll. It might as well have his name printed on the article instead of the so-called journalist who wrote it.'

'What makes you think he's had a hand in it?' Rowan was curious.

'One or two of those thinly veiled "comments" from a "source" are remarkably similar to what he threw at me when I turned him down after he hit on me.'

'Chris made a pass at you?'

Bobbi grinned at Niamh's old-fashioned turn of phrase. 'He came on to me when Alex was in hospital, having their baby. I told him to get lost but he wasn't happy about it.'

'It shouldn't surprise me,' snorted Niamh. 'But that's vile, even by his standards.'

'He's taken things too far this time.' Bobbi's face was set.

'What are you going to do?'

'It's time I spoke to a few people.'

20

It was a Friday night in late October, and summer had eventually given way to a crisp, clear autumn. All around the country, people were putting on kettles or opening a few beers or a bottle of soothing red wine and settling down to a night of television. As it was half-past nine, that meant the vast majority would be switching over to the *Late Late Show*. Tonight the ratings were going to soar through the roof. Because tonight, Pat Kenny had, by some extraordinary turnabout, secured the first ever public television interview with Bobbi Levinsky. The talk had been of nothing else all week.

At Grovesbury Hall, Nellie, Niamh, Alex, Steve and Rowan were gathered in the kitchen in front of the vast flat screen television that hung on the wall. The children were in bed and out for the count after a busy day. Bruiser lay beside the Aga, head on his two crossed front paws, snoring contentedly.

'I hope she knows what she's doing,' Rowan said, taking a swig from his glass of wine.

'There was no dissuading her,' Steve said.

'Of course she knows what she's doing.' Niamh was indignant. 'Sure didn't *Time* magazine call her "the Superbabe with an even sexier brain"?' Niamh had been doing her research on Bobbi's fascinating life when she had learnt of the impending interview.

'That's not the point, Niamh. This is Dublin, it's an awfully small place and Bobbi needs her privacy. She's going out on a limb here to get at Chris Carroll, and it may be too high a price to pay. He won't take it lying down you know. Sorry, Alex, but you know what I mean.' Rowan didn't look contrite.

'It's okay, I'm not going to defend him,' Alex said quietly. 'As far as I'm concerned, Chris deserves everything he gets. But you're right – he won't take it lying down. If she says anything even mildly unflattering about him, he'll be on the war path.'

'Shh,' said Nellie, smoking her cigarette furiously. 'It's starting, look here's Pat. Isn't that a lovely suit he's wearing?'

After a few brief words of welcome to his audience, Pat cut to the chase. 'My first guest tonight, ladies and gentlemen, needs no introduction. As famous for her business acumen as she is for her beauty, she has recently become an Irish resident, and I'm delighted to have her on the show tonight for her *first ever* live interview. Would you please give a big welcome to Bobbi Levinsky!'

The studio audience clapped and whispered to each other excitedly. And, as Bobbi walked onto the set, an expectant hush immediately descended. Even Pat seemed unusually taken aback at the vision that strode gracefully up to him, shook his hand and, smiling, sat down, crossing legs that seemed to go on forever. Bobbi had chosen a red Calvin Klein dress to wear, which was deceptively simple and lent a glow to her beautiful olive complexion. She looked, quite simply, radiant. She chatted easily with Pat as he began the interview, asking her about her early life in America. Explaining that she was of Polish American descent, with a touch of Cherokee

Indian on her grandmother's side, Bobbi spoke about her traditional and rather strict upbringing and how she eventually left home to pursue her dream in New York of becoming a make-up artist.

'And the rest, as they say,' Pat said with a smile, 'is history.'

'Pretty much,' Bobbi continued. 'I didn't really want or need to sell Bobbi L Cosmetics, but in the end, I was outnumbered. I really didn't have a choice.'

'But you did extraordinarily well out of the sale, Bobbi.'

'Yes, that's true, but it left a big gap in my life that I'm still working out how to fill.'

'Is that why you came to Ireland? Have you any Irish roots? Most Americans have some vague Irish connection.'

'Nope, not me I'm afraid. Actually it was my lawyers who suggested the move – for tax reasons obviously. It wasn't so much a positive choice on my part as much as a why-the-heck-not kinda thing.'

'And how do you find living here in Dublin?'

'It's taken a little getting used to.' Bobbi grinned. 'But I think I'm finally settling in.'

'Your home, Grovesbury Hall, used to belong to the late Lord and Lady Grovesbury. I believe you've totally renovated the place?'

'Yes, Pat, I have. Sean O'Rourke handled the project for me, and he's done a spectacular job.'

'It's possibly the most magnificent house in Dublin, Bobbi. But isn't it awfully big for just one person?'

'It's a big house, for sure, Pat, but funnily enough, it doesn't feel as large as it is when you're inside. That was one of our concerns when we were doing the renovations. I was quite clear to Sean in my brief that I wanted a home and not a house. A lot of it's very cleverly designed open-planned space.

'According to a recent newspaper article about you,' Pat was getting down to the nitty gritty now, having already cleared with Bobbi what he could and couldn't mention in the interview, 'you are not living alone?'

'No, Pat, I'm not,' Bobbi smiled. 'I happen to have, let's see, one, two, three,' Bobbi counted on her fingers, 'no, four adults and two adorable children staying with me at the moment.'

'Are these permanent house guests?' Pat pretended astonishment.

'Who knows? But, for the moment, they're all welcome to stay as long as they like. All of them have run into difficulties with their home situations in one way or another. We've all become very dear friends and, as you so rightly mentioned, space is not a problem for me.'

'How do you feel about the way you were portrayed in that recent Sunday newspaper article?' Pat inclined his head enquiringly as Bobbi smiled broadly.

'When you acquire a certain amount of wealth, you automatically become an object of curiosity, Pat. People love to speculate on how you live your life, and if you value your privacy, as I do, what they can't find out about you, they make up. I've learnt over the years not to let that kind of cheap publicity get to me. Although I have to say I was surprised at the level of viciousness in the article. I mean, why? I can understand people being curious about me, but other people's lives are being affected by this. People who've been unfairly dealt with and had to leave their homes under duress – that's not easy for anyone. I find it despicable that some so-called journalist and his sources', Bobbi said dryly, 'would use that as fodder to construct some sort of prurient slant for a salacious article that was a thinly veiled and unwarranted personal attack.'

'Are you going to take the matter further?'

'No, Pat. I'm pretty sure I know who the "source" is, and I prefer to deal with these people in my own way.'

'You haven't been here long, Bobbi, but you've already experienced the not-so-friendly side of an Irish welcome. As a nation, some would say that we have occasionally been prone to begrudgery, particularly when one of our own does well. In your opinion, do you think our recent affluence will eradicate that – or do you suspect it's an indigenous part of our society?'

Bobbi paused thoughtfully before replying. 'I think any society – just like any person – has to be constantly vigilant about how money and wealth affects them. Rapacious property speculation can destroy the fabric of any society. Take Dublin 4 for instance, where I'm living. It's very beautiful, very exclusive, but it's in danger of being turned into a middle-class ghetto. A whole working community is being driven out, and as far as I can see, before long you're going to end up with a lot of Dublin kids speaking Filipino.' There was an appreciative titter from the audience to this reference to the ever-increasing number of Filipino nannies and staff being employed in the area. 'But what really annoys me', Bobbi continued, 'is underhand tactics being employed to pick on small people. It's just not acceptable.' This remark was greeted by a resounding round of applause.

'Well said, Bobbi!' Rowan hooted with laughter at the prospect of the publicity that Bobbi's remarks would be generating on their behalf. 'I do hope Chris Carroll is watching,' he said, as Pat finally wound up the interview to thundering applause from the audience.

'I'd say the chances of that are pretty good,' remarked Steve. 'There's been enough press coverage drawing attention to it for the last two weeks. I can't imagine he'd miss it.'

'She's certainly giving him a run for his money,' said Niamh admiringly. 'I bet he didn't expect this.'

'I doubt that he did,' said Steve. 'But what worries me is what he's going to do about it – and what Bobbi's let herself in for.'

'Something tells me we won't be long finding out,' said Nellie.

Ce

In the space of a few hours, Bobbi lost whatever hope she had had of living a remotely anonymous life in Dublin or, indeed, in Ireland. The papers were full of the interview, radio stations were discussing it hotly, and sacks of mail were arriving daily at the Hall. Unfortunately, the media had got hold of her residential phone number, and it was all Alex could do to keep up with the calls, which she was endlessly trying to field on Bobbi's behalf.

Everyone, it seemed, had an opinion on the matter – from politicians to hairdressers – and everyone constantly debated whether or not Bobbi was abusing her wealth and position by daring to comment on the social implications of living in Dublin 4, or anywhere else, seeing as she had only been in the country a wet weekend.

But the real story the media were after, of course, was what Bobbi had referred to as the difficulties her house guests were encountering with their home situations. There was clearly a story there, and it had every whiff of being a stonker. The fact that an international celebrity was getting involved in the local situation only made it all the more riveting.

Throughout the furore, Bobbi remained surprisingly calm, disinterested even, as Alex commented to Niamh one evening as they sat in the kitchen. 'If that was me, I'd be going berserk by now.'

'I know, me too,' said Niamh as she helped Cindy brush the hair of one of her dolls vigorously. 'I suppose she's used to it – being famous, you know.'

'All the same, I'm surprised,' said Alex thoughtfully. 'It's almost as if she's preoccupied with something else.'

'Like what?' Niamh paused, holding the brush in mid-air.

'Oh I don't know. I just hope she's not having second thoughts about moving here.'

'I think it would take more than a bit of media flurry to affect Bobbi *that* much. Anyway, wasn't she only saying the other night how glad she was she had made the move here? And you'd have to be deaf, blind and dumb not to notice she's head over heels with Steve,' Niamh pointed out glumly.

'Who could blame her? He's gorgeous and as nice a person as he is good looking. I just hope he feels the same way.'

'Why on earth wouldn't he?' Niamh sounded incredulous. 'Sure he's mad about her.'

'Absolutely no reason – but you never know with men. And I'd hate to see Bobbi getting hurt. She's been through a lot, more than she lets on.' Alex chewed her lip.

'Well, I'd like to meet the eejit of a man who'd turn down Bobbi Levinsky – that would give me a really good laugh! Confirm my theory once and for all that they're completely mentally defective.'

'You already have,' said a calm voice from the doorway.

Niamh and Alex looked around to see Bobbi come into the kitchen.

'What?' they chorused.

'You heard me,' said Bobbi quietly, as she went to get a glass of water from the fridge. 'Steve has just finished with me. I'd rather you heard it from me, but you'll forgive me if I don't want to talk about it right now.' With that, she turned around and walked back out, her face uncharacteristically pale.

ℭ

'I saw your friend Bobbi on the *Late Late Show* last week, she was really brilliant,' the young journalist breathed admiringly to Nellie as she sat at the little table by the window in Nellie's room. Under the guise of having her cards read, the reporter had not only gained entry to the most talked about house on Grovesbury Road, but had also managed to secure a riveting interview with the old woman, who seemed more than happy to chat about what was going on.

'Bobbi's a very special person.' Nellie smiled. 'She's come into our lives for a reason. I remember well the day I foresaw as much in the tea leaves.'

'You read in the *tea leaves* that Bobbi Levinsky was coming to live in Dublin?' The journalist double-checked to make sure her new digital recorder was switched on – this was going to be even better than she had hoped.

'Oh yes,' Nellie replied airily. 'Of course, I didn't know it was *her* then – but the tea leaves told me a stranger would be coming into our midst. A woman with her own troubles, who would play an important part in the upheaval that was about to unfold in our own lives.'

'This upheaval wouldn't have anything to do with the trouble Bobbi referred to that you are all having with your respective home situations?' The reporter held her breath as Nellie considered the question.

'As a matter of fact, it does. But that's only part of the story.' Nellie paused for an agonising few seconds while she lit a cigarette. 'You don't mind if I smoke, do you love?'

'No, not in the slightest. In fact, if you don't mind, I'll have one myself.' The girl grabbed a fag and lit it, inhaling deeply. 'You were saying,' she prompted Nellie.

'Oh yes, the cottages.' Nellie exhaled thoughtfully. 'Old Lord Grovesbury must be turning in his grave.'

'Who?'

'Lord Grovesbury, he built the cottages at the turn of the last century to house the families who worked as staff in the big houses on Grovesbury Road. Most had been sold on, but a few have remained in the same families more or less ever since. But now, of course, they've become valuable because of their development potential, and there's not too much of that left in Dublin 4.'

'Someone's interested in developing them?'

'More than interested. I'd say unstoppable – at any cost.'

'How do you mean?' The girl was intrigued.

'Well,' Nellie dropped her voice, 'between you and me, there's been very strange goings on in Grovesbury Gardens lately. My house was set on fire, Niamh ní Cheavin's cat was nailed to her front door – oh, he was all right, someone rescued him in time,' Nellie added hurriedly seeing the look of horror on the girl's face. 'Rowan Delaney had drugs planted in his cottage, and Steve Sorenson's place, our local vet, it was ransacked. You see our cottages were the last four remaining in the way of anyone developing the site.' Nellie watched the girl's face carefully to make sure she understood the implications.

'You mean someone, whoever wants to develop the site, is forcing, *has* forced you out of your homes?' The girl was incredulous.

'Exactly.'

'But that's outrageous!'

'If it wasn't for Bobbi, I don't know what we'd have done.' Nellie sucked her false teeth and sighed meaningfully.

'This, person, the developer, do you know who it is?' The girl's eyes were bright with anticipation.

Nellie smiled enigmatically. 'I have my suspicions. But that's not really the issue here. What's important is that people have been forced out of their homes by foul play. Homes that were built for them to live in for their lifetimes, by a good, kind philanthropist, a man far ahead of his time. Grovesbury Gardens is an important and historic part of Dublin 4 and part of the late Lord Grovesbury's legacy to us. No jumped up property developer should be able to deprive us of our rightful heritage like this.' Nellie blew out an emphatic cloud of smoke.

'Absolutely not. It's utterly scandalous.' The girl couldn't wait to start her research on property developers in the area. This was going to be one hell of a piece of journalism. Just wait till her editor saw what she was going to come up with.

'Now, we'll have to end it there, dearie. I'm feeling a little tired these days.' Nellie shifted in her chair.

'Oh, of course, thank you for the, er, reading, it was very interesting.' The girl stood up and opened her handbag to get her purse. 'How much do I owe you?'

'Oh that's all right, dearie.' Nellie winked at her. 'I don't charge any more now that I'm living in such luxury here at the Hall.'

The girl was taken aback. 'Really, well that's very kind of you, if you're sure?'

'You'll find a way of thanking me.' Nellie winked at her and then followed the girl's disbelieving gaze towards the wall behind them, from where a scraping noise was emanating.

'Oh, Mother of Divine God!' The girl's mouth dropped open as she watched a painting on the wall swing slowly back and forth of its own accord.

'Don't worry, love, that's just our resident ghost. He's a wee bit unsettled at the moment, what with all the carry on.' Nellie chuckled as the girl grabbed her coat and fled from the room.

'Now really,' she said reprovingly to the wall, 'there was no need for that, no need to scare the poor girl out of her wits! Sure didn't I know well she was a reporter. I haven't lost my marbles completely you know. Anyway, Bobbi could do with a bit of support at the moment. We need to draw attention to what's really going on here, don't you think? I know I'm a bit old and slow these days, but I think I know what you're getting at laddie. Just be patient for a little bit longer.'

As if in agreement, the painting slowly came to a halt.

Steve drummed his fingers on the steering wheel and tried to remain patient as he sat in the continuous stream of traffic heading to the Curragh. Overnight, it seemed, the weather had turned and winter had set in with a vice-like grip. Pale fields shimmered under a generous coating of frost, and a watery sun tried hard to break through the low-lying mist. It was a Saturday, and one of the biggest race meetings of the year was about to begin. He turned up the volume to listen to the sports commentary and tried to remember which of the runners in the big race were comfortable with the going, which would be hard after several freezing nights. But he found it impossible to concentrate.

Since breaking up with Bobbi, nothing much was making sense. It was the look on her face that haunted him. He had known for a while now that he was going to have to say something – things had been getting far too serious, far too quickly. But he hadn't been planning on blurting it out quite as unexpectedly as he had. They had been sitting in his kitchen, having a quiet after-dinner drink, when Bobbi had casually asked him to come and visit the doggy cosmetics factory in County Laois with her and suggested that maybe they could stay somewhere nice overnight. Before he could check himself, Steve heard himself saying that maybe it wasn't such a good idea. There had been just the merest fraction of a pause, and then Bobbi had said quietly, 'I see.'

From there the usual platitudes came tumbling incoherently from his mouth: 'I'm not sure I'm ready for this', 'we don't really know each other', 'we come from such different worlds', and his crowing *pièce de résistance* of originality, 'I just need some space.' God, Steve thumped his forehead in frustration as he replayed the scene for the umpteenth time, what an infantile, mind-numbingly pathetic performance. No wonder he had chosen a career working with animals. Dealing with people, never mind women, had never been his strong point. And Bobbi wasn't exactly your average woman, he reflected wryly. She was spectacular – on every level. Which made it even more ridiculous to think that he had been as incapable of articulating his real concerns to her as he was of confronting his true feelings.

The turn into the racecourse loomed ahead, and Steve felt the familiar rush of adrenaline as he concentrated his thoughts on the job in hand. He would cope the way he always did. They way that Claire, his ex-wife, had said would eventually destroy everything and everyone he touched. Steve grinned. He was doing all right so far. The big race would be a close run one, and since he had a hundred grand riding on it there was everything still to play for.

'Why don't you take him to the beach?' asked Rowan, leaning casually on the fence as he watched Bobbi canter round the paddock on Old Chestnut. The horse and rider made an unusually handsome pair now that the animal had recovered fully. His coat shone with health, and his previously wasted muscle tone was building up day by day. He snorted happily now, tossing his head as they passed Rowan, blowing cold bursts of air into the pale winter sunlight.

'What?' Bobbi pulled up and came over to where Rowan was standing.

'He looks like he could do with a good run. Why don't you take him down to Sandymount and let him have a gallop?'

'Sandymount Strand?'

'Doh!' Rowan eyeballed Bobbi. 'Yes,' he said with deliberation. 'The strand, you know, the one at the end of the road here. You can walk down easily from here, take him through at the Merrion Gates, and off you go.'

'They allow horses on the beach?' said Bobbi, slowly turning the thought over in her mind.

'There's no law against it. I've often seen horses down there, well not often, but sometimes. Why not? Anyway, wouldn't sand be good for building up his muscle? I bet he could do with a change of scene. As could you probably.' The comment hung in the air innocently.

'Maybe.' Bobbi dismounted and patted Old Chestnut, who blew noisily into her ear.

'See? He's telling you he wants to go.' Rowan grinned.

'I'll think about it.' Bobbi was unusually curt as she led the horse back to the stable courtyard, followed closely by Rowan.

'You know he's crazy about you. Don't you?'

'Sorry?'

'Steve. You do realise he's in love with you. Completely smitten.' Rowan looked her straight in the eyes.

Bobbi regarded him coldly. 'Is this a quaint little custom for you Irish to send another man to do your romancing for you?'

'Ah, now come on, Bobbi, that's not fair.' Rowan looked

hurt. 'It's just, well, there's things you don't maybe understand about Steve. About any of us Irish men really, I suppose.' He rubbed his chin thoughtfully.

'Make that men in general, honey. But I'm beginning to get the drift – believe you me.'

'Now what's that supposed to mean?'

'That you're all a bunch of snivelling cowards when it comes to anything even resembling an emotion. And I thought *Irish* guys were supposed to be romantics.' Bobbi gave a hollow laugh. 'Boy did I come down in the last shower!'

'You don't mean that Bobbi, you're just ...' Rowan searched for an appropriately sensitive term, ' ... overwrought. It's understandable.'

At this, Bobbi threw her head back and laughed loudly. Rowan looked bewildered. 'Now what have I said?'

'Nothing remotely unpredictable, that's for sure.' Bobbi settled Old Chestnut in his stall and made for the house, with Rowan hot on her heels.

'Now, Bobbi. Wait a minute.' Rowan couldn't understand why his well-intentioned diplomatic skills were being so unceremoniously hijacked. 'You don't understand.'

'Oh, but I do, Rowan. That's just it.' Bobbi turned back to smile at him as he followed her in through the conservatory and then into the kitchen, where Nellie, Niamh and Alex sat companionably over coffee and breakfast TV.

'What is it?' asked Niamh, looking worried at Bobbi's set expression and Rowan's frantic gesticulations to the others behind her back.

'Oh, nothing at all, Niamh,' said Bobbi airily. 'Rowan just happens to think I'm not treating the male population – oh, and Steve *in particular* – with the due consideration and sensitivity they're entitled to.'

Three sets of eyes darted warily towards each other across the table.

'That is absolutely *not* what I said.' Rowan sat down at the table and poured himself a cup of coffee. 'That's my point exactly! We men try to explain how we feel, and you jump all over us and twist everything!'

'Back up a minute there, Rowan,' said Niamh, eyeing him cautiously. 'Just what exactly were you implying to Bobbi?'

'I wasn't implying anything.' Rowan looked bewildered. 'I was just telling Bobbi that Steve is mad about her but –'

'But what?' asked Alex.

'Well, it … it's difficult for him. You know?' Rowan looked uncomfortable.

'Why don't you just come right out and say it? Like *he* should have done.' Bobbi's eyes flashed. 'It's the money, right?'

'Well, it's sort of understandable, Bobbi,' Rowan muttered, as everyone studied the table intently.

'What am I supposed to do? Give it all away? Call him up and say, hey Steve, it's safe to come back, babe. I'm broke. Things'll be really great between us now!'

'Ah, now Bobbi, calm down. It's just that Steve's proud, you know. He wouldn't be very good at playing "Mr Levinsky".' The words were out before Rowan could stop himself.

'What did you say?' Bobbi looked incredulous. 'Who the hell was asking him to play Mr Levinsky – or anything else for that matter? All I wanted was a mutually loving relationship with an emotionally mature man.'

Niamh snorted loudly. 'That particular species didn't make it on to the ark – never mind to our little country.'

'He just needs a bit of time to get his head around the whole thing,' Rowan protested. 'It's no big deal, really.'

'He can have all the time he needs. A couple of centuries will suit me just fine. Now can we please discuss something else?'

Cee

Early next morning, Bobbi jumped out of bed, pulled on her riding gear and quietly made her way downstairs while the rest of the house was sleeping. Outside, frost gleamed on the lawn and the gravel crunched beneath her feet as she walked towards the stables. Old Chestnut heard her approaching and whinnied in greeting, his beautiful head turned eagerly in her direction.

'Hey there, handsome,' said Bobbi, rubbing his velvety nose as she opened the stable door. 'We're going for a little adventure, you and me.' Old Chestnut stood patiently while she put on his bridle and mouthed the bit, blowing as she fastened the girth on the well-waxed saddle. She led him out into the courtyard where he pricked up his ears and looked about, seeming to sense the excitement, although he obligingly stood stock still as Bobbi mounted him.

Then they set off, walking around to the front of the Hall and out the gates onto Grovesbury Road, where a few early risers paused to listen to the long-forgotten sound of a horse's hooves echoing slowly into the distance. At the top of the road, Bobbi turned left onto Ailesbury Road, where she allowed Old Chestnut to break into a gentle trot. There was no traffic as yet, and the odd car that passed by didn't seem to bother him. On the contrary, he seemed alert and energetic, shaking his head and blowing trails of warm air into the early morning light. The lights were with them as they crossed the Merrion Road intersection and went on into Sydney Parade Avenue, arriving at the sea front. Bobbi continued right along Sandymount Road heading, as Rowan had suggested, for the Merrion Gates, where they could easily access the beach. Here, Bobbi pulled him up, pausing for a moment.

The sun had come up and the day ahead seemed fresh and full of promise. The tide was on its way out, and a good stretch of sand was exposed, along which a few early morning dog walkers strode briskly. Otherwise, the place was deserted. As she urged Old Chestnut gently onto the sand, a thousand memories clamoured in her head. Here was a beach, ahead was the water's edge along which she had ridden before, so long ago, on another horse, in another place, in another lifetime. And here she was doing what she had sworn she would never do again.

As if sensing her unease, Old Chestnut quivered beneath her, tossed his head and mouthed the bit. She patted his neck, feeling him tense and alert, as he broke into a trot and began to sidestep skittishly as he neared the water. She let him canter, slowly at first, holding him back, not sure if he was ready for this. After all, a slow canter was all she had allowed him around the paddock at the Hall, but already she could feel the pent up energy within him, the desperate longing to break free, and every fibre of her being identified with it.

'Okay, boy,' she whispered, leaning forward and running her hand through his silky mane, 'I'm ready if you are – let's go.' It took the merest squeeze of her legs to urge him on. Ears pricked forward, Old Chestnut lengthened every stride. Stretching his neck gracefully, his powerful hind quarters rippled as he broke into a full gallop.

Bobbi gasped as the wind whipped her hair about her face and the salt spray flew up around them as they thundered along the water's edge. Faster and faster they went, into the wind, scattering feeding gulls to the air and leaving the distant sound of dogs barking far behind them. Holding her breath, Bobbi waited, ready for the onslaught of guilt and remorse to strike, steeling herself to relive the horror of that last gallop along a beach. The helplessness, the futility, the never-ending fall into the hollow aftermath.

But it never came. With every stride, another shackle to the past was broken. With every stride, both she and Old Chestnut seemed to gather strength and unity.

Silhouetted against the pale winter sun, horse and rider were equally oblivious to anything but the intensity of the moment, and early morning onlookers were treated to a particularly beautiful tableau in motion.

21

Back at the Hall, the inhabitants were rousing themselves to face the day.

Niamh had brought Nellie breakfast in bed before setting off for her office. Alex was bathing Cindy and three of her dolls, and Rowan was supervising the hanging of the portrait of Lady Arabella and Monty, which was being repositioned to face the door of the inner hall. Here, it would hang regally, dominating the beautiful square hall with its flagstone floor from which five polished mahogany doors led off into various other reception rooms. Above the mantelpiece, where the portrait had previously hung, a magnificent Renaissance Venetian mirror was now in place. Rowan peered deeply into this, checking his reflection as he shouted instructions to the builders, who were levering the portrait into position so the man from the gallery could hang it with due care from the appropriate chains.

'That's it, gently does it lads.' Rowan stood with his head to one side.

'Jaysus, this thing weighs a bleeding ton.'

'Nearly there, just a bit to the left. Then the chains will be in position.'

Rowan strolled over, watching closely. He had never really looked at the portrait properly, and he took it in now for the first time, marvelling at its grace and luminosity.

'She was some looker, eh?'

'Hmm?' Rowan was only half-listening. Something had caught his artist's eye, and he now looked at the painting intently. 'What? Oh, yes, Lady Arabella was stunning, but it's the horse ... There's something familiar about it. Something I've seen before, I'm sure of it.' Rowan ran a hand through his hair distractedly.

'Orpen did do rather a lot of society portraits at the time,' Mr Whyte from the gallery pointed out. 'He was a war artist too you know, in the first World War. His style is very distinctive.'

Rowan was now peering directly into Monty's luminously beautiful eyes, his face contorted with concentration. 'That's it,' he exclaimed, snapping his fingers, 'The star! Look at the star on his forehead. I knew I'd seen it somewhere before!' And leaving the bewildered group looking after him, Rowan grabbed his jacket and ran from the hall, through the kitchen and down towards the stables.

*

Chris Carroll couldn't believe what he was reading. Sitting in his study in Grovesbury Road, he clutched the pages of the morning paper with increasing anger. 'GROVESBURY GARDENS, D4 DEVELOPERS BULLDOZE HELPLESS RESIDENTS OUT OF HOMES.' Taking a gulp of steaming coffee left by Maya, he nearly scalded himself and cursed liberally as the hot liquid burned a trail down his throat. The article gleefully continued to elaborate on the misfortunes of the residents of the four remaining cottages in Grovesbury Gardens now residing in Grovesbury Hall, thanks to the generosity of Bobbi

Levinsky who had taken them in when they had been cruelly forced out of their rightful homes. Jesus! Chris's throat constricted as he raced through paragraph after paragraph. This could be absolutely disastrous. He was just about to pick up the phone to his solicitor when it got worse. The words began to blur before his eyes as he read the name of Alex O'Gallagher and her two children, Cindy and Christopher, whose father was well-known property developer Chris Carroll. Alex was described as a 'close girlfriend' of Bobbi's and was staying with her due to a 'rift' with her aforementioned partner.

The rest of the article paled in comparison as far as Chris was concerned. He was being made the laughing stock of the neighbourhood. And all because of that bitch Bobbi Levinsky. Flinging the paper aside, he was just about to storm out of the room when the phone rang. He picked it up. It was his solicitor, Malcolm, sounding uncharacteristically firm. 'Chris,' he said, 'you'd better come into my office. We need to talk.'

Cee

By the time Rowan reached the stables, Old Chestnut had been washed down, watered and was busy thrusting his nose into his morning feed of warm oats. He looked up as Rowan whistled, turning around to greet his visitor and leaning out over the stable door to blow into the hand that Rowan held out.

'Howya, big boy?' Rowan reached up and brushed Old Chestnut's forelock back from his forehead. And there it was. Just as he had known it would be. The white star with five points was not so remarkable, but the trail from the bottom right-hand point that led to another smaller star, connecting the two like a comet's trail, was. And it was absolutely identical to the one on the forehead of the late Lady Arabella's horse in the portrait painted so many years ago.

'Oh man,' said Rowan softly. And wondered why he suddenly felt goose bumps up and down his spine.

Co

'It's appalling, that's what it is,' Carmela Walshe said, nostrils flaring with disapproval from the head of the Victorian dining table as she sipped a glass of red wine. She had organised a select ladies lunch, just twelve of her oldest, and suitably deferential, girlfriends, on the strength of the article in this morning's paper. They sat around the table now, nodding sagely, their collective chins quivering in agreement. 'I've lived on this road for over forty years now, and I can't believe things have come to this.'

'Thank God at least there's *someone* to maintain moral, not to mention elegant, standards on the road, Carmela,' said Betty, her elderly sister-in-law, who was getting stuck into the wine with gusto.

'Thank you, Betty, it's very sweet of you to say so.' Carmela nodded meaningfully at the houseman to refill Betty's glass. 'One tries to do one's best.'

'What's the story with that chap Chris Carroll and his, er, girlfriend?'

'Partner, Eileen,' chimed in Nola. '*Partner* is the term one uses nowadays, I believe, for these live-in arrangements.'

'What? Like a business partner?'

'It's the *nature* of the business that concerns me.' Carmela shuddered. 'They might as well put up a red light outside some of these houses and be done with it. It really has gone beyond the beyonds. It's *such* a bad example for my Marysol, not to mention Padraig who finds it *deeply* upsetting, being so spiritually inclined.' Carmela bowed her beautifully coifed head and sighed.

'Well, poor Lady Arabella Grovesbury must be spinning in her grave, that's all I can say,' Belinda, who did the flowers for the church with Carmela every week, added. 'That beautiful house might as well be a – a hippie commune.'

'And those young children of Chris Carroll's up there with God knows what going on around them,' said Eileen reprovingly.

'And I'll wager they haven't even been baptised,' Nola mused.

'All we can do is remember them in our prayers,' said Carmela, shaking her head sadly.

*

'Pascal, did you hear about the article in the paper this morning?' Melissa had been alerted by her hairdresser earlier that day.

'Sure I've been hearing about nothing else.' Pascal yawned widely.

'You didn't get involved in that venture with Chris Carroll, did you?' she asked anxiously. Melissa didn't fancy any adverse publicity seeing as the whole of Dublin seemed to be up in arms about the Grovesbury Gardens' residents being chased from their homes.

'No, I told him I wasn't interested in the development scheme. Although he was welcome to the cottage in exchange for an apartment.'

'Do you really think he's behind the goings on?'

'It's a pretty heavy insinuation to make about anyone, even Chris. But there's no doubt there's something funny going on. I think he just might have bitten off more than he can chew this time. Anyway, don't worry your pretty little head about it, love. Grovesbury Gardens was bound to be developed at some stage or other. It might as well be Chris Carroll as anyone else.'

*

'Rod?'

'What Tanya?'

'All that fuss about Grovesbury Gardens.'

'What about it?'

'People are really getting upset.' Tanya chewed her lip. 'The road's getting a lot of adverse publicity because of Chris Carroll. I was at a charity lunch today with Melissa, and we could really tell people were talking and whispering about us.'

'Don't worry. The security system's just been serviced. Even if a mob was to descend on us, they wouldn't get past the front gate.'

Tanya didn't look convinced. 'Nathan,' she called to their six-year-old son, playing with the latest Gameboy that money and every bit of Rod's influence could purchase. 'Come on, it's time for bed.'

'Dad?'

'Yes, sport?'

'What's a greedy, new-money East-end spiv?'

Rod and Tanya looked at each other, for once lost for words.

Cee

'See?' said Rowan, pointing to the portrait of Lady Arabella and Monty around which a bewildered household had now gathered.

'See what exactly, Rowan?' Bobbi asked. 'It's the same portrait it always was.'

'Look at the marking on Monty's head. The star and the trail of white leading to the smaller star.'

'What about it?' asked Alex, trying to stop Cindy wriggling out of her arms.

'Look carefully at it, then follow me.'

'Do you know what this is about?'

'Beats me.'

'Is he always like this?'

'That's artists for ya,' said one of the men.

'I heard he was on the drugs,' whispered another.

One by one they all trudged out into the frosty morning, following Rowan who led the way like the pied piper.

Old Chestnut heard them approaching and gave a low whinny in greeting. His beautiful head appeared over the stable door, ears pricked forward at the unexpected activity.

'Allow me to demonstrate,' said Rowan. 'If you'll all just stand back where you can get a good look.' Reaching up, he brushed back Old Chestnut's forelock to reveal the identical marking on his forehead. 'I'm no horse expert, but don't tell me this is a coincidence.'

'Wow,' said Bobbi, stroking Chestnut's nose as he tried to nibble her shoulder. 'I can't believe I never noticed this. You're right, Rowan. It's completely identical to the original Monty's markings.'

'What are you implying?'

'That's just it. I don't know.'

'It *is* strange.'

'Would somebody like to explain what this is all about?' said Alex, shivering. 'I'm frozen.'

'I think I might be able to,' said a quiet voice.

'Nellie!' exclaimed Bobbi, as the little group turned around to find Nellie wearing Rowan's duffel coat over her dressing gown. 'What are you doing out here? You'll catch your death!'

22

'I've been racking my brains trying to remember the incident, and then it came to me,' said Nellie as she sat around the kitchen table with Bobbi, Alex and Rowan.

'Go on,' said Bobbi listening eagerly, her chin propped in her hands, as Alex poured coffee.

'It's only a theory mind, but I just have one of my feelings.'

Alex shot Rowan a look as he raised his eyes to heaven.

'Do you remember?' said Nellie. Then she looked at Bobbi. 'Well, of course, *you* wouldn't, seeing as you were in America at the time.'

'What?' asked Alex, chewing her nail.

'Well, it was about twelve years ago or so. The Horse Show was on, so it would have been the first week in August.' Nellie paused to light up and inhaled deeply.

'Go on,' urged Bobbi.

'Two young scallywags got into the RDS, found their way to the stables, hopped up on one of the show jumpers – the pair of them mind you, no saddle or anything – and hightailed it out the Anglesea Road entrance before anyone could stop them. They were seen galloping up Anglesea Road, and that was the last that anyone heard of them – or indeed the horse.' Nellie paused to draw breath.

'They never got the horse back?' Bobbi sounded incredulous. 'What happened?'

Nellie looked at her and smiled. 'Nobody knew, sadly. But the Aga Khan was devastated, not to mention the horse's famous show-jumping partner, Freddie Martin. They won everything together, you know, they were unbeatable in Europe.' Nellie paused for effect. 'The horse, you see,' she said, blowing out a cloud of smoke, 'was Montyson III, a direct descendant from Lady Arabella's beloved Monty.'

Cee

Chris sat down in the leather chair opposite Malcolm's desk, from where his solicitor regarded him coldly. 'This', Malcolm said, pointing to the newspaper article with his fluttering, bird-like hands, 'could be disastrous.' He fixed Chris with his most reproving stare.

'Thanks so much for pointing out the bloody obvious,' Chris drawled, his voice laced with sarcasm. 'It might have escaped your notice, Malcolm, but it's actually a little late in the day for me to do anything about it now.'

'On the contrary, Chris. It's vital you do something about it. We cannot have any more of this sort of unwelcome attention being drawn to the development. Before we know it, we'll have planning authorities breathing down our necks, and once they start digging, God only knows what they'll ask for.'

'Don't worry, I'll sort out anyone who might have any ideas about getting in my way. I can't afford any hold-ups, not at this stage in the game.'

'Delays will be the least of your problems if the planning

people smell a rat.' Malcolm gave a wry smile. 'They'll go through everything with a fine-tooth comb. It would only be a matter of time before they started researching the leasehold situation – then we'd rightly be in hot water. I cannot afford to have the firm associated with any irregular activity, Chris. I made that clear to you from the outset.' Malcolm pursed his lips meaningfully.

'Neither', said Chris menacingly, 'can you afford for me to tell any interested parties, in the event of any problems arising, that I was advised incorrectly by my trusted solicitor.'

Malcolm glared at him. 'I am merely cautioning damage limitation in what you are well aware are *extremely* sensitive circumstances, Chris. The fact that your personal life is in considerable disarray is not helping things. If I were you, I would be trying very hard to get Alex to come home with the children. That American woman could be dangerous to us.'

'Leave her to me, Malcolm.' Chris smiled. 'There's a nugget or two of information I'll be passing on to her imminently regarding the company she's been keeping. Nothing like upsetting the love life to knock a bird off her perch. Even one with as many millions as she has. And if Steve Sorenson has his way, she won't be holding on to them for long,' Chris gave a mirthless chuckle. Standing up to leave, he turned back to Malcolm, 'Oh and by the way, I assume that letter I instructed you to send to Alex went out?'

'She should get it today, Chris.' Malcolm looked at him over his glasses. 'First thing.'

'Good, I'll give her a few hours to digest it, then I'll be in touch.'

Alex was just back from a stroll in Herbert Park with Cindy, when the doorbell rang. Polly went to answer it, as Alex headed to the kitchen to make herself a cup of hot chocolate.

'This has just arrived for you, Alex,' Polly said. 'It was sent by courier.'

'Oh,' said Alex, taking the innocuous-looking white envelope from her. 'Thanks, Polly.'

Five minutes later, she was still reading and re-reading the official letter with trembling hands. Upstairs, she could hear Polly hoovering away and wondered how it was possible that such normality could continue as she felt the very life being knocked out of her. The phrases began to swim menacingly before her eyes: 'unfit mother', 'we must draw your attention to associations with dubious characters', 'children exposed to persons with possible criminal records'. Alex sat down weakly and tried to take deep breaths. This was it, she was going to lose the children.

What had she been thinking of? The last few weeks she had been living in a fool's paradise. Of course, Chris had never been going to take it lying down. But somehow, the longer time went on without her hearing from him, the more she hoped that maybe, just maybe, he would begin to see that an amicable separation was the best way forward for everybody. Now she felt the full force of his bullying personality. She was just another possession to him or, more correctly, just an accessory to the possession he really valued, his children. The threat was made abundantly clear. *Get yourself and the children back home now or I'll make sure you never see them again.* The letter may have been signed by that mealy-mouthed solicitor of his, but it was Chris's voice ringing out loud and clear from between the lines.

Bobbi had been doing a lot of research on the net regarding equine bloodlines and breeding ever since Nellie's extraordinary account of the missing Montyson. In itself, the story wasn't all that bizarre. After all, Shergar, the famous racehorse, had been stolen and never recovered. But it was the possibility, albeit a remote one, that Old Chestnut and Montyson III could be one and the same that really blew her mind. She pulled on a waterproof jacket and set off down to the stables, humming to herself despite the weather. It was late afternoon, and the drizzle that had begun earlier was adding to the chill in the air. By the time she reached the courtyard, they had seen her, and it was too late to turn back. Steve and Rowan were deep in conversation outside Old Chestnut's box, and they turned now at the sound of her approaching footsteps.

'Bobbi, hi.' Rowan ran a hand through his hair. 'I was just telling Steve about Montyson and Nellie's theory.'

'Hello, Bobbi,' Steve said quietly, meeting her eyes.

'Hi,' Bobbi's stomach lurched as she fought to keep her face impassive. She had managed to avoid bumping into Steve since he had ended their relationship. Now she cursed herself for not checking to make sure the coast was clear before turning up. *Don't be ridiculous*, she chided herself. *It's your bloody house, let him worry about keeping out of your way*, but somehow that only made her feel worse.

'What do you think?' she asked curtly, as Old Chestnut looked out enquiringly at her, pleased at the unexpected visit.

'It's unlikely,' Steve patted the horse's neck, 'but not impossible.' He met Bobbi's eyes again, and she felt a white-hot bolt of electricity shoot through her.

'Well, see ya,' said Rowan over his shoulder as he turned to go. 'I've got work to do.'

Bobbi fumbled with the bolt, hoping Steve wouldn't notice her trembling fingers that suddenly seemed to be having difficulty following the most basic commands. Finally, the bolt obligingly shot back, and she turned on the light in the stable, walking over to check on Old Chestnut's food. Steve followed her in and she immediately felt claustrophobic. Watching him running his hand along the horse's flank, Bobbi was filled with a sudden longing to change places with the horse. 'I could make some enquiries from a bloodstock specialist I know,' he said, bending down to feel Old Chestnut's leg. 'The age seems about right, but without any DNA evidence, we wouldn't have any real proof, even if it is the same horse. Either way, he's made a great recovery. Which is the main thing, isn't it?'

'Sure,' said Bobbi, wishing he'd go. His presence was unsettling her, and she felt ridiculously awkward.

'Bobbi?'

Hearing the question in his voice, she looked up over Old Chestnut's back and immediately regretted it as a pair of turquoise eyes regarded her intently. 'We need to talk,' Steve said quietly.

'I think you made yourself crystal clear Steve.' Bobbi could hardly believe her petulant tone as she continued. 'I understand perfectly.'

'No you don't. You don't understand at all.'

'Of course I do. It's the money. It's always been the money.' She looked at him defiantly.

'That's only part of it, Bobbi.'

'Well you know what? It's part of *me*, the money. We're a package. I give large chunks of it away, Steve, but I can't divorce myself from it completely and I wouldn't want to. And if your feelings for me are so … inadequate that they can't accommodate that, then, you know what? You did exactly the right thing. So there's really nothing more to say on the subject except …'

'Except what?'

'Except that I thought we really had something special.'

'Bobbi!' The moment was broken as Niamh's voice called out urgently. 'Come quickly.' And then, seeing Steve, 'You too.' Niamh fought to catch her breath after running from the house. 'It's Nellie,' she gasped, 'she's collapsed upstairs.'

By the time the ambulance arrived, Nellie was still unconscious, although mercifully Steve had been able to maintain her breathing with mouth-to-mouth resuscitation. A tearful Niamh sat with her in the ambulance, thinking how frail she looked, while Bobbi followed behind in her car.

Minutes later, they arrived at St Vincent's Hospital, and Nellie was taken immediately to Casualty where it was pronounced that she had suffered a stroke resulting from a cerebral haemorrhage. She was brought to intensive care where she would remain for several days.

'I'll stay with her for a while, Bobbi,' Niamh said firmly. 'I'm the closest thing to family she's got.'

'If you're sure you're okay.' Bobbi was concerned. Niamh had been through a lot lately herself. 'I'll get her things together and have them sent down as soon as I get back.'

By the time Bobbi got back home, it was half-past six, and the house seemed strangely quiet. In the front hall a huge log fire crackled invitingly. 'Hello-o,' she called out. 'Anybody home?'

She walked down the three steps to the kitchen following the delicious smell. Peering into the oven, Bobbi found a casserole simmering away that Polly had obviously left for them. Opening the fridge, she pulled out a bottle of white wine and uncorked it, turning as she heard footsteps on the stairs. 'Rowan! You heard about Nellie, I guess?' Bobbi filled two glasses.

'Yeah. Polly told me.' Rowan shook his head, 'Poor Nellie, but she's a good age.' He sounded distracted.

'Are you okay?' Bobbi handed him the glass, thinking now that she noticed it he looked a bit worn out. 'Where's Alex? Has she taken the kids out?'

'She's taken them home,' Rowan said, sitting down at the kitchen table and taking a drink of the wine.

'What? To see Chris?' Bobbi sounded startled.

'Nope. She's gone back to him. Polly said a solicitor's letter arrived this morning and an hour later she was packed and out.'

'You're kidding.' Bobbi looked disbelieving.

'I wish I was. She left a letter for me, asking me not to contact her or she'd lose her kids.' Rowan looked gaunt. 'And she said to say she'd be in touch with you, and to thank you for everything, but that going back to Chris was for the best.'

'Better for Chris, for sure,' said Bobbi, shaking her head, 'but not for anyone else concerned.' Bobbi sat down beside Rowan and sipped her wine. 'He can't take the children from her, you know.'

'I'm not so sure. If he can prove she's an unfit mother, and God only knows what lengths he'd go to to do that, he might be able to get custody, and that would kill her. I can't risk putting her in that kind of danger.'

'You really do love her, don't you?' Bobbi said softly.

'More than I ever thought I could love anybody.' Rowan met her eyes.

'There's a casserole Polly left for us in the oven,' said Bobbi getting up briskly. 'You look like you could do with something to eat. I'll have what's left when I come back.'

'Where are you going?'

'To have a word or two with Alex.'

'Do you think that's wise?'

'I won't know till I talk to her. Someone's got to stop that bastard brainwashing her, and it might as well be me.'

~

By the time Bobbi drove in to Chris Carroll's driveway, her blood was up.

Inside, several rooms were lit from behind heavy curtains, while outside, all was quiet. She was pleased to see there was no evidence of Chris's silver Porsche – which, she reckoned, meant she might be able to catch Alex on her own and talk some sense into her. Jumping out of the car, she strode to the front door and pressed the buzzer, waiting impatiently for what felt like an interminable length of time. Finally, she heard quiet steps approaching and Maya answered the door and peered out anxiously. 'Oh, Miss Levinsky,' she said, sounding worried. 'Er, please come in.' She ushered Bobbi into the hall.

Bobbi got straight to the point. 'I'm here to see Alex, Maya.'

Maya, if possible, looked even more perturbed. 'Miss Alex is not to see, er, that is, she is not seeing anybody, Miss Levinsky.' Those were my instructions.' Maya chewed her lip nervously.

I'll bet they were your instructions, thought Bobbi, *and I can tell exactly who issued them. Bloody Chris Carroll.* Keeping her thoughts to herself, she smiled her most beguiling smile and spoke firmly but quietly with all the assurance her business dealings and many millions had brought her over the years. 'It's very important that I see Alex, Maya. Please let her know I'm here and that I won't be leaving until I see her and can reassure myself that she's all right.'

Maya hesitated for only a second. What were the orders of an obnoxious man like Chris Carroll (even if he did pay her a generous salary) who made his girlfriend and children miserable, compared with a genuine request from one of Alex's true friends.

'Of course, Miss Levinsky, I'll let her know you're here right away. Please make yourself comfortable in the small sitting room.'

Bobbi smiled warmly. 'Thank you, Maya. I appreciate this.'

It was about fifteen minutes later, and Bobbi was about to give up hope, when she heard footsteps approaching. The door to the sitting room opened quietly and Alex appeared. 'Hi, Bobbi.' She came over to kiss her. 'I'm really sorry about leaving the way I did, but things, well things started happening and I felt it was for the best …' She trailed off unconvincingly, not meeting Bobbi's eyes.

'You mean *Chris* started happening, right?' Bobbi sat down on the sofa beside her and took her hand. 'Look, Alex, you don't have to pretend with me. We've always been straight with each other, right?'

'Oh, Bobbi, no one could have been kinder to me and the kids than you. If it hadn't been for you, I don't know what I'd have done.'

'But that's just it, Alex, you were doing so well. Why on earth go back now?'

'He's issued legal proceedings, Bobbi. I got a letter today

from his solicitor accusing me of being an unfit mother and subjecting the children to contact with people of dubious character and possible criminal associations.' Alex sounded completely worn out. 'I can't fight him, Bobbi, and I can't risk losing my children. It would kill me.' A tear rolled down her face that she quickly tried to brush away. 'You don't know what he's like. He'd go after Rowan and make his life hell. There's nothing he'll stop at when he wants his own way. I can't be responsible for that. I just can't … I don't have the strength to fight him.'

'But I do, Alex.' Bobbi was adamant. 'And so do you, you just don't know it yet. Come back with me to the Hall, and bring the kids. Tomorrow we'll get you the best lawyers money can buy and we'll take it from there.'

'I don't know, Bobbi. There's no knowing what he'd do. He's forbidden me to see anyone at the moment. If he even knew you were here –'

'But he doesn't, does he? You can't possibly go on living with a man who treats you like this, Alex. He doesn't own you, or the children. Now hurry! Don't bother with clothes or anything, just get the kids and come with me. Tomorrow we'll get you everything you need.'

'If I do, then that will be it, Bobbi. It'll be out and out war, honestly,' Alex said.

'You don't really have a choice, Alex. Think about it, if you stay, he's won and he'll walk all over you for the rest of your life. Is that the image you want for your kids to have of you? If, on the other hand, you leave, you have the chance to start a new life, on your terms. I know which one I'd choose.' Bobbi looked meaningfully at her.

'I'll be as quick as I can.' Alex smiled for the first time.

'Good, I'll wait in the car.'

True to her word, Alex was on the front steps five minutes later carrying Christopher while Cindy held on to Maya's hand as she helped her clamber into Bobbi's Range Rover. 'Hi, Bobbi.' Cindy looked pleased to be off on another adventure. 'I told Mummy not to bring Christopher, but she said we had to.'

Bobbi grinned, 'I think Mummy's probably right, honey. He'd get lonely for you if you left him behind.'

Just then a spray of gravel announced Chris's arrival as the silver Porsche pulled up abruptly and he took in the situation in a glance.

'Oh, God, Bobbi. Quick, he'll call the police or something, hurry!'

'Relax, Alex. Leave this to me.' Bobbi spoke quietly but there was steel in her voice.

In a flash, Chris was out of his car and banging on Alex's window, demanding that she get out immediately.

'Stop it! Chris! You're frightening the children,' Alex cried as Cindy clutched her teddy tightly to her.

'For Crissakes, Chris.' Bobbi lowered her window and leaned out. 'This isn't going to help anyone. Give it a rest.'

Chris came around to the driver's window and smiled cruelly, 'It most certainly isn't going to help Alex, *or you* I might point out, when I add abducting my children from the family home to my list of complaints. If I were you, Alex, I would get out of that car right now. Do you hear me? Now!'

Alex began to cry as she fumbled for the door handle. 'It's no use, Bobbi. Can't you see?'

'Don't you dare get out of this car,' Bobbi hissed at her uncharacteristically. 'You are *not* going to put yourself and your children at risk from that belligerent excuse of a man who has −' she said, looking pointedly at Chris '− clearly been drinking. If you like, Chris, I'll call the guards right now. I'm sure they'd love to get involved. We could invite the whole road along for the party while we're at it,' Bobbi added astutely. 'What d'ya think, big guy? Huh?'

'Please, Bobbi.' Alex couldn't believe her ears. 'It's not worth it, really.'

'I think', said Chris menacingly, 'that you are a very stupid, woman who interferes in other people's lives because she doesn't have one of her own. You are making a bad situation for Alex infinitely worse. Family law is an expensive business at the best of times, and Alex cannot afford to go up against the best lawyers in the country. Who will, I might remind you, be representing me.'

'Oh, but *I* can, Chris,' retorted Bobbi. 'Even if it means paying them quadruple the fees you do. In fact it'll be a pleasure for me – a real blast. I'll pay them *not* to represent you. And you don't need me to remind you that I have considerably more money than you have.' Bobbi grinned wickedly as Alex put her head in her hands and groaned.

Chris's eyes hardened. 'Not if Steve Sorenson has his way.'

'I beg your pardon?' Bobbi's voice was ice, and suddenly she had the feeling what was coming next was not something she wanted to hear.

'Steve Sorenson, your, er, consort.' Chris was relishing relaying his information. 'Clearly your emotional life is ruled by your heart, neatly bypassing your brain.'

'Please, Bobbi. Let's go,' Alex begged.

'What exactly are you getting at, Chris?'

'Surely you can spot when a man is after you for your, um, considerable assets?'

Bobbi snorted. 'Wrong again, Chris. Steve isn't remotely interested in my money. If anything it's a deterrent.'

'Is that what he says?' Chris smiled thinly. 'A clever ploy, I grant you, given his pastime.'

'What pastime?'

'Gold-digging primarily. His first wife's family will testify to that. How else do you think he set up his surgery and built that house? Oh, and did I mention Steve's a compulsive gambler, Bobbi? Surely you know that much? Getting his hands on your money would be like letting a kid loose in a sweet shop. He gambles everything – can't help himself.'

Bobbi looked at Alex incredulously. 'Is this true, Alex?'

'I … I don't know Bobbi, I do know his ex-wife was very wealthy – and, well, there was talk about his divorce –'

'Divorce! Hah! He took that poor girl to the cleaners,' Chris snorted. 'I do hate to disillusion you, Bobbi dear, but the only interest Steve could possibly have in you is money – whatever slick patter he's coming up with. I'm surprised you didn't pick up on it yourself. But I suppose it must become tedious for you wondering if the only reason people are interested in you is your money. At least, I suppose, you can afford to buy a few friends and house guests. To tell you the truth, you're welcome to Alex, I'm well shot of her. But watch out, even she's managed to cultivate some expensive habits since I introduced her to the good life. Good luck ladies, and Alex, don't think for a moment you'll get away with this. Not only will I make sure you never get to see your children again, but I'll make sure you don't get a penny from me, not one single penny. But Bobbi will need a companion when Steve and her money run out – and one won't be long after the other.'

'You're some sick bastard, you know that?' Bobbi closed her window and manoeuvred the car out the gates, where she turned left and drove back to Grovesbury Hall, silently quivering with rage.

23

A few days later, Nellie was drifting in and out of consciousness. She tried desperately to relate the labyrinth of images that wove their way around her fragile psyche. But as her power of speech had been affected by the stroke, the vital information she was trying to pass on was dismissed as unintelligible ramblings.

'Don't try to talk, Nellie darling,' Niamh whispered, soothing her, as she stroked her snow-white hair back from her wrinkled forehead. 'Everything's fine. We're all here and your things have been sent from the Hall. You have everything you need. I'll be here, right beside you.' Niamh sighed, as she stood up to stretch. She had immediately taken a couple of days' leave of absence from work to stay with Nellie around the clock and was now beginning to feel the strain. She felt sure Nellie could understand her, and was appreciative of her presence, but nonetheless, she seemed inexplicably agitated. Bobbi had been back several times to see her, and Rowan and Alex had also visited, but Niamh refused to leave her side. It was six o'clock in the evening and suddenly Niamh found that, apart from feeling dog tired, she was ravenously hungry. The insistent ringing of her mobile phone brought her back to the present with a jolt. It was Bobbi.

'Niamh, how's Nellie doing?'

'She's the just the same, Bobbi. She sleeps a lot of the time, but when she's awake she's talking gibberish. I can't understand a word. It's so upsetting. I'm convinced she's trying to tell me something.'

'The doctor said that's to be expected, Niamh, under the circumstances. We'll just have to let time run its course. Look, why don't you come back to the Hall for dinner? You need to keep up your strength too you know. I'll drop you straight back down after.'

'Well,' Niamh hesitated, 'maybe just for an hour. I suppose Nellie won't mind.'

'Of course she won't. She's getting the best possible care. Come on home for dinner, then we'll go back to sit with her together.'

'You're right. I'll see you in twenty minutes or so.'

'Good,' said Bobbi, sounding relieved as she hung up.

Cee

After Niamh had left, Nellie saw him again. He had been there all along, of course. It was funny, she thought, now that the edges of reality were becoming so blurred, his aura was in sharper focus than ever. In the little private room that Bobbi had made sure she was transferred to, Nellie noticed the television on the wall that had been burbling in the background suddenly switched off.

He stood now, just at the end of her bed, watching her expectantly with the speculative expression the young reserve for the unpredictable actions of their elders.

'It's no use.' Nellie shook her head wearily. 'I'm too weak. You'll have to do the best you can yourself.'

'All right, Mrs Murphy?' The nurses came in and checked on Nellie, chattering away ten to the dozen. They checked the drips, plumped up Nellie's pillows and patted her hand that lay on the bed clutched in spasm. 'Poor old dear,' said one to the other as they left the room quietly. 'She's talking away to herself, but you can't make out a word. It's all gibberish.'

Cee

'It's raining, Mummy,' said Cindy, squealing as a drop fell straight onto her head.

'Don't be silly, Cindy,' Alex smiled. 'It can't be raining inside.'

'It is, Mummy. I felt it.'

'She's right.' Rowan looked up towards the ceiling. 'There must be a leak. I felt a definite drop there. Uh, oh, look, there's trouble all right.'

Sure enough, as Alex looked up she saw a large patch of damp was gathering, puckering the plaster, from which a steady drip was emerging.

'Better call one of the guys up. If that's not stopped soon there'll be serious damage done. Where's Bobbi?'

'She had to go into town,' said Alex, looking concerned. 'I think she's at some meeting. She said something about a bank manager or something. I'll call her.'

'The sooner the better.' Rowan ducked as another drop almost got him.

Half an hour later the builders were on the case. Alex left them to it and went upstairs to give Cindy a bath and put her down for her afternoon nap. After all the recent upheaval, she was feeling fragile too and had been hoping to lie down and have a quiet rest herself. Somehow, with all the thumping and banging coming from the floor above, Alex doubted very much she would get any sleep.

Cee

At twelve forty-five on the dot, Bobbi strode into Patrick Guilbaud's restaurant in the Merrion Hotel. Her table was ready, and she chose to go straight to it rather than wait and have a drink upstairs. Her dining companion had not arrived, which was not surprising as she was deliberately fifteen minutes early. She needed to think her approach through quietly just one more time.

Finding out who Steve banked with hadn't been difficult. She had remembered a cheque he had written to her for an advance (on his insistence) on the rent for the stables. It was clearly marked 'Private Banking at New Hibernian Bank'. After that it had been easy. The president of the bank himself had insisted on dealing with her when he had learned who the famous prospective client of the bank was. Money sure opened a lot of doors Bobbi thought to herself wryly as she ordered a Champagne-cocktail aperitif.

At five-to-one precisely, Mr Fitzgerald arrived and was shown to the table, where he greeted Bobbi profusely. 'I must say, Ms Levinsky, it's a very great pleasure to meet you. A very great pleasure indeed.'

Bobbi liked him on sight. 'Call me Bobbi, please. I do hope you'll join me in an aperitif?'

'I'd be delighted. I'll have whatever you're having.'

Bobbi gave the waiter their order and settled down to enjoy what she hoped would be an informative lunch. She didn't have long to wait.

'Of course, Ms Lev–, I mean Bobbi,' Mr Fitzgerald, or Eamonn as he insisted Bobbi call him, was effusive. 'I would be more than honoured to take you on a guided tour of our facilities. I feel sure we can offer you the most up-to-the-minute, second-to-none and, of course, intensely *exclusive* banking service available in this country. A woman of your, er, means and experience will appreciate how necessary it is for one to choose the right people to deal with.' Eamonn wasn't sure whether to salivate more over the excellent Chablis Grand Cru Valmur 1998 Bobbi had ordered or the prospect of having this ravishing and obscenely wealthy woman as a client.

Bobbi recognised her chance. 'Actually, Eamonn, it was a good friend of mine who recommended your bank to me. A vet – Dr Steve Sorenson. Do you know him?' Bobbi gazed innocently into Eamonn's eyes as she toyed with a succulent scallop.

'Steve!' Eamonn beamed with pleasure. 'Steve's a friend of yours? Well, Bobbi, you couldn't ask to meet a nicer chap! And a very good client of ours – very good. Of course we're always on hand to advise him, you know.' Eamonn winked knowingly at her. 'Quite a character our Steve, quite a character. I've had many a good day out with him on the turf.'

Bobbi was taken aback – she hadn't expected this. Clearly Eamonn knew of Steve's gambling tendencies and seemed to find the whole thing hugely amusing.

'You say he's a good client?' Bobbi ventured.

Eamonn swirled his wine around his glass knowingly as he warmed to his theme. 'Well he wouldn't be quite in *your* league, Bobbi, but put it this way, we wouldn't like to lose him.

'He's doing well then?' Bobbi's eyes widened enticingly. 'I'd, er, heard rumblings to the contrary.'

'Doing well?' Eamonn laughed heartily. 'If you rate an account that averages at about ten Lotto wins doing well, then, yes, Steve's doing exceptionally well. Of course, he likes the occasional flutter, but it's his dealings on the stock exchange that have made him a rich man – a seriously rich man. And one, as I'm sure you well know, who keeps a refreshingly low profile. None of your poncing about in sports cars and building mad houses for Steve. He loves what he does for a living, and he's a man who takes risks. So far, they've paid off for him. It was a pity about his marriage – though, between you and me, he's better off without that girl, far better off,' Eamonn said firmly. 'It almost ruined him financially, you know. He bailed her father out to the tune of two and half million when the family business got into trouble, and they stitched him up appallingly. Poor old Steve had to walk away without a penny.' Eamon shook his head disapprovingly.

'She was a doctor, wasn't she?' Bobbi asked, trying not to sound too curious.

'Yes, that's right, still is probably. Although she could have been struck off.'

'How do you mean?'

'Well her family's business was pharmaceuticals, and let's just say that it was an unfortunate irony that she had an unhealthy relationship with more than one drug that I know of. The last I heard of it, she was living in the States. Like I said, Steve's better off without her. She was very attractive, very brilliant but very unbalanced.'

'Poor Steve,' Bobbi said thoughtfully.

'Indeed,' said Eamonn. 'He certainly came out of it the worse, not just financially, but Dublin being Dublin, well, people love to gossip you know. Her family were quick to put about the rumour that Steve had been after *her* money. Can you imagine?' Eamonn chuckled. 'Steve Sorenson a fortune hunter? Well it's a ridiculous idea, but I can see how the whole business must have left a very bitter taste in his mouth.'

'I can understand that.'

'He's a simply marvellous chap, and I must say I owe him a debt of gratitude for putting you in touch with us.'

'Oh, please don't say anything to Steve about this,' Bobbi said hurriedly. 'He, well, you know how he hates any attention being drawn to himself. I promised I wouldn't actually mention his name.'

'Oh, quite, quite, Bobbi.' Eamonn tucked into his lamb with relish. 'You can count on my discretion. Mum's the word.'

Later that afternoon, Bobbi was driven home deep in thought.

So Steve *was* a gambler, but not quite the one Chris Carroll had made him out to be. According to his bank, he was a very valued client and certainly didn't appear to be under any financial strain – quite the contrary. No, the problem was more complex than that, and unfortunately money was at least *part* of the issue – it *always* was. She sighed, sitting back into the deeply soft leather seats as her driver negotiated the early evening traffic. Why was she even vaguely surprised? Men's egos were as fragile as they were large. A woman who was far wealthier than the man in her life was bound to be in for a hard run romantically. Never mind a man who'd been through it all before – to his detriment.

But what was new about that? All her life Bobbi had been taking on men in and out of the boardroom – and mostly coming out on top. If Steve was bothered about being considered a fortune hunter, he was just going to have to get over it, because Bobbi had realised months ago she was head over heels in love with him, and she was sure he felt the same way. A feeling like this didn't come along often in any lifetime – and if it meant going out on a limb and taking a risk to make him realise this, she was the woman to do it.

Niamh was on her way home from the hospital when she decided to take a detour. It had been weeks since she had been down to the cottages, partly because of demands on her time and partly because she couldn't face seeing her little home again knowing it was about to be brutally demolished.

It was early December, and as soon as she pulled her car up outside her cottage, she knew it had been a mistake. The row of cottages looked infinitely forlorn. Where once there would have been Christmas wreaths on doors, and the merry twinkle of Christmas lights on trees and a welcome candle in a window, there now was nothing but an atmosphere of abandonment. The cottages were sectioned off by tapes, and a makeshift site office had been constructed at the entrance to the little green where, on many a summer's day, they had all sat. Several skips were full of the debris of previous lifetimes and a bulldozer sat ominously waiting to be galvanised into action. Niamh sat in her little car and furiously brushed away the tears that she had been keeping at bay for so long. Turning on the ignition, she drove away, vowing never, ever to look back.

Ce

Niamh drove in to Grovesbury Hall seconds after Bobbi had pulled in and got out of the car wearily to join Bobbi who was waiting on the steps for her. 'You look all done in. How's Nellie doing?'

'She's pretty much the same as yesterday,' Niamh said, as they went in the front door. 'She's stable, but still very weak.'

'Bobbi! Niamh!' Alex called down to them excitedly as she peered over the banisters from the first return. 'Come quickly, you're not going to believe this.'

Bobbi and Niamh followed her as she ran back up the vast staircase taking the steps two at a time.

'What on earth's going on?' asked Bobbi, taking in the trail of water damage that began on the ceiling of the first floor and appeared to lead to a trail of further exploratory damage as they ascended to the top of the house.

'It started at lunch time, when you were out,' Alex explained breathlessly. 'When the builders came to fix it we left them to it. But they had to follow the trail to its source which was in here.' They all traipsed into the little turret room that Bobbi had turned into her office. 'Oh my God!' Bobbi gasped in horror as she looked at a three-foot hole in the wall. 'Was this really necessary?'

'Ho-*oh* yes!' said a deep voice Bobbi realised belonged to a head that was now peering out of the hole in the wall. 'If I hadn't seen this with me own eyes I wouldn't have believed it myself, Missus. This piping is all top notch and brand spanking new, but it looks like some smartass has deliberately opened up a pipe here – although how they could have done that and then plastered the thing over is beyond me.' The builder shook his head in disbelief.

'It's weird. That's what it is, just weird,' said his workmate. 'Like something from *Tales of the Unexpected*.'

'That's the best bit, Bobbi!' Alex could hardly get the words out she was so excited. 'Look what they found under the plasterwork.'

Bobbi followed her directions but, peering into the hole, could see only darkness until the builder shone a torch in. 'See this panelling? Well I was feeling around for the pipe and lo and behold the wall started to move! It didn't half scare the gizzard outta me!'

'It's a secret room, Bobbi! Think how old it must be,' Alex said. 'We didn't feel it was right to go into it until you were here. So go on, take a look.'

'Rather you than me, love!' said the builder, handing her the torch. 'These old places have seen some pretty hairy goings on in their time.'

'Yeah,' said his pal. 'Watch out for the Boogie Man!'

'We'll be right behind you, Bobbi,' said Niamh, crossing herself silently.

Bobbi took the torch, and a very deep breath, before climbing in through the broken plaster. For a moment, all she could take in was the musty smell of sealed-off air as she cast the torch around the tiny room. Then she gasped.

'What is it?' asked Alex sounding terrified.

'Look!' Bobbi's hand began to tremble as she motioned with the torch. 'Over there, by the wall. Can you get some proper flash lights?' She nodded to the builders. 'Looks like we're going to need them.'

One by one, they all clambered through the hole.

'It's a trunk,' said Niamh breathlessly, as Bobbi went over slowly and got down on her knees to try it.

'No good, it's locked.' She looked back at Niamh and the others who were watching with bated breath. 'What's that noise?' she added, cocking her head to listen to the small, scraping, repetitive sound.

'Looks like it won't be locked for long,' said Rowan, who had just come up with a powerful flashlight from his studio. 'Look at that,' he said quietly, directing the light to a spot on the wall.

As Bobbi looked, she saw a large, black key hanging on a nail in the wall above the trunk. She watched – they all did – mesmerised, as it swung slowly back and forth until, before their very eyes, it came off its nail and fell on to the trunk, before dropping onto the floor in front of Bobbi.

'Holy Moly!' said Rowan.

'Jesus, Mary and Joseph!' said Niamh, crossing herself.

'I'm getting out of here,' said Alex.

'Bring me the other light,' said Bobbi calmly to Rowan. 'I'm going to open this.'

24

The key fitted perfectly. Just as she had known it would. It turned, stuck for a moment and then, with another twist, unlocked. All the lights were fixed on the trunk, which now stood eerily illuminated in the otherwise darkened room. Bobbi lifted the bow-shaped top slowly, and it creaked backwards, coming to rest on long unused hinges.

'What's in it?' whispered Niamh.

'It looks like clothes,' said Bobbi, carefully lifting out the items one by one. First a small jacket, followed by a white stock with a gold tie pin still inserted. Then a pair of riding breeches, and a pair of still muddy boots.

'Who do you suppose they belonged to?' wondered Rowan.

'Lady Arabella, maybe?' ventured Alex, who had managed to stay in the room – avid curiosity overcoming her earlier misgivings.

'They're way too small for an adult. Maybe it was her childhood hunting outfit?' Bobbi held up the small jacket and looked at it thoughtfully.

'Look, there are photos and news-clippings,' said Rowan curiously.

Slowly, Bobbi laid all the items out carefully on the floor. The clothes, the photos and news-clippings, a few old faded papers and the strangest item of all, a bracelet made out of what looked like hair wired together very carefully, with a small white label attached to it by a thread.

'Let's get these outside into the light where we can get a proper look at them,' said Bobbi. 'Here, you take the photos Rowan. Niamh, the papers, and I'll take the clothes.'

Back in Bobbi's office, everyone crowded round to have a look.

'What do you make of it?' Rowan asked.

'Be careful,' Alex said anxiously, 'they might be valuable.'

Bobbi smiled up at her. 'I think they were only valuable to the person who stowed them so carefully. And if we're lucky, we're about to find out who that was.'

'This photo is definitely Lady Arabella. You can recognise her from the portrait,' said Rowan. 'Look on the back, "Arabella and Monty, July 1929".'

'And this, look, it's a clipping of her wedding day. That must be Lord Grovesbury.' Niamh pointed to a handsome-looking, heavily moustached man gazing adoringly at a young Arabella in a glorious wedding dress.

'Who's this?' Alex pointed to another faded photo of a child of about nine or ten grinning broadly as he sat proudly astride a horse. Bobbi picked up the photo and turned it over. 'Bertie on his ninth birthday with Montyson, given to him September 1940.'

'Bertie must have been their son,' said Rowan. 'Look, there's that marking again on the horse's forehead. It's the same star shaped pattern – just like Old Chestnut.'

'So what became of Bertie then?' wondered Niamh aloud. 'The title died with Lady Arabella.'

'Oh, God,' murmured Alex, 'look at this.' She held one of the news-clippings in her hand which now shook slightly. In a halting voice, she read quietly, "'TRAGEDY OF HEIR TO GROVESBURY ESTATES: In a freak accident on the hunting field, Bertie Grovesbury, only son and child of Lord Albert and Lady Arabella Grovesbury, was killed instantly on Saturday when he fell from his horse and broke his neck. He died in his father's arms. Lord and Lady Grovesbury remain inconsolable." It's dated 1941, he must have been only ten years old.'

'Read the others,' urged Niamh, as a sudden hush descended on the room.

'It's more of the same,' said Bobbi quietly. 'Here are the official death notices from *The Irish Times* and the London *Times*, and this, oh Lord, how sad.' Bobbi shook her head as she read. "'THE END OF AN ERA, HORSES LEAVE GROVESBURY HALL: In a sad development following the tragic death of Lord and Lady Grovesbury's only son and heir last week, Lord Grovesbury has decreed that all horses be banned from his family seat, Grovesbury Hall. The National Stud and the Aga Khan are believed to be negotiating for most of the immensely valuable bloodstock, lovingly bred over the last twenty years by Lady Arabella and her family before her. Montyson, by Lady Arabella's famous Monty, was shot by Lord Grovesbury himself on the hunting field, following the tragic death of his son when he fell from the horse."'

'These must be his clothes,' said Bobbi quietly, folding the small jacket carefully. 'She must have locked everything away when he died – how tragic.'

'Man, it's heavy stuff,' said Rowan. 'What about the papers, Niamh?'

Niamh glanced down distractedly at the papers she held in her arms and flicked through them. 'Hard to tell, they look like some old maps and stuff. I'll take them into the Land Registry – I'm back to work on Monday – and see if they're anything interesting, but I doubt it. They mostly seem like old legal letters.'

'Good idea,' said Rowan.

'And what about this?' asked Alex, handing the bracelet of hair to Bobbi. 'Do you think it's … you know, her son's hair? A memento.'

Bobbi took the bracelet in her hands and fingered it. 'It's a memento all right, but I don't think it's the son's hair.' She held the circle of hair to her nose and breathed in. 'Wait a minute, there was a label on this wasn't there?'

'There, look it's on the floor beside you.' Niamh pointed to the small white label attached to a piece of thread that had fallen off.

Bobbi picked it up and looked at the immaculately scripted words in ink and read slowly, '"Monty, my beloved friend, 1915–1942". But this is wonderful!' Bobbi said, looking up with shining eyes. 'This must be a piece of Monty's mane.'

'What's so wonderful about that?' chorused Rowan, Alex and Niamh, looking completely puzzled.

'Don't you see?' Bobbi leapt to her feet. 'If this is Monty's – the *original* Monty's – mane, then we have an answer!'

'To what?' Rowan looked at her as if she was mad.

'*My* Old Chestnut – all we have to do is send a sample of Old Chestnut's hair in with *this* bracelet, get them DNA tested and we'll know if he's Montyson III, stolen from the RDS all those years ago. Just like Nellie said.'

Bobbi was sitting in the small library where a warming log fire was crackling when she heard Steve press the front-door intercom. She knocked back a quick gulp of champagne and tried desperately to ignore the insistent thumping of her heart. How ironic it was that she, one of the most successful businesswomen in the world, who had clawed her way up the career ladder to take on the big boys, could be reduced to a jittery mass by one emotionally confused, if undeniably handsome, Irishman.

'Dr Sorenson to see you, Bobbi.' Polly the housekeeper

showed Steve in to the cosy room smiling broadly. She had a soft spot for Steve and couldn't help thinking what a handsome couple he and Bobbi made.

'Sorry I'm late.' Steve eased himself into a large brown leather armchair opposite Bobbi. 'I came as soon as I could when I got your message.'

'That's okay.' Bobbi was cool. 'Drink?'

'Er, yes. Thanks. I'll have whatever you're having.' Steve's eyes followed her as she got up to fetch another glass. The cream cashmere wrap dress she wore clung like a second skin and showed off her fabulously long-limbed body in a most unsettling way.

'Cheers,' said Steve, unsuccessfully trying to avert his eyes from the enticing inch of cleavage that could be glimpsed from the deep V-neck, particularly when Bobbi leaned forward ever so slightly to reach for her glass as she did now.

'Cheers,' she said, crossing well-toned legs and stretching them out in front of her, making infuriatingly distracting circles with one elegant foot encased in a brown suede high-heeled shoe.

Steve forced himself to concentrate. He was beginning to feel edgy. If he hadn't known better, he would have had the distinct impression that Bobbi was laughing at him. He cleared his throat and tried not to think about the loosely tied knot at her side that, if undone, would unravel the whole, infinitely gorgeous package.

'I, uh, sent off the two samples of horse hair to UCD for DNA testing. It'll be about a week before we get results,' he said, running a hand through his hair.

'Great,' said Bobbi, looking him directly in the eye as she twirled a strand of hair around her finger.

She didn't attempt to fill the silence that ensued. Steve found himself shifting uncomfortably in his chair.

'It would be an extraordinary coincidence if Old Chestnut *did* turn out to be the missing Montyson. Despite the similar markings, you do realise what a long shot it is?'

'I like long shots. It's how I made my fortune.' A slow smile played around her mouth.

Steve was taken aback at the sudden reference to money. It was most unlike her to mention it, but then the Bobbi sitting across the fire from him seemed distinctly unfamiliar. It wasn't that she was being cold or unfriendly or even businesslike – all of which he could have dealt with – it was more as if she knew something he didn't and was enjoying every minute of her new-found knowledge. 'Its okay, Steve. I know how uncomfortable my money must make you feel. After all, it can't be easy if you're struggling to get by. I guess having an obscenely wealthy woman in your life didn't help things,' Bobbi said, sounding genuinely sympathetic. 'I fully understand why you couldn't cope.'

Steve nearly choked on his drink. 'What?'

'You heard me.'

'Look I have no idea how you got it into your head that I'm … I'm *struggling*, as you put it, but that is most certainly *not* the case. Who the hell have you been talking to?' Steve leapt from his chair and began to pace the room.

'Nobody,' Bobbi said innocently. 'I'm just assuming that your practice must have high overheads. Then you've been through a divorce. Then there's your free animal clinic and everything, which is laudable by any standards – but, well, it can't be easy.' Bobbi held her breath. She knew she was pushing it and there was a very thin line here that would be disastrous to cross.

Steve turned to look at her from the far side of the room. 'I may be short of certain things in my life, Bobbi,' the even tone failed to disguise the anger in his voice, 'but money certainly isn't one of them. I could retire in the morning if I wished to. And very comfortably, I might add.'

Bobbi chewed her lip and tried very hard not to laugh. It was now or never. She put down her drink, got up and walked purposefully towards him. Slowly she untied the knot of cashmere at her side and shrugged the dress off her shoulders, from where it slipped soundlessly to the floor.

'What are you doing, Bobbi?' Steve was finding it hard to speak as he watched her unhook her bra while holding his gaze, leaving only a silk suspender belt and a whisp of a thong clinging to the glorious body that had invaded his days and nights since he had last seen her. Despite himself, he caught his breath. She was face to face with him now and slipping the fingers of one hand suggestively inside the top of the shimmering silk stockings that clung to the never-ending legs.

'I'm taking a gamble,' she said suggestively.

'On what?'

'On you having the best night of your life.' Her glance was provocative. 'If you don't – you walk away.'

'And if I do?' Steve swallowed hard.

Bobbi smiled evilly. 'It comes at a price.'

'How much?' Steve reached out to hook his hand around her neck feeling seriously turned on.

'How much am I worth, Steve?' Bobbi arched away from him. 'You name the price. Until then, you can look, but no touching.'

'Don't be ridiculous.' Steve felt himself get rock hard.

'I never joke about money.' The suggestive smile still played about her luscious mouth. 'And it *is* only money, Steve. I've got plenty of it, you say you could retire in the morning – so what's the problem? Unless you insist on making it one of course.' Bobbi held her breath.

'What are the odds?'

'On what?'

'On us making it?' He trailed a finger along her jaw, making her shiver.

'Who knows? But right now, they're leaning considerably in your favour.' Bobbi allowed her glance to drop pointedly. 'If you're up for it, that is.'

'I think you can safely guess the answer to that. I'm willing to take a risk if you are.'

'Money up front,' demanded Bobbi as she knelt down and unhooked his belt.

'I'll write the cheque now,' Steve groaned.

'I was hoping you'd say that.'

Cee

Niamh was at work and enjoying her mid-morning cup of tea and a digestive biscuit when the telephone rang. From the extension number that flashed up, she could see it was Eileen in deeds.

'Niamh.' Eileen was as brisk as ever. 'Those papers you gave me?'

'Did you get a chance to look over them, Eileen?'

'I did, and there's nothing earth shattering in them.'

'Oh,' said Niamh, feeling deflated. She wasn't sure what she had hoped for, but somehow the whole trunk incident had seemed portentous to her.

'Mostly maps of the original estate and old legal corres-pondence. I don't imagine they'll be of much interest to anyone except the present owner, you know. If she wants to get a couple of them framed or something. Oh, there was something rather curious though, now that I think of it.'

'What?'

'Well, it's probably nothing, but there was one letter from a firm of solicitors – McBride & Whitaker, I think. Wait a minute till I get it … Here it is … Yes, addressed to the second Lord Grovesbury, dated 1903.'

'Go on.'

'Well, it's referring to changes in the deeds having been amended "as your Lordship requested" … Where are we?' Eileen paused infuriatingly as she flicked through more pages. 'Oh here we are, yes, "regarding the properties comprising thirty-four newly built cottages known as Grovesbury Gardens".'

Niamh had a sudden sharp intake of breath. 'What else does it say, Eileen?'

'That's it. There's nothing more. You'd have to have a look at whatever deeds they were referring to.'

'Where would I find them?'

'They could be with the solicitors, if that firm are still around. If not, well, you know yourself, Niamh, a lot of that old stuff would have been destroyed in 1922.'

'Thanks, Eileen,' Niamh said thoughtfully. 'I appreciate you taking the time to look at them for me.'

'No problem. I'm sorry I can't be more specific.'

Niamh put down the phone and immediately reached for the phone book on a shelf beside her desk. She flicked through it quickly, her eyes scanning down the pages of business listings until she came to it. It stared back at her, clearly printed in large type. McBride & Whitaker, Solrs, 46 Fitzwilliam Square, Dublin 2.

Cee

Steve was in the surgery when the call came through.

'It's UCD for you, Steve,' said Lucy, popping her head around the door. 'The DNA lab. I told them you were busy. Will I say you'll call them back?'

Steve put the final touches to the dressing he had applied to the injured paw of the handsome gundog he was treating and shook his head. 'No, Lucy, I'll take it next door.' Lifting the dog down from the table, he showed patient and owner out and went in to the small room off the surgery to take the call.

'Dr Sorenson here.'

'Steve, it's Julia. We've got the results of the horse hair samples you sent in.' Steve listened to voice of his old friend and colleague.

Steve smiled. Why was it that people giving test results always seemed to enjoy that split second of prior knowledge? 'And?'

'It's a match. Straight up, ninety-five per cent compatibility. Same bloodline definitely. Is that significant?'

'Yep.' Steve was grinning from ear to ear. 'That's great, Julia. I think we can safely say it's significant. Thanks a lot, I appreciate you giving this priority. You'll fax me through the details?'

'For you, Steve, anything.'

25

Old Chestnut, or Montyson III, now that he was officially recognised, was enjoying his new-found notoriety greatly. Once his bloodline had been confirmed, events had gained momentum by the minute. As his rightful owner, the Aga Khan himself had been alerted immediately and had sent a message of thanks and congratulations to Bobbi. News of the extraordinary story was spreading like wildfire, and not just in bloodstock circles. Since his disappearance had been just over twelve years ago, most people remembered the story. Now, Montyson's reappearance and the realisation that he had been nursed back to health through the dedication of one of the most glamorous women in the world was catching the imagination of the national and international press. It was one heck of a feel-good story – and just in time for Christmas. Already reporters were clamouring on Bobbi's doorstep with camera crews hot on their heels.

Bobbi recounted the story a hundred times and answered

the endless questions as best she could. In the meantime, Montyson was walked around the courtyard, stopping occasionally to pose regally for photographers.

It was one such particularly charming shot of Bobbi standing beside Montyson while he nuzzled her shoulder that Chris Carroll found himself staring at while he sat in Malcolm McBride's office. The article was effusive in its praise for Bobbi and, along with the story of Montyson's rescue and recovery, was quick to link in to the theme of 'waifs and strays' residing at Grovesbury Hall. Written by the same reporter who had been to see Nellie, the article referred to Bobbi as the "millionairess with a one in a million social conscience" and mentioned again the proposed, and much objected to, development of Grovesbury Gardens.

'I warned you that woman would be trouble.' Malcolm drummed the desk nervously. 'I told you we should have got her on board.'

'There's nothing she, or anyone else, can do now, Malcolm. The builders are already underway with the demolition. They started on the cottages today. By this time tomorrow, Grovesbury Gardens will be the Ground Zero of Dublin 4.' Chris sounded bored, 'And not before bloody time.'

Ce

'We can't just sit here and let him get away with it!' Rowan paced the kitchen floor furiously.

'There's nothing we can do Rowan.' Steve frowned. 'It's all legit. I don't like the idea of it any more than you do, but you might as well accept it.'

'Niamh was really upset after she called around to the cottages the other day.' Alex sipped her wine. 'She said she wished she hadn't.'

I know the feeling,' said Bobbi sympathetically. 'There's nothing worse than trying to recapture the past. Steve's right, Rowan, just let it go. Grovesbury Gardens is history.'

'It's been quite a week,' said Steve, articulating all their thoughts. With all the hullaballoo over Montyson's re-appearance, the fate of Grovesbury Gardens had been put on the back burner. Now, sitting in the kitchen after dinner, the sense of anti-climax weighed heavily.

'It may be too late to stop Chris in his mercenary tracks,' Rowan sat down with a grin, 'but it's not too late to make it painful for him in the process.'

'How do you mean?' Alex looked worried.

'I think a little demonstration is in order. A tribute, if you like, to part and parcel of *real* Dublin 4, and the people who made it what it is. A fitting farewell party. The 4s fighting back so to speak.'

'I'm not sure I like the sound of this.' Bobbi grinned as she shook her head. 'But I'm up for it if you guys are.'

'Roll up your sleeves then, people, it's going to be a long night. We're talking serious strategy here. Speaking of which, where's Niamh?'

'She's working late,' said Alex. 'She said she'd be back by nine.'

'Good, let's get started then. We haven't a minute to waste.'

A couple of hours later things were well under way. While Bobbi scribbled a selection of rousing slogans, Rowan organised the various placards and banners to be carried, and had called in a few delighted art students to help draw them up. Alex and Steve were making phone call after phone call to round up as many friends and call in whatever personal favours they could to drum up support.

By the time Niamh arrived home, Bobbi's designer kitchen resembled the hub of a political party on the eve of a presidential election. 'What on earth is going on?' Niamh looked around in bemusement.

'Just a little farewell demonstration we're going to stage to give Chris and his cronies something to think about.' Rowan grinned as he held up one of the more lurid placards.

'Any luck at the land registry, Niamh?' Steve asked.

'I'm afraid not.' Niamh sat down wearily 'There was something – at least I thought it might be some sort of a lead – but it turned out to be a red herring.'

'What was that?' Bobbi was curious.

'A letter from a firm of solicitors called McBride & Whitaker referring to some sort of change to the deeds relating to Grovesbury Gardens.' Niamh paused to take the cup of coffee Alex handed her.

'They're the firm Chris uses,' Alex said, chewing her lip. 'Malcolm McBride is his solicitor. I can't stand the little creep.'

'Are you sure?' Rowan frowned.

'I ought to be. It's on the letterhead of that charming piece of correspondence I received from him.' Alex threw him a look.

'Of course.' Rowan looked contrite. 'Sorry, I should have thought of that.'

'Alex is right,' said Niamh. 'I rang them anyway and spoke to the secretary. She was very nice, but said that any papers dated earlier than 1921 would have been destroyed when the firm's offices were burnt down, and the letter we found in the trunk was dated 1903.'

'Well, that's that, I suppose,' Bobbi sighed. 'Anyway, we've done all we possibly can, under the circumstances.'

'Is there anything I can do?' Niamh asked.

'Nope, we're pretty much all done – apart from the art department.' Bobbi smiled as she watched Rowan and the students painting furiously. 'I'm going to have a long hot soak and get some sleep. You should too, Niamh. You look exhausted.'

'I think I will.' Niamh drained her coffee and got up. 'I've got a thumping headache that I have a horrible feeling is turning into a migraine. I haven't had one for years, but this one is showing promising symptoms.'

'Off you go,' said Rowan. 'We'll reconvene tomorrow at ten o'clock sharp, and make sure you're wearing comfortable shoes, girls, you're going to be on your feet for quite a while.'

Alex followed Bobbi and Niamh upstairs to check on the children and left the guys to finish up in the kitchen.

'Oh, by the way,' Bobbi said, turning to Niamh, 'I had Lady Arabella's trunk put in your room, underneath the window. Polly had it cleaned and polished. It's a nice old piece, and it looks good there. I couldn't think where else it could go. Feel free to use it for storage or whatever.'

'Thanks, Bobbi,' Niamh placed her hand on Bobbi's arm, 'for everything, you know, I never, well, I - I never thanked you properly. And I don't know what I, what any of us would have done without you.'

'No need.' Bobbi smiled. 'I'm happy I could help. I just wish things could have turned out differently.'

'Me too.'

'Now go and get some sleep. Have you got any pills for that headache of yours?'

'Yes, I do, thanks. Night, Bobbi.' Niamh went into her room and closed the door softly behind her.

Once inside, she undressed quickly and went straight to the bathroom and took two Nurofen Plus, then washed her face and brushed her teeth and clambered wearily into bed. Exhausted though she was, sleep eluded her. The thumping in her head was now accompanied by blurred vision and nausea, and she lay still in the darkness willing the pills to take effect. She hadn't had a migraine in years, but given all the stress of the last few weeks, and considering most of the day had been spent pouring over all the old documents from the trunk, she supposed it wasn't surprising.

She thought about the demonstration Rowan and the others were organising and smiled despite herself. Nellie would have loved to be part of it! Then it struck her. She hadn't been to see her today. She had meant to call in on her way back from work, but the headache was taking hold by then. When she did get home, all the talk about the demonstration had distracted her. Oh well, poor Nellie wouldn't mind. Niamh resolved to call and sit with her for a while tomorrow. Whatever else, Niamh knew she wouldn't be able to face joining the demonstration. It would be far too upsetting. She would prefer to remember her little cottage and the others as they had been – cheerful, pretty and warmly welcoming.

As a cool breeze blew the muslin curtain back from the window, Niamh watched in the darkness as the old trunk was silhouetted briefly by a shaft of moonlight before she drifted into a disturbed sleep. Tossing and turning through the night, she dreamt fitfully, waking every couple of hours. At one stage she was sure she felt someone in the room, but turning on the bedside lamp saw nothing but the curtain blowing softly. Worn out from the migraine that was now thankfully abating, she took two more pills and fell finally into exhausted oblivion.

In her small room in St Vincent's Private Nursing Home, Nellie had taken a turn for the worse. But, as she prepared to make her final exit from this world, Nellie was not alone. 'So you're still here,' she whispered, looking at him standing beside her bed. 'I suppose you're going to hang around to see it all through, but I'm just too tired.' She smiled, reaching out to take the hand he offered her.

'Mrs Murphy?' the night nurse whispered as she leaned over her and checked for a pulse.

But Nellie had quietly slipped away. The nurse noted the time of death. It was four-thirty a.m.

Bobbi got the call that Nellie had passed away and decided there was no need to tell any of the others until the morning. She put down the phone and settled back to get some sleep. Wherever Nellie was, she felt sure she was at peace.

The next morning dawned bright and clear. In the kitchen Polly was cooking a full Irish breakfast to give sustenance for whatever travails the day ahead would bring. She was looking forward to the demonstration herself, particularly as head-quarters were at Grovesbury Hall, which would give her version of events immense credibility when the time came to share them.

Rowan was the first down, followed by Alex, and it was there that Bobbi joined them and told them the sad news of Nellie.

'Niamh will be so upset,' said Alex. 'Have you told her yet, Bobbi?'

'No, she's still asleep. I knocked on her door earlier. I'll go up again after breakfast, but I think it's best to let her sleep on for the moment. She wasn't in good shape last night.'

'Well,' said Rowan, raising his cup of steaming coffee, 'here's to Nellie, wherever she is I'm sure she'll be with us in spirit.'

26

News of the demonstration had reached the media and Melissa was the first on the road to be troubled.

'Excuse me, Mrs Sheehan.' Maria, knocked respectfully on her door. 'There is someone who ask for you from TV2000. You want to talk to them? Or I tell them to go?'

'Oh, Jaysus.' Melissa was not expecting any callers at eleven o'clock in the morning. Nonetheless, one couldn't afford to miss a media opportunity. No one understood better than Melissa the fickle nature of the press – and she wanted them on her side. She tried frantically to think what they could possibly want to consult her about and played for time. It was probably just some forthcoming charity event or fashion show. 'Ask them to wait in the informal drawing room, Maria. I'll be down as soon as I can.' Jumping quickly into J-Lo type sweat pants and a cut-off top, Melissa peered in the mirror and assessed her newly dermo-braisioned complexion. Deciding it just might pass for a post-workout glow, she risked going bare-faced, save for a quick daub of Bobbi L lip gloss, and hurried downstairs.

'Hi there!' she said, bursting into the room with verve. 'How *are* you guys?' Melissa took in the videocam and recognised the reporter from Carol Dalton's slot *Carol Calls*.

'Melissa,' the reporter gushed, 'it's *so* good of you to talk to us at such short notice. But we felt you, if anyone, could give us a true, heartfelt account of the devastating demolition going on in your backyard. What are your feelings about the soon-to-be-no-more Grovesbury Gardens?'

For a split second Melissa was stymied. She tried desperately to remember whether or not Pascal was involved in the proposed development and seemed to remember he had backed out – much to Chris Carroll's anger. Safe in this knowledge, she launched forth with gusto, like the veritable media prima donna she had become. 'Quite frankly,' she began, 'I'm appalled at what's happening.' She sank down gracefully into a suede-covered sofa and crossed her legs, forgetting the price tag was still reassuringly fresh on her platform runners. 'Of course, my husband and I were against it from the beginning. The minute Chr– that is, *our neighbour* proposed the scheme we objected *strenuously*.' Melissa paused for breath. 'To think that those poor people are being evicted from their homes just because of some greedy property developer's insatiable appetite is just unthinkable.' She shook her head sadly.

'Your husband, Pascal Sheehan, is a heavy hitter among the property boys, Melissa. How does he feel about it?'

'Pascal and I, share the same convictions.' Melissa looked meaningfully to camera. 'We both know what it's like to value a roof over our heads. Pascal and I have worked hard to provide the lifestyle we enjoy today, but we are resolute that nothing but *nothing* is worth causing, or indeed adding to, the distress of another human being. As you know, Pascal was responsible for the recent development of the St Rita's site. He provided additional housing and a leisure centre for single mothers out of his own pocket, I might remind you.'

'Will you be playing an active part in the demonstration yourself, Melissa?' The reporter blinked innocently at her.

Melissa hesitated only for a nanosecond. 'Why I thought that would have been obvious from my outfit, Clodagh,' she giggled. 'Buildings may topple, bricks may crumble – but it'll take more than a bulldozer to flatten the spirit of true Dubliners. One of whom, I might add, I am proud to count myself as. If I were you, I'd watch this space, Tiananmen Square will have nothing on Grovesbury Gardens. Now, if you'll excuse me, I really must dash. I have a demonstration to attend.'

Carmela Walshe was walking back from ten o'clock mass in Donnybrook Church when she swept onto Grovesbury Road. At first she didn't notice the commotion taking place in her driveway. Then, drawing near to her home she saw a couple of Jeeps and what appeared to be a cameraman and various reporters watching in delight as Marysol was filmed lounging nonchalantly in the doorway, holding forth her opinions. From an upstairs window, Padraig was waving frantically to warn his mother off, but by the time she saw him, it was too late. The collective pack had sensed even meatier quarry and they rounded on Carmela excitedly. 'Mrs Walshe, is it true you and your husband are involved in the development company responsible for the demolition of Grovesbury Gardens?'

'Your daughter tells us you and your husband are involved in an ongoing vendetta with Bobbi Levinsky and her house guests. Would you care to comment?'

'Is it true that you and your husband were responsible for putting an old-age pensioner out of her cottage?'

'Is it true Marysol and Rowan Delaney are planning to marry in the New Year?'

Tanya Sykes was strongly considering going into the panic room she and Rod had fortuitously installed. After Melissa had rung her to warn her of reporters on the prowl, and the imminent demonstration against the development in Grovesbury Gardens, she had battened down all hatches securely. That was one of the perks of being a telecoms millionaire: there were more high-tech security systems in the Sykes' home than in the latest Bond movie. Rod never took any chances with their privacy, and would be livid if he thought any adverse publicity might be created.

Satisfied that nothing bar a scud missile could gain entry to her home, she took several deep breaths and went upstairs to relax in an oxygenated whirlpool bath.

Downstairs, Nathan had easily escaped his nanny's clutches by telling her they were making a movie outside and were looking for pretty extras. Now, from the control room in Rod's private office, he was watching proceedings on the road with interest. Any threats of prospective punishment that might be meted out by his parents happily dissolved on seeing Rowan Delaney walk by with a large placard, followed by an exotic crowd of chanting demonstrators. With impeccable timing, Nathan pressed a button and the electric gates opened, followed swiftly by the front door.

It was therefore with a certain element of surprise that Tanya Sykes, almost, but not quite, submerged in bubbles, greeted the eager crowd of reporters and cameras that her son, Nathan, led proudly into her state-of-the-art bathroom. 'Mum,' he said gleefully, 'there's some people who want to talk to you.'

Cee

It was noon when Niamh awoke with a start to the soft knocking on her bedroom door.

'Niamh? It's Polly. I just wanted to check that you were all right? Can I come in?'

'What? Oh, yes, sure, Polly.' Niamh sat up in bed feeling

drained, but thankfully her migraine seemed to have gone. 'What time is it?' she asked, feeling confused as sunlight flooded the room. 'I must have overslept.'

'Niamh,' said Polly, sitting down on the bed beside her, 'I'm afraid Nellie passed away last night – well, at four-thirty this morning, actually. Bobbi didn't want to wake you to tell you, so I ... Well, I said I would. I'm sorry, Niamh. I know how close you were to her.'

'Oh, no,' whispered Niamh, her eyes filling with tears. 'I meant to go and see her. Yesterday was the only day I didn't go to see her, and now she's gone.'

'The nurse said it was very peaceful. Really, Niamh, you mustn't upset yourself. Sure she wasn't even conscious for the last two days. Honestly, she just slipped away in her sleep. She wouldn't have known a thing – and she wouldn't want you to be unhappy. You know that's the last thing she'd want.' Polly patted Niamh's hand.

'I knew she was dying in my heart I suppose,' Niamh sniffed. 'I just didn't want to admit it to myself. She was the last link I had to my own mother, you see.'

'Of course, and you were as good to her as any daughter could have been – better even.' Polly smiled. 'Now you have a good rest. I'm going to bring you up some tea and toast, and you're to take it easy. Bobbi said so.' Polly was firm. 'How's the head?'

'The migraine's gone – but I'm feeling a bit washed out, I suppose. I can't believe I've slept for so long.' Niamh rubbed her eyes.

'You've been through a lot lately, Niamh. You all have.'

'Oh, the demonstration. I forgot, have they –'

'The others left this morning. Bobbi said there was no way you'd be up to it and you were to take it easy. It sounds like good advice to me.' Polly got up and made for the door. 'Now I'm going to bring you up that tea, I'll be back in a jiffy.'

Niamh sank back against the pillows and closed her eyes. She felt somehow as if events were overtaking her, and there was nothing she could do. She thought of all the times she and Nellie had spent together and smiled. Nellie had had a good life and in many ways an extraordinary one, considering her psychic talents. In the end, she had had the best possible care among people who loved her. Niamh would miss her, of course, but she was glad that Nellie hadn't suffered a debilitating old age and had been sprightly right up to the stroke. It was funny, she thought, how everything came to an end sooner or later. Today would see the end of Grovesbury Gardens and another era, and no amount of demonstrating was going to change that.

Mentally shaking herself out of her maudlin reverie, she opened her eyes to the sunlight flooding in through the window and then gasped, her hands flying to her mouth. There, under the window as it had been last night, was Lady Arabella's trunk, but it stood now with its top wide open on its hinges. For a moment Niamh was frozen. She knew it had been shut last night, locked, with the key still in it, and she hadn't so much as touched it. Just then, Polly came bustling back in with Niamh's tea and toast. 'Now, here we are. Why whatever's the matter, Niamh? You look as if you've seen a ghost.' Polly put the tray down beside Niamh, concern written all over her face.

'The trunk,' said Niamh, slowly.

'What about it? I polished it myself yesterday, it came up a treat.'

'It was shut. Last night it was shut and … and now it's open.'

'Niamh,' Polly shook her head and smiled, 'you must have opened it last night yourself. You probably don't remember, what with your headache and all.'

'I never touched it. I swear,' Niamh said emphatically.

'Look, if it's bothering you, I'll shut it.' Polly made for the window.

'No. No, Polly, don't. It doesn't matter, really. You're right, I'm just being silly.'

'Niamh, are you all right? Will I get the doctor? Bobbi said if there was any –'

Niamh cut her off mid sentence. 'No, Polly, I'm fine, really. I'm just a bit overwrought. Don't bother about me. I'll have my tea and get up and have a nice soak in the bath and I'll be fine. Go on, I'll be down in about an hour, and thanks for the tea.' Niamh smiled encouragingly at Polly, willing her to go.

'Well, if you're sure.' Polly hesitated.

'I'm positive. If there's no sign of me in an hour, you call the men in white coats with my blessing.'

'Well if you need anything just shout.' Polly left the room closing the door behind her. Really, she thought to herself, the sooner all this business with Grovesbury Gardens was over the better. Then they might all be able to resume some sort of normality.

As soon as Polly had gone, Niamh pushed aside the breakfast tray and got out of bed. She went straight over to the trunk where she stood for a minute or two looking at it thoughtfully, her arms folded and a frown of concentration on her face. Could she have opened it last night? She considered the possibility and then dismissed it. The very thought was daft. Of course she would have remembered. It wasn't as if she had even had a drink.

Kneeling down, she ran her hands over the worn and polished wood and leather, marvelling at the quality of the workmanship. Inside, the trunk was lined with softer leather, once, she supposed, a deep red, now faded to pink, fastened by brass studs to the solid wood. Reaching over to pull the top down to close it, she noticed a small tear in the leather of the inner left-hand side as it creaked slowly on its hinges.

Running her fingers along it, she felt something hard and cold. At first she thought it might be a ring of some kind and scrabbled further inside the leather to try and grasp it. Her finger slipped right into it, but the ring was not loose. Hurrying to the bathroom, Niamh grabbed her small nail scissors and then cut quickly into the worn leather, apologising mentally to the late Lady Arabella. She cut a small neat flap and pulled it back, and then took a sharp intake of breath. Behind the leather flap was not a ring, at least not the kind she had supposed. The cold, hard object she had felt was clearly a lever. Holding her breath, Niamh hooked her finger into the brass circle and pulled. As she did, the lever came out, twisted and, before her eyes, released a panel of wood to reveal what was obviously a secret compartment. Inside was an envelope. With trembling fingers, Niamh opened it, taking out the sheets of folded paper stiff with years. Running her eyes along the faded typescript, the first sheet appeared to be a copy of the same letter found in the trunk from McBride & Whitaker. Underneath, however, was another set of papers of thicker parchment, which she began to read hungrily:

> *In accordance with your Lordship's instructions, we hereby amend the deeds to the properties known as Grovesbury Gardens, comprising thirty-four cottages in the Grovesbury Estate as follows: The cottages shall be leased to the neighbouring houses of Grovesbury Road to house their members of staff for a period of ninety-nine years, after which time it is my wish that the leaseholds will revert to the current owner of Grovesbury Hall. It is my further wish and instruction that at this time the owner of Grovesbury Hall offers the cottages for sale to their respective tenants for the sum of five hundred pounds each.*
>
> *Signed Lord Herbert Grovesbury, dated November eleventh, nineteen hundred and three.*

'Oh God,' said Niamh aloud, tears streaming down her face, 'I don't believe it, I can't believe it.' Looking at her watch, she saw it was already half-past twelve. It could be too late. Flinging on the nearest clothes that came to hand, she grabbed the deeds, whispered a prayer to Nellie to hold off the demolition and raced downstairs and past an astonished Polly towards the front door.

'Niamh? What on earth? Where are you racing off to?' Polly shouted above the drone of the Hoover.

'There's no time to explain, Polly. Just say a prayer I make it in time,' Niamh yelled back at her before disappearing out the door.

C&

Grovesbury Gardens was playing host to pandemonium.

Rowan, looking every inch the revolutionary in a black Che Guevara-type beret and combats, was eagerly rousing the rabble to action. The builders, who had been taken unawares, stood by helplessly as a large human chain formed around their machinery.

Between them, the residents had gathered quite a crew. An Taisce had turned up along with a crowd of architectural students, who were vociferously protesting about losing an integral part of old Dublin 4. Thanks to Steve, an impressive group of animal-rights supporters were lending their collective voice to proceedings. The local councillor was on hand, quick to spot a media opportunity, as were several friends of Alex's from her modelling days who were lending a welcome touch of glamour to the unfolding scenario.

The press were having a field day. As word spread, more camera crews and photographers turned up. As usual, the main attraction was Bobbi. With Bruiser standing protectively by her side, she shouted to reporters over the increasing chant of the crowd. 'As you can see, this is an issue a lot of people feel very strongly about. Not only are we witnessing a unique part of old Dublin 4 being destroyed, but in the process, people are losing their homes. I may be the new kid on the block here, but even I can see that's a travesty. I'm lending this demonstration my full and unequivocal support.'

Melissa was having the photo opportunity of a lifetime.

She lay on the flat of her back, in a sea of mud, her legs

raised in a Dolce & Gabbana clad V-sign of victory against an oncoming bulldozer.

'You'd better get out of the way, Missus,' one of the builders advised her, as the crowd chanted with renewed vigour.

'Fuck you, arseface! I'm not moving a fucking muscle,' she spat at him under her breath, before turning to her other side to smile valiantly to the cameras. 'I refuse to move an inch. If they want to knock down this little cottage that is someone's dearly loved home, they'll have to get past me first!'

'Way to go Melissa!' yelled Rowan.

Carmela was standing at the back of the crowd clutching her rosary beads. She had been unsure of what course of action to take but on reflection had felt it would be better to play the part of concerned onlooker. Her stricken expression was ironically heartfelt as she caught sight of a scantily clad Marysol climbing up a ladder to join protestors on the roof of one of the cottages, cheered on loudly by two burly looking labourers, while her son, Padraig, gazed at the men with what looked uncannily like ill-concealed lust.

Totally out of breath and lost in the sea of demonstrators, Niamh frantically searched for Bobbi in the crowd. 'Please, please. Has anybody seen Bobbi Levinsky?'

'Sorry, love,' said a harassed guard. 'You'll have to keep back. Things could turn ugly here. I've just called for back up.'

'You don't understand, I've got a piece of paper that will stop all this. You've got to do something!'

'Bit late now, love. Best thing you can do is run along home. Now move back, please!'

Just then she caught sight of Bobbi, being interviewed for television. Pushing and fighting her way through what seemed like endless rows of people, Niamh finally reached her.

'Bobbi!' She clutched at her coat sleeve urgently. 'I'm sorry to interrupt, but you've got to see this!'

'What on earth? Niamh, are you okay?' Bobbi looked at Niamh's distraught face as she turned away from the camera and said to the reporter, 'I'm sorry, can you give us a minute, please?'

'What is it Niamh? Slow down. I can hardly understand a word you're saying.'

'Look at this!' Niamh thrust the paper into Bobbi's hands. 'This changes everything. Read it Bobbi! The cottages – all of Grovesbury Gardens belong to you now! *You're* the legal owner. Chris Carroll has no rights whatsoever!' Niamh held her breath as Bobbi quickly scanned down the legal document.

'Oh, my,' said Bobbi, hardly believing her eyes. 'Is this for real?'

'It's signed by the second Lord Grovesbury and legally witnessed.' Niamh pointed to the signatures.

'That's good enough for me,' said Bobbi, looking up. 'Where's the foreman? You,' she said, grabbing one of the builders, 'get your boss over here *now*.' As the man scurried off, galvanised by the authority in Bobbi's voice, the sound of sirens could be heard as four more police cars pulled up alongside the demonstrators. Chris Carroll appeared from the crowd with a face like thunder, followed by his solicitor, who rushed over to speak with the guard in charge. Chris, catching sight of Bobbi striding over to the harassed foreman, intercepted her. 'I've had quite enough of you and your sad little group of followers. As you can see, I've called the police in. You can do your chanting to them. Now get off my property or I'll have you dragged off myself.'

'Sorry to disappoint you, Chris.' Bobbi smiled up at him. 'But I have a piece of paper here that rather scuppers your plans.'

'Miss Levinsky?' It was Fred, the foreman. 'You were looking for me?'

'Yes I was,' said Bobbi. 'I have a legal document here proving this site, and the cottages on it, belong to me, not to

Mr Carroll. I'm instructing you this minute to cease any further demolition to the site.'

'How dare you!' Chris bellowed. 'Fred, pay no attention to her, she's off her rocker. The police are here to get rid of this mad lot. Just get on with the job I'm paying you to do.'

'Do that, and you'll have me to answer to.' Bobbi showed him the document. 'As you can see, *I* am the owner of Grovesbury Gardens, and I'm telling you to get your men off my property, *now!*'

Fred looked at the document and scratched his head. 'I'm no lawyer, but I'm not getting me or my men into any trouble. Mr Carroll, you'd better sort this out.'

'Malcolm!' Chris shouted to his solicitor. 'Get over here!' And then to Bobbi: 'You'll be sorry you ever heard the name of Grovesbury Gardens by the time I've finished with you.'

'You're the one who's finished, Chris. At least as far as Grovesbury Gardens is concerned.'

'Chris, what is it?' Malcolm hurried to his client's side.

Bobbi held the document up for him to read. 'Take a look at this, and don't for one moment think I'm going to let you get your grubby hands on it – you can read it perfectly well from there.' Bobbi and Chris watched intently as Malcolm's face turned white and then flushed deep purple.

'It's a scam,' said Chris, leering at Bobbi. 'A cheap, pathetic last-ditch attempt to delay us. She's bluffing. Malcolm,' he demanded, 'tell her I'll have her arrested for this!'

Malcolm cleared his throat and searched for words that seemed to elude him, his pursed mouth working impotently. 'I, um, I'm afraid it's not that simple, Chris.' He strived to regain his equilibrium.

'What the hell are you saying man?' Chris's eyes narrowed.

'I thought as much.' Bobbi's voice was like ice. 'I'll see you both tomorrow in *my* solicitor's office. In the meantime, get your men off my property.' She smiled at Chris before turning to go. 'I think you'll find you have a building project on your hands here, Chris, but not, perhaps, the one you intended. If this means what I think it does, you're going to have to rebuild every one of the cottages you've demolished illegally. Should keep you busy for quite some time I imagine.'

As Chris stood with his mouth working in speechless fury, he watched the guards call a halt to the demolition and order the builders off the site until further notice, and he listened to the cheers of the demonstrators ringing in his disbelieving ears.

EPILOGUE

August 2004

Niamh ní Cheavin, soon to be Niamh O'Buachalla, had bought a new hat for the occasion. With her impending nuptials in September, she thought it a justifiable investment. Although she and Fergal were having a church wedding (he was a widower *and* a cat lover), she had decided to wear a nice suit for the ceremony and, of course, a hat. She still had to pinch herself at the turn her life had taken since dear Nellie had died. Not only had she been able to purchase her *own* cottage in Grovesbury Gardens, thanks to Bobbi honouring the late Lord Grovesbury's wishes, but Nellie had also bequeathed Niamh *her* cottage. Niamh was now the proud owner of two very desirable properties in the much talked about location.

She checked her reflection in the mirror and smiled, wishing Nellie was there to see her. The large picture hat lent a softness to her features and set off the elegantly cut navy and white suit to perfection. Who'd have thought it? If anyone had told her this time last year that she'd be off to a posh luncheon given by an American billionairess before setting off to the Aga Khan Nations Cup at the Horse Show, accompanied by her very own fiancé, she'd have laughed out loud. But it was real, all of it. Right down to the small, sparkling solitaire diamond on the third finger of her left hand. As Nellie would have said, 'It just goes to show, you never know what's around the corner.'

Rowan and Alex had flown in especially for the week. They were currently living in New York, where Rowan's portrait style (of Alex in particular) had taken the art world by storm, meaning he was in constant demand.

Naturally, they were staying with Bobbi for the visit, and the celebrations were already well underway.

The charges against Rowan for possession of drugs had been dropped spectacularly when it had been discovered that the cocaine found at his cottage had been, on inspection, nothing more innocuous than a mixture of glucose and expensive Italian laxatives. If Marysol's mother, Carmela, had known that this had been the price of her prized three-carat solitaire, she would have had even more reason than usual to supplicate heaven.

As it was, she had a more pressing problem to deal with. The fact that Bobbi was giving a pre-Nations Cup luncheon in Grovesbury Hall meant she had been seriously upstaged. So much so that she had been forced to cancel the luncheon she and Liam had given on the same day for over twenty-five years. That she had been invited to Bobbi's was cold comfort. Carmela felt she couldn't possibly be seen to attend. It would be altogether too humiliating. Especially that word was now out that she and Liam had accepted one of Chris Carroll's apartments in exchange for Nellie Murphy's cottage prior to this unbelievable turn of events. Truly it had been a sad day when this American woman had come into their lives. Until then, everything had been going along as it always had. Now, she hardly felt able to show her face – even at ten o'clock mass at Donnybrook, where she sensed acutely the snide expressions thrown in her direction. Carmela shook her head and sighed. What had she, a devout practising Catholic and upholder of moral fibre, done to deserve this?

☙

Chris Carroll was probably the only person of note in Dublin who would *not* be attending Bobbi's prestigious luncheon. Since the fateful day when the amendment to the deeds of Grovesbury Gardens had been discovered, his life had taken a very definite turn for the worse. Not only had he lost his lucrative development scheme, but he had also been instructed in court to undertake the reconstruction of the cottages that had already been demolished. Under the circumstances, Alex had been granted custody of the children, and he was allowed visitation rights which, at the moment, meant a fortnightly trip to New York, which he could very well do without. The banks were closing in and Meredith Lacey, with impeccable timing gleaned from her years in public relations, was moving out, claiming she 'needed space'.

Worst of all, it looked as if he was going to lose his home on Grovesbury Road. His silver Porsche had had to go too, and without that to swish around in, his chances of appearing vaguely attractive to the opposite sex were looking slim – which he, unfortunately, was not.

☙

The lunch had been an unequivocal success. Grovesbury Hall, in all its newly refurbished finery, had basked in the glow of a warm summer's day. A vast open marquee had been erected on the lawn where lunch had been served and, afterwards, guests had wandered lazily around the sumptuously elegant surroundings.

The *pièce de résistance*, of course, had been the official opening, by An Taoiseach, of the newly restored stables, which were to house, once again, some of the finest bloodstock in the country. With its ten acres backing on to the grounds of the RDS, Grovesbury Hall was ideally equipped for the purpose and Bobbi had, with Steve's help and encouragement, acquired a fine collection of brood mares, from which she intended to breed.

Now though, it was time to leave for the RDS, where the competition for the Nations Cup was about to take place. As various cars and limousines pulled up on the gravelled front drive, guests hurried to claim their drivers. Bobbi and Steve, along with Niamh and her fiancé and Alex and Rowan, preferred to walk the short distance, strolling along Grovesbury Road and into the side entrance of the RDS.

Minutes later, Bobbi and Steve took their place as guests in the President's Box, at the top of the Grand Stand. The crowd stood to the rousing sound of the national anthem, then the president joined her guests and everybody settled down to enjoy the competition. The excitement was palpable. From the far end of the arena, each team emerged, escorted in front by the army band. Magnificent horses danced skittishly, sidestepping with excitement at the cheering crowd and the rousing playing of the band. Their riders fought to keep a dignified seat and removed their riding hats in salutation to the president as they passed her box.

Finally, it was Ireland's turn. In they came – four team members clad in their immaculately cut green jackets, seated on the finest of Irish bred show jumpers. But, as the band played before them, it was no ordinary cheer that brought the crowd to their feet. For, in front of the team, leading them in proudly, was Montyson III, accompanied by his old show-jumping partner Freddie Martin.

Despite his twelve-year absence, Montyson looked as if he had never been away. His coat glistened over carefully sculpted muscles, and he walked calmly and serenely, ears pricked forward, tossing his beautiful head occasionally as if to acknowledge the roar of the crowd. Looking down from her vantage point in the box, with tears of emotion streaming down her face, Bobbi could have sworn Montyson looked straight back up at her as he completed a lap of honour.

And then, all too soon, it was over. The horse and rider whose legendary show-jumping record was still unbeaten exited the arena and left the current competitors to battle it out. Montyson posed regally with his partner for photographers, before he was led by his new groom the short distance to his home.

Back at Grovesbury Hall, the stables slumbered peacefully in the warm evening sun. Montyson was washed down, watered and then fed in the comfort of his ancestor's stable. Later, when he had been left alone, he looked out over the top of the open half-door, ears pricked in anticipation of the footsteps that would come to greet him as Bobbi always did before turning in.

For the moment, though, all was quiet. Not so much as a leaf stirred in the still of the evening. The sun was setting, casting shadows that played on the surrounding cobblestones. Soon, very soon, Montyson would be joined by new companions in the stables. But for now, it was the presence of past occupants that haunted the moment. That, and one last visit from his young friend, who, hovering as he did at the back wall of the stable, was invisible to any human eye. Montyson sensed his presence, though, and whickered gently, enjoying the company.

But for young, ten-year-old Bertie Grovesbury, killed so tragically on the hunting field all those years ago, it was time to move on. His beloved horses had been restored to Grovesbury Hall, and his work was done. Pastures new were beckoning.

ACKNOWLEDGEMENTS

It was the best of times and the worst of times ...

No one is more surprised than I that *Sold* ever got to see the light of day. It was written during a particularly difficult and stressful time, and on several occasions I almost gave up. Heartfelt thanks are due to the following people who helped make it happen.

To everyone at New Island, particularly editor Emma Dunne, who is every fragile author's dream to work with.

To Claire Rourke for blissfully painless editing and pointing out that not all redheads come under the label of 'titian'!

To Kate Thompson for being ... well ... Kate.

To orthopaedic surgeon extraordinaire John McElwain (Big Mac) who said 'I'll fix it' and did – when everyone else said 'you're buggered!'

To Nathalie Landers of Tallaght Hospital, who always made sure I was top of the list when it came to getting plastered.

To Louise Wilson of Sandymount Physiotherapy Clinic, for getting me back on my feet – literally.

To Simon Ensor of Sherry Fitzgerald for keeping me abreast of wildly climbing D4 property prices (truth *is* stranger than fiction).

To my wonderful family and friends (you know who you are), particularly in this instance Catriona O'Neill – currently residing in Marbella – whose home is always as much a haven of acceptance and hilarity as the first 'apartment' we shared in Merrion Village.